STORM MAKERS

STORM MAKERS

E.L. CHAPPEL

For information,
E.L. Chappel
1611 S. Utica #201
Tulsa, OK 74104

www.elchappel.com

ISBN-13: 978-0692665855
ISBN-10: 0692665854

Library of Congress Control Number: 2016905385
LCCN Imprint Name: Tulsa, OK

First Edition: April 2016

CHAPTER 1

"Wall cloud, twelve o'clock!" I shout to the team.

I scramble from the passenger side of the storm chasing rover, angle between the bucket seats, drop to my knees, and shimmy like a chimpanzee along a narrow metal catwalk.

I clench the thin side rails of the gangplank.

Don't look.

I will my eyes away from the bottomless floor, unsure that if I lose my balance, the crisscrossed net fastened to the frame will keep me from a fate worse than roadkill.

An epic bolt of lightning cracks.

The back of the mobile weather center lights up.

An electrified bolt strikes the wet road.

"Hold on," our meteorology professor yells. The rover swerves, and my fingers slip from the rails. My chest crashes against the catwalk. Wide-eyed, I stare at the two-lane rural road.

The world tilts as the asphalt blurs past. Nausea climbs my throat. *I'm not afraid of heights. I'm not afraid of...*

The rover's thick treads swerve over the solid yellow line, and when the vehicle jerks back, I cannon from the walkway.

Heights.

I soar—Superman style. The road markings below smear. I tense my muscles. *Any second now.*

The stiff hatches of the woven safety net snap against my skin.

After two loosely tucked rotations, I roll to a stop, belly up, gravel pelting like BBs against the back of my waterproof jacket.

Couldn't have stayed in the lab and written a paper on temperature and dew point spread, could you, Lyre?

I exhale with the force of a violent gust front and grip the nylon straps, knowing that the temperature/dew point project would earn me, at best, a C midterm grade. KC was right; with this professor, the safe route is a guaranteed GPA sinker.

I blow my bangs from my forehead. The question is, are the risks that come with chasing tornados worth the chance to get an A grade?

Clenching my fists, I squeeze my eyes shut and silently thank the engineering club for spec'cing a heavy-duty harness when tricking out our school's weather-hunting Hummer.

"I see it. I see it," Trigger calls from the Doppler station. My lids split to see my best friend secured in an ejection seat salvaged from a fighter jet. "Epicenter building…three miles, dead ahead." His sky-blue eyes glom on to the radar.

Bright-red scallops forge across the screen, pulsing with green thunderheads. Outside, tornado sirens shrill.

"Spotter…report." Professor McVie's voice climbs a notch, and I hear the rover's big-block engine rev faster. "Tana?"

Wiggling like a bug on its back, I pull my knees to my chest, rock to regain my footing, and then push to a wide-legged squat. I thread my wrists through the overhead subway lanyards and clench the leather loops. "Searching, sir."

A blustery gust lifts the rear tire in the air, and my thick rubber boot soles dig into the cross straps to maintain balance.

I paste my face against the picture window and scour the gray-black cloud mass until I spot the thunderstorm's pointed ledge. "Got eyes on the anvil," I shout over the howling wind. I release one overhead handle and trace the sharp point of a cloud resembling a miner's pick.

Golf-ball-sized hail pelts the shatterproof glass.

"Pressure readings, wind speeds." Our professor weaves, dodging another lightning assault. Undeterred, the weather hunter redirects the rover straight into the storm's path. "KC, any rotation?"

Along the back width of the vehicle, the fourth member of our team hangs upside down from the ceiling, strapped in a recliner, swiveling side to side like a bombardier gunner. My second best friend, KC, rides the semicircle track, unaffected by McVie's erratic maneuvers, and cycles from one end of the vehicle to the other as if she's at home on the couch, dominating in a virtual game jam. "Pressure's falling; dew point's steady," she says, viewing at least a dozen isobar maps.

I scurry across the remaining walkway, well aware of what's coming next. I revert to my monkey bar ways, swinging from overhead harness to looped harness, my feet grazing the gangplank grate. I stretch over the last two handholds and drop into the second ejection seat welded next to Trigger's. With my shoulder harness fastened, I tilt my head back and stare into the belly of the billowing storm monster that hovers over our pitted moonroof.

Crack.

Flash.

Thunder rumbles. In its wake, a rainbow of color burns.

A neon-green band of ribbon shoots from the festering supercell.

Shuddering, I nudge Trigger.

His surfer tan pales.

"The aurora borealis." I blink, and the majestic curtain of light vanishes. "But how?" I mouth, aware the northern lights aren't associated with this kind of weather. My earlobe tingles, and an image of blood, spit, and phlegm sprays in front of my eyes. "Aaaaaah."

"T?" Trigger's perfectly arched eyebrows spike.

"It's nothing." I shake my head. As quick as it came, the gore flash goes away, and I divert my view to the rover's side window.

"Nothing? You look like you've…Tana, you aren't seeing—"

"No," I snap, well aware of what he's about to ask. I'm not having visions from the afterlife, and I'm *not* hearing whispers from my dead father.

The howling winds fall off. Soaking rain lightens into a foggy, eerie mist. The roaring charcoal monster seems to have retreated. But it hasn't.

"I've got rotation!" KC screams.

"Incoming!" McVie bellows. "Brace for impact."

I want to look away. Seal my eyes tight. Cower with fear. But for some reason, the beast's greatness calls to me.

Thrills.

Entices.

Terrifies me beyond death.

My heart pounds like hail on pavement.

Water seeps from the cracked moonroof and splatters across my forehead. I stare as a decrepit funnel finger extends from the churning wall cloud. The wretched spindle whirls, pointing like a parochial school nun. Its punitive funnel spins and engulfs our armored rover.

"Brace, brace, brace! Cover your heads!" McVie hollers.

I hunker down on my shoulder straps.

"Lift-off in three, two, one…"

CHAPTER 2

Airborne, the Hummer tumbles end over end, spinning in the dust-ridden air. My neck snaps forward and then thrusts back. We somersault from the front battering ram bumper to the rear reinforced-steel tailgate. My eyes split and then squinch. Rain, dust, and debris prick like a thousand sharp needles. I force my lids shut. Muted tornado sirens roar. My head slams against the seat back. I see spots.

Although I'm certain we're spinning at top speed, my thoughts slow to the pace of an idling propeller. My earlobe stings, as if lit on fire. In the darkness, a spark of blue-green light flashes. On. Then off. A steady buzz follows, echoing like static over a loudspeaker.

Bang, bang, bang. Metal clangs metal.

Gunfire. My hands fly to my ears. *Guards. Help. Eddie, where are you?* My lips quiver.

A timer ticks. Flames explode before my eyes.

Lightning, an airplane, stars, needles, piercings, and a beacon tower flash in my mind like an emergency strobe. A sugary taste fills my mouth. A figure in black knifes through the air. The smell of rotten eggs fills my nostrils. A tattered, leather eye patch appears. I cower.

Run! My instincts shout.

My feet stomp. I charge forward. The darkness whisks by as if I'm riding a roller coaster.

My heart thrusts against my rib cage. The vibration stops. Quiet settles. *This isn't real.* I shake my head.

In my mind, I slow to a walk.

My hands fall limp to my sides.

An incandescent ceiling light cycles.

Startled, I leap into the air.

The light burns long enough for me to see a sheet of dingy plastic hung over an open doorway.

Panting, I skulk forward.

I move toward the sheet, smeared and dotted with crimson blobs. I push through the curtain, and a sticky dampness streaks my arms. *Blood.* I shiver and reach for my shrapnel neck scars. Caressing the raised skin, I stumble ahead. With arms waving in front of me, I knock into what feels like a metal cone.

I stumble to a knee and use a hand to break the fall. Sharp shards slice my palm. Blood trickles toward my fingers. Ahead, a dull lantern burns, and my eyes narrow to adjust.

I rise and ease forward, glass crunching beneath my heavy boot soles. As the lantern's cast widens, shapes appear on the floor—smashed goggles, a shredded lab coat, and what looks like crumpled sew-on decals. As I edge closer, the light brightens, and I tiptoe up to a second sheet of heavy-duty plastic.

Slipping past, I suck a steadying breath, bend down, and angle my neck around the corner. Four boys in tailored business suits are huddled around a lump on the floor. I squint and look closer.

"Tell," a deep voice shouts. His shined dress shoes kick at a limp body trapped in the corner. The hoodie-covered torso writhes and then retracts back into a ball.

"Us." A second pinstripe-clad thug strikes a drainpipe with an aluminum bat. *Bang, bang, bang.* Metal clangs metal, sounding like gunfire. He twists, ratchets a thigh, and delivers a pile-driving blow to the solar plexus. A weak, raspy wail comes from the lump. A wheeze, a cough, and then the balled figure spits blood.

The third boy jumps in the air, and with the momentum created by his stocky frame, he executes a crushing elbow to the collarbone. "Your code."

The lump's legs jerk, and the camping lantern topples over. All light goes out.

The heat fades from my earlobe.

What is this? Panic flashes over me. *Am I backsliding?* The last time I saw images that weren't there and heard voices that weren't real, I did something horrible—an unforgivable act in Trigger's airplane, one I will forever regret.

After a final thrash against the storm-chasing rover's headrest, the whiplash stops. I gather we've hit ground. Water sheets across my face, and I wipe my eyes. Through the rover's shattered observation window, I see charcoal soot, as thick as chimney smoke. *The twister must be done with us.* When my vision clears, however, the sinister finger reappears.

The whirling digit scoops up the rover and curls it back into the tornado's gusty grip. "Hold on!" I shout to warn the others, but the swirling wind whistles, drowning my words.

After toying with the vehicle for a dozen more dizzying loops, the fierce funnel spits out our three-ton rover like a sour grape.

Another surging downdraft thrusts my body against the safety harnesses, and our six-thousand-pound steel coffin plummets toward the red Oklahoma dirt. Angled like a lawn dart, the rover hits ground.

My neck snaps sideways as the vehicle ricochets and arcs back into the air. We crash onto the front bumper, flip, and then lift airborne again. My brain fires, *You should be scared!* while my body tingles with excitement.

"Kind of reminds me of your landings, T," Trigger manages to say despite the rover's porpoising.

To most, I'd guess the act of chasing storms might seem terrifying, but to a brand-new licensed private pilot, the wild ride in an F1 tornado has hardly caused me to break a sweat. "Any touchdown you can walk away from is a good one," I banter and clench my teeth as the rover's steel frame slides across the crux of a deep retention ditch. Clumps of crimson clay cake on the few remaining shards of window glass and slow our forward momentum like a ship's anchor chain.

The wet dirt builds, and our storm-chasing behemoth surrenders, beaching on its back. Crumpled and broken, the rover lumbers to a stop.

Dangling by my canvas shoulder straps, I glance at Trigger.

"Are we dead?" He quotes his signature line with no emotion, almost as if he accepts that his death is somehow inevitable.

I'm uncomfortable and confused. But I don't dare tell Trigger—or Gran or my mother, or anyone for that matter—since up until a moment ago, I'd been making serious progress. No hallucinations. No more nightmares.

A warm surge burns, reheating my left ear. *It's not real,* I chant in my head. A tingly buzz chases and beats in time with my heart rate.

To date, my only experience with death was an explosion that killed my father. A second close call, however, was the night Dad's fiery image returned from the afterlife—a night I wish I could do over again.

Looking back, it's hard to believe I tried to take my own life in Trigger's homebuilt airplane. Never mind his. Trigger saved me that evening. And in the process, he became my best friend. I owe him a life debt. I hope to repay him someday.

Scanning the command center, I check on the rest of our storm-chasing team. KC waves, and by the easy way Professor McVie's shoulder-length ponytail flicks, I assume everyone's OK.

No sign of Dad's ghost channeling through their mouths like before.

I suck in and hold my breath.

No flittering yellow butterfly bursting into flames either.

I allow my gaze to sweep around the rover. Flush, lively skin coloring glows back at me. *It's all good.* I blow out.

My team is alive and acting themselves, as far as I can tell. Zero casualties—unless you count our mangled rover.

"Definitely not dead," I answer Trigger.

Trigger's smile stretches into his surfer grin. He unhooks his seat straps and reaches to reboot the radar. With his head turned from me, I notice a familiar glow—a turquoise halo beaming from his right ear, the piercing the government-sponsored school required—not the National School where KC, Trigger, and I are currently enrolled, but an elite prep school we stumbled upon four weeks earlier, stealthily hidden in the desert. A campus called Pioneer.

Could it be real? I touch my helix, rub the earth magnet receiver, and then bask in the warm rush that follows while connected to Pioneer's secure intranet. I picture the blue light and relish in the comforting euphoria that, with the exception of a few minutes ago, I haven't felt for nearly a month—since the night we escaped from the administration at Pioneer Academy and their twisted security, Chief McDunney.

KC must have noticed it too, because even hanging inverted, she eyes our matching trip souvenirs. "What?" She crinkles her nose. "Matching earrings? Are you two together?"

"Us, ah, no," Trigger stammers, fingers fumbling from the computer's acknowledge buttons. "You know I'm with Brooklyn." His voice lowers. His eyes drift back to the dull, blank monitor.

"Guess I just thought…" KC says, even though I remind her at least once a day that Trigger's status remains *currently in a relationship.* "With the coordinating blue lights and all…" she adds.

"My light's on?" Trigger's ocean blues dart to me.

I angle my neck to show my earlobe.

"Pioneer's intranet?"

I nod.

"How? The instant we escaped from Pioneer, we were permanently disconnected."

I'm about to try to explain something I don't understand myself when Professor McVie tumbles like a boulder from the front seat, rolls along the crooked catwalk, and pops to his feet, arms wide, palms open, as if readying to sumo wrestle. His eyes jut around the back of the rover, reminding me of a hunting tiger. "Stay calm." His arms close, and he folds his hands in yoga-prayer position. He takes a gigantic breath and funnels air through puckered lips. "Didn't I teach you anything? Easy Victor," he says and *ohms* like a monk.

KC, Trigger, and I trade a shrug.

"Flough, Lyre, this is no time for relationship chitchat," McVie says. He lunges forward—ninja style—delicately planting the ball of his foot on the cracked moonroof. After a couple of catlike steps, he arrives at what is left of the rover's rear end. McVie releases KC's seat belt, lifts her from her recliner, and lowers her to stable footing.

"The storm is circling back around." Any balance of a disciplined black belt vanishes. "Easy Victor!" he shouts. "Everyone evacuate. Pronto."

In a full sprint, he hurdles a pile of high-tech barometers and then shoots like a log through the tear in the mesh safety net. "Take cover! Now! Bury yourselves in the ditch." Pancaked against the wet, red dirt, he bear-crawls along an irrigation trench.

Trigger and I disconnect our safety harnesses, and following the professor's lead, we worm through the muck.

After a series of commando crawls, I lift my chest from the cool ground and peek over the trench's edge. The straight-line winds prick my face. I collapse spread-eagle and lie flat, submerging my slicker in a murky mud puddle.

Water splashes as Trigger and KC drop to the ground and pancake on either side of me.

"Do you hear anything?" Trigger crawls closer and glues his hips to my side. *Zing.* A spark shoots through my body.

Best friends, I remind myself, even though I feel his invisible tractor beam lock onto my chest.

He taps my ear piercing. "I mean over your receiver."

Mixed in with the howling of the rumbling storm, an easygoing reggae riff drums in the background. *Maybe I am losing it.* I bunch my face up, doubly confused—first about the visions, but also about hearing this calming, feel-good, every-little-thing tune each time Trigger is around. I thought we had a more-than-friends moment when we returned from Pioneer in the cab of Trigger's pickup truck. But at school the next day, he was back in Brooklyn Dehavilland's arms. *Crossed wires.* I ignore the reggae riff. *It was just an adrenaline moment. Move on.* Divert and distract. I use evasive emotional maneuvers, stare into Trigger's bright blues, and shout over the wind, "Transmissions are line of sight. No way they can reach this far."

The sky surfer shimmies closer. His lips press against my cheek, sending a tingle rippling to the tips of my toes.

"Then why is the light on?" he asks. "No way it would glow blue if we weren't picking up a signal."

Thunder booms overhead, and the soupy overcast shimmers with purple veins of static electricity. KC throws her hands in the air and sinks her face in the pooling water.

"The Weatherman?" I yell, matching my cheek to Trigger's so he can hear.

"Henry's genius-grade gray matter is off the charts; I guess he could have developed some sort of booster."

"I don't know. Pioneer's firewalls are super secure. Even for someone as smart as Henry." A pungent, earthy scent stings my nostrils. I sniff. "Smell that?"

Trigger breathes in and samples the air. "Stinks. Like mulch."

"Air's getting heavier."

"The dry line is approaching."

From the west, a fierce squall wrinkles the rover's pliable outer skin, crushing it as easily as an aluminum pop can.

"Oh my goodness." Professor McVie springs to his feet. "The storm logs are still in the Hummer." He slaps his forehead, swings his hand forward, and stiff-arms the storm.

"Wait!" I belt. The words slap back into my face.

McVie levers forward, elbow locked and head down, muscling against the force of the raging gust front.

I hear a familiar sound. It's vague at first, like a train chugging off in the distance. Pistons pumping. Horn howling. Chugging faster and faster.

"Here comes the eye." Trigger flattens.

I bend my neck and stare at the sky.

From the cloud base, a second scraggy hand claws in our direction.

"McVie's in trouble." I shout to KC and Trigger. Pushing to a plank, I scurry forward like a four-legged crab.

"Tana, no!" Trigger's voice echoes from over my shoulder. I feel his fingers scrape against my ankle, but he is unable to hold on to my rain pants.

Slipping and sliding, I scramble to get my footing, and once my soles have traction, I match McVie's stumbling speed.

With the benefit of forward momentum, I throw my weight, thrust my free hand into the powerful airstream, and swat at the professor's boot tread. *Gotcha.* I catch a notch of his rubber sole.

McVie's legs cross and tangle, tripping over one another. He timbers and then plunges flat against the soggy ground.

Just in time. I breathe a shallow sigh.

A second later, a fist of funnel fingers arrives.

Unraveling, they scoop up the rover, whisking the bent steel skeleton into their winding grip.

The twister tightens, swirling faster and faster.

"Cover your heads!" Professor McVie hollers, half submerged in a mud puddle.

I layer my arms over my skull and hunker down as the dry line passes overhead. A rain shower of sand sprays. I squeeze my eyes shut.

Blind, with my face buried against my slicker's collar, a bright glint lights my inner lids. Lightning, I assume. But the glow doesn't fade. In fact, it gets brighter. Although my lids are sealed, my view is filled with black-gray static similar to the picture I've seen on granddad's TV when the cable goes out.

What the heck?

I slide my arms down and knuckle both eye sockets, well aware that the storm above my head is filled with dark thunderheads.

Heat warms my cheek. My earlobe buzzes. I touch my piercing.

Impossible. My skin is hot. *Pioneer doesn't have an antenna tall enough to send a signal this far.* I fight the only logical conclusion, the fact that my halo receiver is lit.

The camping lantern flicks on again, and I see bile-colored walls, a turbine engine, shattered chemistry beakers, and four boys in dress shirts and neckties circling the same balled body from the prior vision.

"Where are your friends now, freq geek?" the thick-chested boy shouts and thrusts his shoe into the whimpering lump.

"What was that?" A second stocky frame hovers and puts a hand to his ear. "Didn't quite hear you, butt-kisser. Say again." He kneels on the boy's groin.

I hear a squeal chased by a groan. The hood covering the lump's head folds back, revealing a pair of black eyes, sullen cheeks, and a shaved head. The boy says, "Sir Newton was right." Blood drips from the side of his mangled jaw. "For every action, there is an equal and opposite reaction."

"Henry!" I scream, recognizing the voice of the friend we left behind.

Dirt, sand, and water fill my mouth. What sounds like a locomotive chugs in the background.

"For such a little rodent, you can sure take a beatdown, Mr. Aska Gu." The boy, whom I now recognize as Tap, the head of Pioneer's Future-of-Wall-Street clique, taunts. "Tell us your secret, you little weasel." The Streeter grabs Henry's sweat shirt collar. "It's the only thing that will save your life."

Is this real? I ask myself again. Despite all the support from my family and friends, I know I still suffer from PTSD. *It's a process,* I remind myself as my pupils dart over the inside of my eyelids for some sort of clue, a location, or a time stamp to clarify what exactly is going on, since the only way I could be receiving this message is via virtual streaming—a feature of my ear piercing that could only work if I was still connected to Pioneer's in-skull network, which I'm not.

Despite my rationalization, cackling voices echo in my head. I see the image of a third Streeter, who lifts a knee, preparing for another assault of stomps and kicks.

A door creaks.

"Enough," a voice shouts.

Thank goodness. Whether it is real or not, I feel a sense of relief wash over me. Distracted, I ignore a second heaviness—the sensation of something piling on my arms and legs.

Light from the camping lantern flickers. The image disappears. I see static. *No, no, no.* I shake my head. A blue screen blazes, and when the light clicks on again, I see a tattered, leather eye patch inches from Henry's swollen cheeks.

Chief McDunney? I gag and throw up in my mouth.

"Tana, if you can hear me, please," Henry says, "help me." Spit bubbles from his lips.

I wiggle my arm loose from whatever is piling on my jacket and reach for my ear piercing. Even though I know it won't work, I pinch the wireless booster. Clumps of what feels like mud, rock, and dirt pelt my raincoat.

"They abandoned you, loser." My eardrum echoes with a Streeter's laughter.

Pioneer's security chief, McDunney, grabs Henry by the back of the neck and drags the Weatherman's limp body across the floor.

Grit clogs my nostrils.

Tap says, "The chief will get you to talk without uttering a word."

Whispers from Pioneer's in-skull network echo in my ears. *Don't get caught alone with McDunney. The chief's been in prison. McDunney's a perv.*

A single tear tracks down my cheek as I'm buried beneath the Oklahoma dirt.

What have we done? More important, is it real?

CHAPTER 3

Shivering, I stretch my fingers and scratch the surroundings. Trigger's and KC's slickers are no longer against my thighs. A heaviness settles around me, as if I'm packed in snow.

In the distance, I hear a muffled voice and piece together words sounding like *all clear.*

When I open my eyes, I see black—no sky, no stars, and no remnants of the stunning harvest moon.

I shudder.

Over here. I open my mouth to shout.

Grit piles on my tongue.

My lips reseal, and I heave my arms toward my face. The weight, however, keeps them pinned to my sides.

I'm buried.

My heart races. I will my arms to swim and my legs to kick. *Too heavy.* I squirm. *Feels like wet cement.* I suck in through my nose and inflate my chest, expecting that any second, I'll run out of fresh air.

Dig. I claw the earth with my fingernails.

"Please no." I squeal through pursed lips. *I don't want to die. Henry's in trouble, Dad's killer is at large, and I have an unpaid life debt.*

Despite my begging, an excruciating pain weighs on my neck. My chest collapses. The last trickle of stored air slips from my lungs.

I think of my mother. *Just when things were getting better…*

My muscles clench.

"Tana." Faintly, I hear my name.

"T, where are you?" I twitch at the muffled voices.

Here. I'm here, I holler with my mind, picturing what I hope is a rescue effort.

The pressure on my face eases. The darkness beneath my lids lightens to gray. Fistfuls of warm knuckles knead my damp, icy cheeks.

"T!" What I guess are Trigger's stubby fingers make sweeping passes over my eyes. A large hand wedges behind my neck and lifts me from the muddy grave.

Sitting up, I spit grit from my mouth, cough, choke, and gasp for air.

KC pinches my nose. "Blow," she says. God knows what dislodges from my nostrils. She wipes and then drags the boogered cloth over my mouth.

"Remain calm, slow breaths." Professor McVie scoops his arms toward his chest. "In." He holds for a second and opens his arms as he exhales. "Owwwww-ut." Once the air funnels through his lips, McVie reaches for the rain slicker tied at his waist and smacks it against my torso as if I'm on fire. "You're fine. No problemo."

Remnants of my muddy coffin clunk to the ground.

Trigger runs his sleeve over my lips and gently dusts my lashes. KC's thin arms loop over my head and fall around my neck.

"Just like new," McVie reassures, and then kneels in front of me. He straightens my collar and wipes sweat from his brow. "Quite a pair of hands you have there, Miss Lyre."

His catlike eyes glisten, signaling, I think, how much he appreciated my diving rescue. "Occasionally, I miss the thunderhead, staring at the light show," he says. Tears well.

"Something in your eye, Professor?" I knock his shin with my clunky hiking boot.

"Red dirt, Miss Lyre." Using the checkered bandana around his neck, Professor McVie dries the dampness from his eyes. He stands up and glances around, appearing to survey our situation. Downed power lines, broken branches, and wood and metal siding from a silo block the rural highway. The retention ditch overflows with water, circling us like a castle moat. The corner of McVie's eyelid twitches. "Reports?" he says.

KC licks her index finger and holds it in the air. "Wind's shifted; pressure feels steady."

I add, "Sky is clearing; no sign of convective activity. Outlook— promising."

Professor McVie smiles, props fists on his hips, and swings his matted ponytail over a shoulder.

Trigger says, "Ah, sir…"

"I realize your Doppler equipment is inoperative, Mr. Flough, so let's just skip your part of the briefing."

"It's not that, sir." The sky surfer points to the last-known location of the rover and uses his spare hand to cover a grin. "The rover is gone," he says and snickers.

McVie smiles. "Way to point out the obvious, Mr. Flough."

Despite the bad news—the inconvenience of our team being stranded over a hundred miles from Tulsa without a ride—McVie seems unconcerned. Maybe even a little amused.

He reaches for his shin, hikes his pant leg to his knee, and tears a Velcro case from his calf. He unfastens a second seal, palms a bright-orange walkie-talkie-sized device, and thrusts an arm in the air like the god of thunder and lightning. "Spot." He squeezes the center rubber button. A green light pulses. "Never go chasing without it."

"This is our rescue plan?" My eyes roll toward my friends.

KC shrugs. Trigger draws the universal wacko finger circle around his ear. We wait, skeptical, and count about a dozen or so flashing pulses on the emergency locator, and we consider that Professor McVie's neurons may have gotten fried during the storm.

We are wrong.

Inches above the horizon, flat paddle-like blades appear. Their angled airfoils *whup-whup* and propel closer. McVie's extended arm drops to his side. He widens his stance and then sticks out a hitchhiker's thumb.

In triangle formation, three National Guard Huey helicopters hover overhead. Mud slings as one chopper floats to the ground. Once its rails are firmly planted, a uniformed weekend warrior jumps from the rear compartment, jogs over, and shakes McVie's hand.

"Need another lift, Professor?"

CHAPTER 4

Even without the Internet, news travels fast. Clearly not by my hand though, because when it comes to electronics and storms, I have learned my lesson—tough-love schooling that came several weeks ago on a flight where Trigger and I were accidentally sucked into a mystical geomagnetic storm.

Believe me, when Mother Nature plays the power card, be smart—leave your cell at home. With another radical weather event under my belt, I kind of get why my grandfather says, "At times, it's best to go prehistoric."

The helo crew communicates via two-way radios, announcing the successful recovery and imminent return of our third-hour storm-chasing class—accounted for and safe, without injury.

Mom's probably having a stroke. I hope they notified our parents.

"Only casualty," I hear the pilot say, "one faculty-issue rover."

KC's hand shoots up, undoubtedly to correct him. Truth be told, this is the second totaled weather Hummer this semester. A worried look on Professor McVie's face leads me to believe that tidbit of information isn't worth rehashing.

Pretending to pluck a hair from KC's cheek, I knock her arm to her side and flash a wide-eyed glare.

"What?" KC asks.

I drag her stare to our professor.

"Oh, got it. Mum's the word." She pretends to lock her lips.

In the twenty minutes it takes to hitchhike back to National's campus, the entire student body has assembled on the lush green lacrosse field, which when the season finishes, I hear, converts into a drone launch strip.

Our classmates crouch as the Hueys skim the tree line and buzz the Olympic-length pool. Waves from the blades slap against the airline jet fuselage moored for water rescue class. In our wake, the gutted trainer bobs.

A grinding noise rings, and the tail rotor tilts. A *swoosh* sounds as the razor-like blades twist into the airflow, chopping louder, as if the pilot has pressed the airbrakes. The crowd splits, and the helo settles in the gap. When the landing skids sink in the Tennessee bluegrass, the copilot edges from the cockpit, slides the passenger door open, and guides us from the chopper.

"Nice touchdown," I whisper to KC.

"Yeah." She eyes McVie as we climb from the back. "How do you think these guys know our professor?"

I shrug.

My feet have barely hit the ground when I'm deafened by a high-pitched squeal.

"Triggs!" A leggy gazelle, the hottest girl in school, nicknamed BB, the "bouncing blonde," sprints from the crowd. Trigger cups his fingers around his mouth to cover an ecstatic smile and lowers his aviator glasses to hide his ooey-gooey gaze, but I see through the diversion. He is, without a doubt, mesmerized by the likes of Brooklyn Dehavilland.

"You're OK." She lassos her arms around his neck, and he swings her like a carousel. Forehead to forehead, they coo.

"Oh, please." KC chokes her neck. "Toss me back in the middle of an F1 twister, but *puh-lease* don't subject me to this gross violation of National's no-public-displays-of-affection-on-campus policy." For extra effect, she gags and holds her stomach.

"Extenuating circumstances," I say, unable to peel my gaze from the perfectly matched couple. Secretly, though, I listen for a hint of a reggae riff and wait for the invisible tug of Trigger's tractor beam. *Crickets.* The dead air reminds me that Trigger and I are nothing more than friends. *A misunderstanding.* "We were nearly crushed to death at the hands of at least three tornadoes," I say, quashing the does-he/doesn't-he coin about to flip in my head.

"Big whoop," KC says. "The class is called *Storm Chasing,* so what does Miss Heiress to a Pipeline Company think? We're going to collect data for our midterm at home on the couch watching the Weather Channel?"

My attention shifts to KC, and I frown. "You know that's not remotely true." *Brooklyn is annoyingly perfect.*

"OK, you're right. It's ridiculous to think we would ever gather data from television."

This time, I make a disgusted wince. "BB is studying to be a petroleum engineer. She's top of the math group, funny, and a ruthless field hockey player, not to mention, she looks like a supermodel. A complete package. And if she wasn't dating Trigger, you know we'd choose her as a friend." As the words leave my lips, my innards twist into knots.

"Still, her family's business is not very environmentally conscious." KC wrinkles her nose. Embarrassed, I'm guessing, she looks away and adjusts her almost-edgy purple frames, confirming what I knew the moment we met. KC's heart is golden, and she always speaks her mind—a quality I wish, by the way, that she could share through osmosis. Despite her uncanny knack for saying it how it is, once in a while she gets tripped up in the tidal wave of school scuttlebutt.

I mean what I say about Brooklyn, I really do, but I have to admit that part of me wishes the gossip were true. Then Trigger would have a reason to discount her. Then I wouldn't have to feel so guilty about how I get all tingly around her boyfriend.

What is it about Trigger? When he's near, for some reason, I know everything will be all right. Kind of like the way I feel around Eddie.

Not cool, Lyre—jonesing after someone else's boyfriend. Like KC, I sometimes struggle to accept that, in such a short time, Trigger has a serious girlfriend.

Anyway, why would anyone want to date someone like me? I see things that aren't really there and…I choke, the guilt ball building in my throat. Despite endless hours of rationalizing, I can't come up with a single reason why Trigger and BB don't belong together.

Hooking an arm around KC, I drag her toward the picture-perfect couple.

A few feet away, KC slows and lowers her voice. "Thought you two were getting close, I mean, after that whole Pioneer ordeal. The pink-dress compliment. What happened?"

Wish I knew.

KC says, "Maybe he got scared."

"Scared I might kill him in an airplane."

"Technically, you were trying to take your own life, T, not his."

"But the end result is the same, Kase. If one person in an airplane has a death wish, then everyone else becomes collateral damage."

"We all have shortcomings." She grins and layers her hand over mine. "So one brush with death, and he opts for safe and goes back to Brooklyn?"

I turn and look at KC. *She really is my friend.* "We probably wouldn't have worked out anyway," I say.

KC scans the sky surfer. "I see what you mean. Lean muscles, great smile, strong sense of integrity, and a killer pilot. You're right. Train wreck."

I look at Trigger, and my entire body tingles. Steel drums rumble, and that darn calypso beat rattles in my head. *Stop!* I think, before my hips start to sway.

"What I meant was"—I clear my throat—"we're really different."

"Maybe." KC shrugs. "For the record, I'm going with he chose safe and uncomplicated."

I squeeze her fingers.

"Speaking of things that can give you heartburn." KC eyes the happy couple.

"Hey." I tap Trigger's chiseled shoulder. When he splits from Brooklyn, he blushes and unhooks her petite hands from his neck. BB's face twists, and she leans her narrow hip against her beau. Behind me, I hear KC blow air.

"Can you give us a few minutes, Bea?" Trigger reaches for a strand of the gazelle's waist-length hair and pinches it between his fingers until reaching the golden tip. "Midterm brainstorming." He winces and promises to find her the minute we finish.

Brooklyn glides away, pausing every other stride to turn and look back at Trigger. He watches her, every reluctant step, until her silhouette fades behind a rolling hill of plush grass.

"All right." KC snaps her fingers. Both Trigger and I twitch. "Back to reality. Our midterm?" Her tone is strictly business. "Not to mention those matching blue rings glowing from your ears?"

Henry. The video clip. What's wrong with me? I fist-smash my forehead. *The blood, the gore—his plea, begging us to come and rescue him. Do I risk telling KC and Trigger about what I think I saw?* My lower eyelid twitches. *What if the image was another glitch in my traumatized skull?*

I touch my neck scars. An imaginary coin flips in my mind. *Heads, it was real. Tails, I'm losing it. Again.*

The coin flattens. *Heads.* I gulp, drape my arms over KC's and Trigger's shoulders, and huddle us into a closed circle. I suck my stomach muscles tight. "Henry needs our help."

KC seems disinterested. If I had to bet, I'd say she's focused on our failed midterm project.

Trigger says, "Needs our help how?" His forehead furrows. "Wait, T. How do you know Henry's in trouble?"

"I saw him." *Please let this be real.* "His image, I mean." I squint, recalling the details. "A video stream, I think, while I was buried under the mud." I skip over the flashes I saw in the rover. *No need to appear extra crazy, right?*

"From Pioneer? Not possible." Trigger backs from our circle and glances to the spot on the hill where Brooklyn disappeared. "Are you two holding out on me?" His brows arch. "Because unless you've found a mega-power booster, built a skyscraper antenna"—he bends his neck and scans the horizon—"or modified National's artillery of weather balloons, there's no way a signal came through."

"But our piercings lit," I say. "We all saw them."

The sky surfer lowers his gaze and toes the turf. He looks up, wide-eyed. "The storm. Of course. With the lightning and the electricity in the air, I'm sure the ear glow was a fluke."

"I saw Henry." My upper lip quivers. Echoes of kicks, punches, and moans ring in my ears.

Trigger scans me the same way he would an instrument panel, back and forth, searching for a sign that something's not quite right. After one last eye sweep, he steps forward and cups my elbow.

"T," he says, "you sure you're not just—"

"No," I snap and knock his arm away. "I'm not seeing things. I'm telling you I heard Henry beg for help." *At least I'm pretty sure.*

"What exactly did he say?" KC interrupts.

I shut my eyes and picture the überscientist who single-handedly helped Trigger and me escape from the messed-up, crazy security chief, McDunney, and his boss, the president of Pioneer Academy.

I see Henry's image. Terrified. Trembling. Surrounded by boys dressed in suits. "He said…" My memory skips ahead, and I repeat his plea. "'Help me, Tana. Please.'"

"Help him how?" Trigger's words quicken.

Shots of shined shoes, neckties, and a tattered eye patch pulse like strobe lights beneath my closed lids. "More like with whom."

"Streeters," Trigger says, as if our thoughts are reconnected. I hear him grind his teeth.

"The Future-of-Wall-Street clique was in the stream." I open my eyes. "And…and Chief McDunney."

"McDunney?" Trigger's face flushes as red as flames from a solid rocket booster.

I whisk away the image of the chief's ratty leather eye patch, ignore the memory of his rotten-egg breath, and focus on what else I saw. "At one point in the transmission, the feed cut out, and I saw static."

KC taps a finger on her nose. "Then the stream continued?"

I nod.

She circles around Trigger and leans in until she's centimeters from his ear. She retrieves a tiny magnifying glass strung around her neck and rasps on his Pioneer ear piercing. "Earth magnet," she says and tugs on the sky surfer's ear helix.

More of a statement than a question, if I know KC.

She angles closer, resting her chin against Trigger's neck. "There's a tiny micro receiver embedded in the halo." With a twist of a knob, she fine-tunes the eyeglass. "So where's the antenna?"

"Not sure." Trigger swats KC. "Besides, it's Tana's stud that picked up Henry's SOS." He steps back, waving both hands as if being attacked by a swarm of irritating gnats.

A coy, mischievous, maniacal grin spreads across KC's lips. She fans herself and winks. Quirky personality, yes. Obsession with gossip, without a doubt. But she rules when it comes to anything with a power button, the school, the state, and the entire nation as it relates to the Internet. She is so dominant, in fact, she has been solicited not once but twice by men in dark suits claiming to be recruiting for the government.

"You're not seeing things, T," KC says. "Not this time. I'm 90 percent sure Henry tried to send you a message."

"A message?" Trigger stares at me. "What kind of message? A way to find Pioneer's airfield? The formula for the storm brew?" Sweat beads on his tanned forehead.

Henry getting his butt kicked is what I want to say, but I know nothing good would come of it. "No, nothing that specific."

Trigger's shoulders sag.

KC shuffles over and taps her magnifier against my ear stud. "I suspect he embedded an attachment."

My eyes bug, and I'm sure my jaw slackens.

KC says, "I don't quite understand the design or how images are transmitted, but if there was an attachment, it has a processor."

"And if it has a processor, you can hack it."

"Boom."

KC and I trade a fist pound, chased with our signature five-finger spread. Trigger's ruddy skin fades back to surfer bronze. Our resident techie has just given an impossible scenario a viable shot in the arm.

"If I know Henry, there's a clue in the attachment." I tromp over the grass, relieved my friends believe me and I won't have to join National's after-school cuckoo club. This time, what I saw was real. Confirmation, I guess, that the counseling sessions are helping.

"What kind of clue?" Trigger joins me, matching my strides.

"Maybe an upgraded signal. Or like you said, the formula to make the storm-particle brew." *Wishful thinking.* I rub my neck scar. "Some way to guide us back."

Trigger takes my hand and moves it from my neck. "Don't worry, T. We'll find a way." He presses my palm.

"Time out." KC blows a whistle, another accessory on what she refers to as her utility string. "Call me a script kitty, but I don't get why you can't just fly around over the desert until you see a couple of long stretches of concrete and a control tower. Nevada isn't outer space." She shrugs. "Heck, if you have a license, you can drive there."

Trigger and I exchange a can-we-trust-her glance. Without a word, we decide to share.

"There's a jamming net, Kase," I explain.

"The megabrains at Pioneer have discovered a way to create geomagnetic storms," Trigger adds.

"They shoot a bunch of combustible goo in the air, and once ignited, the residue acts as an electrified shield."

Trigger stops pacing and runs his fingers through his hair. "A shield that can only be breached by a signal sent out by some tricked-out compasses with special directional cards."

"A card we had, but it was removed while Trigger's plane was stored in Pioneer's student hangar."

If KC's surprised, she doesn't show it. She stares off for a minute and blinks back to us. "What about GPS? Unless there's clouds, dust, or fog, the campus should be as easy to figure as a six-letter password."

I glance at Trigger. "Guess that's why Henry's dad was so desperate to create cloud cover." It seems the sky surfer's instincts weren't so far off after all. Pioneer may very well have greater aspirations than just early warning for devastating weather.

"They know how to create fog," Trigger says. "We saw that firsthand."

KC's eyes become as wide as flying saucers. "Didn't see that one coming."

"But there has to be another way they cloak the school and airport," I say. "When we arrived last time, the weather was CAVU—clear skies and visibility unlimited."

"Odds are, they're jamming in-and-out signals from the ground," KC says.

"Not sure." Trigger picks up a pebble and volleys it between his boots. "We saw all kinds of cutting-edge tech while we were at Pioneer. Piercings, in-skull chat streams, magic cloths that take on the shape of whatever they touch, 3-D contacts." He lobs the stone across the field and cocks his head to show KC his lenses. "Surgery is the only way to get these out."

"Lenses?" KC straightens her purple eyewear. "Even though you have twenty-twenty vision?"

"Eighth wonder of the world."

KC's eyes glaze. "A question just begging for the Screen Slayer to conquer."

Here's another one, Slayer. How did Trigger's plane fly cross-country in less than ten minutes—not once, but twice?

Another puzzle for another time. Helping Henry is top priority.

"First things first." The Screen Slayer pinches her lower lip. "We have to find the attachment Henry sent."

"Whatever it takes." Trigger's ocean blues shift to me. "If what Tana saw is true, Henry's in trouble. He stuck his neck out for us, and there's no way we're going to let him down."

CHAPTER 5

"We need a game plan." Trigger pulls a pen from his pocket and twirls it around his fingers.

"I agree, but—"

A drill sergeant voice interrupts. "Plan for what?"

"Hey, Dad." Trigger freezes. Our Fundamentals of Flight professor, a.k.a. Trigger's father, steps into our brainstorming circle.

My throat goes dry. KC's four eyes bug out from their sockets.

"Heard you got mixed up in some weather?" Flough says.

"Solid wall cloud, couple of twisters." Trigger's posture remains stiff. "And we lost another rover."

"Garden-variety storm then."

Although his dad answers all casual and unconcerned, I notice a deep line furrow across the war hero's leathery forehead. He looks his son over. "So what's this plan you're talking about?"

"Midterm project," KC blurts. "Data was in the rover. Didn't have a chance to back up. Way too turbulent." A tiny bit of drool trickles from the corner of her mouth.

Professor Flough's jaw locks.

He isn't buying it. Not at all. After eyeing each of us, he faces Trigger. "Don't suppose you're planning a research trip to the desert?"

KC gulps, and I swallow, leaving my best friend on his own to offer an explanation.

"The thought has crossed our minds."

To say I'm shocked is an understatement. Well aware of his dad's bias against the Pioneer Academy and their philosophy of distributing pills to students to predict their future careers, Trigger went ahead and told his dad the truth—head-on, without hesitation. Add guts to the long list of things I admire about T. Xanthus Flough.

"We discussed this." Trigger's dad scowls and gnaws a soggy toothpick. "Your first visit, the geomagnetic storm, all an unfortunate accident. When I left that dust bowl of a campus, they swore to remove our compass homing chip. But going back intentionally?" He eyeballs his son. "Not an option."

"Even if it means a man gets away with murder?"

For a moment, I think Trigger touched a nerve and challenged the sense of justice inherent in every soldier.

But I'm wrong.

Trigger's dad shifts his weight and grinds his jaw, and the toothpick dwindles to a stub. He focuses somewhere off on the horizon, acting as if Trigger has said nothing at all.

"So the weapon of choice today is the silent ultimatum, Dad?" Trigger says and rolls his fingers into fists. His golden skin turns red. "Didn't you raise me to honor justice and accountability above all else?"

His dad nods. "That's right."

"Stick up for people who can't fight for themselves?" Trigger wraps his thumbs over his knuckles.

"Affirmative."

"Then…"

Professor Flough spits the remaining wood shards from his cracked lips and widens his legs to double shoulder width. "Final answer," he grumbles with the crushing weight of an armored Humvee.

Trigger bites his lip.

The white noise of the student body grows louder.

"Tana." My mother pushes through the crowd and cuts across the lawn.

Behind her is a man who looks like a mix between a lumberjack and a rodeo bull.

Now at my side, Mom squeezes my arm and combs her fingers through my bangs. Specks of red mud flakes fall and settle on my boots. "I got the your-daughter-is-back-safely text from the school, but I thought I'd come see for myself."

"We're fine, Mrs. Lyre." KC wedges in next to my mom and rests a temple on her shoulder.

"Lamar." The redheaded bull of a man opposite Mom draws Professor Flough's uncompromising glare away from his son.

"Gunner," Flough says. His rigid shoulders soften, and if I'm not mistaken, a genuine smile crosses his stiff, career-military upper lip. "It's been too long." They man hug. "What brings you to Tulsa?"

"Came to see Linnea," the stranger says.

I'm not sure whose head snaps around first, but I am certain of whose brain is quickest to engage. *See my mother because?* Although my mind is firing on all cylinders, my tongue can't get out of first gear.

My friend's motormouth, however, has already shifted into second. "KC McKenna." She finger waves to Mom's acquaintance.

"Gunner Clark," he says, his tone strong—a match, by the way, to his rock-solid physique. "You're the up-and-coming computer specialist." He shoots a look of admiration. "I follow your programming work, Miss McKenna."

"Ah, it's nothing." KC turns as pink as the rising sun. Her hands twitch like she has OD'd on sugar.

"And you must be Tana." The man-bull steps toward me. His steady pupils make it difficult to read what's behind his blank expression. "From what your mom tells me, you're a girl who never backs down from an adventure."

"Guess so." I shuffle my feet and conclude that he must be more than an acquaintance, and then I raise an eyebrow at my mother.

"Gunner and your dad were roommates in college," Mom says. "The best of friends."

"Don't remember seeing you at the funeral," I say, having left my diplomat daughter's filter in London. My words, I must admit, come across more biting than I intend.

"Tana," Mom snaps.

"No, Linnea." Gunner Clark laughs. "She's right." He trades a warm smile with my mother and chuckles again. He makes solid eye contact. "You speak your mind, just like your father." Mr. Clark's head bows. The sides of his mouth droop. He coughs, clears his throat, and then speaks. "Regretfully, I was away on business when your dad passed, Tana. Halfway around the world in a remote town with no access to phone or Internet."

I watch his pupils dilate. His eyes glisten. His frown deepens. *Sincere, I suppose. Or a very good actor.*

"By the time I heard the news," Gunner says, "Benjamin had moved on to the next place." His voice fails. He chokes out a few more words. "I'm so sorry for your loss, Tana."

Feeling like a jerk, I press my lips together and strain to offer an apology. Clearly my earlier comment was a rash lapse in judgment. *Be kind, Tana.* Gunner Clark suffered a loss. Just like mom and me. *He deserves condolences, even if I don't really know him.*

Awkwardly, I shake his hand and force a gracious smile—the way I always do when someone mentions my father.

"Any friend of Dad's is a friend of ours, right, Tana?" Forever the diplomat, Mom knows exactly what to say—a skill set I missed out on in the Lyre family gene pool.

"Care to join us for breakfast?" Mr. Clark says. His blank expression returns, erasing any signs of sadness. He steps closer to my mother and rests a hand on her shoulder.

"I'm in." Professor Flough, rumored to never pass up a free meal, accepts the invitation.

Gunner Clark checks with the remainder of our circle.

"Midterm project," KC says.

"Starting from scratch," Trigger piggybacks.

"Due tomorrow," I say and then feel the disapproving weight of my mom's Miss Manners stare. "But thanks for the offer," I add, hoping to avoid another social faux pas.

"Maybe next time." Mr. Clark sort of grins, guarded. I get the impression he's disappointed.

"Grandma's making goulash." Mom dusts dried mud from my jacket sleeve. "I'll be gone for dinner, but let's meet at our usual spot at nine. Be home by six. At the latest."

You're going out? This is new.

Mom says, "You can tell me all about the storm later tonight."

"On the roof?"

"Nine o'clock sharp." My mother waves and walks off with Mr. Clark.

Professor Flough lingers for a minute and adjusts his aviator glasses. He angles his head at Trigger. "Flight-team competition is in a week. Air force cadets—our toughest comp yet. So if you're searching for something productive to do, get up in the air and practice your maneuvers."

Although Trigger holds his tongue, his body shakes, and I suspect, if pushed a millimeter further, he will explode and rocket into orbit.

Flough's attention turns to me. "Miss Lyre." He lets his glasses slide midway down his crooked nose. "Just because you're a natural flyer, doesn't mean you are up to speed. Getting a private license is just the beginning. You are a latecomer to the flight team, and if you want to remain an alternate for this season, you best get your two half moons in the sky with Trigger and practice."

I swallow and nod.

"Miss McKenna."

"Sir?"

"Team managers are supposed to post stats."

KC says, "Yes, sir."

Professor Flough's eyes narrow. "If that's the case then, when I looked online this morning, why did I see blank rankings?"

"We were out chasing...there was a storm...the rover..." she stammers.

Flough raises a stop sign palm. "No excuses." He pushes his aviators over his eyes, spins on a heel, and strides away.

KC shakes her head. "That man is impossible to please."

Trigger's gaze follows his dad. "Tell me about it."

Professor Flough stops, checks the sky, and then shifts his mirrored lenses toward the admin building. "Oh, and, Miss McKenna…" He pauses, his back to us.

KC cringes.

"The next time you tell a lie, try to keep the spit inside your mouth. You'll be far more convincing." He continues toward faculty parking.

Any positive momentum we might have created deflates like a ruptured weather balloon.

KC dries the corners of her lips. Trigger kicks a hunk of grass. My heart sinks, realizing we've just been officially forbidden to return to Pioneer.

"No trial for my dad's murderer and no reinforcements for Henry." Defeated, I drop to the ground and tear out handfuls of thick grass. All the things that are important seem millions of miles away, without the slightest chance of ever being resolved.

"Go practice your maneuvers," Trigger repeats. "Yes, sir." He salutes even though his superior is nowhere in sight. "Anytime I make a logical point…" The sky surfer stomps across the field. "Act in a way he's taught me to be…" He stops and then shouts, "If it goes against his pigheaded opinions, it's keep your trap shut and go practice your flight maneuvers." Trigger bends down and with both hands, unearths another section of sod, lifts it over his head, spins in a circle, and chucks the crumbling mass. "I need to get out of here," he bellows. The force of the throw sends him to his knees. Breathing heavy, he balances on all fours.

"You know…" KC fidgets with the strings on her splash jacket. "Correct me if I'm wrong…" She twists the braided cords around her index fingers. "Didn't Flough say going back to Pioneer *intentionally* is not an option?"

"Not just said it, ordered it!" Trigger yells.

"Perfect." She grins.

"Huh?"

KC's words surprise me too, and when I notice her drifting into a trance, blocking out every single sound around her, I know we are well on our way to a viable solution. Her lips start to move in the typical gone-figuring McKenna way. Reciting formulas, her extraordinary mind runs multiple scenarios. Amped from being up all night, her megabrain works quadruple time.

In a blink, her lips smack, and she shakes off the mind fog. "Technically," KC says, "it isn't our intention to go back to Pioneer." She speaks at breakneck speed. "As a matter of fact, I know for sure none of us are interested in attending that freak show of a school."

She allows dead air to linger, I think, to field any objections. When both Trigger and I offer none, she smiles. "Our sole intentions are to help a friend and hold a guilty party accountable."

Reasonable enough. We all nod in agreement.

"The way I figure, our intentions are outside the parameters of Professor Flough's orders." KC points to the bronze statue, a recreation of the school's founder reading from a forged scroll. "Fairness, integrity, and accountability, the foundation of National's honor code. Isn't one of our graduation requirements to uphold the code of ethics taught right here by our instructors?"

Leave it to KC to find a loophole, one that if challenged, actually makes sense.

"Way to go, Kase." We knock exploding fists, well aware of the challenges ahead, knowing this small victory is just the first of many hurdles before we are able to get back to Pioneer—the most pressing obstacle being figuring out how to create a geomagnetic storm at will and save a friend. The more daunting, however, is how to capture a cold-blooded murderer.

CHAPTER 6

"It's blank." KC blows out, looking defeated, her purple-streaked hair spread across her laptop's keyboard. After three hours of continuous attempts to open Henry's encrypted attachment, she has failed to find one clip of video or a single line of usable text. As far as I know, this is the first time the Screen Slayer has confessed to being beaten by a program. Even temporarily.

"Maybe you need a jolt of caffeine." Trigger offers to make a vending run.

"I'm not tired," KC snaps. "I mean, we've been up all night, of course, and I need sleep, but that has nothing to do with why I can't read Henry's attachment."

"Then what's the problem? I thought you were good at this?"

KC scowls. "Breaking the code is the easy part. Kindergarten variety. Almost as if Henry wrote a simple strand so even an amateur script kiddie could figure the hack. But when I crack through his firewalls…" Her bony fingers glide over the keyboard. "Attempt to approach the cyber back door…" Pictures of barbed wire screens appear after each keystroke. "And breach the perimeter…" The sound of an antique hinge creaks over the speaker. "I find myself idling alone in a virtual closet."

Over her laptop speakers, I hear metal hangers clanging, knocking as if someone packed in a hurry. Her screen is opaque, as solid as an overcast sky on a moonless night. No glint of a light cord, no virtual window latches or hidden techie knobs to point to a cyberspace exit.

"There's nothing here." KC enters a sequence of commands, shifts, and controls. Despite her patented ciphers, the screen remains dismal.

"Now what?" Trigger's temper flares. "Without Henry's help, there's no way to get back to the desert."

"We need a weather expert," I say, hoping to shift his focus in a more productive direction. Forward. Moving us closer to another possible solution. "Someone with intimate knowledge of magnetic storms."

KC spiders her fingers against her neck. "What about Professor McVie?"

Perfect, I'm about to say. But something in Trigger's body language tells me it's a terrible idea.

"No way. If we tell McVie, he'll help us," Trigger says. "If he helps us, he'll likely get fired."

Trigger's right. Already on probation for not respecting the school's strict Safe Distance Policy when it comes to studying storms, our professor has been cited for putting his students at risk. Throw in last night's tornado close encounter and loss of another rover and, at best, McVie's job at National is precarious. His passion for the hunt far exceeds his concern for the consequences—a handicap we both share.

KC says, "No sacrifice is too large in the pursuit of knowledge. Isn't that what McVie always tells us?"

"Come on, Kase," I say. "We all know that every cent of McVie's paycheck goes straight into research, leaving him scraping by, living week to week in that beat-up old camper on the far edge of the airport. He needs his job. We can't put Professor McVie in that position." Although based in fact, the words sting my tongue as I discount the only person capable of helping with our plan.

"You have a better idea?" KC says, never compelled to hold back from stating the obvious, even when unnecessary and grossly unpopular. "So far, we have a general idea where the school is, a magnetic compass without a GPS card, and no foreseeable way to create a geomagnetic storm." Spittle bubbles from the corner of her mouth and dribbles down her chin.

"Yes, thanks, Miss Tell-It-Like-It-Is." Trigger's irritation ratchets up. "We already know it's practically hopeless."

KC ignores him and types another series of systematic keystrokes. "Just stating the facts."

"Nothing's impossible," Trigger says and paces from one end of the lab to the other. I watch him, searching for signs of truth behind his bold words. But even amid his anger and a geyser of can-do adrenaline, I see him floundering, a fighter jock fish drowning in high-tech water.

"I refuse to let Henry down." He strides. "Let Tana down. Allow that coward Dr. Harb to get away with murder."

"I'm listening." KC's eyes remain trained on her computer screen.

Trigger glares at the back of her head. "Am I the only one who ever has any ideas?" He doesn't wait for an answer. Instead, he clomps toward the door and exits the lab.

No, you're not the only one, I think as he disappears down the hallway.

I have an idea, one I don't dare mention.

***

I never have any trouble speaking up when it comes to my grandmother's cooking. The goulash is extra spicy tonight, and I didn't hesitate to ask for seconds.

"Heard you had quite a day." Gran spoons the thick stew into my bowl and adds an extra dash of paprika. Fiery as rocket fuel, just the way I like it.

"We were well on our way to mapping the most intense storm of the season and then—" I stop, remembering what my mom says about grandmothers and worrying.

"Then?" she twists a flat noodle around her fork.

"Then, our professor decided to fall back. Put some distance between us and the wall cloud." I dig through the vegetables, scouring for a potato. "You know, for safety and all."

"I see." Gran's brows scrunch. "That whole part about you being buried alive was just a piece of fiction?"

I fumble my fork to the table, and when I scramble to recover it, my hand hits the prongs, flipping it in the air. "How?" I wonder if the ability to know everything that goes on in my life is somehow genetic. Very little, if anything, gets past Gran and my mother.

"I do have access to the Internet, dear."

The Internet. Hold on. There were only four of us lying in the retention ditch, hiding from the storm. No way McVie leaked a word. His actions, at the very least, showed questionable judgment. Being born and bred in the military, Trigger's lips are perpetually sealed, making him not inclined to spill in person or, even less likely, online. That leaves...

"I follow KC's blog," Gran says. "Although I don't completely trust everything I read on the web, there's a lot of good stuff floating in cyberspace." Her eyes edge up, and I assume she's waiting for an explanation.

"It's just, well, Mom asked me not to worry you."

"Pish." Gran waves her hand in the air. "I'm not made of porcelain." She rips a piece of bread from a crusty loaf and drags it across the inside of her empty bowl. "Really, you two." She shakes her stylish gray bob. "Where do you think you got your sense of adventure? I was first runner-up to Miss Oklahoma, you know."

After another pass with the sticky sourdough, she glances into the great room at my grandfather seated in his favorite chair, TV muted, completely engrossed in the daily crossword puzzle. "From him?"

Now looking at my soft-spoken, even-tempered, steady-handed, can-fix-anything grandfather, I realize how ridiculous the notion that any strand of my warrior DNA spawns from Pop. Gran, however, is a different story altogether. She's genetically engineered to run like a locomotive—similar to me, but exactly like my mother.

"OK, being my first buried-alive-in-mud experience, I have to admit that I was scared. But only for a second. My friends rallied to my rescue."

"Being a little afraid is good, Tana. It elevates us to a level of peak performance."

Although it is kind of strange advice coming from my near-eighty-year-old Gran, something deep down in my insides stirs, perhaps explaining my attraction to danger.

"Where's Mom?" I push from my chair and carry our bowls to the sink.

"Mr. Clark invited her to see a visiting political speaker. Considering his line of work, I suspect he's trying to lure her back into the mediation business."

"What does he do?"

"Some muckety-muck union negotiator for the Department of Transportation."

Makes sense why I struggled to read him. He's trained. He probably only reveals what he wants seen—a strategist, just like my mother. As I picture the two headstrong negotiators together, I amuse myself by envisioning them posturing against one another—her talking about the hot Oklahoma weather and him pretending to care, all the while, Mom watching for tells; The real reason why Gunner Clark is here. I'm so glad I excused myself earlier. *Score one for the gut-o-meter.*

"Might be good for her." I rinse the plates, scrub the stewpot, and load the dishwasher. As I rinse away the soapy bubbles, I flash back to our life when my parents worked for the UN—long days, after-hour parties, fundraisers, and continuous travel. I shudder as I compare the old days with my current social schedule—incidental time with my friends and quiet dinners with Mom, Pop, and Gran. *Maybe Molassesville isn't so bad after all.*

"Do you think she's ready?" I ask.

"To move forward?" Gran answers. "Yes. But to go back to the way things were before, when your dad was around? That I don't know."

CHAPTER 7

"Do you think Dad's out there?" I squint an eye and align my thumb against the night sky to the center of Orion's star belt. Cicadas rattle from the bushes. Tree frogs croak.

Mom lies next to me on our sunroom's flat roof. From my periphery, I notice her close a lid and match a stiff arm to mine. But instead of lingering, her thumb traces the mighty hunter's bow and arrow until reaching the horns of the neighboring star cluster, Taurus the bull. "There's no doubt." Mom smiles.

"I guess Dad could be intense when he had something on his mind."

"Something?"

"OK." I giggle. "*Everything.*"

Her hand flies to her stomach, and we both belly laugh. "It was on or off with your father. For as calm and cool as he might appear as a mediator, at home he was all bucking and blowing."

"Like a bull," I say.

"Bullheaded."

We practically bust our guts.

How strange. Less than a month ago, even the slightest mention of Dad's name sent Mom and me spinning into a heated debate—so much so, I avoided the subject altogether. But here we are, thirty days later, hanging out on our rooftop beneath an inky-black sky filled with stars, talking about him, laughing even, as if he's still around. *How cool. Maybe family counseling is making us closer.*

As the gut-buster dies off, the cicadas' buzzes intensify. My chest rises and falls. My breathing slows. "Do you think Dad knew?"

Mom drags her attention from the sky, rolls onto her side, and props her head on an elbow. "Knew what?"

"That he was going to die?"

Mom's eyelids flutter. She touches her lip to stop a twitch. "Your dad was so intuitive, Tana. It was almost like he had some superhuman way to get into other people's heads and know what they were going to say before they spoke."

Every muscle in my body tightens. "So he knew."

Mom flattens and exhales. "His intuition was probably warning him. Did he trust it?" She squeezes an eye shut and matches her thumb to Taurus's horns. "Who knows? He was so—"

"Bullheaded?" I say.

"Pigheaded also." This time neither of us laughs.

The winch I haven't felt for a while cranks down on my heart. "Why did he do it, Mom? My whole life, he preached family comes first. Why would he risk his life for people we'd never met?"

Lines I've never noticed before wrinkle around my mother's eyes. She rolls her lips together and then says, "People were being wronged, T. Damaged. Furthermore, they were kids." Her mouth tightens. "Kids your age."

"So he was lying when he said family above all else."

"No. Yes." She shakes her head. "Honestly, I really don't know." Her chin falls to a shoulder. "There was something about the BioDynamics mediation that he couldn't leave alone. After the break-ins, we discussed whether winning this case was worth the risk to our family. He said to trust him. He had a reason. An urgent reason."

"What reason, Mom?"

She twists her neck. "He never told me. To this day, I don't understand."

I feel that all-too-familiar chest winch ratchet tighter. Mom must sense the pull because she places a reassuring hand on my forearm.

"What I know for sure"—Mom's pale-brown eyes lock onto mine—"is you were always on your dad's mind and you will forever be in his heart."

My eyes fill and tears track down my cheeks. "For real?"

"No doubt."

Mom's fingers lace through mine. "We were wrong. Your father and I."

I swallow.

My mother frowns. "We should have talked about the break-ins and the death threats."

The sensation of being buried in mud weighs on my chest.

"We…"—Mom exhales—"I…thought it best not to focus on the negatives. I told myself that if your dad and I showed all the good that came from our work, well…" She pauses and half laughs. "The good would overcome the bad."

"Worked for a while," I lie.

"Until it didn't." She swipes my bangs across my forehead. "Still having nightmares? Flashbacks?"

I reach for my neck scar. My stomach somersaults. "They're better." I cough. "Fewer, I mean."

Mom moves my hand away and touches the incisions on my collarbone, my cheek, and my forehead.

"I realize they feel huge to you, Tana, but the reality is, they're hair thin."

I know. But at times, it feels like there's lava bubbling under my skin. "The plastic surgeons did their jobs." I resist the urge to touch the stitch marks. "No one even mentions them."

"What about the visions?" Mom asks.

I squeeze my eyes shut and picture Henry. My head starts to throb. *Divert and distract.* I know Mom wants me to change how I handle stress, but I've been this way all my life. It's not like flipping a light switch. I shift focus and think back to the storm and the rover. No exploding butterflies. No images of Dad from the afterlife. And I did just pass my private pilot's license test. *That's progress, right?*

"Not lately," I divert and throw in a viable distraction. "But I really wish Eddie could have stayed. I miss him. Feel safer when he's around."

"Me too." The corners of Mom's thin mouth curl. "And that crazy retro Caesar haircut."

I say, "What's up with that shag?"

"He *is* a diehard Beatles fan."

"A half-Italian and half-Latino John Lennon?"

Mom winces.

"I'm not seeing it. Does he think it's cool?"

"Hard to say." She *tsks*. "Women sure flock to him like bees to pollen."

"Young women, old women, married women," I say. "I don't get it."

"Hero syndrome," Mom says. "The fact that he's tall, muscular, and carries a gun."

Yuk. I cringe, thinking of Eddie as a chick magnet. "I guess if you're in to that upside-down triangle, body builder physique." I scratch my head. "At least he doesn't still wear socks with his sandals."

"You cured him of that."

"Does he like the new family he's protecting?"

"I think so." Mom glances over a shoulder. "You realize he requested a diplomatic couple with no children?"

"I heard." My spirits lift. I feel a little less forgotten. "He gave me a burner phone in case I get into a jam."

Fear flicks across Mom's eyes. "What kind of jam?"

"*Take this, T,*" *Eddie said before he left for his overseas assignment.* "*Call if you need me. Your risk tolerance seems to have climbed a few notches.*" A conversation, I think, that's best kept between the two of us.

"Nothing," I reassure her. "Probably wants to check who I'm texting. He promised to come visit the first chance he gets."

We both snap up as a white blur soars overhead. A makeshift paper airplane loops and shoots straight through my bedroom window.

Crap. I look away and then allow my sight line to ease back to my mother.

"UFO?" she says.

"Huh? Did you see something?" I sit up and search the darkness. "Where? I must have missed it." *Terrible aim.* For someone who has such great hand-eye coordination, Trigger couldn't hit a freight train with a slingshot.

A grin splits Mom's lips. "You best get going. I have a sneaking suspicion someone is waiting for you beneath the magnolia tree."

Positive I look like a deer caught in high beams, I shade my brow and climb to my feet. "How did you…"

She points to egg-sized cameras tucked under the roof eaves.

"Let me guess, Pop again?"

She nods, smiling. "I know everything that goes on around here."

CHAPTER 8

A balmy September breeze blows through my open bedroom window, swirls, and lifts the gauzy sheers. The hem waffles and then sinks back toward the hardwood floor.

A second paper airplane, folded to resemble a military fighter jet, shoots between the split in the airy fabric. Arcing like a long bow, the makeshift airfoil cuts to the left, rolls belly up, and crashes to the floor. *Like I said earlier, all thrust and no vector.* Admittedly, though, this model flew a second longer than the one the night prior.

Jenks, my amber-colored tabby, leaps from the pillow-top mattress, stretches like an accordion, pounces, and buries his claws in the uninvited guest.

I cross the room and inspect the crash site.

"Good boy." I lure the crumpled frame from Jenks's hunting grip and scratch him behind the ears to acknowledge his kill. He howls. His back bristles. With the paper plane's underside exposed, I notice two shiny quarters glued beneath each wing. Long-range fuel tanks, I assume. A modification that explains why the folded notebook paper glided a little farther than usual. *An upgrade. Nice.* I open the edges and see a handwritten message.

"In the mood for a show?"

I smile, recognizing the sketchy scribble, and marvel to what extent a guy will go to get a girl out past curfew.

Does this mean the funk is over?

Grinning, I hurry over to the windowsill and slip in between the tea-stained sheers.

Using the flashlight on my cell, I aim five quick light bursts toward the tall gray shadow looming under the hundred-year-old magnolia, signaling that I'll be down in five. It's our own code, which KC developed so we could all message without leaving any electronic footprints. "Never know who's watching," she always warns.

A single beam flicks back, and I know Trigger received my signal.

Being aware of what has to be done but having no idea how to do it is the most frustrating thing on the planet. I dive on the bed, pop open my laptop, and use the technique KC taught me to partition our home wireless network.

I type in an encrypted password and then run her Reflection program that projects an image of me working on my math homework with a virtual tutor onto any computer linked to our network. *Maybe you don't know quite everything, Mom.* Jenks coils at my side.

When access to the protected partition is granted, I type Dr. Abraham Harb's name into my taskbar and search for any reference to the man who killed my father.

Same-o.

Once again, the search engine comes up empty of any new data. Links to Harb's job history—security chief, scientist, head of a classified project at the pharmaceutical behemoth BioDynamics—appear onscreen, facts I already know. But when I dig further—industry publications, science symposiums, speaking engagements—I see no reference to the renowned researcher. It's almost as if he evaporated into the dry desert air.

Where are you hiding?

I scan the web page one more time. No trail. No leads. No clues to help catch a killer. Like an Olympic sprinter sidelined with a sprained ankle,

I lie on my pillow-top bed, helpless, destined to watch my gold-medal opportunity from the bench. Jenks, my official tiger-tabby mascot, meows.

Or am I? I roll onto my back. For the second time today, my mind drifts to the forbidden option. The powdered taboo, an advantage Trigger and I vowed never to explore.

Double or nothing. That was our pact. Either we both took the fortune-telling pill or we didn't—that was the promise we made to each other in the nurse's line at Pioneer while waiting to receive a glimpse into our futures—the pact I didn't hesitate to break at the first sign of duress.

A sting of residual guilt cuts beneath my rib cage as I struggle to think of a reason Trigger keeps me as a friend. I let him down, not once but twice. I haven't figured out why he's giving me a third shot to screw up again.

Double or nothing, my mind repeats our mantra. I swallow. *There must be another way to help Henry and also get justice for my dad.* I rerun every possibility. Truth is, there isn't.

Inside, my chest pulls, aware of what I'm up against. I'll have to ask Trigger to do the unthinkable, the one thing he swore was out of the question.

I can't ask him to do it. Guilt cuts again. Compromise on something he feels so strongly against. So it's decided. Although it might be our best chance to get back to Pioneer, there is no way I'll even suggest that he take Henry's parting gift—a powder-filled pill that, if swallowed, shows the future.

Comfortably dressed in yoga pants and a coral-colored T-shirt, I opt for the exit less likely to attract attention. I tiptoe across the room, slip out the double-paned window, climb down the rusty fire escape, and land on the roof of the rotunda room. A few short steps and I turn backward to shimmy down a section of patinaed-copper guttering.

Just as my feet hit the ground, Trigger skulks from the tree's protective cover and latches onto my arm. "Sure is tough to get anything past Gran and your mother." The sky surfer releases my elbow and points at his pickup truck. "I really need to talk to you."

A short block away sits a vintage Chevy pickup, nicknamed the Creamsicle due to the fact it's painted the color of orange sherbet and accented with a coconut-white stripe. The dessert on wheels is parallel parked against the curb.

We scurry down the tiled walkway, weave through the moon garden, pass underneath my grandmother's snarly wisteria trellis, and round the speared iron fence. Once on the cracked sidewalk, we both run. Fireflies flicker in our path. I step onto the sleepy street and approach the first-generation drop-center ladder short-bed pickup. Trigger wanders to the driver's side.

In the front seat, he leans across and jiggles the interior door pull. I squeeze the chunky chrome handle from the outside and yank on the passenger door. When the creaky hinges give way, the sky surfer sets the shifter in neutral and hops out, leaving one hand gripped to a steering wheel big enough to steer a bus.

"On three," he whispers, and after a short count, we both use our body weight to heave against the boxy steel frame.

I lift on my toes in order to get better traction, lean farther forward, and stomp against the ground. Our feet chop, and after a series of sighs and grunts, the thick white-walled tires begin to roll. The Creamsicle gains momentum.

Three blocks away, we reach a steady glide and jump onto the bench seat, and Trigger pops the clutch. The engine whines, clanks, and then turns over. Now with the truck firing on all cylinders, he shifts into second gear and checks the rearview mirror.

"Think we made it undetected." He angles over both shoulders to see if we've attracted any neighborly attention. Luckily, all the porch lights stay off.

"Under three minutes," I report, reading from my dive watch. "We're getting faster."

"Practice makes precision." Trigger's attention alternates between the road ahead and the rearview. With the engine roaring, he transitions into third gear.

I avoid the temptation to fill the dead air and instead, listen to gravel *pitter-patter* against the corroded, Swiss cheese floor. My gaze drifts to the rectangular side mirrors, tall and wide enough to power a medium orbit satellite. *Tonight marks the fourth evening this week a paper airplane crash-landed in my room.*

The big-block diesel motor revs faster. Trigger downshifts, challenging all 220 horses under the hood to climb the steep First Street Bridge. Nearly at the top of the hill, the carburetor sputters, coughs, and gasps for air. As a last-ditch effort, the sky surfer reaches to flip off the air conditioner switch.

"Lean forward." Trigger's ocean blues narrow.

I scoot forward to the edge of the bench seat, put my head against the windshield, and will the grinding transmission over the asphalt peak. We teeter like a seesaw, front wheels pulling forward, rear axle slipping back, and when Trigger butts his muscular shoulders to the dash, the scale tips.

Tires teeter forward. The massive hood dips. The truck's prehistoric engine spits a heavy sigh of relief, and the Creamsicle coasts to the intersection of the river's frontage road.

"Never gives up." Trigger rubs the old Chevy's dash. "A typical Flough."

The panel lights brighten, and the suspension seems to ride higher. *Everything Trigger touches assumes his swagger.* As one, he and his motorized horse glide down the paved trail.

At the bottom of the slope, Trigger turns at the flashing yellow traffic light, parallels the muddy water of the Arkansas River, circles the oil refinery, and curves through the gas storage tanks. He cruises past the fenced electrical grid and maneuvers around the demolished gate to the boarded-up entrance of an abandoned open-air amphitheater.

Our low beams light the weed-riddled gravel, and Trigger parks the Creamsicle in an unmarked stall. Outside the truck, we track on foot across the tall grass. A steady buzz hums overhead from live electrical wires.

Trigger is uncharacteristically silent. Normally, he yammers nonstop, only pausing to check if I'm keeping up with him. We usually rehash the pros and cons of school, flying, and what comes next. Life stuff. The overwhelming prospect of the future. Plans I prefer not to think about. At times, though, it feels like he's about to open up and share something difficult or important. But at the last minute, he always goes radio silent. Still, four weeks of nightly walks have shown me there is far more to Trigger Flough than his glistening white teeth and above-average flying skills.

Tonight is different. Absent is Trigger's *Flough swagger*. His cocky surfer grin remains dead flat like waves at low tide. If I didn't know better, I'd guess he preferred to be alone.

But it was his paper plane that flew through my window and drew me off the roof, away from stargazing with my mother. I shoo off any doubts that Trigger wants my company.

As the brittle prairie grass crunches beneath my boots, I consider what could be bothering my friend. I list standard go-to categories: school, girls, flying, or family.

Shaken by the tornadoes? Nah, Trigger's nerves could rivet steel.

Brooklyn? Can't be her either. Just a few hours ago, they were literally joined at the hip.

And despite the fact his father suggested otherwise, Trigger's aerial maneuvers are perfected for the flight team's next competition. I know. We practice together.

Speaking of Professor Flough…my mind discredits the conflict between Trigger and his dad, due to the mere fact that it is a daily occurrence.

That leaves friends. Or friend. Specifically, our failed attempts to help Henry.

The gnarly brush beneath my feet transitions to freshly seeded grass. Sprinklers fan back and forth, soaking the landscaped foreground. An attempt, I'm guessing, for the land seller to spruce up the place a little.

An easy wind blows from the south and mists my skin. Even though the blue-black sky provides little light, I can read the painted sign nailed to two rotted fence posts. "Land for auction. Ten acres. No trespassing. Violators will be prosecuted to the fullest extent of the law." A clip-on slot overflows with "For Sale" flyers and a real estate broker's business cards.

Trigger stays true to form—tight-lipped, ignoring the warning. He walks toward the opening in the stone wall. Reluctantly, I follow.

CHAPTER 9

Beyond the crumbling entrance, a dilapidated amphitheater appears—open air, built to resemble a Shakespearian theater in the round. Steep aisles of bedrock stairs divide rows of bench seats chiseled from the same charcoal-colored rock. I jog down the jagged steps, move front and center, and sit in the third row. I prop my elbows on my thighs and examine the floating stage anchored in at least four feet of water. It's a platform built to be worthy of a castle and surrounded by a man-made mote. I sense Tana following.

Before long, she climbs over the backless stadium seats and squats next to me. Hairs I didn't know I had stand at attention. Downtown, church bells chime eleven times.

"When I come here…" I say, figuring by now that Tana thinks I've gone mute. She doesn't seem to mind though. I like the fact we can hang out and be quiet. "I always expect to see two dueling knights charge on the stage and fight to the death. One dressed in black armor, the other white."

"Good versus evil." Tana smiles. I'm guessing she's aware of how I struggle to relate to anything in between.

"You'd think one time I'd envision something else."

"The battle is ongoing." Tana hugs her knees to her chest. My eyes trace the shape of her soft jawline. A loose strand of hair blows over her eyes. I reach to brush it away, and then decide against it, remembering she tried to kill me in my plane. More important, I remember I have a great girlfriend.

Tana tucks the wavy strand behind an ear. "If history really repeats itself, a conflict not to be resolved anytime soon."

"Still…" My thoughts drift. This place reminds me of medieval times. The curved exterior walls have cracked and fallen into disrepair like the Colosseum in Rome. I kind of wish I was born back then, where differences could be resolved with a sword, brute strength, and heavy armor.

Tana squints at the clamshell stage that's tethered to the shore by metal cables, equipped with a retractable top. She says, "I see a drum set and a hardcore metal band."

"Volbeat?"

"More like AC/DC." She cups a hand over her Pioneer ear piercing. "Can you hear it?"

I shake my head. At times, Tana and I are so in tune, finishing each other's sentences; heck, sometimes I know what's about to come from her mouth before she speaks. But other times, like now, I have no clue what she's talking about.

"A snare drum thumps." Tana plays air sticks. "Guitar strings twang." Her fingers strum a pant leg. "The lead singer screeches." Tossing her bangs, she sings into a clenched fist.

I squint at the empty venue and close one eye the way I do when trying to see things from a different perspective. "Old school heavy metal?"

Tana laughs. "Exactly."

I spin around on the stone slab and lie flat on my back. With no ambient light for miles, the stars seem within arm's reach. "I've been racking my brain all day, but I just can't figure how to get back." My fists pound stone.

Tana must have stretched out since the crowns of our heads touch. I feel unsteady, like I'm flying in the clouds without a compass. My throat tightens.

"Henry?" she says.

"No…I mean…yes," I stammer. My tongue feels triple sized. *What's my problem?* I clear my throat. It's not like me to get tongue-tied. "Of course I want to help Henry."

Tana worms closer, and her soft skin brushes over my razor stubble until her forehead meets my chin. The sky above tilts sideways. The stars in Orion's Belt bunch up. *Brooklyn Dehavilland. Smart, beautiful, athletic, the girl every guy in school wants to have on his arm. I'm so lucky to be with BB. She adores me. When we're together, there's no one else in the world. So why does Tana have this effect on me?*

I'm a knucklehead; that's why. It's like the guys on base say; the jet you're not flying is always faster. Get your head straight. I rub the exhaust smoke from my eyes and look at the girl who is as volatile as a stick of dynamite on the Fourth of July. "I've run every scenario known to meteorologists, and I still can't find a way back to Pioneer."

Tana gestures like she's shot an arrow from a bow. "Bull's-eye," she says. "I know what you're thinking."

I hope not.

She matches her thumb to the North Star and covers the dull glow. A grin wiggles across her plump lips. "Just as I thought, a circumstance the fearless Flough can't swoop in and fix."

A heavy sigh slips from my mouth, louder then I intend. *That's it.* Why I'm drawn to her. I don't have to be perfect, über, and on top of everything when Tana's around. For as unpredictable as she can be, Tana is capable of handling herself. I can hang back, relax, even let my guard down, *a little*, confident in the fact that whatever I do, Tana doesn't judge me at all. "OK, Miss Mind Reader, how do we help Henry?"

She says, "And get justice for my dad?"

"Goes without saying."

"Since we're on the same page, the question is, do we continue down the safe path or plunge into the unknown?"

By the smug look on Tana's face, I assume she has an answer in mind.

I'm aware of her bias, given the proven fact that she'll sacrifice just about anything to catch her dad's killer. What I'm not sure about, however, is how far my friend will go to get what she wants. My chest cycles again, quick and shallow—unsure of what to do next.

"There is a way." Tana stares into the endless black sky.

I swallow. "What do you mean?"

Her gaze drifts back to me, and I see what looks like conflict churning in her brown-green flecked eyes.

"You could"—she rubs her lips over one another—"take your future pill."

A burst of wind blows, the clamshell marquee rattles, water ripples, and dried maple leaves bob over the wavy pond. In the distance, a freight train fires a warning blast. As if struck by lightning, my body flinches. I sit up. Both hands grip the stone ledge and tighten like socket wrenches. Tana steadies my forearm.

"It's the only way," she says. "If you want to help Henry."

I shove trembling fingers into my cargo pocket. I dig around until I feel the translucent pill case, jiggle it a couple of times, and then raise the tinted plastic against the moon's light. I pop off the safety cap and pinch the squishy, powder-filled capsule from the jar. The gel-covered crystals twinkle. In my periphery, I see Tana's face bunch.

"You have the pill with you?" she asks.

The ebb and flow inside the shimmering capsule makes me feel crooked, like when I'm in a turn in an airplane for a while, and when leveling, I feel like I'm leaning in the opposite direction. "There's something about this that doesn't feel right," I say as spots dot in front of my eyes. I curl the window to my future in my palm. *Double or nothing.* "We agreed looking ahead wasn't a good idea. Besides, you said it didn't work, right?"

Tana's pupils widen. "Not exactly." One hand reaches for her stomach. The other scratches her nose.

She's lying.

"What aren't you telling me, T?" My skin feels as hot as Oklahoma's red dirt. "We made a pact." My heart thumps against my rib cage. "When we got back from Pioneer, we swore no more secrets."

Tana looks as if she's been turned to stone. "*You know…*" I snap in front of her dead eyes. "Remind me again what you saw before I traded myself to that perverted monster McDunney in order to save your backside?" Anger erupts in my gut.

A zoned-out zombie expression covers her face—the one that comes right before she sees or hears things that really aren't there. Exploding butterflies. Whispers from her father. What I wouldn't give right now to have an implant that could not only see but also hear her thoughts.

"Never mind." I hop on top of the bench and sprint up the stone slabs, skipping every other row. *This thing with Tana—way too complicated.*

"What if Henry gave your pill back for a reason?" Her voice ricochets off the curved walls. "In the hangar, before we left, when he gifted you the capsule, what was it he said?" Her words are steady and lucid. "Just in case you ever needed to return to Pioneer."

My heart seizes, but my legs keep climbing. My arms pump. My feet stomp rock.

"And what if he figured out how to embed a message? Discovered a way to alter your future pill?"

At the top tier, my ankles twist. I stumble, regroup, and rest my hands on my knees. "Not possible," I pant. "Pioneer uses the pill to see years in the future." I poke holes in her logical-but-flawed train of thought and then drag an arm across my forehead. "Not what might happen over the course of a few months."

"Why not?" Tana's voice is even. "Henry managed to invent a chameleon chamois, bootleg intranet frequencies, and when we challenged, he even created a geomagnetic storm."

I shut an eye but still struggle to see her point of view. "Henry Aska Gu is the smartest kid I've ever met, but he's a meteorologist, not a chemist." I search my pocket for the amber pill bottle. "There's no way Henry hid the layman's guide to creating a geomagnetic storm inside this minicapsule."

Tana stomps up to the cheap seats and stands as sturdy as a century-old magnolia, inches from my face. She layers her arms. *Talk about guts.*

"Unlikely." She stares into my eyes without blinking. "But what if he found a way to help us get past the jamming net?"

"Not only would he have to send the CliffsNotes on how to build the storm-making brew, since our direction card for our compass is MIA, but he would also need to stream Pioneer's missing airport coordinates." I bend my neck to search the inky abyss. "Pretty tall order, even for a weather genius."

"What if our receivers glowing during last night's storm was a signal?" Tana presses on as if she hasn't heard a word I said. "A code. Like KC's flashlight sequences. A beacon of hope. Henry's SOS. Just *in case* he needs backup." Tana sticks a stiff finger in my chest. "Are you really willing to take that chance, you chicken-shit quitter."

***

The ride home in the Creamsicle is unusually quiet. Neither of us, I guess, is willing to give an inch. Two bulls, horns locked, clashing about whether to crash the electric fence. *Tana can be so pigheaded.*

I'm not a chicken. I grind my molars. *I just have more sense than to go up in a plane on a harebrained whim.* I drive the long way home just in case she comes to her senses.

The brakes squeal as my dream on a stick rolls to the curb and stops at Tana's front walk. *Screw the Buttinski neighbors.*

"So that's it?" Tana clicks the latch, unbuckling her seat belt. "You're going to leave Henry all alone based on a technicality?"

I grip the jumbo steering wheel. "For the record, I'm not afraid. Taking a pill to see what comes next feels like cheating, T. We're supposed to conduct ourselves with integrity. Take it as it comes, not ingest some magic pill and get the answers to life's tests."

Tana spins on a heel and stomps two steps, turns, marches back to the passenger window, and ducks in. "You don't get it, do you? Our friend's in trouble, and the man who murdered my father is living it up in the desert. Extenuating circumstances, don't you think? Well worth a moral code deviation." Tana searches the landscape like she's looking for something. "Do you see any swords? Horses and men with lances? These are modern times, Trigger. Things aren't always black or white."

CHAPTER 10

Faced with the reality of never getting justice for my dad and burdened, knowing I'm about to abandon a friend, I wake the next morning with an overwhelming sense of dread. I know Trigger drove the great circle route home, hoping I would fess up to what I saw when I swallowed my future pill. But how can I explain something I don't understand myself?

What I know for sure from the vision is that I dove out of the back of a camouflaged cargo plane even though I'm terrified of heights. I understood radio transmissions in Russian. I was older and had an affection for black neoprene. The truth Trigger wants isn't a truth at all. My pill-induced vision was incomplete. Foggy. Fractured. Interrupted by Chief McDunney. I have no idea where I was, or why I was riding in an airplane cargo bay with a parachute strapped to my back. I've played the image over a hundred times in my head, but the glimpse into my future was cut short. Thanks to Chief Creepy, I only ingested half the pill.

None of this information will help me convince Mister There-Are-Only-Black-and-White-Knights to take his pill. In this case, the truth isn't applicable. Right now, there's no truth to tell.

My stomach knots. A heaviness settles. Likely side effects of knowing I've tested our friendship one too many times.

Speaking of hopeless causes. My chest pinches as I picture the image of Henry—outgunned, weak, and alone. He's the kind of person Dad dedicated his life to protecting. How disappointed my father would be that I failed to help someone in need, especially a friend.

That's right, Lyre, choke it down. What's better first thing in the morning than a double-decker guilt sandwich?

In the bathroom, I leap over cold tiles, hopscotching until I land on the cushy bathmat in front of the pedestal sink. I tie my hair into a high ponytail, lean into the vanity mirror, and tilt my head until the light reflects off of Dr. Lindy's topaz-rimmed contacts. I skim a fingertip across the hard lens that I was told could only be removed with surgery. *What's the use of having 3-D-enhanced vision if it only works on Pioneer's campus?* Sure could use the advantage of boosted vision right now— a crystal-clear line of sight to help see a path back to Pioneer.

"Options?" I ask the reflection in the shabby-chic mirror. With Trigger on the bench, who can I count on?

Snatching my cell from the charger, I speed-dial KC's number.

"Achoo." KC answers with a sneeze.

"Who do we know who can figure out how to make a geomagnetic storm?"

Anyone else may have paused, but the girl armed with the World Wide Web forever firing in her head answers faster than a 8.429GHz processor. "Duh, Professor McVie."

"Too risky," I say. "It's no secret he's on the verge of getting canned."

KC sniffles and then sneezes again. "You have a better idea?"

I focus hard, willing my idling contacts to spark up another viable option.

No such luck.

"OK…" I exhale, torn, not comfortable putting our best professor in a compromising position. "We'll meet at McVie's office first thing this morning." I look away from my reflection.

I hear KC hack on her keyboard. "I'll message Trigger."

"Don't bother," I say. "Trigger won't be coming."

***

"Tana," Gran shouts from downstairs. "Your ride is here."

Ride?

I step into my boots and shuffle to the window. Through the tea-stained sheers, I notice the Creamsicle rattling at the front curb. Trigger leans against the hood, arms and legs crossed, speaking with my mother. *Is he smiling?* I squint. *And talking with his hands?*

My mom laughs at every other word he says. I'd hate to even guess the topic of conversation. *Since when is Trigger funny?* After last night, he's the last person I expected to see at my door.

Frontal lobotomy? Long shot. As a rule, military pilots avoid doctors at all costs, with the exception of mandatory flight physicals. Trigger told me that the fewer times pilots are around doctors, the better chance they have of keeping their medical certificates. *Kind of ironic.*

"On my way," I answer Gran, scoop up a school blazer, and heave my pack over my shoulder.

Rushing, I stumble and trip down the stairs. As I stagger off the last step, Gran's crossing-guard arm flies out and stops me midair.

She shoves a nutty scone in front of my face. "Take it," she insists and touches my midsection. "Young motors can't run without premium fuel."

I examine the seed-speckled pastry. "What's in it?"

"Whole grains, wheat, raisins, and almond butter, all the necessary ingredients to keep a body running regular." A proud grin stretches across her painted lips. "Just ask Pop."

I crane my neck into the living room to see Grandpa in his favorite reclining chair, snoring with a vengeance. *Yep.* Here are the scone's aftereffects firsthand. A nutrient-rich body laid out, almost firing on all cylinders. Maybe next time Gran should add a bit of sugar.

"Pass." I hand back the brick-like bakery item and grab a banana from the fruit bowl centered on the console table, I can't afford to be bloated. Today is going to be a big day—one way or another.

"At the very least, offer one to your male suitor." Gran swings her silver bob toward the lead glass windows framing the front door and winks.

"He's a friend, Gran," I say. *At least, until yesterday.*

I unlock the dead bolt and open the solid carved door.

"Friend, suitor, whatever." She winks again. "Offer it to him anyway." Gran drops the scone in my jacket pocket. "I don't mind if you tell him you made it yourself."

Seriously? Coerce him with baked goods? I freeze in my tracks, spin, and glare at her. *Is it throwback Thursday?* Goose bumps prick my skin. "Wait. Rewind." I shake my head. "Yesterday you told me to be strong, independent, adventurous, and today…you're saying that the best way to win over a boy is through his stomach?"

Gran's face bunches.

"Because I'm sure Trigger will fall head over heels after he spends the better part of the morning in the bathroom reaping the effects of the body-balancing ingredients. Sheeze." I circle the crazy finger around my ear. If I didn't know better, I'd swear there were two people living in Gran's head. Closing my eyes, I whisper, "Please, please don't let it be genetic."

I take the scone from my pocket and slap it onto Gran's palm. "I'll take my chances."

Tracking down the front walk, I approach what could be yet another mind bender. My backpack slides and jerks my shoulder forward. *Who will launch the first emotional stinger? Mom or Trigger?*

"Good morning, dear." Mom reaches down and centers my pack. "Trigger was just telling me about an outing he's organizing for the weekend."

We have a winner.

"Outing?" I try not to sound surprised. My eyes slide to Trigger.

"You know, like my dad suggested, T. A cross-country trip to practice our *flight* maneuvers." Every muscle in his cheeks clenches.

What's this all about?

Curious, I nod in agreement.

Mom scans me with a critical eye. Her professional eye. If I know her, she's looking for some sort of tell—dilated pupils, shaky hands, nose scratching, stammering—any sign of nervousness that shows I'm not being honest. I stand as I was taught. Frozen. My face as blank as the concrete sidewalk. A technique, if she recalls, she taught me herself.

"Flight comp's in a week, and you know how I feel about coming in second place." The sky surfer's posture remains easy and relaxed, as if he has nothing to hide. *Since when is the son of the living legend so skilled in how to say one thing but mean another?*

Mom's arms fall to her sides, and she smiles. "I think it's a fantastic idea. Flying to different airports. Exploring varied terrain. Hiking trailheads and building campfires on a mesa." Her forehead crinkles. "There will be supervision where you spend the nights?"

"Of course, Mrs. Lyre." Trigger grins.

"Adults?"

"Hundreds. Soldiers actually. I've planned our route so that the last landing of the day will be at airports near military barracks. We'll stay in the guest bunks." He stiffens. "Separately, of course."

"Perfect." Mom's eyes edge to mine. "You'll be protected by an army then; what's safer than that?"

Huh? I have to admit, Mom's reaction surprises me. Did she just say I could travel all weekend with Trigger? Overnight? Is it the scones? Perhaps I should trot back to Gran and reconsider.

Trigger says, "Tana can come then?"

"Yes," my mother says without hesitation. Strike two by a mind winder. "Are you leaving tonight?"

"Right after school."

"And KC is going?" Mom says.

"Still has to clear it with her parents." The lies continue to roll from Trigger's honor-ridden tongue.

"What about Brooklyn?"

"Midterms. She's booked with tutors all weekend."

"Probably for the best." Mom sounds relieved. I'm guessing she thinks it's better to have friends than couples. She flashes *the look*. "You *will* check in each night this time?"

I choke down the wad of tension building in my throat and make a promise I'm not sure I can keep. "Definitely."

"Be home in time for Sunday dinner."

"You have my word." Trigger sets the timer on his chunky dive watch. "Be back in about forty-eight hours." He ushers me into his pickup.

I wave to my mother as the Creamsicle crawls from the curb. I notice that something about her is different—the giddy smile, her glowing skin, and the easiness about her, evidenced by the fact that a) she didn't freak out about our storm-chasing incident, and b) she gave me permission to go on this trip. Something is going on. Maybe she signed up for yoga.

Trigger turns on Riverside Parkway and merges into traffic. "Welcome to the gray area," I say, part irritated and half curious. "Didn't realize white knights are allowed an occasional hall pass."

"I deserve that." The sky surfer signals into the turn lane and joins the queue at National's entrance. "But the most fantastic thing happened last night." Trigger's grin stretches the width of the Arkansas River. He looks as giddy as my mother.

"I figured out how to get back to Pioneer."

If my jaw gapes any wider, my chin will hit the rusted floorboard.

Trigger says, "I took the pill."

CHAPTER 11

"You did what?" I say, stunned.

"Took the future pill." Trigger's grin stretches the length of his sun-kissed cheeks, resembling what I envision is a soldier disobeying a direct order.

He had the frontal lobotomy, I guess. "And?" I ask, dizzy.

The frozen four-wheeled dream on a stick edges to the head of the traffic line. Trigger crosses the intersection and steers up National's steep hill.

"What?" he plays dumb.

With my nerves about to split skin, I blow my bangs and talk through my teeth. "What did you see?"

"Not what I expected." He exhales. "No glimpse at my future career, no insight into whether I need to major in engineering or economics." The Creamsicle complains, groaning and grinding. The sky surfer shifts gears and rests his hand next to mine. I fidget in my seat.

Is it possible each pill is different? There was no doubt I saw my future, and if the images prove true, I should register for Russian next semester.

"It wasn't at all like Pioneer's headmaster said at orientation." A deep frown overpowers his longboard smile. "I didn't see tomorrow, next week, or years ahead. As a matter of fact, it's more like I saw a flash from the past."

I examine his face. He looks off to the left, a telltale sign he's recalling something that's already happened. His actions match his words, so I gather that Trigger is being honest.

Why would he lie? Guilt pings in my chest. Perhaps for the same reason I'm withholding my future-pill vision.

Trigger's hand jerks away. "Isn't that what you saw?"

He knows. I straighten and look away, guessing he thinks I'm holding back. If I change my story now, tell him what I saw, he'll know I lied, and I doubt our friendship will survive another deception.

"Can't really remember." I squeeze my eyes shut and keep up the act. Erase the image of myself, much older, darker, with some massive burden strapped to my back. Couldn't have been the past. My vision was definitely years in the future. "The image is still fuzzy." I massage my temples, seeing automated frames. Highlights of being face-to-face with my dad's murderer play like an upcoming movie trailer. I touch the thick scar on my collarbone.

I say, "After leaving Soraya and Dr. Harb, I was so angry…"

Double or nothing. You promised.

About to spit out my arsenal of excuses of why I broke our pact and took my future pill, I realize not a single one is true. *Time to fess up, Lyre.* My chest heaves.

"I wanted an easy way out," I say. "I thought knowing who killed my dad would make me feel better. It didn't…Fact is, I chickened out. Swallowed the pill on purpose."

There. I said it. I blink and look at Trigger.

"I'm so sorry." Ashamed, my eyes drift to the Creamsicle's mile-long dash. "I never thought you would have to trade yourself to handsy McDunney."

The corner of Trigger's mouth twitches.

What really happened with McDunney, Trigger? I ask with my eyes since any mention of Pioneer's security chief sends the sky surfer hightailing it for the nearest exit. I'll bet he thinks whatever went down with McDunney is my fault. I don't blame him. I wish he would tell me what happened. Maybe I could help.

"Trigger." I dust his knuckles. "I only absorbed half my pill. I didn't see the future."

He knocks my fingers away. "I remember everything. Clear and crisp, as if I'm standing opposite Henry while he tinkers in his lab."

"Wait. You saw Henry? In your pill vision?" A wave of panic pushes my heart against my ribs, as I relive the image of our friend's bloodied body cowering in the corner. "Was he…"

"As far as I can tell, he's fine. At least at that moment, whenever it was. Sporting his patch-covered jumpsuit, windshield wiper goggles, he looked to be in the middle of some sort of presentation. A demonstration, probably, to defend his junior thesis."

That's not what I saw. I rub faster across my neck scar and glance around, searching for any sign of a yellow butterfly. *Am I imagining things again?*

Regardless, until I figure out what's real and what's not, I need to play along.

"How does Henry's thesis give us a road map to Pioneer?" The words have barely left my lips when Trigger cracks up. He belly laughs to the point that I consider he's the one who's going bonkers.

"The whiteboard…" he says between the gut crunches. "In his lab." Trigger's eyebrows spike, like he's touched a loose electrical wire. "Henry wrote Pioneer's airport coordinates as the location for his thesis project."

"In plain sight?" I say.

"In bold, block letters. Right under Chief McDunney's and the review board's noses."

Trigger's vision must have been from before. Or was it after what I saw when buried in the mud? *Is that even possible? Can future pills go backward?*

"His humor is still intact." Trigger shrugs. "I'm guessing Henry's OK."

"Unbelievable," I say, even more confused.

In between Trigger's short breaths, I hear a sigh of relief. He angles off into the student lot and parks the pickup beneath a canopy of sprawling oak trees. "I'll have KC hack Pioneer's coordinates onto a new GPS navigation card. With a little luck, the flight computer will accept the location, and we'll be on our way to help our friend." He holds for a second, glances at the Creamsicle's orange floorboard, and says, "And get justice for your dad."

Trigger climbs from the car, slams the clunky door, and trots toward the science building in full Flough swagger. His chest puffs out, and the warrior persona surfaces. On the next step, however, his ankle rolls, and he stumbles on the otherwise smooth pavement.

The warrior dubbed "Sky Surfer" by his fellow flight-team members appears to have a moment of doubt. Recovering, he stands stiff, and his sharp jaw tightens. He turns around. His shoulders slump, and he says, "We still don't have any idea how to cook up a magnetic storm."

Double or nothing. In a blink, we're a team again. *Welcome back on board the emotional roller coaster that is T. Xanthus Flough.*

With my partner floundering, I realize it's my turn to step up. After all, three brains are better than two.

"I have an idea." My insides tingle.

Trigger's ocean blues widen. "Do I really want to know?"

CHAPTER 12

KC is waiting for us inside the science building. We trek down the main hall, past the classrooms, to the observation dome for our school's planetarium—the temporary location of Professor McVie's weather lab. KC, Trigger, and I cut through the sky-show theater, weave around the display of potential inhabitable planets, head down the curved corridor, and enter the observatory—the unofficial location of storm-chasing central.

The far corner of McVie's makeshift office is sectioned off with plastic tarps and pole-mounted zip walls. His previous space, so I hear, was an unfortunate casualty of last semester's storm-surge experiment.

A miniature blackboard is duct-taped to the plastic to the left of the entry zipper. Handwritten in chalk are times for sunrise, sunset, and the forecasted surf conditions.

"Three feet at four seconds. Insignificant waves."

Does McVie realize the closest ocean is fifteen hundred miles away?

I traipse over piles of rubber boots and splash jackets, breathe in the scent of pineapple and coconut, and notice a freshly waxed surfboard. *Not.* He must still think he's in Florida and the head meteorology expert on staff for the Army Corps of Engineers.

Trigger unzips the thick, milky-colored sheets; tracks to the tripod work lights; and drags a few lawn chairs away from the indoor fire pit.

He scoots next to KC, who's seated at our professor's petrified-log desk—a fulgurite, he explained during the first day of class. "The combustible reaction after lightning strikes sand. A symbol of natural beauty."

More like a piece of rotted driftwood.

I take the folding seat next to KC. Across from us, Professor McVie stands and thrusts a hand in the air. After a click with the remote control in his palm, the retractable dome overhead motors halfway closed.

McVie appears more unhinged than usual. I notice a few extra singed strands mixed in his shoulder-length hair. Maybe the near-death experience yesterday has tempered his rumored adrenaline addiction.

"Miss McKenna." McVie snatches an elastic band from a desktop barometer and twists his hair into a ponytail.

Trigger and I stiffen.

Our professor eyeballs our trio. "Why are you here?"

"If you recall, Professor, we've come to discuss some alternatives for our midterm project."

Although staring straight ahead, I manage to shoot KC an eye sidewinder.

Midterm? I scrunch my face. KC angles the cell in her lap and shoots two quick bursts of light code at my sideways glare.

Got it. I nod. *Play along.*

McVie whips his stringy pony and checks over both shoulders. He hunches forward, back humped like an angry tomcat.

"An experiment concerning geomagnetic activity perhaps?" McVie whispers. His catlike eyes dart around the room.

To think for a moment that I doubted Go-To McKenna—a girl notorious for being hyperprepared and redoing her homework for sport.

The tarp walls crinkle, and our professor shudders. With remote in hand, his arm flies up again, and he motors the sky dome completely shut. "Just a little wind," he says. His pupils widen, and once his heightened eyes make another security sweep, he grips a rubber stress ball. "You were saying, Miss McKenna?" McVie's fingers clench the gooey material.

Trigger and I exchange a smile. Leave it to KC to concoct a roundabout way to get right to the point. She'd arrived early and laid the groundwork.

"A topic that would really make our midterm project stand out, don't you think?" She plays the role of the eccentric science nerd flawlessly.

Because she is one.

A crooked smile crosses McVie's lips. What teacher would pass on the opportunity to encourage bright, innovative students thirsting for knowledge? I cross fingers behind my back. *Hopefully not McVie.*

KC scribbles the layers of the earth's atmosphere on a piece of scrap paper. "Wouldn't it be something if we could create a geomagnetic storm?"

"Artificially incite the aurora borealis," I say.

"You know, the northern lights," Trigger adds.

"Yes, Mr. Flough, Miss Lyre, I'm familiar with the phenomenon." McVie's pale-green eyes shift side to side and then roll back in his head. He mumbles, chanting like monks in Tibet, reciting rounds of equations and formulas in his hymn. Then, he stops.

His eyelids pop open. He stands and wanders around the tent—erratic, like an ant with no obvious destination.

I wager whether McVie's scattered brain is up to the challenge. *Odds are fifty-fifty at best.*

"Of course you do, sir," Trigger says, respectful and official, the way he speaks to his father. "We figured you're the only one who could come up with an answer."

More numbers, verbal symbols, and a noise like a flushing toilet whistles from McVie's motoring lips. A delete function, I figure. A deposit in the science recycling bin.

Now flat-footed, Professor McVie faces us. "It's never been done." His throat gargles. His tongue pokes in and out like a lizard's. Another verbal toilet flushes, and then he whistles. "So far."

I weigh the pros and cons. If we tell McVie about Henry, the fact that a month ago I witnessed a seventeen-year-old student cook up a successful batch of geomagnetic particle brew, would he believe us? I size up our professor: wild eyes that border on manic, a wacky neck tick, a no-need-to-look-before-you-leap mind-set.

"It's a chance to explore uncharted territory, Professor." Trigger gives McVie a nudge and then winks at me.

A challenge. I catch on to the sky surfer's approach. *Candy for adrenaline junkies.* Which I don't get, because if I had to guess, our weather professor's toes are already dangling over the I-dare-you ledge. *Maybe it's a guy thing.*

Trigger says, "You'd be the first."

"Numero uno?" McVie's eyes bulge.

"If anyone has the guts, sir, it's you."

That's right, my friend; seal his fate. Give him the final jolt from National's protective awning and coax him straight into the meteorological abyss.

"Only if you want." My conscience powers in, well aware of what's at risk for our favorite professor—his position, his livelihood, and his reputation.

KC and Trigger twist around, scowling. *Have you lost your mind?* I interpret from their expressions.

Probably. My lips stretch into a cheeseball grin. By the time they turn back, McVie has disappeared.

"Professor?" My throat cinches.

"Now you've done it," KC scolds. She springs up and rushes to the back curtain.

A loud crash thunders from behind the divider. Go-To McKenna ducks and covers her head. A symphony of pots and pans clangs. Metal grinds. Glass shatters, and a series of yellow tennis balls bounce beneath the ballooning curtain. The rubber balls roll to a stop, and the banging subsides. The room becomes quiet enough to hear the bar fridge hum.

KC peers around the corner. "Everything OK back there, Professor?"

A stream of green goo shoots from a tear in the curtain and splats into her hair.

"Gross." KC fingers the sticky mess.

"Locked and loaded." McVie emerges from the storage area, one foot in a mop bucket, wearing a ball cap with shiny foam lightning bolts attached above both ears, a flare gun in one hand, and a crate wedged beneath his armpit. I can't pull my eyes away—not because of his insane getup, but because of the storage crate of neon-green test tubes tucked under his arm.

Could it be?

My eyes sweep to Trigger. His ocean blues sparkle. Then he does that thing—he guesses my thoughts.

"Yes." Trigger clenches a fist and pumps an elbow.

I stare into the shimmering liquid tucked under McVie's arm. "But it's the wrong color."

"My apologies about the misfire, Miss McKenna." Professor McVie raises the tip of the flare to his lips and blows a puff of dust. "Cartridge needs cleaning." He inhales and chokes.

KC squeegees the soapy mess glommed in her purple-hued hair.

"What's with the bug juice?" I ask, my gaze fixed on what I hope is a batch of electron-and proton-enhanced particle fluid.

Please, please be the brew that will get us back to Pioneer. I double cross my fingers.

"One sip of this, Miss Lyre, and you'll shoot like a rocket, thirty-six thousand miles above the earth." McVie heaves the old milk crate onto the fulgurite desk. He eases one of the dayglow tubes from the carrier and raises the luminous contents into the light.

I dig my nails into Trigger's cargo pants.

McVie leans in, and his words fade to a murmur. "I've been following this weather blog. Really obscure, cutting-edge stuff." His hands tremble as he slides the test tube into the crate. "Coincidently, a month ago, the blogger posted about the principles behind geomagnetic weather. He claimed solar-charged particles use magnetic ropes to travel between the earth's upper atmosphere and the sun."

Coincidence? No way. As much as I want to remind him that scientists don't believe in happenstance, I can't drag my eyes from the weaving and churning of the iridescent test tubes.

"A supercharged connection from earth to the sun? P-l-e-a-s-e," KC says and rolls her eyes. "The heat from the solar flares would give our planet a killer sunburn."

McVie frowns. "Have you already forgotten my lecture about the magnetosphere, Miss McKenna?"

"After a week's worth of classes on how the solar winds shock the earth's protective shield and create geomagnetic storms, believe me, I know all I need to know about the magnetosphere." KC sneezes three times in a row. "But ropes that tether the sun and Earth together?" She grabs a tissue from her pocket and blows her nose. "Sounds like fringe science to me, Professor."

"I thought the same thing, Miss McKenna." The lightning bolts on McVie's hat appear to shimmer. "Until now." He pulls the crate of glowing test tubes to his chest. "I started following the blogger's daily posts as any respectable meteorologist would," McVie says. "Quickly realizing that whoever's posting must be some heavy-hitter, possibly from NASA."

Or a teenaged überscientist.

"Brainstorming anonymously, off the professional grid. Wanting to avoid attracting attention from all those hoity-toity science organizations. There's a reason they call themselves aaaaass…" McVie looks at KC and me. "Beg your pardon, ladies." His cat eyes narrow, likely on the verge of a full-blown cerebral kill. "From that moment, I'm hooked. Every week, the blogger asks pointed questions. The answers—my conclusions—led to materials that could potentially incite geomagnetic activity." McVie's lizard tongue cycles. "I read between the lines. Followed the breadcrumbs, gathered the ingredients, and voila!" He utters a tidy bowl flush. "A storm recipe."

Our mouths gape.

"What?" McVie says. "As a professional, how could I resist?" He pounds his chest.

Any guilty feelings I have fall away. Fact is, we could never put our professor at risk. He does that all by himself—storm chasing, explosive experiments, and concocting homemade storm-making brews; escapades that are really his ideas, but not for the reasons I originally thought. He really isn't an adrenaline junkie. He's a storm-chasing Christopher Columbus.

"We've known…" McVie's neck bends, and he gazes at the sealed observation dome. "Let's see. When did we know? How long have we known?"

"You were saying, Professor?" KC snaps her fingers.

McVie shudders. "Oh, right." He knocks his head. "Stay on task." His eyes reconnect, and he straightens his lightning bolt cap. "Anyway, for as long as I can remember, the earth's iron, nickel, and cobalt DNA has acted as a giant magnet, attracting powerful charged flares from the sun that create geomagnetic storms. But what I didn't put together was those storms can cross an entire polar time zone in less than sixty seconds."

I nudge Trigger. "No wonder we were able to fly back and forth to Pioneer in a matter of minutes."

"Yeah," the sky surfer says. "The amped energy of the geo-storm acted like a supersonic afterburner."

"With a little trial and error…" Professor McVie gathers a flare gun hooked on his cowboy belt and empties one test tube into its cartridge barrel. Then he widens his stance like a western gunslinger.

McVie points the barrel at the overhead dome, cocks the hammer, and mouths *pow.* "One geomagnetic fire starter."

KC shuffles over and speaks into my ear. "Henry?"

"Who else?" I say.

As McVie loads a second flare gun, his sleeve lifts, and I notice a tattoo of an eagle against a shield.

"The 101st Airborne Division." Trigger's bright blues widen. "The army's elite paratrooper division."

McVie jumped out of airplanes? I swallow and think of my future pill vision.

"I did take one liberty," our weather professor says. "To make it my own." His hands wave like an illusionist, unveiling his marquee trick. "I decided to dye it green, like the aurora."

Trigger glues himself to my side, and KC loops her arm around mine. McVie came through. With the final obstacle gone, nothing can stop us from returning to Pioneer.

"So what's the plan?" The gunslinger persona resurfaces, locked and loaded, tool belt slung low on his hips.

All three of us gulp.

KC says, "The fewer people who know about our plan, the better."

"But we need McVie's help," I say.

"Which leaves us with no choice but to let him in on our scheme," Trigger adds.

"I've got this." Go-To McKenna straightens her glasses. "As far as our midterm project, Professor…" she says in such a way that if I didn't know better, I'd swear we were switched at birth—her not being the offspring of an oil executive and a socialite, but the quick-witted, think-on-your-feet daughter of two world-renowned negotiators.

"Since it's fall and all." KC's words glide as if memorized from a script. "Do you think gathering data on the northern lights is more practical?" She dabs the corners of her mouth. "From an academic standpoint, of course."

McVie's lips pucker. "Your midterm assignment. The one due this morning."

"The twister, the lost rover," KC reminds him. "Completely out of our hands. What if for our makeup midterm, we test the blogger's hypothesis?" She adjusts her glasses. "Fire your storm mixture into the sky and then record the results?"

McVie drops the cowboy facade, and a spark of excitement lights his face. "Interesting." His tongue shoots in and out. "When might you want to conduct this little experiment?"

"How about tonight?" Trigger says.

McVie's ready hands hover over the sparkling green flares, flex, and reposition as if preparing for a quick-draw duel. He whistles the theme from an old spaghetti western. "Tonight it is."

"Riverside Airport?"

"Sunset." McVie glances at the surf report scribbled in white chalk. "Six forty-six."

Our trio reaches for our wrists and synchronizes watches.

"Appreciate the help, Professor." KC walks over and shakes his hand. "Need to keep our grades up. College applications are due before long."

"College, yes, that's right." McVie twists his pony around a finger. At any minute, we're sure to hear another verbal toilet flush.

With our arms linked, KC and I move toward the zip door. Trigger trails. Once out of earshot, KC says, "I think we fooled him."

I glance over my shoulder to see Professor McVie shoving a change of clothes and handfuls of antenna cords, and spare battery packs into a duffel bag. He looks up at me and winks.

"Doubt it." I face my friends. "I think he's on to us."

We exit the way we came in and huddle in the reinforced corridor— the alternate living accommodations for humans in case of a zombie apocalypse, otherwise known as a tornado shelter.

"Meet me at the hangar right after class." Trigger has moved past the storm challenge and shifted into flight-planning mode. "We need to borrow some equipment from flight operations." His warm ocean eyes ice over like a glacier. As he checks off the to-do list, he reminds me of his father. He points at KC. "Laptop, spare USB drives, and if you can find one, get an extra signal booster."

She nods.

"Tana, you're in charge of Dr. Harb's last-known whereabouts, a Pioneer uniform, and"—Trigger touches his forehead—"bring that pink dress."

CHAPTER 13

The pink dress? What's the deal? First, we were kind of friends and then pretend brother and sister. When we got back from the Pioneer ordeal, it felt like more, but the minute Trigger saw BB…I squeeze the bridge of my nose. *Hang on.* My mind rewinds to what Mom said about Eddie during our rooftop chat. *Hero syndrome. Could Trigger's military no-man-left-behind mind-set make him feel obligated to stick by me? A girl who's traumatized and, at times, dangling by a thread?*

That would explain the nightly talks. The rides to school. His hot-and-cold personality when it comes to Brooklyn and me. He's not scared of me like KC thought. I'm a goodwill project.

Near the end of eighth-hour physics, I stare at the clock. With less than two minutes to go, the seconds stretch the time continuum for what feels like forever, leaving me way too much time to think.

Correction, worry.

She'll come through. I'm referring to Gran, not my mother. Already at school, with no time to go home and pack, I had no choice but to ask for backup. With Mom, bringing a uniform might slide, but a request for a dress would certainly throw up a warning flag. "What do you need a dress for if you're going to stay in military barracks?" she'd undoubtedly ask. So I chose the path of least resistance and called my eighty-year-old grandmother.

It's not like she's less inquisitive, just a tad more flexible. She's a hopeful romantic who may have a different perspective on whether a girl should ever leave home without a fancy outfit. After thinking on it a little more, I figure the dress Trigger asked me to bring is probably for Pioneer's month-long Aurora Celebration—in the spirit of being prepared for anything.

Earlier this morning, Gran called Trigger a suitor, so when I messaged between classes, I let on that her instincts might be on target about him being more than just a friend. I left out the details, allowing her to draw her own conclusions. She's delighted, I imagine, since she harps on me about finding a boyfriend. Bringing a dress on this trip might appear to further the cause. I mentally cross my fingers, hoping Gran comes through.

And she does.

With formal wear and my Pioneer uniform packed in my duffel, I ride the shuttle to the Riverside Airport. The bus is empty, just the driver, Sam, in front, and me a few rows back. As we wrap around the airport ring road, I see the flight team's planes readying for practice and wonder what excuse Trigger gave in order for us to miss mandatory maneuvers.

I check my watch. Ten past three.

The shuttle jerks as Sam jackknifes at the flight-line entrance; the back end of the shuttle swings and tips. As we skid on two wheels, I consider for the first time ever that it may be safer to drive with my mother. A plastic baggie spills from the duffel and thuds on the floor. I recognize the stowaway—a bag of Gran's body-balancing brick scones. *Terrific.*

Sam corrects, appearing unaccustomed to the light load. He cusses and then apologizes in the next breath, since swearing violates National's honor code.

"No worries." I knock his arm with my bag and duck through the bifold door. "Everyone slips once in a while."

Red-faced, Sam stammers a series of regrets and kisses a medallion on his neck.

"See," I finger my scars. "Safe and sound."

***

With our school's undefeated flight team on the ramp, the inside of the hangar is deserted. Full motion simulators squat like grasshoppers, idling in the center of four thin hydraulic legs. Two trailer-mounted turbine engines stand static, the pressure chamber's door is unlatched, and every computer monitor in the weather center is abandoned.

I duck under the shell of a jet fuselage and track a course for the far corner, up to a row of tall storage lockers painted caution-cone orange. I drag fingertips down the backside of the dayglow cubbies and curve around the corner of the last tall locker.

"Trigger!" I shout and jog toward his limp body crouched on the floor.

The sky surfer's head is slumped forward like his neck is broken. His arms are wrapped around his knees and clenched to his chest. Pasty and gray, he resembles a corpse, his complexion the color of a building thunderhead. His skin drips with sweat. *No, no, please, he can't be dead.*

My duffel falls from my shoulder, and I drop to my knees. A surge of heat flushes through my body, and I'd swear I smell smoke. I jostle his arm and lift his chin. "You're fine." I drag my sleeve back and forth over his forehead and wipe the dampness from his skin. *Don't leave me, Trigger.* My fingers tremble.

"Wake up," I grit my teeth and shake his shoulders, and when he doesn't move, I slap his cheek.

His neck twitches. Slowly, the sky surfer's eyes open.

"Trigger?" I say, my lips quivering.

Groggy, he doesn't seem to recognize me. His arms drop to his sides, and his legs stretch. With his boots flat on the floor, Trigger leans against the locker and shimmies to his feet. After knuckling an eye, he squints and steadies a hand against the steel door.

His eyelids slide together. His head falls to his hands. He rakes his skull and then perks up as if soaked by a bucket of icy water.

My heart pounds.

"Tana, good." Trigger checks his wrist. "You're here." He scoops the opened flight bag from the bench and starts collecting the electronic components scattered around his feet. "We need to get over to McVie's lab and see if he'll help us figure out how to create a geomagnetic storm."

Am I dreaming? I rub my neck scar and steady my racing heartbeat. *Or having a bad case of déjà vu?* I pinch my arm, and when the indentation reddens, I know I'm wide-awake. *It's not you, Lyre.* This time, it's Trigger who has had the brain fart.

"Good one," I say, assuming he's goofing around. But Trigger's expression remains as serious as an engine fire.

I say, "McVie agreed to help us, remember? Here, at sunset."

"Oh, right." Trigger shakes off the mind fog. "You know how focused I get when I'm rehearsing flight plans in my head." He gathers up two satellite phones and night-vision goggles, plus a few handheld GPS units, and tucks the bundle in the utility bag. "I zone off into another world."

What I know for sure is that pilots do have rituals, similar to professional athletes—a favorite pair of shoes, lucky socks, or specific routines they must perform in order to be game ready. Trigger's ritual is to sit in a chair and run through every segment of the flight plan in his mind. He repeats the dry run over and over, so by the time he gets in the air, it's as if he's flown the route a hundred times.

But this is different. No-Fear Flough's chiseled face is coated with sweat. The only other time I'd seen him this anxious was while being chased by Chief McDunney and his goon detail the night we escaped Pioneer.

*And...*flashes of our round robin flight float in front of my eyes—the thrashing storm, the radical turbulence, and how Trigger hit his head hard enough to be knocked out not just once, but twice.

Did he suffer some sort of head injury, and the symptoms are just showing up now? Or did the electric shock from the instrument panel leave some delayed side effects?

Knowing Trigger is not one to admit weakness of any sort, instead of being direct, I try a circling approach.

"A lot of details to sweat—flight plans, weather. Who knows what will greet us if we get back to Pioneer." I pick up a flashlight and check its batteries. "I imagine it's pretty easy to get bogged down."

"Not sure what you're talking about." Trigger appears to have shaken the head cloud. "Piece of pie in the sky." Staring me straight in the face, he points to his chest. "Bulletproof."

Despite his attempts to cover, I know something is wrong. *Terribly.* My thoughts spin toward the incident with Chief McDunney. Could it have something to do with…*Nah.* I quash the thought. That was a month ago.

The sky surfer palms a two-way radio and a pair of walkie-talkies. "While I was prepping, I remembered something else from the pill flash," he says, as if the whole brain fog moment never happened. His sudden willingness to share knocks me further off balance.

"What's that?" I say.

"Henry left a second hint. A way to land at Pioneer's airfield undetected."

And you're remembering this now? Despite the fact you have no recollection of what happened earlier this morning? I twist my mouth and consider that there might be another explanation for Trigger's memory mishap. *Could Henry's special past-future-pill cocktail be causing Trigger's memory glitches?*

But with no clue what Henry added to the powdery mixture, I decide to wait and get the facts before making unfounded accusations.

"Let me guess," I tease. "He suggested a stealth approach."

Studying Trigger's bright-candy-red homebuilt plane, I point at the racing stripes and the roaring turbo-charged engine and raise both eyebrows. "We're going to land quietly and scoot past McDunney in this hot rod?"

"Exactly." Trigger's easy smile returns.

"And *exactly* how did Henry's past-future-pill vision suggest we accomplish this impossible trick?" I say, and my chest tightens. "Shut off the engine and glide in for a landing?"

Trigger touches his ear and caresses his Pioneer piercing. His gaze wanders my way, and I feel compelled to check my receiver to see if it's glowing. In some weird, unexplainable way, it seems like our receivers are connected, and I can still hear his thoughts. Admiration swirls in his sky blues as if I had kicked on the afterburners and busted the sound barrier.

"Right on," he says.

It doesn't take a rocket scientist to realize that without engine power, Trigger's front-loaded bird is more a sinking submarine than a soaring glider. "An engine off landing is an emergency procedure," I say.

Trigger nods and packs a box of snack bars. "Henry's situation is urgent."

There it is, proof again that he's not quite himself. Although known to push the envelope while flying, Trigger is never reckless. I try logic, hoping to steer him back to procedure. "Meaning if the engine fails, then you have no choice but to glide to a landing site."

Another agreeing nod, and Trigger straps water bottles to the flight bag's Velcro holders.

"The manual says nothing about killing the engine on purpose." My voice spikes. "Believe me, I've read it."

"Actually, it does." KC corners the row of student lockers, McVie plodding like a packhorse beside her. "Supplemental Part IV of the operations manual, subsection B—simulated power-off landings for the purpose of flight instruction."

Trigger looks at KC and grins. "Listen to your friend."

"You're taking flight lessons, aren't you, T?" KC says, aware that I passed the test for a private pilot's license.

I flash her the stink eye and then throw the specifics of the subsection she quoted back in her face. "But the spirit of the procedure is to be used only in an actual emergency."

Lightning, strike me now if I didn't just sound like my mother.

"Which is exactly what this is." Professor McVie drops the heavy saddlebags from his back and collapses on the bench. "It's the only viable option. Miss McKenna and I calculated numerous trajectories and figured the best pitch-to-glide ratio."

Although KC agrees, a look of reluctance crosses her freckled face.

Trigger pulls a card from his pocket and reads off our weight and landing numbers. "I worked out the most balanced center of gravity for two people and all of our equipment…"

"Wait, only two?" My eyes draw to KC like metal to a magnet.

The script kitty rubs her nose and then starts to sneeze. "I can explain." She holds up a finger and continues to spray at least a dozen times. As the interval between *achoos* lengthens, she says, "Mom said I can't go." A silent hack shoots a light spritz from her nostrils. "Dad's back from Qatar." She seals her lips, holds her nose, and squeaks. "Have to spend time with family…*Achoo*…What a joke, right?"

A senior executive for an oil company, KC's dad travels most weeks. On the weekends, he comes in town for what he considers "family time," which for the McKennas means two days packed with fundraisers and corporate events. KC is forever watching her socialite mother drown in chardonnay, while her dad remains chin down, focused on his phone, typing e-mails twenty-four seven.

Honestly, I don't see anything funny about it.

"Here's the compass card, complete with Pioneer's not-so-secret coordinates." KC slaps the chip onto Trigger's extended palm. The sky surfer's eyes bug and blink to McVie.

"Don't worry, Mr. Flough," McVie says. "KC told me everything."

"Sorry," KC puts a finger to her nose to thwart what looks like a sneezing attack. "I'm terrible at keeping secrets."

Trigger's gaze connects with mine, and I do a palms up.

"Bygones." KC removes her cell from her pocket and connects a black magnet the shape of a fun-sized candy bar to its back. "I made these from earth magnets." She touches my earring. "The material is similar to your piercings. Attach this to any cell, and you'll be able to gain access outside Pioneer's closed intranet."

"Kase, you are amazing," I say.

"Amazingly stuck in Tulsa. Again." Her eyes glass over, and she sniffles.

"You know," McVie says, "if I fire these flares, how will I be able to record the footage for your midterm data at the same time?" He acts stumped and runs his fingers over his coarse razor stubble.

KC jumps up and raises a hand. "I can help." A hint of hope breaks through her frown.

"Yes, I understand you're an expert with anything with a power button." McVie holds out his pinky finger, and when KC latches her own to it, he proclaims the partnership a done deal.

Trigger nudges me and tosses a look toward the hangar door. "Time to fly."

I agree and stand next to KC. "I feel better knowing you'll be here, computer ready, tracking our every move."

"It's what I do best, I guess." She fidgets with her purple frames.

Trigger steps around me, leans over, and kisses KC on the forehead. "You never cease to surprise me, Kellan McKenna."

KC blushes, knowing the best-looking guy in school just paid her a massive compliment. I prop myself against her for support as she watches Trigger swagger toward the ramp door.

"Miss Lyre." McVie tugs on the sleeve of my bomber jacket. "Be ready for the electrical surge once you enter the storm. Power stations on the ground will go dark, and transformers are certain to blow."

I nod, acknowledging something I'd experienced but never understood.

"More importantly"—McVie clenches my bicep—"all electronics in the airplane will temporarily black out. And when you launch into the upper atmosphere, be sure to stay calm, since you'll both pass out."

CHAPTER 14

Out on the ramp, the beacon light circles the airfield. A green stream chased by its ghostly white shadow signals that the sun has set. The plan is for Professor McVie and KC to drive a mile north and position themselves atop Turkey Mountain. The peak is less of a mountain and more of a hill, but it still offers high-enough elevation to launch the storm flares into the required orbit.

The evening sky is an endless canvas of smeared blues and swirling, peachy pinks. Smooth and calm—most aviators' dreams. Not ours though. Tonight, we need moist, volatile air and gusty wind conditions to create the perfect storm. I sure wish the Flough swagger could change the weather.

Stepping on the left wing, I stack my duffel on two others packed in the backseat. No doubt about it, this time we're prepared.

I lower inside, run the final preflight checks, and then slide out of the captain's seat to let Tana climb into the copilot's post.

"Ladies first," I say. By the look on Tana's face, I'm guessing she thinks I'm old school. Or maybe she thinks I'm being condescending? I watch as she scoots around the throttle. *Doubt it*. I'm pretty sure she knows in most ways we're equal. Either way, my dad would kill me if I didn't respect a lady.

Once belted in, I secure the locks on the gull door and switch on the tail-mounted strobe light to let everyone on the ramp know we're about to crank the propeller.

I use one hand to push the key into the ignition, my other to grip the throttle, and make sure to push on both toe brakes. I'm about to yell, "Clear," when Tana grabs my arm and says, "Wait."

"What's the matter?" My hand drops from the silver start key. My eyes dart around the tarmac. "Is something blocking your wing?" I lean across her to get a better view.

"No." Tana shakes her head. "It's just…I still don't understand."

Here we go again. "What's there to be confused about? We've run the start procedure hundreds of times." I roll my lips together and clench the throttle. *Stay calm.* She hasn't wigged out since the first time we flew together. Regardless, no matter how often we go up to practice, part of me wonders if someday there will be a repeat performance. *Not if you're with her. You saved her once; you can do it again.*

Tana looks away.

You created this, T. Still, I can't help wondering how I'd feel if I were in her head. Guilty. Embarrassed. Scared. Humiliated.

Forcing a grin, I reach for her shoulder. But before I get a chance to reassure her, she says, "Let's pretend McVie's flares work. We create a storm, activate the magnetic compass, the airport coordinates actually work, and we land safely at Pioneer."

Man, am I off base. I say, "That's how I practiced the flight in my head."

"How do we let Henry know we're coming?"

I raise a fist to my forehead. "I keep forgetting. You didn't see my pill flash. During Henry's project summary, he sent one final message, a cryptic trail of breadcrumbs."

"Let me guess, the code to break through Pioneer's impenetrable intranet?"

I feel like a brick dropped on my head. "Do you remember when Henry said he goes out to the airport every night looking for signs of geomagnetic activity?" *Speaking of which…*I clear the wings and crank the engine.

Tana's mouth twists.

The motor turns over and rumbles, interrupting the conversation. I radio for a departure clearance with the control tower—first, to get the go-ahead to take off and second, to signal McVie and KC, stationed up on Turkey Mountain, where they monitor a two-way radio. "Cleared for takeoff" is the signal, the secret code word, and once they hear my transmission, KC and McVie will ready the flares.

"Your takeoff." I eye Tana from my periphery. "You're legal now, right?"

"Two-day-old temporary-pilot certificate in hand." Tana pats her bomber jacket pocket. "Check." She takes the controls. Her mouth stretches into a mile-long grin.

I do like flying with her. I let go of the side yoke and throttle handle. *She might even love airplanes as much as I do.*

Fifteen seconds later, Tana lifts the airplane from the ground. From over my left shoulder, a green stream screams past like a bottle rocket. The light streak sails overhead and then sparks in the air.

"Flare number one," I confirm, and Tana banks the airplane ninety degrees. West—a straight track over KC and McVie's launch site.

The fiery flame ignites and explodes into a cascading bloom of fireflies. Hundreds of particles collide, splitting, smearing, and oozing into a thick band of yellow-green ribbon. Their effervescent light speckles the night sky.

"It works," I say.

Tana rocks the wings side to side in celebration.

I cycle the landing light once as visual confirmation.

McVie replies with one quick click of a boosted flashlight.

"Sixty seconds to launch number two." I set the timer on my dive watch.

The candied band ahead weaves and slithers like a snake across the horizon, expanding until it engulfs the nebulous sky, mysterious and mystical, whisking the breath from my lungs.

"Straight ahead," I call out.

Tana holds a steady track into the waving curtain of light.

The second flare explodes through the light show, and we enter the first layer. Inside, the brightness dims and a textured veil falls. Darkness descends as thick as chimney smoke.

Lightning cracks.

I reach for the GPS knob to confirm Henry's coordinates.

Turbulence rocks the plane.

Tana struggles to hold the controls.

I touch her hand and give a reassuring squeeze and then refocus on the instrument panel.

All systems normal.

We wait for what's certain to come next.

It doesn't take long.

After an instrument scan, I see the radar screen pulse red.

Severe storm—dead ahead.

CHAPTER 15

McVie was right. I did pass out. I figure that the lack of oxygen when our plane catapults into the upper atmosphere is the reason why we go unconscious. *Stay calm.* I hear Professor McVie's ninja voice in my head. Sound advice since my pulse is beating at a tornado-chasing rate. *Speaking of things I'm grateful for—thank goodness airplane engines run without electrical power.*

I look out the window and see the airplane's wings aligned with the horizon, flying level as before, on our first trip to the Pioneer School. The autopilot is miraculously engaged, and with all signs of the aurora and the geomagnetic storm gone, the stars pulse against an onyx sky.

Trigger comes to, his expression confident, showing no obvious signs of concern. *Maybe he's starting to trust me a little.*

As we glide through the smooth air, I loosely wrap my hands around the control stick, back up the autopilot, and scan the instrument panel.

The temporary power outage is over, and lights are on—engine, cruising. The compass is activated, needle arrowing at Pioneer's airfield.

Everything is as it should be, except…I stare at the upper corner of the windshield and notice a hairline crack. *Impossible.* I choke a hailstone-sized lump down my throat. I blink and lean forward, squinting to be sure. *Not just one crack, but a spider-web-like cluster.*

Trigger doesn't see it yet, the unexpected fracture in our already iffy plan. His focus remains pinned on the outline of the rocky mesa less than five miles ahead.

Crap. I fall back against my seat, well aware of what we're already up against. It's one thing to idle a perfectly running engine for training, with the propeller windmilling, knowing that in an instant, a quick shove on the throttle lofts the plane back safely in the air.

But to kill an engine by cutting the fuel and bringing the propeller to a dead stop? Forcing an otherwise perfect airplane to plummet like a stone chucked into a river? And if that isn't hard enough, why not try to land in the dark, on a strip of pavement no wider than a sidewalk? I swallow. Definitely a maneuver that exceeds my current skill set. *Maybe Trigger should do the landing. Since he has a lot more experience.*

I peek at the creeping crack on the windshield and decide whether or not to alert Trigger. *Loose lips could definitely sink this airship.* With the challenge ahead, I keep quiet and choose not to add any additional stress.

Trigger calls out surrounding landmarks. "Freight cars. Silt Railroad Station. We're on track."

Did he just say he sees the crack?

"Say again?" I ask, hyperfocused on the split.

"T?" His neck twists over to me for a second and then returns front and center. "You're as pale as a full moon."

I suspect what he means is as white as a ghost, cryptically asking if I've had another paranormal encounter with the memory of my dad.

"Nerves," I explain. Half fib, half truth. Again, I've placed myself in the uncomfortable position of having to lie to Trigger.

"My landing?" he says.

I nod to trap another fabrication from escaping my lips, and notice dull lights spark on the ground. *The power grid must have rebooted.* What I assumed was an early Christmas gift last trip was explained away by Professor McVie and good old-fashioned science. "Airport eleven o'clock," I say.

As if he's been hit by a shot of nitrous, Trigger manhandles the controls. "I've got this," he says, and in one sweeping motion, he yanks the throttle to idle, switches the fuel off, and moves the propeller lever to feather.

The engine seizes, and a stone-cold stillness settles—the same eerie quiet, in fact, we'd experienced before the tornadoes hit. "What I wouldn't give for my splash jacket and a water-filled retention ditch," I say.

The edges of Trigger's mouth curl.

Powerless, we plunge like a kite made of lead.

Once we are at best glide speed, Trigger angles for the ground.

Passing four hundred feet, the sky surfer holds 110 knots, and all I can do is hope KC and McVie double-checked their math.

"Three hundred feet," I call out.

Our craft sinks.

With the precision of a NASA engineer, Trigger holds speed, aware every knot means the difference between life and death.

"Two hundred feet."

A crumbling strip of pavement comes into view, unlit and painted with a bold-yellow X.

"It's closed!" I shout.

Trigger banks to the right. "No worries," he says. "I'll land on the taxiway."

"You mean that bike-path-looking strip with troughs of water on either side?"

"You're the one who wished for water."

"One hundred feet, fifty, forty, thirty…" I say and then hold my breath, hoping my filled lungs might help slow the descent.

"Twenty, ten feet to go…" I squeeze my eyes shut.

The landing gear hits with a firm *thud*, and my lids blink open.

The nose of our plane splits the sliver of pavement.

"Woo-hoo!" I punch a fist in the air.

Trigger blows out his breath. "Just like I practiced it in my head."

Really? I twist and glance at the sky surfer.

As we roll into a sand berm, I notice a tiny sweat bead bubble on his upper lip. Although he fakes the Flough swagger, I see right through it. No X-ray vision or in-skull network required. I guess every once in a while, even an überpilot gets scared.

The plane jerks to a stop, its wheels stuck in grainy sand. "Now what?" I say.

Trigger grins. "We wait."

CHAPTER 16

I should have been surprised when a one-ton tug the size of a wrecker appeared out of thin air, but I learned during our last visit that anything is possible at Pioneer.

The sand piled in front of us ripples like a mushy ocean wave. And once it runs its course, the edge of the mound lifts.

"Eureka!"

Beneath what I now realize is a painted tarp bursts Henry Aska Gu, sitting on a jacked-up monster tow truck.

He's still in one piece. I breathe, easing the tension on one of the two vise grips clamped around my heart.

No sooner does the sense of relief settle than curiosity interrupts. "How in the world did he hide that mega tug?"

As Henry gathers and folds the paper-thin cloth, I see the tanned hide's underside.

"The chamois, of course." I fist slam my forehead. Based on the cloth's massive size and impeccable color match, I assume Henry has tweaked the prototype.

"What took you so long?" Trigger says, even though we haven't waited a full minute. He hurries out of his seat and leaps from the wing.

Henry drops the desert-camo-printed chamois, jumps from the tug's captain's seat, and runs toward Trigger.

I scoot across the cockpit, deplane, and join them.

By the time I arrive, Henry's arms are wrapped so tightly around Trigger that I don't dare cut in. Instead, I hang back and watch as the most resourceful person I've ever met unravels. Tears streak his cheeks.

"I can't believe you came," Henry says and gnaws his lower lip. The Weatherman's arms fall from Trigger's shoulders. He starts to wheeze and then reaches for a pocket. "It's been hard since you guys left." Henry retrieves his inhaler and takes a steroid hit. "Everything changed." When he wipes away the dampness, I notice splotches of black-purple bruises patching his cheeks.

What could have possibly changed in a month? I want to ask. But seeing what I'm assuming are the repercussions of our narrow escape hyperventilating in front of us, I roll my lips together and keep my trap shut. *Man, did we mess up.*

"We're here now." Trigger steps back and rests a reassuring hand on Henry's neck. "Tana and I—"

Henry spins like a top. "Tana," he blurts my name, now realizing I'm standing opposite him. He runs to my side, stops, shuffles his feet, and slugs my arm. "I knew when I sent the message you would be the one to hear."

"Me?" My hands clench.

"Who else?" Henry's chest heaves. He lifts his inhaler to his swollen mouth and pumps. He traps the air in his lungs for a second and then releases a breath through funneled lips. His panicked expression shifts as quickly as the steroids opened his airway. The Weatherman straightens. An air of self-assuredness follows, the sort of confidence I've witnessed when he talks about science.

Henry appears taller than I remember, grown up, stronger in the way that comes from surviving something horrible. I should know. I used to, sometimes still, carry a similar posture. I search for any signs of the goofy boy I met a short time ago. *What happened to you, Henry?* I shudder.

"Despite your efforts to hide it…" He speaks like a robot. Any tears have long since dried from his chocolate-brown eyes. "I see it," he says in a thundering tone.

"See what?" I ask, unsure of what we're talking about.

"Your kind heart, T."

A surge of electricity sizzles beneath my skin—the wild rush that flows when something said is so real that it becomes uncomfortable.

I take in the compliment. I feel awkward and calm all at the same time—a sensation that compares to nothing else, not even the delight of being around Trigger.

"Kind, but guarded," Trigger says. "Cased in kryptonite."

The exhilaration I feel flushes from my limbs. Icy chills chase it. I glare at Trigger and brush my hand over Henry's cut-and-swollen forehead.

"So?" Henry shrugs. "It's not like you're Superman, Triggs."

More like supermoody. "Hold still," I say and drag my knuckles over the Weatherman's uneven complexion, noticing new cuts, healing scars, and squishy knots filled with fluid. *Enough.* I can't hold my tongue any longer.

"What's happened to you?" My fingers circle the navy-blue ring beneath his left eye.

Henry raises his chin and then shies away, revealing razor stubble where his bushy head of curls used to be. My hand falls from his cheek. "I don't understand. Where is your dad?"

Henry shuffles a few steps before his feet tangle, and he tumbles to his knees. Trigger grabs one arm, I circle to secure his other, and we help Henry to his feet. Trembling, Henry straightens his horn-rimmed glasses, shakes off our assistance, and limps toward the tug. "We need to hide the plane," he says, "before anyone else realizes you're here."

CHAPTER 17

"This is your idea of hiding?" I stand outside a neglected shack of a hangar, the last in a row of ancient storage buildings before the edge of the airfield blends into the vast, cracked desert.

Thin walls of silver corrugated metal waver as a steady breeze blows from the south. Even though the rectangular space is packed floor to ceiling with helium tanks and other spare airplane parts, my pearl-white homebuilt, airbrushed with red and black racing stripes, remains obvious. All Pioneer's security chief and his goons need to do is open the bifold door, and the winged elephant in the middle of the hangar will trumpet our unscheduled arrival. That creep McDunney will find us soon enough, for sure, but later is better than now.

"What's with all the helium tanks?" I ask.

Henry cranes his neck over his shoulder. "For the annual hot-air-balloon fly-in at the end of summer." He scratches his nose. "That's why there're so many, stockpiled, I mean." He gulps. "Hey, T, watch this." The Weatherman unrolls the chamois strapped to his backpack. I can't help but feel like he's creating a distraction. *What's the real deal with the helium, my friend?*

Henry lifts the cloth over his head and shakes the featherweight material.

His arms swoop to his thighs and flit back through the air—up and then down, like an eagle flapping its giant wings. His arms cycle, fingers clenching the fabric's edge, and with each flutter, the cloth expands until it stretches wide enough to cover the entire polished floor.

Henry thrusts his hands up one last time and then lets go, leaving the magical cloth untethered and hovering overhead. Streams of dim starlight drip from a single window cut in the corrugated wall, highlighting a pattern of pin-sized specs that match the hangar floor.

Gravity tugs on the cloth, and it drifts like a falling leaf and covers the airplane, tail to wing tip, with a blanket of sand-colored snow.

"Not quite." I stare at the airplane shape pushing from the slip-covered dune. "Covered doesn't mean hidden."

No sooner do the words leave my lips than I regret what I've said.

Before my eyes, the tan tarp sparks, shimmers, swirls, and mixes into a creamy-mocha color. The fabric churns, and the sheet transforms into an iridescent-pearl color. Then, as if a magician has waved a wand, the distinctive shape of the plane oozes in the way warm butter melts over waffles, and it fades into the brilliant-white floor.

My eyes bug. My brain scrambles for an image I can no longer see. "The plane's gone?"

The Weatherman grins. "Disguised as a concrete hangar floor."

"The perfect cover," Tana says.

"Don't worry." Henry kicks the vacant space where the tires once were.

"And where is the plane it took Dad and me seven years to build?" I say.

"Right here, Triggs." Henry's foot appears to bounce off an invisible tread. He takes a few running steps, jumps, twists backward, and then seat-drops in midair.

"How?" slips from my lips.

I watch Henry, impossibly perched from what I estimate is our vaporous wing.

"I've programmed microscopic cameras to project whatever I want the viewer to see."

Feet dangling, the Weatherman peels a tiny corner of fabric from the wing tip, showing his intricate design sewn into the seam. "Two hundred different images of the hangar floor project three dimensionally." Henry burp-snorts. "As you can imagine, I've had a lot of alone time on my hands."

Tana and I exchange the same look. Although he has been physically beaten down, Henry's mind seems unaffected, heightened actually. If the evolution of the chameleon chamois is any measure, being taunted has kicked his genius IQ to DEFCON 1 level.

A wiry smile crosses Henry's face, taking the place of his puffed-up grin. He cracks into a full-blown gut buster. Bent at the waist, his window-washing goggles slip and tumble to his feet.

I find myself air laughing, unsure of what's so funny. We roar on, whooping and snorting, and when Henry straightens, my hand flies to my mouth.

"Your piercing," Tana says. She points at Henry's ear. "It looks like fire."

Henry's elbow curls. He reaches for his earlobe. But it's too late.

From behind us, a familiar voice thunders. "That's because we're here."

"Chief McDunney." I grind my teeth, recognizing his craggy drawl.

Like Henry's, the chief's ear receiver is glowing like a bonfire.

"Not good," Tana belts.

I clench my fists. Red, blue—it really doesn't matter. All I know is that if the earring lights match, the wearers are connected, and anyone linked to Pioneer's intranet can track our position.

"Run!" Tana shouts, and we both spin, take a few steps, and are met by a dozen uniformed soldiers. They fan out, dressed in desert camo, looking like...*Could it possibly be?*

"Who are they?" Tana asks.

"US Marines."

As the soldiers fall in line, elbow to thick, beefy elbow, they form a mile-long roadblock of solid muscle. I grip Tana's forearm and anchor her at my side. "Forget about trying to run."

Chief McDunney saunters over—his jaw as wide as a pit bull's, his head attached by a tree-trunk-sized neck, and his shoulders still too thick and broad to see around. He lowers his pocked face inches from mine. The stench of rotten eggs floods my nostrils. I gag and look away.

"Mr. Flough, Miss Lyre," McDunney snarls and pushes a finger into my chest.

I slap it away.

The chief chuckles. "I warned you two to never return to Pioneer."

"Get your hands off me, scumbag."

I tighten my fists and swing at McDunney's overstepping gesture. Every inch of my skin crawls.

With little effort, he bats my punch away. He's still head and shoulders taller than I am and old-man strong. *Just wait, Chief.* I glare at him. *A few more hours in the gym and I'll be bulky enough to beat you down.*

What were we thinking?

Questions overpower my anger. *That we'd glide in, hide a three-thousand-pound airplane, and blend into the student body as if nothing happened?*

Something did happen, you overgrown pervert.

I zero in on the chief's good eye, ushering away the memory of his ID badge dragging over my chest.

What was the game plan once we got here?

I avert my eyes to the chain of muscle backing up the chief—Number One and McDunney's regular security team of six, a dozen oversized marines, and a fleet of jeeps and Humvees.

"Beefed up security, huh? Sucks to get beat by a bunch of candidates, doesn't it?"

McDunney snarls.

I scan the surrounding landscape—not another soul around. I gulp. *This is so not like me.*

Caught up on finding the airport and creating the geomagnetic storm, I hadn't figured a plan once on the ground. Even if we could get past the blockade, there's nowhere to go.

I shake away the dull pain throbbing in my head. *Tana tried to warn me. Why didn't I listen?*

I rub my eyes and picture my dad's disapproving mug once he gets wind that I dragged Tana on a suicide mission. Then there's KC and

McVie in the weather lab, monitoring the sat phone and waiting for a sign that we arrived safely. And toss in the earful I'd get for lying to Tana's mom and then taking the future pill.

Ugh!

I rub my temples. All of a sudden, our valiant mission for justice and friendship seems to lack one iota of common sense.

How irresponsible. What's my problem? I knock my fists on my forehead. *I know better. This was so not a good idea.*

"Take them to the detention area," McDunney barks at his second in command.

"Aye-aye." Number One jogs over and latches onto my arm. I point my elbow to the ground and yank. Numero Uno doesn't flinch.

His minion follows, securing Tana's wrists.

"Detention area? Wait a minute," Tana shrieks. "I want to go to medical. Better yet"—she stomps on Number One's boot—"take me to Dr. Lindy's office." She wiggles a hand free, pinches her ear receiver, and blinks like she's having a seizure.

"What are you doing?" I say, as Number Two regains control of her wrist and ratchets it behind her back.

"Activating Dr. Lindy's emergency signal. Hold the disk and blink for reinforcements."

"We're not connected anymore, T." I see panic in her eyes. "Besides, I think it's going to take more than a shot or magic contacts to save our butts."

Almost as if perfectly timed, a pair of high-beam headlights shines in our eyes. Tana looks away. I squint. Henry dodges from behind us and runs—lame attempt, since Number One's long reach snags the hood of his sweat shirt.

"Bring the genius to me!" McDunney shouts. His nostrils flare, and the tattered eye patch lifts from his scarred cheek. The guard restraining Henry drags our friend to his commander.

Chief McDunney hovers over Henry's slight frame and scowls. He flicks Henry's ear with his crooked finger. The Weatherman cowers and buries his bald head in his sweat shirt.

The chief raises a fist, and Henry curls into a ball. Laughing, McDunney throws a look to a jeep flanking the soldiers. "Get him out of my sight."

"Trigger!" Tana shouts.

Call it instinct, but for some reason, I can't tear my eyes from the approaching headlights. "It's going to be all right."

"Are you out of your mind?" she says. "How?"

Head ticking in short intervals, McDunney surveys the airfield. "Gu, to my jeep," the chief mumbles, calm and collected, far more in control than the last time we were here. Number Two nods at the marines dressed in tan-and-brown desert fatigues. Two men move out of line and jog over to secure Henry.

"No one can help you now, lab rat," McDunney taunts.

True to his accused nature, rat or ant, Henry squeals and wiggles, desperate to get away. The marines easily thwart his efforts.

McDunney licks his lips and flicks Henry's ear. "Not even your buddy Headmaster Funkhouser."

Henry's feet scurry—front, back, side to side—fretting in any direction that might provide a chance to break away. The enlisted men lift him off the ground; his boots hover a foot from the sand. Henry flails like an ant about to be crushed by the sole of a government-issue boot.

Now equal in height, the chief's eyes launch daggers into Henry's terror-ridden gaze. "This defiance." He sneers. "Final nail in the coffin."

Every centimeter of Henry's tiny body shakes. McDunney grunts, and the soldiers carry him away.

I stand and stare.

"Leave him alone," Tana says, squirming like a caged crocodile. She twists her forearm and breaks free. "Trigger—help him."

"Stop," I say and tear my gaze from the funneled beams. I grab Tana's wrist and pull her close so I can whisper in her ear. "This doesn't make sense."

"You're right; Henry doesn't deserve this," she says, shifts her weight, and readies herself to run after him.

"That's not what I mean." I refocus on the streams of light growing wider as they approach. "McDunney isn't military."

"So?" Tana says.

"So there's no way US Marines are under his command."

From the expression on her face, I can tell she's thinking, analyzing the armored Humvees circling McDunney's jeep, noticing the way the uniformed team moves with such ease and precision, as if they are a single unit. I hope she's wondering why Pioneer would need an elite group of soldiers of this caliber to protect the future minds of America.

That is, unless she's seen the future.

The blinding headlights shine through arm gaps in the muscleman barrier. The surrounding area brightens, and a camouflage-painted Humvee appears.

"A-tten-tion!" a drill sergeant tone booms from behind the hazy glow. Faster than a gunshot, every soldier salutes with stiff fingers.

Slicing the headlight beams, a skyscraper-sized shadow projects forward. The outline grows. The figure stops, assumes a shoulder-wide stance, and layers thick arms over a uniformed chest.

"Red Rover, Red Rover." Authoritative syllables echo as if he was yelling down a well. "Send the son of Lamar Flough right over."

"Mac?" I shade my eyes and trace his athletic shape. His head seems to almost touch the night sky. And despite the fact that his extra-large uniform matches the rest of the bulky marines', he nimbly moves forward. "Mac Numereau? Is that you?"

His long strides quicken, and less than a foot away, his veined arms unfold.

"It is you." I hustle forward to meet his open embrace. We clench a solid man hug and then separate.

"Let me guess, brother, you're happy to see me?" Mac smiles his all-American grin and cracks a wad of gum.

With the light at his back, I recognize his clean-shaven face and his standard-issue dishwater stubble that is buzzed high-and-tight around his skull.

"Understatement," I say and twist my neck toward McDunney. I glance at the soldiers and then back to Mac. "Surprised, I mean." I scrunch my brows together. "What are you doing here? Last I heard you were staked out in the Middle East."

The ex–air force officer turned marine, who is the closest thing I've had to a brother, nods affirmatively, which doesn't help explain any further. His full lips purse like he has something to say, but then he changes his mind.

You're right, bro. This isn't the time for catch-up.

Mac scans the perimeter, the chief, the soldiers, and the four men crowding around us.

"I'm here on assignment. A joint civilian/military project with Pioneer." Mac's straight talk catches me off guard since he used to subscribe to the same loose-lips-sink-ships communication philosophy as my father. Apparently, I'm not the only one. McDunney's cloudy eye bulges.

"That's classified information, Sergeant," McDunney says. "These two are not sworn students. They are fugitives. My prisoners."

Mac's jaw circles like a rotor. He snaps his gum and grins. "These two." He points at me and Tana. "Not possible."

McDunney throws his shoulders back and puffs out his chest.

Mac stands surefooted, unaffected by the chief's challenging gesture. "My operation, my decision. I dictate who does or doesn't get information. Trigger is like a brother to me, born and bred in the military, straight out of the womb in red, white, and blue. Believe me." Mac's purplish-green eyes resemble the aurora's particle brew. He says, "Trigger knows how to keep a secret."

Even in the dim light, I see the chief's olive complexion redden. The tattered eye patch wrinkles. His shoulders slouch, and he falls back into the ranks of the enlisted men. Not quite in line, he pauses, turns, and points a thick, accusing finger in my direction. "What about his so-called sister?"

"Sister?" Mac's gaze shoots to me. He shakes his head and chuckles. "More like girlfriend."

Chief McDunney clenches his fists.

"I'm not his girlfriend," Tana says.

A ping spikes my chest. In my head, I hear a door slam and a dead bolt latch.

"I guess a baby could have come after Trigger's mom split," Mac says. "But I doubt it. That woman had one goal in life—to become a general's wife." His eyes slant to me.

I shove my hands in my pockets and kick a tiny sandstone.

"Don't be embarrassed," Henry says. "Sometimes I make up reasons why my mom took off too."

The deep crow's feet around Mac's eyes wrinkle. His face shifts, as blank as a sand dune, making it an impossible read. He stands solid and captures my gaze. A second passes, and I nod, understanding his silent question. *Is she trustworthy?* Mac asks in our wordless language, a series of expressions we made up when we were kids. We exchange our secret blood brother look, and when I bob my head, Mac says, "I trust her too."

McDunney's eye patch lifts touching his bushy unibrow. "No way," he says.

"In charge." Mac points to himself and widens his stance, refolding his drumstick forearms over one another. "Ask around, Chief; I don't tolerate insubordination."

Every soldier on the ramp gives a subtle, agreeing nod.

Chief McDunney winds a round-'em-up finger over his head. Obeying his signal, the Pioneer security force breaks formation and retreats back to their jeeps with Henry in tow. They manhandle the Weatherman into the backseat and stuff him in between two of the chief's guards. Four engines turn over, and the caravan drives off, in box formation, toward the airport exit.

"At ease," Mac hollers. His men relax and file behind him.

Tana grabs my sleeve. "We can't let them take Henry."

Mac glares at me, his commanding jaw tightens.

I give him a look to convey that she isn't familiar with chain-of-command protocols. "What she meant to say was, 'Permission to help our friend, sir.' She's right, Mac." I straighten my spine, stiff as a lightning rod. "Henry's the reason we came here."

From the corner of my eye, I see Tana's cheek twitch.

"At least"—I kick another stone—"most of the reason."

Mac doesn't answer for what seems like an eternity, and then his steel jaw cranks open and stretches into a true-blue wince. "McDunney does kind of have it in for that kid." He works his gum. "I get it though. He's odd."

"Henry Aska Gu's the smartest guy I know."

"Mind may be A-rated, but physically he's a D or an F. He needs to nut up if he wants the bullying to stop."

"He's not like you and me, Mac."

"Does he have a Y chromosome, an appendage between his legs?" My military brother adjusts his own bulging package. "Then he's a man. Give him a few months in my unit, and I'll whip him into shape."

I blow air, wondering when Mac grew up to be my father. He used to make fun of the colonel's rigid thinking and snap judgments. Now if I close my eyes, I hear my father. *OK, Lamar.* I shrug, going along, not agreeing, knowing better than to jab Mac in front of his men.

"Shame he didn't get a father like yours," Mac says.

Geez. Just as I suspected, he's become my dad. I clamp my teeth together, resisting the urge to make a bunker-busting quip about one of the greatest pilots to ever live.

"Masters, McNeal," Mac booms like a blow horn. "Go retrieve Mr. Aska Gu. Gently. Bring him to our camp. Preferably unharmed." My half brother grinds his gum and faces me. "Speaking of the old man, does he know you're here?"

CHAPTER 18

Every tent in Camp Numereau is colored desert beige and tan. The shape of each bunk's pitched roof reminds me of my grandparents' single-car garage. Rows of matching pup tents speckle the entire northeast corner of the airfield, resembling a caravan of RV campers at an extraterrestrial convention.

Tents qualify as barracks, don't they? I rationalize. And they must be occupied by men and women in uniform. So, we didn't really lie to my mother when we told her we'd spend our nights in military dorms. I mean, what's safer than sleeping surrounded by hundreds of marines?

Blame it on the excess testosterone in the air, but my ability to divert and avoid is amped. Check that off as one less lie we'll have to cover with our parents.

Sort of.

"Welcome home." Mac angles his bulging shoulders sideways to fit through the tent's makeshift door. Inside, he spreads his legs wide and layers his thick arms. "There are your racks." He fingers two cots on opposite ends of the narrow room. Single poles at either end support the pointy roof.

"There are only two," I whisper to Trigger. "Where's Henry going to…"

"Ladies." Mac's eyes settle on me. He arcs an eyebrow. "You are a lady, right, Miss Lyre?"

Is that a trick question? Afraid to ask a follow-up, I nod.

"Good, you can hang out here during the day, but you'll sleep in the guest bunks next to my tent." Mac's glare flicks to Trigger. "This is a marine camp, not a college dorm."

The sky surfer stares straight ahead, avoiding any eye contact, and answers with a hearty, "Yes, sir."

"Showers and the head are at the end of this row." Mac points to the right. "Mess tent is in the center." His stubby thumb angles over a shoulder. "Three clicks east and then half a click north. Honestly, though, the food at Pioneer's café is much better." Mac's right eye blinks as if he's ticking items off a memorized checklist. His jaw holds steady and his slit gaze shoots to me. "Ladies' facilities are at the far end of camp. The last tent before the mesa. For privacy. Marines don't intermingle."

I swallow a lump growing in my throat.

"Masters or McNeal can take you there in a jeep. Just give me a heads-up."

"Thanks, but I'm sure I can find my way," I reply, certain I don't want to have to tell two buff marines every time I need to pee.

"You think?" Mac's lips pucker. "Military camps can be confusing. Same tents, same uniforms, identical haircuts." He runs a hand over his head stubble. "It's pretty tough to tell anything a part. Especially if you didn't grow up blue or green."

"Don't worry about her, Mac," Trigger assures him. "Tana possesses a super sense of direction."

"Built-in GPS?"

"More like a heat-seeking missile."

"I see." Mac's sight line ping-pongs between us. His forehead wrinkles. "How is it you two know each other?" A subtle grin creeps across his lips.

"School," I say.

"In Tulsa. We're just…"

"Friends." I finish Trigger's sentence.

"Explains a lot." His smile stretches. Barely. "Well, it's nice to finally meet one of my baby brother's friends."

Marine Masters pushes through the tent opening and heaves our duffels onto the cracked, dusty ground.

"Planning an invasion?" Mac frowns and toes our exploding duffels, stuffed with enough gear to equip a special-forces unit. He rolls his lips together and cracks his gum. "Get settled, grab some shut-eye, and we'll meet in the morning and get better acquainted." Sergeant Numereau struts toward the fabric door. "My office. Zero eight hundred."

"Zero eight hundred, your tent," Trigger confirms. "Permission to speak freely, sir?"

The sergeant hesitates and looks back with slitted eyes. "What's on your mind?"

The tension in Trigger's shoulders releases. "We really appreciate you taking us in."

Mac's chin bobs.

"And getting us out of trouble with McDunney. Man"—Trigger blows out—"that was above and beyond."

"Nothing your dad didn't do for me." Mac grimaces. "You know I owe him, big-time." Numereau turns.

As one tree-trunk thigh disappears through the makeshift door, I say, "Sir?"

Mac sighs. The tent flap laps against his forehead.

Yeesh.

"Sergeant Numereau?" I say in my best apologetic voice.

His palm flies up like a stop sign.

Outside, I hear an engine knock, what sounds like a parking brake set, and muffled voices.

"Bring him here," Mac says. He draws the tent flap.

"Henry!" I spring to my feet, close the space between us, and lift his loaded backpack from his shoulder. "Sit." I signal him to the cots, and he collapses on the taut wool blanket. "Are you all right?" I inventory his face. The ring around his eye remains a yellowish green. His split lip is dried over, and his forehead is knotted and splotched purple. No new marks as far as I can tell. Or at least none that are visible.

I hand him his pack, and he wastes no time checking its contents. Appearing satisfied, he collapses flat on his back. "Did I mention how glad I am you guys are here?"

Trigger and I sit on the remaining racks surrounding Henry. A double-layer friend sandwich. I flop flat and stare at the sturdy poles supporting the tent. My intuition tells me Trigger is doing the same, so I don't bother to check.

"You weren't kidding," Trigger says. I roll to my side, propping my head on an elbow. "Things are really different."

Henry clutches his pack like a security blanket.

"Why are the marines here?" I say.

Wouldn't have anything to do with the hangar full of supposed cloud-seeding drones Trigger saw before we left Pioneer the first time, would it?

Not quite sure who is friend or foe, I stick to the basics, what I assume won't raise suspicion if overheard by a passerby in camo pants. "Since when are ear receivers red? And why can't I hear anything on the intranet?" Questions roll off my tongue as fast as they pop into my head.

Henry's eyes meet mine and then turn to Trigger. I'm guessing he makes the what's-up-with-the-spastic-girl face, because when his neck centers, Henry exhales. "So she hasn't eased up on the interrogating?"

"Nope." Trigger shakes his head. "I don't think she can help herself. Since I've gotten to know her family, I think it's genetic."

I sit up, cross my legs, and cuddle my knees. "If I'm going to be labeled, I might as well live up to my reputation. Tell me why the Streeters are beating on you?"

Henry's body tenses. "Guy stuff."

Frames of kicks and punches and blood flash before my eyes. "Seriously?" I frown.

Henry tightens his grip and rocks back and forth. But that doesn't deter me.

"Pretty iffy explanation for a scientist," I say, aware the ultimate insult to any lab guru is to say his thoughts aren't clear or based in well-researched facts. A low blow, I know, but I'm desperate to understand if what I saw was real. I need to make sure I'm not losing it.

"Where's your dad?" I press harder, annoyed just by mentioning Henry's obnoxious father. "Why is he letting the Streeters beat you?"

The Weatherman's eyes fill. He bites his cut lip. His crooked teeth dig in farther, and blood trickles down his chin.

Now you've done it, Lyre. I'm about to apologize when Henry transforms. His eyes dry and a hard expression covers his soft, baby features. Like he said when we arrived, everything, including our friend, has changed.

"Give the guy a break, Tana. Can't you see he's not interested in talking right now?"

"If not now, when?" I glare at Trigger. "We don't have much…"

Henry's eyes bug. "Time?" he says.

"Henry, listen…" Trigger shoots up like a rocket and steps between our friend and me.

"My father left with Dr. Harb," the Weatherman says. Short, puffy breaths intertwine with his words.

My heart throbs. "Left where?" I say, and my throat tightens.

The flashbacks return. In my head, I hear the timer beep and the bomb explode, and I feel the sensation of blazing heat as my dad's silhouette disappears. My view fills with billowing black smoke.

When Henry doesn't answer, I climb to my feet, shove Trigger aside, and grab the collar of Henry's hoodie. "Harb can't get away, not this time. I won't allow it." I grind my molars. "He will pay for his crimes." My fingers flex. "Tell me, where are your dad and Dr. Harb?"

"I…I…don't know." Henry quivers. "He left. Ditched me. Said he and Harb's work is far too important to be held back by his disappointment of a son."

My fingers unravel and release his collar. "Henry…" I ease back, not daring to look at Trigger. Remnants of my self-serving frenzy exit through my fingers like electric sparks.

The Weatherman dry heaves and coils into a fetal ball. He rocks, and his heavy breathing shortens into an air-seeking wheeze. I pry his pack from his arms, retrieve his inhaler, and fold it into his quivering hand. I help him match it to his lips and then squeeze the pump on the aluminum can once. "Easy," I say as much for him as for me.

Henry's neck stretches back to help his airway open.

I slide onto his cot and cradle his head. "I'm so sorry." I stroke his forehead. "I don't know what came over me."

Maybe all the diverting and denying eventually bubbles up.

The Weatherman sucks a huge steroid-infused breath, sits up, drags his sleeve across his face, and unzips his backpack. "With that out of the way, let's get down to business."

"Business?" Trigger says.

"The real reason you came back here."

"You think we came all this way for only one reason?"

A twang of guilt thwacks my chest. My heart beats double time, certain that the Weatherman now regrets sending me his SOS message.

"Henry." I reach for his arm. He knocks away my hand.

Trigger wedges in between us, creating a buffer, just enough space to shelter me from Henry's line of sight.

"We came back to help you." Trigger bumps our friend's shoulder.

Henry's body jostles and then centers upright.

"Don't get me wrong, holding Dr. Harb accountable is also part of the mission, but when Tana saw your video clip, the one you so stellarly streamed to her receiver, she pledged to never stop searching until we found a way back here."

Henry leans to look around the sky surfer. "You came back for…me?"

"Of course," I say. "You sent the message knowing I would come and help. Remember?"

"Then all it took was for Tana to convince me to take the pill." Trigger's mouth twists. "You can imagine how easily I went along with her suggestion." He chokes himself with both hands around his throat and pretends to gag.

Henry grins. "Not." After a few rounds of snorts and giggles, he says, "I assumed when you left that you might have some unfinished business. So…"—he does a palms up—"I made you a special pill."

I *so* want to ask what he changed, whether it was tested, how he knew the doctored pill would work, and why in the world Trigger saw the past while I got a glimpse of the future. But I recognize Henry's fragile state, still recovering from my last filter-free interrogation, so I decide to wait. Save the future pill inquisition for another conversation.

"If it wasn't for Trigger's pill-induced vision, we would have never discovered the coordinates for Pioneer's airfield."

From Henry's puffed-up expression, I see he's pleased. "The GPS coordinates modulate. They aren't static. The school updates their mainframe servers at the end of every day."

I *thunk* my forehead, remembering how KC's mirroring software remains anonymous, despite Pop's obsession with our home computer's software updates. "Every time Pioneer updates, their server's IP address changes."

"And?" Henry bicycles his hands.

I think for a second and then make the virtual connection. "The IP update must shift the airport coordinates somehow."

"Right on, T. Except the actual lat/longs never change. The jamming net cloaks the airfield's position and allows the modulated signals to be sent to satellites."

"Which tricks the GPS boxes in planes into thinking the airport doesn't exist," I say, knowing KC would pass out if she knew what she was missing.

Henry says, "Even if the onboard computer had stored the field's coordinates from a prior landing—"

Trigger shoots to his feet. "The next day, the lat/longs are different."

"Airport not found," I say.

The sky surfer points at me. "That's why the numbers I wrote down didn't work when we were back in Tulsa. Why I couldn't lock onto Pioneer's location in order to get back."

Henry's fingers spider toward his inhaler. But instead of taking a hit, he sucks a deep breath. "I knew you'd come back." He exhales and wipes his brow. "That's why I streamed video to Tana and left virtual footprints all over the Internet."

I rest my hand on my heart and smile at Trigger. His surfer grin flashes back.

"Makes sense," I say. "The shadows of his bread crumbs were what KC chased all over the net, but she always wound up stuck in a virtual closet."

I expected Henry to retreat into some complicated, techie explanation but instead he asks, "Who's KC?"

"A friend."

"What kind of friend?" Henry fidgets with his horn-rimmed glasses. "Not only did she find her way into the cyber house, but she managed to hack into the coat closet." He moans. "As luck has it, I'm in the market for friends."

"You'll meet her." Trigger moves to the duffels.

"I will? When?" Henry licks his fingers to smooth his head stubble. "Where? She isn't packed in one of these bags is she?"

I glance at our luggage pile and consider if any of the ski-length bags could hold a body. Perhaps even a prisoner.

"Relax," Trigger says. "She's back in Tulsa, family commitment, couldn't make the trip."

Trigger retrieves KC's tweaked cell encryptor and passes it to Henry. Instantly, the scientist runs a diagnostic. He thumbs over the smooth plastic and then weighs it in his palm.

"Light. Magnetic. Let me guess, it can work around Pioneer's closed network and connect any phone to the intranet regardless of the firewalls?" Henry turns the booster end over end, scrutinizing the work of someone who could quite possibly be his intellectual equal. He brings the booster to his nose and squints through his bottle-thick lenses. "No visible seams." His words quicken. "No prongs or input plugs." Cords on his neck thump faster. "Not even a recessed serial number."

Certain he might hyperventilate at any second, I ready his inhaler. With the booster in his left palm, he reaches for his cell with his right and matches each wrist within an inch of each other. With the pull of some invisible force, the booster and phone clap together. The cell screen lights, and the handset vibrates. Henry groans again, and his dim eyes brighten. "I need to meet this girl."

As fate would have it, KC McKenna's contact flashes across the caller ID.

"Introduce yourself," Trigger says.

Unanswered, KC's call continues to buzz.

"Go ahead. Answer."

Henry's hands shake. His lips glom together as if dipped in a jar of peanut butter. "Uh, um…" He thrusts the phone at Trigger.

All in one motion, Trigger grabs the cell and then flips it to me like a hot potato. With no real news to report yet, I kick the call into voice mail.

"Why didn't you pick up?"

I glance at Trigger. "Before we report in, I need some answers."

"Like?"

"How are we going to find Dr. Harb and Henry's dad?"

No longer tongue-tied, Henry says, "I have an idea, but you're not going to like it."

"What other options do we have?" I say.

The Weatherman shrugs. "None."

"Then you might as well tell me."

Henry tugs on his collar and clears his throat. "Ah…" he says.

I open my eyes wider. "Well?"

"You need to make up with Soraya."

"That liar-deceiver-manipulator-accomplice-fraud?" I say in one breath. "You mean the earring thief who pretended to be my friend?" Each toxic syllable stings my tongue. I'm unsure what hurts worse, the fact she said I could trust her or that I believed it. "Out of the question." Dust flies as I stomp the ground, searching for something to kick.

"Calm down." Trigger stands and reaches for my arm.

I bunch up my face, sending a sharp warning to back off. I assume he gets the message because he falls back onto his cot.

"Just listen," he says, palms motioning to slow down.

"This is me being calm," I say through a locked jaw.

"That's calm, huh? Remind me to never be around when you're really mad." Henry's voice trembles. "The working theory is that Dr. Harb wouldn't have gone far without his wife and daughter."

"And?" I wind my hands.

"Here's the thing." Henry coughs and then wheezes. "I think Soraya knows where her dad is hiding."

I glare at both of them. "Burrowed beneath the ground no doubt, hiding like a pathetic little weasel. Big whoop. Next."

Henry eyes Trigger and adjusts his goggles. "We could capture her and then hold her captive here in our tent." He stands. "Odds are Sergeant Numereau has at least one prison interrogator in his unit."

"Or"—Trigger joins him. The steadiness of his voice feeds my irritation—"we can reactivate the bootleg network, pretend to forgive her, and then watch every move until she leads us to her dad." His ocean blues brighten.

Henry twists his head. "No dice, Triggs. Two problems with that plan. First of all, bootleg frequencies don't exist anymore. After you guys left, McDunney grilled me for days. No sleep, no food, and…" He layers his arms over his chest.

"And what?"

"Never mind." Henry pulls his hood over his shaved head.

"It's OK, man." Trigger rests a reassuring hand on his shoulder. "Whatever it is, you can tell us."

"No water, I had to pee in a pot…" He hugs himself tighter. "And, you know, other interrogation-type stuff." His lips quiver. "After a week or so, I cracked."

I remember the virtual SOS—Henry in the corner, shivering, bloody, and alone.

"An entire week?" I say. Horrified. Embarrassed. Guilt-stricken.

Henry avoids eye contact.

"Once they had my work-arounds, Pioneer hired outside consultants—a solid group of computer geniuses who cracked my code and plugged the virtual holes in their intranet."

Trigger says, "Explains the run-ins with the Future of Wall Street."

Henry touches the blood knot on his cheek.

"I get it." Trigger knocks a fist on his forehead. "With no bootleg frequencies to sell, you're no longer any use to them."

"Doesn't matter anymore." The Weatherman eyes his inhaler. "All the receivers have been upgraded."

"Hence the red glow," I guess.

Henry nods. "Want to hear the second glitch in our plan?"

"As if that isn't enough?"

"There isn't any actual proof Soraya knows where her dad is hiding."

I grind my molars.

"I do, however, know from a reliable source that our corporate-risk officer in training might have a way to contact him."

"There's our loophole." Trigger squints with one eye, indicating he's shifting perspectives. "We make peace with Soraya and then mention something that sounds important. Urgent even. A tidbit so compelling that she won't be able to resist telling her father."

"If she really knows where he is," I say. "Don't forget, she's an extraordinary actress."

Henry ignores my snip and builds on Trigger's assumptions. "Then we follow like her shadow, observe her every move."

"There's no way." I cringe. "I'm not capable of even fake forgiving her, never mind rekindling a friendship."

"All right, so I miscalculated." Henry tosses an obvious look in my direction. "There's a third flaw in the plan."

"Tana." Trigger identifies me as the weak link. "But I'm certain she's up to the challenge." His voice cracks on the last syllable.

If this is his idea of a pep talk, I suggest he step down as flight-team captain.

"Stop blowing smoke up my stack." I exhale, scattering my bangs.

"Fact is," Trigger says, "we can't do this without you. Henry and I can't go everywhere Soraya goes. We're not exactly, you know…" He grins. "…the right gender. We need you, T."

"Speak for yourself." Henry snickers. "I've always kind of wanted to see the inside of the girls' bathroom."

"Cheeseball." I slap his arm. "This is far more important than a lame sneak-a-peek prank."

Henry cowers as if I threatened him with a baseball bat.

"See, Tana," Trigger says, "you're the only one who can make this plan work."

"She'll see right through me. I don't forgive her. Not for a single thing, and on top of that, I'm a horrible actress."

"I guess that depends." Henry's voice is faint.

"On what?" I say.

"How bad do you want to catch your dad's killer?"

Speechless, I whirl around, scoop up my duffel bag, and then barge out of the tent.

"What's up with those two? Have they lost their minds? Me, befriend Soraya? How friggin' unbelievable." I'm about to rant on, but then I realize every pitched bunk along our aisle is dark and quiet. Not a single camo-clad soldier roaming around. "Where is everybody?" I check my wrist. "I guess when Mac says lights out, he means it. Sure." I stride. "Overlook the fact she's the daughter of a murderer." I spin on a heel and retrace my steps. "Skip over the obvious." I tromp over the sand. "I mean, everyone knows there are well-documented studies that prove violence is genetic. And manipulation? Ha! She learned from the best." *Liar, manipulator, deceiver, cheat.* I squeeze my fingers into my palms and envision a perfect BFF head butt.

As if somehow still connected to the intranet, I hear Trigger's voice of reason mingling in my thoughts. *It wasn't her fault,* the distant words say. *Soraya didn't plant the bomb, and are you even sure she was aware of what her father did?*

"Can you say cross earrings?" I argue against the phantom logic. My strides lengthen, and my boots slosh through the soft sand as I picture the proposed *kiss and make up*. The forced hug. Soraya's emerald snake-charming eyes weeping with faux dampness.

"While we're at it, why not go shopping and then go to the fall dance?" Even the thought of this exchange makes me want to throw up. I jog around to the side of the tent, kneel, my head hurling forward. My stomach dry heaves, and after a few false starts, I realize I haven't eaten for hours, my last meal being a corner of Gran's cleansing scone. As the nausea subsides, I rock back on my heels and push to my feet.

That's when I see a flicker. A driveway length away, a beam of light darts across the biscuit-colored tent. As the stream narrows, a towering soot shadow appears and glides against the canvas backdrop like a wisp of chimney smoke.

The shadow skulks along the sidewall and shines a flashlight on the entrance to Sergeant Numereau's bunk.

Tap, tap…tap, tap, tap. Metal hits wood.

"Who is that?" I whisper. *If only there was a sliver of a moon.*

Inside the tent, a dim lantern glows, and the door unzips.

Light spills through the flap and a statuesque figure dressed in head to toe black is backlit. Before I get a chance to see a face, the figure ducks through the opening and disappears into the seam.

Inside, images cast on the flexible walls, outlining two men shaking hands. One I assume to be Mac. The identity of the other man—unknown.

CHAPTER 19

It's midnight. *Who has meetings at this hour?*

I may not be able to see, but I can try to hear. Hunching down, I tiptoe across the sagebrush and crouch beside the adjacent bunk.

"Thought we were on the same page?" the shadow says.

From where I squat, the man's voice is muffled, making it hard to tell if I've heard it before. When the second voice replies, though, I recognize it loud and clear.

"We are," Mac Numereau says, his commanding tone difficult to miss. Seated in a chair, Mac's shape eases back and puts his boots on his desk.

"Then why did you defend those derelicts?"

"Trigger and his friends?" Mac rocks. "I'm afraid it's obvious why you were ejected from the military."

"I have flat feet," the solid shadow says.

"And a one-track mind."

"That happened when I was sent away by the almighty Colonel Flough."

"Is that what you're calling it?" Mac says. "You mean sent to prison. When you were found guilty of—"

"Some he-said-she-said nonsense."

"Maybe you should have joined the marines."

"Maybe I should've been under a commander who backed up my word."

Mac wastes no time correcting the soot shadow's insubordination.

"Lamar Flough may be a lot of things, but he's honest and loyal above all else."

The shadow grumbles something else I can't quite hear.

"I take formal complaints in writing. If you have something to report, put ink to paper. Understood?"

The shadow twitches.

"In charge." Sergeant Numereau's image points to himself, the curved line of his proud stature stands and moves across the thin wall. He leans into his auxiliary. His voice drops to a murmur.

I waddle, my knees cycling against my shoulders. At the edge of Mac's tent, I catch the last few words. The subordinate says, "Wouldn't it be something if we could convince him to join us? Imagine the resources we'd gain by recruiting the heir apparent?"

"Everything is going as planned." Mac straightens. "Dr. Aska Gu and Dr. Harb both agree."

Hold on. Henry's dad and Harb are still here? I scoot a foot closer. *Go on; say it. Say it. Please. Tell me where they are.*

"The pills are nearly ready for a field test," the unidentified man says, not giving up any clues about the scientists' location. "We don't need him to complete the mission."

"You're still wearing blinders." Mac's featureless face turns in my direction.

"What do you mean? I'm briefed daily and well aware of what's at stake here."

"Need-to-know basis, Private," Mac says. "You don't need to know the second phase of the plan. Yet. When the time is right, you'll understand the tactical advantage of having another valuable resource. For now, you'll have to trust me. I command you to leave him and his friends alone."

"You're not the only one with a code of conduct," the soot shadow retorts. "And I'm not just another peon in your unit."

"Correct. But according to service records, you would have had to donate a limb to get into the corps. How many times were you rejected? If memory serves, at least three."

The unidentified man's voluminous shadow expands.

Mac says, "Not a hand on those kids, understood?"

The shadow's heels click together. "Yes, sir."

Be still. I squeeze my core tight. Because what I just overheard makes the ground beneath my feet seem to spin. *Focus on something solid.* I stare at the rusty tent spike. It, too, blurs.

Doctors Gu and Harb haven't left campus? My hands grasp my skull. *They're making future pills that they plan to give to soldiers?* The heels of my palms squeeze my matted hair. *Is that even possible?*

All at once, everything I believed to be true doesn't make sense. My fingers slide and massage my temples. Trigger's almost brother is running the experiment. Does that mean the sky surfer is aware of this plan?

Confused, I envision two sides of a coin flip. Heads, he doesn't know; tails—*please don't let me find out Trigger has kept this from me. Steady,* I remind myself, my fingers boring dents in my flesh. *Stifle the emotion.* Negotiation tactics 101. *What do I know for sure?* Facts not assumptions.

After careful calculation, I consider all the things I've kept, still keep, from Trigger. So why isn't it possible that he also has secrets?

My skull pounds.

Is this joint Pioneer-military exercise the reason he did an about-face and was willing to take the taboo future pill?

What about Henry? Is he part of the scheme?

Heads or tails? The coin of chance flips, even though my gut says it would be hard to believe an experiment of this magnitude could escape his scientific radar.

A heaviness weighs on my shoulders. *Is it feasible that Henry's SOS was a ploy to get us here?*

Suddenly, everything moves very fast. My thoughts scramble. Fistfuls of imaginary coins toss in my gray matter.

True, false, yes, no. End over end, heads or tails. Authentic or just another elaborate fabrication?

I rub my temples, not wanting to admit I'm unsure which one of my so-called friends I can trust.

None, I decide and wrap my arms over my head.

The bodyweight shift knocks me off-balance. I timber against the tent's staked rope. The braided cord stretches and holds for a second. Straining, the nylon line unravels. The elastic cord snaps, and the corner of Sergeant Numereau's tent sags.

"What in the world…" someone inside says.

A strand of cord twangs and shoots like a rubber band.

Puff. Dust flies as my keister hits the ground. I shake my bangs from my eyes and see two sets of thick black combat boots.

"Miss Lyre," a husky voice grumbles. No longer an apparition, the identity of the soot shadow is clear. Chief McDunney hovers, his enormous frame shading me like a solar eclipse. "What are you doing here?"

CHAPTER 20

Even in the dark, I can feel McDunney's accusing gaze. "What are you doing here?" he repeats.

My mouth goes dry.

Like a ray of sunlight, Sergeant Numereau shoots from behind the chief's shadow.

"You all right, Tana?" He leans forward and extends a sturdy hand. I latch on, and with his free hand, he steadies my elbow and pulls me to my feet.

"Tripped," I say and brush the grit from my pants.

"Out for a late-night stroll?" Mac asks.

McDunney steps closer. "How long were you standing here?" He squares his wide shoulders to mine.

"Oh…ah…not long at all." I cross my legs in a slight curtsey. "Need to use the facilities."

"Please." McDunney sighs.

As fast as you can say tall tale, my head angles toward Mac. "I was looking for an escort to the ladies." I do a pee-pee shuffle. "Sir."

The glow from inside the tent highlights the sharp lines of Mac's tight jaw. His attention shifts toward McDunney, and when he looks back at me, his purplish-green eyes glimmer. "Exactly as instructed." He works his gum. "I'm sure the chief would be happy to show you to the head."

McDunney's lips curl.

"Is there…there must be, someone else," I say.

Chief McDunney sniggers.

"I…I hate to bother the chief with such a trivial errand."

Mac's easy expression vanishes.

My cheeks burn as if lit on fire.

"Anything to help, sir." Chief McDunney seizes my arm and drags me forward. "This way, Miss Lyre."

My feet drag behind McDunney's aggressive strides. Grit and tiny rocks kick into the air. Nearly at the jeep, I dig in with my heels and fight to check over my shoulder. Once turned, I see Mac assume his signature stance—feet shoulder wide, arms layered over one another.

Are you really just going to stand there? I plead with my eyes.

Sergeant Numereau doesn't answer.

∗∗∗

In the jeep, the brisk bite of the air soothes my burning cheeks. Jostling against the roll bar, however, does nothing to ease a queasy stomach or slow, racing heartbeats. McDunney's slicked hair lifts as the jeep bores full speed through the tent grid. *Check your surroundings, Lyre.* I count twelve bunks before we reach the first cross path.

Pay attention to distinguishing features. Even the tiniest details are important. Tips from Eddie's survival lessons flood to the front of my mind. *Gather breadcrumbs. Markers to find your way back.* That is, if I'm coming back.

The chief's lead boot eases to check for foot traffic, and once both sides are cleared, he shifts and the engine roars forward. Another dozen tents fly by, and at the next cross section, McDunney winds the steering wheel and cuts left. West, my internal compass senses. The next groups of tents have paled from the intense afternoon sun, confirming my estimation.

Twenty-four tents tallied so far, and if I count backward to the south, I would be standing in front of Henry and Trigger's bunk. We drive down another identical aisle and then turn right at the flagpole. A quick jog left past three more tents, and the chief skids in order to make a hard right turn. Facing north again, we barrel ahead.

The ground angles up, I know, because the engine grinds faster. Quiet as the night, the chief doesn't say a word. The lack of light from the starless sky allows his ear receiver to blaze brighter. I can see the glow, even from the passenger seat. When the chief's finger touches the piercing, he utters one word. "McDunney."

Now connected to security's stream, I notice his unibrow furrows and wonder if the voice on the other end has suggested he bury me in a ditch. I reach for my own piercing, wishing Henry's bootleg frequency was still up and running. *What is he going to do to me?* I rub the earring between my fingers. The tarnished stud remains icy.

Right at the pile of sandstone boulders, I note, and I continue to keep track of our position. One last jog around at the fork in the road, and the camp disappears behind us. Ahead, all I see is a dark, vast black hole of space.

McDunney clicks off the headlights.

Inside, the jeep goes dark, with the exception of blocked numbers on a dash clock. Midnight. I gulp the lump in my throat, and search the horizon line. I don't see anything resembling a tent. Sand, brush, and darkness fill in the desolate landscape.

Ticktock. Ticktock.

Where are we going? I consider asking, though I think I already know the answer. The chief's lips remain zipped, tight as a pressure seal, his eyes focused, and the red halo illuminates his ear.

Racing forward into the shroud of night, I search for landmarks. No stars, no moon, not a single reference point. The sky and landscape blend. Disorientated, my internal compass spins. *I'm lost,* I admit, as the jeep rockets forward.

Don't give up. My throat constricts. I glance at the ground and hear pebbles kick against the metal frame. *Could this be my last road trip?*

Like a beacon of hope, an idea slaps my forehead—a crazy, wild what-if—one as desperate as the circumstance. *What if I jump?*

A jagged mesa appears on our left, shaped similar to the bow of a grand ship. The perfect place to hide…hide a…*sixteen-year-old corpse.*

My fingers slide across my waist, creeping to the latch on the seat belt.

I suck a deep breath and squeeze my eyes shut.

My thumb beats against the plastic release button.

Leap, tuck, roll, echoes in my head.

My upper lip quivers.

Even if I survive the fall and run like the wind, McDunney has the jeep, and he will hunt me down. My heart thunders beneath my blouse.

I have no other choice. The only hope is to catch him off guard and then pray for a miracle.

"It's nearly finished," McDunney says, and his halo fades. Security's stream disconnects.

Time's up. On one. I grip the latch and steady my hands. *Three, two…*

The chief whips a radical left turn. My thumb slips, smashing the release button. The seat belt retracts from my shoulder earlier than planned. The jeep skids and arcs around a tall rock, creating a monumental force that flings my body to the right.

I eject from my seat and grasp for the roll bar. As I tumble, my arms swim. My legs lift overhead. "Aaaaaah!" I wail.

McDunney's neck snaps around. His arm slices air and latches onto my forearm like a grappling hook. He yanks my flailing body back and then secures me in the passenger seat. The jeep slams to a stop.

Chief Creepy sets the parking brake and then switches on the head lamps. The narrow beams illuminate a single camo-colored tent. "The ladies' facilities." He leans over and sniffs my neck.

Yuck.

His five-fingered winch releases my arm.

I think of Sergeant Numereau's words verbatim. The ladies' facilities are way out. For privacy.

Is McDunney really going to let me use the bathroom?

"I'll just be a minute," I say, swinging from the passenger seat, planning to take off running as soon as I clear the jeep.

"Take as long as you want." McDunney's easy tone stops me in my tracks.

What kind of sick game are you playing?

"Do you know how to use a clutch?"

"Huh?" I say.

The chief shakes his head. "Not a difficult question."

"Sure," I answer, having practiced many times with Eddie when we lived in London.

McDunney pulls a flashlight from his belt and shines the beam against the layered mesa. "You can walk if you like, but if I were you, I'd take the bike."

I bunch up my face.

"Oh…" The chief chuckles. "You thought…" He glances at the ladies' tent and adjusts his ratty eye patch. "You're not that important, Miss Lyre. I've got my eye on a far bigger prize."

Without waiting for a response, he releases the jeep's parking brake, shifts into gear, and doubles back around the tall rock structure. I walk a few steps and see wide treaded tires. *A dirt bike?* I grab the handlebars, straddle the gas tank, kick-start the motor, and rev the engine.

My stomach churns, and nausea bubbles in the back of my throat—likely a side effect from all the testosterone at camp Numereau. *I'm staying here tonight.* I kill the engine and then climb from the desert-style dirt bike. *There are worse places.* I hike toward the ladies' bathroom, choosing what's probably a hard floor over the stiff cot in my assigned bunk next to Sargeant Numereau's tent. *I need some time to think.* I cross the tent's threshold. *Away from Mac, Henry, Trigger, and most importantly, Chief Freaky. Yes, distance and some sleep. That will help me make sense of this circus. Perhaps when I wake up, I might even have a better game plan.*

CHAPTER 21

I wake to darkness, with the exception of a single dull light bulb dangling over a dust-covered mirror. I stand and shuffle to a plastic sink set into a barrel-sized water tub. I swish water in my mouth, run my fingers through my hair, leave the tent, and climb onto the desert dirt bike.

A pit stop and a couple of wipeouts later, I arrive back at Camp Numereau, moderately cut and bruised and not quite getting why girls have to go miles to the bathroom. A little distance from the men, I understand. But way out on the edge of camp seems above and beyond—kind of like Mac's personality.

Miles of riding against the stiff, brisk wind has left my bare arms raw and numb. The sun is not yet visible, but the stark sky is translucent, like glacier ice. By the degree of brightness, I guess it's around 6:00 a.m.—twenty or so minutes before the sun rises and roasts the dehydrated earth. For now, however, the air remains cool and crisp.

Unlike last night, the camp teems with marines—I see hundreds of soldiers in desert camos, jogging in clusters similar to swarming bees. Two by two, the tan-and-cream masses blur, weaving in and out of the tent stakes, repeating rounds of "I've been everywhere, man…" jodie verses. I steer toward Henry and Trigger's bunk, surveying for a place to park the loaner bike.

Next to the air pole or against a Humvee? I decide the urban tank is as good a place as any; I reverse course and point toward the Hummer's rear bumper. Before I reach the idling land yacht, however, a worker bee breaks from his swarm and darts to my side.

"All through, ma'am?" he says, trotting in place while keeping time with his unit's running chant.

I nod. "Was looking for rental return."

"I'll take it from here, ma'am."

I twist the ignition key, and the six-speed transmission sputters.

The camo-jacketed marine commandeers my ride. Once straddling the seat, he shouts, "Ooh-rah!" He cranks the motor, pops the clutch, and arrows across the aisle, as if shot from a harpoon gun. Racing, he angles left and disappears behind Sergeant Numereau's tent, reminding me of something Trigger said once: "There's no dimmer on a marine's on/off switch."

Yawning, I stretch my numb arms above my head. Anxious to share what I've learned, I hustle toward the boys' tent, and split the seam, and when I'm about to enter, I hesitate. I pause and think about what to tell and what to keep from Henry and Trigger.

Throwing up outside the bunk? Unnecessary, since all they'd do is give me a bunch of crap.

The chief meeting with Mac? That tidbit might prove useful. In fact, if I watch closely, their reactions may give a clue if either is in on the secret Numereau-McDunney master plan.

When McDunney mentioned the heir apparent, I assumed they meant Trigger. But also overhearing the part about the son of a program founder, my mind switched to Henry. If that's the case, then why let the Streeters rough up someone so valuable?

Doesn't make sense. Who were the chief and Mac referring to? Henry or Trigger?

I finger the metal door pull, uncertain of whom I can trust. A dull ache throbs in my chest, making me sure of one thing—I can't handle another disappointment.

The zipper grinds, though not by my hand. I try to duck in but knock Trigger's head instead.

"Ouch," I say.

"T?"

We rub foreheads. "Come inside." The sky surfer backs away as I step through. I slip off my boots and then crash on a cot.

About to dig the sand from the corners of my eyes, I notice Henry hovering overhead.

"I was so worried." He kneels and offers his shirt sleeve. Grateful, I use the corner of his cuff to dust away any leftover grit.

"But then Triggs reminded me of how long it takes for your nuclear temper to cool below DEFCON levels."

My arms drop to my sides, and I turn to him and smirk. "Don't suppose you've developed a pill for that?"

"I—" Henry starts to explain, but Trigger interrupts.

"Your arms, Tana." He scoots alongside me, cradles my forearms, and brushes the rocks from the wrist-to-elbow raspberry, half dried and half bubbling with damp blood.

"Long story," I say. "The short version is I wiped out a couple of times riding a dirt bike for miles from the girls' bathroom."

"You can ride a dirt bike?" Henry's eyes bulge.

I shrug.

"Cool." He ogles.

Trigger says, "You went to the bathroom alone? After Mac specifically told you to take an escort?"

"Well…" I seal my lips and wait for the decision coin to flip in my mind. *Heads spill, tails…*

"Then a marine escorted you?"

"Not exactly."

Trigger looks at me sideways, and I fold my scuffed arms beneath the itchy blanket. Even though the coin settles on tails, instead of keeping my fat trap shut, I go against the odds and tell what happened. "I went with Chief McDunney."

"The chief? Wha…why?" Trigger shoots to his feet. "Why on earth would you ever go anywhere with him?"

My mind coin flips.

Heads. It's decided. I will test my so-called friends. I'll reveal another crumb and see how they react. "Sergeant Numereau ordered me to go," I say. My eyes bounce between Henry and Trigger.

"No way." The sky surfer's hands slice through the air like an umpire who's just called a runner out at home plate.

Defensive, I note.

"Must be some sort of mix-up," the sky surfer says. "After the way McDunney was at the hangar, Mac would never send you with him."

Maybe you don't know your brother as well as you think.

I glance at Henry, digging in his pack, showing no interest. He appears singly focused, so much so, in fact, that I suspect he hasn't heard a word said.

Tails. I decide without consulting the coin and keep what I overheard last night to myself until I can gather more information. Still, there's one thing I'm dying to know. How do we find out what the chief and his team are up to? Wishing I still had the enhanced vision that came with my Pioneer contacts, I have an idea. "Last night, when I was riding in the jeep, McDunney got a message via the security stream." I finger my bangs. "Something important, urgent enough for him to leave me alone at the girls' lav." I stand and stride the length of the cot. "If we could reply to the message or listen in like before—"

"Impossible." Trigger steps in front of me. "Like Henry said, the back-door virtual holes in Pioneer's network are plugged."

"What are we missing?" I force my tired eyes open and walk around Trigger. "I know. Let's call KC?"

"You mean Henry." The Weatherman refers to himself in the third person and clenches something tiny between his fingers. "Scientist." He points to his chest, a move borrowed from Sergeant Numereau, and then leans over and attaches something to my ear piercing. As if a light switch has been thrown, I hear voices, layered conversations, not unlike when I first got my stud. I listen closer. The exchanges are short, deep toned, and gravelly. Definitely not students. A husky voice joins, and I know who I'm listening to: the chief, Number One, and the rest of the Pioneer security crew—McDunney and his cronies via the secure stream.

"Security's stream?" I throw an arm around Henry's neck. He shrugs it away. "How? You said it was no longer possible." I fiddle with the add-on receiver, twisting and tapping, waiting for the visual to appear. "Hold on." I blink and knuckle an eyelid. "I can't see anything."

"You won't." Henry frowns. "So far, I've only been able to figure out a way to hear." He passes a second microchip to Trigger. "And if whoever's connected talks over one another, I can't separate conversation. Stupid." He punches his forehead.

"At least we have ears," I say. "It's more than we had a moment ago."

"I did manage to disable the light. This way, we can listen undetected."

"Nice." I offer a fist pound. Henry doesn't raise a hand. "Now all we need is a *viable* plan."

Trigger and Henry trade a look.

"What?" I say.

"While you were in cooling-off mode, T, Trigger and I cooked up a scheme, one that might get everyone what they want."

CHAPTER 22

What I want comes at a huge price—at least, according to Henry and Trigger—a sacrifice I'll have to make if I want justice for my dad. When they left for breakfast, I stayed behind, considering whether I'm up for the task. Not only do I need to forgive Soraya, but I also have to convince her to reinstate our BFF status—in less than twenty-four hours. I flatten myself on a cot and yank a government-issue blanket to my chin.

Impossible, I decide, well aware of my substandard acting skills. A year ago, perhaps, but since Mom left the embassy, my showmanship has become rusty and unpolished. Besides, I never want to be fake and phony again. *There must be another way.*

Feeling sick to my stomach, I crunch into a ball, rock, and bite my lower lip. *Do you want justice or not?*

A vibration buzzes from beneath the wool cover, and without thinking, I touch my ear helix. The metal is cold, and I don't hear any voices. I gather that it's not the chief's security stream. Releasing my knees, I listen for the next stretch of buzzing, and when the tone hums again, I lean over the cot's edge to see our sat phone jumping on the floor. The lit screen flashes with my friend's ID.

"Kase," I say, and after scooping the cell from below, I answer the call. "It's good to hear your voice."

"Tried to call last night, but got voice mail."

"I know. Sorry, unexpected issues came up."

"Spill," KC says. "Every juicy detail."

"Henry's OK. Dr. Harb has gone underground, and Henry and Trigger want me to buddy up with Soraya and see if she knows how to contact her dad." I blow my bangs in the air.

"Did the brain trust offer any suggestions on how to crack the queen of deception?"

"Go shopping and attend the fall dance." I share their dumb idea. "The stuff girls do when they spend time together."

"Is that what girls do?"

"Guess so."

"We never go shopping."

"No," I answer, realizing when KC and I get together it's generally to do homework. "We don't."

"We're girls."

"Yes, but we're different."

"And…"

"Kase, what are you getting at?"

"Just because you woo her with mall chitchat, get all dressed up, and attend some stupid party celebrating the harvest, the aurora, or spew your guts to the solstice—call it whatever you like—that doesn't guarantee she will lower her guard and tell you about her dad."

KC has a point. It's been over a month since Soraya and I have hung out, and the last time we were together, my hands wound up choking her neck. Despite all our girlfriend time, I can't say I know very much about the situation with her parents. "So what would it take? If you were in Soraya's shoes and I was trying to get you to open up about your relationship with your dad?"

The line goes quiet, making me think we've been disconnected. KC is still on the phone, though, because I hear her raspy breaths. "I guess I'd have to really trust you to confide something that personal."

My gut cinches, preparing for an answer I suspect I don't really want to hear. "Trust me how?"

"With the absolute confidence that you'd never betray me, no matter what."

"But I'm going to deceive her," I say. "Bringing Dr. Harb to justice is the main reason we came here."

"Then you must make her believe you wouldn't deceive, even if you intend to."

All of a sudden, I feel very small. In the far corners of my conscience, a voice utters—*liar, manipulator, deceiver, cheat…*"No!" I shout back. "I have a good reason. I'm keeping a promise I made through fiery flames on Dad's death ramp." Although this is solid thinking, I can't help but wonder if the annoying little voice speaks the truth. Am I becoming everything I've sworn to hate?

"No, you're not going to lie?" KC says. "Or no, you don't care about catching your dad's killer?" Her frank words cut, reminding me that I have a choice.

"I know what has to be done. Doesn't mean I like it."

"Then bury your feelings, and join the rest of us in the world of pretend."

Speaking of reality versus fantasy, two sets of technical boots straddle the tent entrance. "Ready to go, T?" Trigger checks his wrist. "Meeting with Mac in less than five."

With KC holding, I eye Henry's rubber boots. "I need a favor."

"Shoot," KC says.

"Any chance you could hack into Pioneer's admission files and do a little digging on a group of students who call themselves the Future of Wall Street?"

"Any chance the earth rotates around the sun?"

"Knew I could count on you, Kase. One other favor—check out Mom's friend Gunner Clark."

"Now that sounds like fun."

"By the way, I've got someone you should meet," I say and wave the phone above my head.

"Who is it?" Henry bends inside the tent. He's about to reach for the cell when KC's voice echoes, "Tana, are you there? Can you hear me?"

"It's her…" The Weatherman turns as white as a cumulonimbus cloud and sprints out of the bunk. Trigger and I trade smiles.

"I'm here," I put my lips to the speaker. "But I have to go."

"Wait, one more thing." KC sounds uneasy. "Well, um, last night my parents dragged me to another fundraiser. Third one this week. Anyway"—she sneezes—"you'll never guess who was seated next to me at our table."

Trigger is here, Brooklyn is locked down with tutors, and as far as I know, KC has no other boy crushes at school. "I give. Who?"

"Your mom and Gunner Clark."

CHAPTER 23

Mom and Gunner? There must be some mix-up. Despite all of our progress lowering the Lyre DEFCON safety level, my mother, Miss Antisocial-Bordering-on-Reclusive, voluntarily out and about in *T-town* two nights in a row? Not a chance—unless everyone at the event was hand-searched and triple background checked.

Despite KC's four-eyed intel, I'm aware of my mother's aversion to massive social events. They are open season for hundreds of guests to ask questions—probing, personal questions—curious to be in the know about why a high-profile international mediator is hiding out in Oklahoma. Besides, Mom thinks crowds are massive security risks.

Now outside our bunk, I realize I'm the last to arrive at Sergeant Numereau's keep-your-mouth-shut-or-I'll-have-to-kill-you confidential show-and-tell. Henry, Trigger, and two marine mountains lean against the Humvee with their ankles crossed and thumbs hanging from their pockets. Sergeant Numereau's weight shifts over his boots, his eyes glommed on a stopwatch.

I scan both ways down the aisle and around the corners of each tent— *Where are you?* I check again, certain after last night that McDunney must be lurking in the shadows. I grip my ear and tap three times on Henry's microscopic booster attached on my piercing.

Here, crazy whack job. Even if I can't see him, perhaps I can hear him. Great idea, but it doesn't work. I hear dead air. Not the chief or idle chitchat. Absent is the low buzz of radio static constantly crackling over the stream, almost as if security's lifeline was somehow disconnected.

"Miss Lyre."

Startled by the sharpness of Mac's voice, I spin and leap a foot in the air.

"How nice of you to join us." Sergeant Numereau claps a gum bubble, leaving tiny bits stuck to his chapped lips. "I was worried you got turned around coming back from the head."

"Not at all," I say and cup my hand around my ear to buffer background noise. Still, no sound vibrates over security's stream. "The camp is a grid." I move closer. "Each block is twelve bunks square. Once I figured out the pattern, well, then it's only basic math."

Mac's eyes slide to Trigger, sparkling with a glint of approval.

My friend shrugs. "I told you she had a natural sense of direction."

The sergeant chuckles and opens another stick of Beemans. "It was my intention to meet with Trigger this morning, alone, to show him why my marines are camped here in the desert, partnering with Pioneer. But at breakfast, when T. Flough told me he wouldn't go anywhere without his friends, I had no choice but to make an exception." Mac winces.

"Here's the deal." He wields a rigid finger. "Not one thing you see or hear over the next hour can be spoken about, written about, or shared with anyone outside this group. Understood?"

Although phrased as a question, the undercurrent is a direct order. He assumes his wide-legged stance, his steel arms crossed like a bulletproof vest. "I said, do you understand?"

"Yes, sir," Trigger belts. I bob my head in compliance. Henry tugs at his ear piercing.

Mac dons a bucket cap and strides toward the Humvee. "Load 'em up!" he hollers. Two marines signal, and we climb into the rear of the vehicle. Numereau assumes the driver's seat, buckles up, and without checking if everyone is in, starts the engine and speeds from the aisle.

We exit the airfield, jostling and rattling down the only road that leads to the Pioneer campus. The words *top secret, classified,* and *don't tell anyone* lead me to believe something stranger than usual is going on behind the Pioneer gates—something even bigger than turbofan engines buried beneath the airfield.

What could possibly be so important to need a platoon of marines to protect it?

Now idling at the security gate, I rest my chin on Trigger's shoulder and talk in his ear. "We're going on campus?"

He faces me. "Obviously."

Sergeant Numereau floors the accelerator, and our urban tank jerks forward. Trigger's mouth smacks my cheek.

Zap.

I shiver as an electric shock ignites every nerve ending in my skin. My fingertips tingle, and I turn away. I stare through the box window, hand on my cheek, tracing the track where Trigger's lips have just been. *Friends*, I remind myself. But something deep inside begs the question—if that's the case, then why does his touch affect me this way?

"Everyone out!" Mac shouts, climbing from the driver's seat. He whistles through his teeth, and the marines disembark, and when he snaps his fingers, they scramble into single file. I shake off the Trigger tingle, unlatch the door, and follow their lead. I sense my friends tailing behind me.

Ahead is the three-story science auditorium, Professor Aska Gu's former classroom—the place where we first saw the video of the weather-seeding drones, when Trigger and I pretended to be student candidates on our first visit to the Pioneer campus.

I glance over my shoulder at Henry and wonder if this building stirs any unpleasant memories. *How could it not?* I picture the clip from Trigger's stream during the candidate-mentor shadowing day, the podium, and Henry's dad saying how disappointed he was in his son.

Outwardly, Henry appears unaffected, not mousy or frightened as he was the last time we were here. Whatever happened in the past month has changed him, hardened him.

I avoid looking at Trigger on purpose in order to kill the possibility of an uncomfortable exchange. Facing forward, I focus on the auditorium's entrance doors and consider what in the world the military could be testing here.

As I am about to reach for the handle, a loud squelch buzzes over my ear receiver.

Static.

A squeal.

Chased by another high-pitched whine.

The security stream is up and running. I tap my earlobe twice, attempting to lower the volume, when a husky voice speaks, one I recognize beyond a doubt.

"Team leader to Number One"—the gravelly tone barks—"the candidates are about to enter the building."

I squat and throw out a stiff-arm to stop the door from opening. *McDunney is in there.*

Rounds of sinister laughter vibrate over the security stream.

"No." I dig my heels into the concrete. "We can't go in."

Like a row of tumbling dominos, Trigger and Henry pile against my back. Off balance, Trigger tugs on my sleeve and steadies himself, wincing. Henry's arms windmill, and his spine arches backward.

"What gives?"

I clench my ear about to mouth the chief's name, but before I get the chance, Sergeant Numereau storms through the entrance. His face flushes fireball red.

"I'm about to let you in on a secret only a handful of very senior officials know, and this is how you repay me? Horseplay?"

With the help of swimming arms, Henry manages to center over his feet. "Streeters?" He gulps. "Where? Inside?" He clings to my arm. "Is that what stopped you, T?"

"No," Trigger says to Henry, but Numereau misunderstands him.

"You mean 'No, sir,' right?" Mac says through clenched teeth.

"Of course, Mac. I mean, no, sir…no more messing around." Trigger's iced glare lasers at me. "You really are determined to screw this up."

"But—"

When I try to explain, he puts his forehead to mine. "Mac would never let anything happen to us."

I pull away, look over his shoulder, and notice Sergeant Numereau showing his teeth like an angry bear.

I'm not so sure.

"That's one." Mac holds up a warning finger. "This isn't baseball. No three strikes and you're out." A second meaty digit waves in front of our faces. "Meaning one more screw-up and the whole team is out. Permanently." His chin angles down at Trigger. "Almost family or not, I'll have no choice but to hand you over to McDunney."

The mere mention of the chief makes Henry shudder. "Not him, no, no, no." He rakes his buzzed scalp and then hides beneath his hoodie.

"No one is going anywhere with McDunney." Trigger puts a hand on Henry's shoulder. "Isn't that right, Mac?"

Sergeant Numereau churns his gum. "Play by the rules, and we'll all stay together."

"Understood," Trigger replies.

Mac's head oscillates like a spotlight, crisscrossing back and forth, pausing on each of us, likely to illuminate any cracks in our commitment.

No one flinches—not even Henry.

After a couple of eye sweeps, Mac seems satisfied. He steps aside and waves us across a narrow corridor and through a set of double doors.

The doors thud shut behind us, and with that, every shred of light leaves the theater. It's a large room, I gather, by the hollow echoes of dead bolts locking. I wave my arms every which way in the darkness, reaching for a solid surface.

"Put these on," a voice says.

A hard plastic material, rounded like a helmet, collides with my midsection.

"On your head."

I lift the bucket over my skull. I hear a soft click, and then what feels like a visor covers my eyes. In a second, I can see everything, clear and bright, as if I'm standing outside on a sunny day. Trigger, Henry, Mac, and his marines wander among rows of empty seats, places where Professor Gu's students sat for the drone lecture—the room I experienced through Trigger's view when we were still connected on Pioneer's virtual-student stream. Today, however, I'm here in person to see the reading lights coiled and the desks retracted and nested flush along the armrests.

"Sit," Mac commands.

Obedient as a pack of trained dogs, we crowd into the closest row— Henry on my left, Trigger to the right—and the sergeant and his soldiers take seats one row back.

"I don't like this," Henry whispers.

I touch my shoulder to his. "Me either."

Reaching under the brain bucket, I tug on my ear and grip the one advantage they don't know we have. I tap until Henry's security-stream listening device reaches maximum volume, just in time to hear a voice utter, "You're on."

Chief McDunney struts onto the stage; his presence casts a volcanic shadow against the blank screen behind him.

"McDunney is here?" Trigger's helmet knocks mine, causing the stream to screech like a microphone. "Why didn't you tell me you heard security chatter?"

I tried, I want to shout. But I sense Sergeant Numereau's eyes surveying my every move. Instead, I dig my fingers into Trigger's arm, my way of answering his question.

Trigger doesn't move.

What's up with him? I push harder in order to get his attention.

His arm remains steady. His helmet stays front and center, reminding me of the zombie state I found him in near the flight-team lockers back home.

Through the dark-tinted visor, I squint and look closer. *He did get a massive jolt of electricity from the cockpit panel last trip. Maybe his brain has short-circuited?*

Trigger grips my hand and peels my fingers from his forearm, turns, and butts his helmet against mine. "What's with you?" he says.

Or is it his history with Mac that's making him different?

Speaking of big brothers…

"Lights," Mac's voice booms. The IMAX screen flickers, and a fluorescent glow changes the overcast-gray backdrop to a bright, regal blue. "Camera," he says, and hundreds of tiny see-through cubes appear and float weightlessly through the air. Henry reaches to touch the 3-D images. "Action."

The virtual cubes cluster over the stage. Then, as if slurped by a powerful vacuum, each block drops inside another, doubling the size of the original. The host square grows exponentially until it equals the size and shape of the floor-to-ceiling movie screen behind it. When the final cube tumbles into the stage-length box, the side splits like a fence gate, and the hinges creak open.

From the box, images of soldiers charge forward. Dressed in full battle gear, they tote assault weapons. The man I assume to be the commander hesitates and then shakes something from his glove. Whatever it is rolls into his palm; he pinches it with gloved fingers and drops it into his mouth. He swallows hard and closes his eyes. His lids flicker, and his lips move like he's talking to himself. Less than a minute later, his eyes pop open. His chin bobs. He tightens the strap on his helmet and then signals his troops to attack.

A surge of virtual men runs through our seats. Their eyes are targeted forward, their faces stiff, showing no signs of fear, erasing any doubt that they're about to engage a dangerous enemy.

Odd. The Lyre gut-instinct alarm pings. For men who are about to risk their lives, why don't they appear more nervous?

As the last line of marines passes my field of view, I pivot in my seat, expecting to see the beginning of all-out carnage. But when my visor steadies, I see the exact opposite.

The raging soldiers slow to a crawl, divide into four groups, and surround a rickety warehouse. They hold position.

With a flick of the leader's hand, the tactical team bursts through the windows and doors.

Glass shatters, and doors crumble as the marines penetrate the building.

At once, hundreds of heads snap up. The workers scramble to their feet and pancake over their workbenches, looking to protect the reels of red and blue electrical wires scattered over each station at any cost. Hundreds of cell phones tumble to the floor. The marines shuffle forward and surround the mounds of putty-colored clay. From the perimeter, the leader moves ahead and stands next to a rack filled with black hunting vests.

"A factory," Henry stutters.

"For suicide vests." I gasp. We watch as the soldiers secure the facility without firing a single round of ammunition.

"Lights," Sergeant Numereau says in the hushed way everyone spoke at my dad's funeral.

The images on my visor vanish, and again I find myself blinded by darkness. A buzz hums, and a bright glint appears below my tinted eye cover.

"Remove the heads-up helmets." Mac's funeral tone drones. I lift the brain bucket from my skull and twist the helmet around to inspect what must be a virtual projector.

"Cool tech," I say, tracing the visor with a flick of my finger. "But this can't possibly be our government's best-kept secret."

Silent until now, McDunney speaks. "Very perceptive, Miss Lyre. Or not. Perhaps you've had an advantage. A vision." His thick unibrow wrinkles, and his eye patch lifts, giving a glimpse at his cloudy eyeball.

I squirm in my seat.

The chief says, "So you really only swallowed half of your future pill?"

I cough, reliving the sizzle of the sweet, grainy powder as it melted on my tongue. I flash to the gutted transport plane, the Russian-speaking pilots, and my reverse swan dive out the aft cargo door. *Use your filter,* I coach. *McDunney has no idea what you did or didn't see.* Shaking the memory, I meet the chief's baiting with a blank-paper stare. *What does my future have to do with Pioneer's experiment?*

"Yes, Miss Lyre," Sergeant Numereau says. His head dangles over me like a jib on a crane. "What exactly did you see in your vision?" Mac's face hovers so closely, I can taste the winter mint on his breath.

The way I see it, I have two choices—lie or lie less. However tempting the all-out I-didn't-take-the-pill fib is, I know McDunney's men recovered the remnants of my half-swallowed capsule. And if I've learned anything about this messed-up school, it's that they have unlimited access to cutting-edge tech, and they are very thorough. So it's not a stretch to assume that they've tested the saliva-covered leftovers and matched it to my DNA from Dr. Lindy's new candidate physical. By process of elimination, I'm left with option number two. I lie *less.* "My pill didn't work for the past, the present, or the future. I didn't see a thing."

The chief's unibrow rises. "The past?"

Mac's face bunches. Veins bulge from his neck.

"I…I…"

Numereau says, "Miss Lyre?"

"What I meant to say is, I didn't see much of anything. I only swallowed an itsy bit of the pill." My cheeks burn. I look at Trigger for backup.

The sky surfer stares ahead, eyes vacant once again. "Trigger." I nudge his elbow from the armrest. His body collapses like a rag doll. Startled, he snaps upright, and his pupils widen as if he just now noticed the lights were on.

I turn to Henry to ask what is wrong with our friend when Trigger leans in and says, "Who cares? You didn't see anything." His tone is indifferent and detached.

"Was that supposed to make me feel better?" *Because now I feel worse.*

"Makes sense," Mac says, strides to the stage, and stands next to McDunney. "Without the entire contents of the pill in your system, it's unlikely you'd see your destiny." The chief's lips split like he's looking to ask a follow-up question, but before he has a chance, Mac clasps his thick shoulder. "The student's pill was designed to be ingested whole. Isn't that right, Chief?"

McDunney nods, but his sole eye narrows.

"I don't get it," Henry says. "There's nothing classified about heads-up technology. It's old news, invented before I was born."

"Ever the astute scientist, Mr. Aska Gu." Although phrased like a compliment, the heavy dose of sarcasm in Mac's tone tells me that he means the opposite.

"The devil is always in the details." McDunney grabs his glowing red receiver and points to Henry's unlit chunk of dull-earth magnet. "Isn't that right, Shoe Gu?"

"Details you had to steal in order to crack the code," the Weatherman says.

The chief's olive skin reddens to the color of the scalding desert sun. Blame it on the virtual effects, but I'd swear smoke streamed from his ears.

"Enough," Mac belts. "Clock's ticking, Chief."

"Ticktock, tick—" Henry mocks.

Numereau snaps his fingers.

"How did the marines find the warehouse?" Trigger's question hushes the room. "Suicide sweatshops are impossible to find; their locations are said to be known by only one man."

For the first time, I see Sergeant Numereau grin—a puffed-up, vigorous smile, one a proud father might bestow on a son. "Go on."

"And if—we're talking a monumental if," Trigger says. "Since as far as I know, no military unit has ever been able to locate a bomb-vest factory. Another thing"—he squints an eye the way he does when shifting perspectives—"where were all the guards protecting their highest-value target?"

"What did I tell you?" Mac speaks to McDunney but loud enough so we all can hear. "Right on, brother. Any terrorist would be willing to die or take his own life before betraying the cause. Especially a bomb maker."

"Then how did you—" Trigger says.

"Get the intel?" Mac interrupts.

"Torture a prisoner?"

"Oh, no, little bro," Numereau says. "This is a new world, new game, new rules. No need for archaic scare tactics anymore."

"I don't understand."

"We have something far superior, 100 percent accurate."

"Amped-up drone surveillance?" Trigger guesses.

"True," Mac says. "The drones have a role, but they're not the main event."

"Then you have a spy?"

"More like a wildcard." Mac's eyes move to McDunney, nodding as if to give him the go-ahead to speak. The chief looks like he's about to break from his skin.

"We have a new pill." McDunney beams. "One that shows the present."

My hand flies to my mouth so no sounds can escape. Trigger's pill showed the past. Mine glimpsed the future, and now the chief and Sergeant Numereau claim to have a window to the present? I gulp.

Trigger doesn't blink. He sits stiffly at attention. "The present?"

"What our enemies are planning at this very moment," Mac boasts. "With around-the-clock research, we've been able to stretch the pill's vision. Now we can see three hours before a terror attack will occur."

McDunney rolls his slimy lips together as if protecting a secret. He smirks, and his tattered eye patch lifts. "Pop a capsule, and after a few seconds, a vision appears identifying any threats to our nation."

"We see every move," Mac says. "Know their plans, almost as if we're implanted in their thoughts."

"An American leprechaun on their shoulder," the chief jokes.

Mac rocks back and forth on his heels—as giddy, I'd guess, as a 250-pound man gets. McDunney offers Mac a fist bump. The sergeant ignores the gesture.

"What if they change their minds?" Like a bunker buster, Trigger blasts a gigantic hole in their perfect plan. "A lot of things can happen in three hours."

I flash to the brain-bucket vision. The team leader's hesitation, the shake of his glove, and the tiny spec pinched onto his tongue. That was the last-minute check. He swallowed a pill to make sure the plan remained the same.

"What's the catch?" Henry says.

McDunney and the sergeant exchange an unsteady look. "Catch?"

"The recip, the trade-off, the rub. What do you have to sacrifice for the advancement of the greater good?"

McDunney opens his mouth, and Mac puts up a palm.

"Maybe like the future pill," Henry says. "You know, the one taken by every one of Pioneer's"—he air quotes with bony fingers—"*candidates.*"

Mac's jaw grinds.

"Not quite perfected, is it? Let me see"—the Weatherman rubs his hairless chin—"How many marines are on medical leave for so-called attention problems?"

Trigger and I whirl around to face our friend, our mouths dangling open. "Reactions?" I say, since less than a month ago, Henry told us there hadn't been a single side effect.

"Ten, twenty—"

"That's enough, Mr. Aska Gu." Mac cracks his gum.

McDunney says, "I'm not sure where you're getting your information. Any adverse effects are—"

Numereau interrupts. "Are post-traumatic fallout from our tour in the Middle East."

"Not one shred of evidence points to a flaw in the pill." McDunney's gaze slides over to Sergeant Numereau.

"So that's the official story?" Henry says with a double dose of sarcasm.

"You would know." McDunney's and Henry's glares clash like a pair of dueling knights.

Although tempted to gang up on the chief, I can't help but glare at Henry. *What do you know that you aren't sharing?*

"Imagine the tactical advantage. Knowing the enemy's plan before they execute it." Mac moves behind the lectern, next to the US flag. He straightens his pressed fatigues and stands tall—a poster of patriotism. "Soldiers' lives will be spared, civilian casualties nonexistent."

"Right." I elbow Trigger. "Let me guess; next he'll claim the pill is the ticket to world peace."

Trigger doesn't reply. His gaze is locked on the skilled orator.

"The mission of our military will shift into a role of global peacekeeper. A dream the founding fathers had when they created this great nation." Mac touches a chunky dive watch that's hashed like the cardinal headings on a compass.

I lean against the seat back and then twist to whisper in Trigger's ear. "Somehow I don't think a pill is what they had—"

"Shhh," Trigger says. "I'm trying to listen."

"So now you know." Sergeant Numereau pinches a piece of fresh gum from his breast pocket and slips it into his mouth. "If all goes as planned, in the next thirty days, every unit commander will be locked and loaded with an endless supply of present pills. Project Déjà Vu will be fully operational."

I wait and hold my tongue, certain that at any second, Trigger will stand and object. But when my friend, the self-proclaimed follower of the highest honor code, makes it to his feet, he does something unexpected.

Swift as a wind gust, he crosses the floor and climbs three steps. *Go, Trigger!* My heart flutters. I scoot to the edge of my chair.

Once onstage, the sky surfer marches straight at Sergeant Numereau and just when I think he's going to unleash the wrath of Flough, he stiffens and offers Mac a gracious hand.

"War will finally be obsolete." Trigger's face glows like the sun. *Trigger! Don't!*

He says, "Wait until I tell my dad."

McDunney's forehead furrows.

"Hold up, my friend." Mac breaks their grip. "Remember, no one outside of this room can know about this?"

"Of course, sure, I get it. Don't tell civilians. But my father? He has the highest level of security clearance."

"No one."

"Don't you trust him?"

"With my life."

"Then?" Trigger's mouth twists.

"The old man will be told when the time is right. You know he's the closest thing I had to a father. But this project is radical, different, and Lamar Flough is not a fan of change."

On this point, I have to agree with Mac. When National's administration suggested changing from flight suits to khakis and collared shirts to accommodate Oklahoma's sweatbox summers, Professor Flough about blew his flattop. "Serious aviators wear flight suits," he had insisted. "That's the way it's always been, and as long as I'm around, the way it will always be."

In one simple statement, Mac summarized every disagreement Trigger had had with his dad.

"I don't need to remind you that you gave your word," Mac says.

"I did, and you have my 100 percent commitment."

What? I glare at Trigger.

"Glad to hear it." Mac Numereau unfolds his arms. "Because there's something else I need you to do."

CHAPTER 24

"Incoming." Henry curls in his seat, hands covering his head.

My stomach tightens in anticipation of information I'm sure I don't want to hear. Sergeant Numereau hangs an arm over Trigger's shoulder. "How would you like to join my team?" he says and pulls my friend close to his chest. "Enroll in Pioneer's exchange program and finish high school on the road. Like the old days, you and me ranging, base to base, traveling all over the globe?"

Trigger's surfer smile stretches as wide as the horizon.

I hug my knees. *This can't be happening.*

"What do you think?" Mac rocks on his heels. "Tell you what, if you come"—he rolls flat-footed—"I'm sure I can find a way to fast-track your backside into a fighter jet."

"Seriously?" Trigger's hand touches his heart. "Fighters take years. How can you make a promise like that?"

"Leave it to me. Our recent success here in the desert has opened many doors."

"Yes…" Trigger's eyes inch toward Henry and me. "I…I mean, I'll think about it, Mac."

"Fair enough. You have until the end of the day."

Trigger nods. I picture the flamed funnels of jet afterburners shooting from his eyes.

I feel as if my insides have shattered.

Having heard enough, I stand, push past Henry, and hightail it for the exit.

"Fall out," Mac commands, even though my hurried strides have put me less than an arm's length from the door. *I don't take orders from you,* I say with a glare. I fling the metal doors open as if they were made of paper, and without looking back, I cross the tiled corridor.

"Tana!" Trigger yells from behind me. I hear at least two pairs of boots pang against the floor. I don't answer and plow ahead, having exceeded my daily quota of friends who say one thing and then do another.

"Wait up," my so-called friend shouts louder. He's getting closer. I hear the intervals of rubber squealing against the tile shorten. I keep pace, barge through the exterior door, and break into a jog. I feel the patter of controlled breaths beat against my neck. *He's closing in.*

"What?" I whirl around.

Full stride, Trigger and Henry shoot past. They skid and trot back to where I stand.

"Something wrong with your hearing?" Trigger snaps.

"Seriously?" My tongue lashes like a whip. "Are you really that clueless?" I notice Henry shaking his head.

"I don't get why you're so upset?" Trigger kicks a sandstone.

Henry slips on his wiper goggles and disappears beneath the hood of his oversized sweat shirt.

"Yes, sir, Mac." I salute, mimicking Trigger's voice. "I'll *definitely* consider quitting National, abandoning my family, and ditching my friends. For what? So you can go off and play with the big boys in the sky sandbox?"

"That's not what I meant."

"It's what you said."

"It's just"—Trigger lofts another pebble—"a chance to be part of something epic, rid the world of wars, centuries of fighting, senseless loss of life."

"And fly fighters?" I say.

"There's that," he says. "Which, by the way, is an opportunity of a lifetime. Everything I've ever dreamed of, a chance to show…" His biting words trail off.

"Show who?"

Trigger's face reddens. He stares at the ground and buries his clenched fists deep in his pockets. "Tana, how can you expect me to say no without even considering the offer?"

"You hate Pioneer, remember. The desert, McDunney—the fury I see in your eyes whenever I mention the chief—how wrong it is that an entitled hypercompetitive nerd herd gets ahead by cheating."

Trigger steps back.

"Your words." I get up in his face. "Taking a pill to get ahead is one thing, but dosing soldiers with experimental drugs is just wrong. Plain and simple. The Trigger Flough I know would never buy off on that drummed-up malarkey."

"Even if it means an end to terrorism? Safety and peace for every human being on the planet?"

"Whose version of peace?" I counter. "Our government's? Our values? Our military's rules? After all, if we are the only ones who have the pill, doesn't that put us in charge?"

"Yes, I guess, but, no…we'll be the peacekeepers, strictly in the spirit of fairness and justice." He stammers, quoting what sounds like the thought bubble from a superhero comic. Any second now, I expect his fist to thrust triumphantly over his head.

"That's Mac's brainwashing talking."

"This is different, Tana. A way to force the most destructive nations to the table to negotiate their differences, peacefully. Can you imagine? I don't understand why you're not more open to this breakthrough. It's similar to the work your parents did for the UN."

Heat surges through my veins. I sense that if I open my mouth, I might breathe fire. For someone who wants to end all conflicts, Trigger is dangerously close to provoking a nuclear event.

I grind my molars. "Don't pretend to know anything about my parents."

Trigger's shoulders sag, and his voice softens. "Even if I were to stay, join Mac, do you really think it would end our friendship?"

"After what I just heard, yes."

"It's not like you to be so dramatic, T."

"It's unlike you to let your self-serving goals cloud your judgment." If the pained expression on his face is any indication, that one stung. I, on the other hand, feel numb. *Has he forgotten about when the situation was reversed?* "So double or nothing has been traded in for a single-seat fighter jet?"

Trigger answers with a blank expression.

Although undeserved, I glare at Henry, too. Guilt by association. Why not? He belongs to the same gender pool. *Like Gran says, if it has tires or testicles, it's bound to be trouble.* I turn on my heel, ready to storm, well, anywhere, when over my shoulder a steady voice speaks, calm and indifferent—the way I wish mine had been.

"This discussion, while insightful, is not getting us any closer to our goal." Henry's logic freezes me in my tracks. "You know, the big picture? Making nice with Soraya so we can catch your dad's killer."

I hold still and think about why I came back to Pioneer. I close my eyes and blow out, allowing my hot temper to simmer. I came here for two reasons: to help Henry and avenge my father—not to save the world or stop Trigger from making the biggest mistake of his life. All the chances we took, risking Professor McVie's job, navigating a storm, landing without an engine, and standing up to McDunney will be wasted if I don't find Dr. Harb.

Neither forgiving nor forgetting, I retrace my steps and rejoin my soon-to-be ex-friends. I unclench my jaw and avert my eyes to Henry. "How can I get Soraya to trust me again?"

"Give her this." He hands me a microscopic disk, identical to the one clipped on my ear piercing—the upgrade that allows access to the security stream and disables the telltale light glow. "As a show of good faith."

You have got to be kidding me.

"Don't worry, T; you'll know when the time is right," Henry says.

I thumb the unassuming spec in my palm. *Will this be enough to convince Soraya, the queen of manipulation?* I curl my fingers into a fist. "All right." I groan. "Where do I find her?"

"Word around campus is that she's committee chair for the Aurora Celebration." Henry points toward the closest of two rocky mesas. "Odds are she's at the outdoor band shell setting up for the kick-off concert."

"A stage?" I search the towering peaks and the razor-sharp edges. "I don't see anything resembling an amphitheater?"

"Pretty rad, actually. You didn't see it last time you were here?" Henry snaps his fingers. "Oh, that's right—you guys blew out before the Spirit Dance and left me to fend for myself."

I swallow.

Trigger gulps.

"Anyway…" The Weatherman cycles his goggle wipers. "The venue looks like a piece of sweet potato pie cut from a layered-rock dish." He licks his lips. "Head straight for the nearest mesa wall, and when you get close, you'll be able to see the stairs."

"Do whatever it takes to connect with her and then get security to bring you back to the bunk," Trigger says. I ignore him. "We'll head to camp and figure out a surveillance plan."

"Here." Henry hands me a sat phone from his pack. "Use KC's piggyback, and call if you need reinforcements. You can count on us. You have our words."

Double or nothing rings through my ears. I raise my eyes to meet Trigger's. "Pass." I stare hard. "Words don't mean anything." Marching away, I glance at the chunky phone clenched in my hand, see the missed calls, and realize there's only one person I can count on. She'll be the one I'll call if I need backup.

CHAPTER 25

Winded, I hike the last switchback of a mile-long zigzagging stretch of stairs cut into the side of the pointed red rocks. I linger at the top and lean over the metal rail to take in the majestic view.

Don't look down, I remind myself.

Too late.

My vision blurs. I white-knuckle the safety rail, sensing that at any moment, I could tumble to an untimely death. "Crap," I mutter, my head spinning. No matter how much I try, I can't get past my fear of heights.

Find a spot and focus—a coping mechanism I learned on a "Face Your Fears" webinar. I raise my line of sight from the rock coffin below and lock onto the horizon.

Clouds wisp across the blurry blue boundary, and as my dizziness settles, a straight line appears where ground meets earth.

"Sure is some kind of view," a deep, soothing voice interrupts my concentration.

Startled, I twist and check my six o'clock, well aware of what happens if I look away from my anchor. *Not good, Lyre.* My vision blurs. Dizzy, I timber to the ground.

With the gap between my face and the red-rock footing narrowing, I will my hands up to break the fall. No luck. They dangle by my thighs like a pair of wet noodles. I squeeze my eyes shut and clench my teeth, readying for ground impact when two thick arms scoop my torso. My cheek brushes warm skin, and my eyes pop open. I look up to see a wide brim, shading soft, steel-gray eyes. Balled biceps flex against my back and roll me closer. *Am I dead?* I steal Trigger's line.

"Whoa-ah," the Good Samaritan's words drag long and slow. My gaze traces past full lips, up a whiskered jaw, to a weathered Stetson hat. I smell cinnamon.

Lordy.

"Easy." The cowboy tilts me upright but doesn't let go. His pressed checked shirt sleeve drags across my neck, and I'd guess, if I look down, he'll be wearing boots.

Nice catch. My mind swims, struggling to tear my gaze from his mouth. I breathe and take in a whiff of cedar and freshly cut grass.

The cowboy grins. "You're not from around here, are you?"

"No…I mean, yes…" I shake off the brain fog. "Sorry, what did you say?" Tongue-tied, I push free of his grip. My eyes dart back to the steadfast horizon.

"What do you reckon is your favorite part?" he says.

"Part?"

"Of the view."

For a half second, I allow an eyeball to edge away from my anchor, and I call out the first landmark I see. "Airport."

"All righty then." His vocal cords strum like a tall string bass. What sounds like boots knock against concrete.

"Truth is…" I say, feeling compelled to explain, "I'm kind of getting my bearings."

A snare drum rumbles, a guitar twangs, and the digitized sounds of an electronic keyboard hum. The cowboy's boots tap faster, matching the thump of the strapping beat. "Have you had a look at the stage?"

"No," I say, and the cowboy dressed in Wranglers and a worn hat lassos my arm. He leads me from the rail, closer to the open-air pavilion. As we approach, the music echoes louder.

Fiddles are picked, banjos are strummed, and what sounds like a four-string bass provides a bottom for the trebly melody.

As we round the red-rock corner, my inner ear steadies, and I get my first clear look at the venue. *A sweet potato slice cut from a sandstone pie baked in heaven.* Exactly like Henry said.

With one piece of the rock pie removed, the triangle-shaped void is filled by rows of tiered pavilion seats bordered by steep stairs on both sides, which descend down to ground level and lead to center stage. The area for the performers is surrounded by two arrowhead slabs of pumpkin-colored stone and open to the vast desert sky.

I exhale, and the light-headedness settles. "I've changed my mind."

"About?" the cowboy says.

"This is my new favorite part."

"So long to the airport." He tips his hat, and when he lifts the rim, I get a glimpse at his face. "Tuck Hunter." He extends a hand. My fingers slide into his firm grip.

"Tana," I say, lost in the steadiness of his eyes. Heat from his calloused palm warms my fingers.

"You like the music?" His words glide like a bow over a fiddle.

There's music playing? Focusing, I become reacquainted with the rocking country tune playing in the background. "It's fine," I answer and brush my bangs from my eyes.

"Fine?" Tuck winces.

"Not bad," I backpedal, noticing his twisted expression, guessing I've said something to offend him. *Use your filter.*

"Pleasant," I mean. "If you're into the honky-tonk thing." *There you go, Lyre. Much more politically correct.* "Personally, I prefer heavy metal."

"Test, test." The drummer on stage blows into a microphone. His leg twitches, and the bass drum booms. "Paging Tuck, anyone seen our lead singer, Tuck Hunter?" A single triangle chimes.

Ding-dong. Hello. I deliver a monster mental head slap.

The percussion triangle chimes a second time.

I gulp. *So the cowboy standing next to me is the lead singer of the band featured at tonight's dance? Terrific.* Someone, anyone, please knock me over the edge. I suck in a long breath and dare to face the country music.

I turn to him. "A singer?"

"Yep."

"And this is your band?"

"My redneck, honky-tonk band." His words snap like a rubber band.

"About that." I roll my lips together, stalling to come up with a clever explanation for my latest social misstep. "I'm sure if I listened a little more, it might grow on me?" I raise my eyebrows.

"Heavy metal, huh?" He groans. "Volbeat?"

"AC/DC."

"Ah, vintage." Tuck's shoulders roll back. A crooked smile creeps across his perfect lips. "You know, we have a lot in common."

"Huh?" *Is his hat on too tight?* I mentally twang the brim. "Metal and country? Polar opposites."

"On the surface, I reckon." He lifts his brim. "Did you happen to see the lumberjack-looking guy sitting behind the drum set?"

"Mr. Microphone?"

"Right on. He's in charge of keeping the band on track." Tuck whistles through his teeth, and the drummer raises a stick in the air. But it isn't really a stick, at least not entirely. A plume of wiry fringe flops from the tip.

"What is—" I say.

The corners of Tuck's mouth lift. "Close your eyes."

I shudder.

"Go on." He cups my elbow. "You can trust me."

Again with the trust. Clock's ticking. I wonder how long this one will last. I shake my bangs in front of my eyes.

Tuck drags a finger over my forehead, brushing the fringe to the side.

I blink away. *Pretty sure you just jinxed yourself, stud.*

"Go on." Tuck presses lightly on my bent arm, and he hums. "Listen."

My lids drift shut. I hear a whistle, and after three clicks of what sounds like clopping blocks, the music resumes.

With closed eyes, every note is heightened. An electric acoustic guitar. Synthesized hammer on piano. The tapping of drums.

"Closer." Tuck's breath blows over my face, as gentle and pleasant as an autumn breeze.

I indulge him. I tune out the main beat and concentrate on the nasally undercurrent. *Killer.*

"Can you hear it?" His voice fades into the music.

"Yes." My eyes flutter open, understanding what the bristled-tip stick is for. "It's a brush." I drink in the distinctive sound the drums make with the strike of a textured tip.

"Yes." Tuck's heels click. "Old-school country. Some might even say vintage."

I feel my smile stretch. "Vintage, with a twist."

"Like I said, we have a lot in common."

"Affection for old and new."

"That"—he laughs—"and the fact we're both students at Pioneer."

CHAPTER 26

"Tana's visiting." Seemingly out of thin air, a voice coos. It's so distinct that even though I haven't heard it for a while, I recognize the tone.

Tuck's neck angles over his shoulder and tracks Soraya as she walks between us. With his head cocked, I notice short blond stubble poking from beneath his hat.

Not a single thing redneck about it.

A standard-issue chunk of faceted earth magnet is pierced through the helix of his left ear.

He's a student. An upperclassman, if I had to guess. To say I'm surprised is an understatement. Tuck is unlike anyone else I've met at Pioneer.

"Mornin', Soraya." Tuck Hunter bows his head. Quicker than a breeze shifts, his attention returns to me. "Visiting for how long?"

"A few days," I say, suddenly burdened by the thought of leaving tomorrow.

Ever the actress, Soraya thinks on her feet. "Tana is here doing research for her thesis, narrowing down possible topics." She flashes me a weighted glare.

Ignoring Soraya, I divert the conversation back to Tuck. "You're enrolled? Here?"

"Officially, yes." He tugs his ear receiver. "The band and I are on tour, though. We took a break from the schedule to come back to play at our last Aurora Celebration before graduation."

Last? I considered asking. But after the country music slur and wanting to avoid another blunder, I opt to use my filter. "Funkhouser and McDunney let you leave campus?"

"A conditional hall pass of sorts." The edge of his mouth dips. "Being that I woke up one mornin' knowing I was destined to be a western singer, how could they refuse?"

"A lot of that going on around here." I glance at Soraya.

"Isn't that the point?" Tuck shrugs.

"Speaking of ideology," Soraya says. "Isn't the point of a rehearsal to practice?" From anyone else, the comment might sound snippy. But the sweet nature of Soraya's songbird tone makes even the most sarcastic words seem nothing more than a mere suggestion.

"I do believe it is." Tuck chuckles and hooks a thumb on his pants pocket. "I'll see you at the concert tonight?" His dancing gaze shyly boot scoots over to me and lingers for a verbal RSVP.

Without as much as a swivel step, I answer with an enthusiastic, "Yes."

"It's a date then." He clicks a heel. "Come early if you can, and I'll show you around backstage."

Although completely out of the question, I nod in the affirmative.

The cowboy lowers his chin and tips his hat. "So long, ladies."

Soraya says, "Lemon-lime soda sipped through Red Vine licorice."

"More like smoke over water." I dab the edges of my mouth and watch as Tuck Hunter walks off into the rock-ridden sunset.

"Future Mr. Lyre?" Soraya rests her chin on my shoulder. When I spin to look at her, I can't help but feel Pioneer's ear piercing may double as a memory wipe. *So we're back to best friends forever? As if nothing happened. Before I knew your father was a cold-blooded killer and I tried to choke you with my bare hands?* Soraya's expression is blank. *Doesn't she remember?* The hairs on my arms prickle. A tingle rushes up my spine.

Liar, manipulator…I shake her from my shoulder, pretending to have an itch. "Tuck, no he's…"

"Another brother?" Her brows lift.

I stiffen. *Is a truth told on top of a lie real or false?* If I choose to be honest about Tuck, does that cancel out the fact that I lied to Soraya about Trigger being my brother? We had no choice. We fibbed for a good reason. Lie or Chief McDunney would have whisked me off to who knows where. *Deceiver, cheat*…Judgment plays in my head. I swallow hard.

Soraya's eyes narrow. "A friend then?"

Either way I answer is bound to be a lie. Yes, Tuck's a friend is ridiculous because we've only just met. No, doesn't quite fit either, since the truth is I'd like nothing more than to get to know him better. Way overcommitted in the half-truth department, I go with an answer that could be true. "Odds are Tuck Hunter has plenty of friends."

"He does." Soraya's head tilts side to side. "But a girlfriend?" Her emerald eyes glimmer. "About that, I'm not so sure."

This is so messed up. I'm standing opposite the daughter of my dad's killer like nothing has happened, dishing about boys. *Deceiver, liar, manipulator, accomplice, cheat, con artist, fraud.* I clench my fists, reminding myself of the words that describe Soraya's true nature. *She lied.* I muster up the memory of seeing Gran's cross earrings on Soraya's bedroom floor. I relive the shock and pain of being played a major fool. As the anger builds, something else bubbles up—a reminder of the debt owed to Henry for helping us escape Pioneer, which is the second, but very important part of why we came back. *Get Soraya to believe you want to be friends again, Lyre. You gave your word.*

Images of Henry's shaved head, bloodied lip, and bruised face pulse in front of my eyes. The task I considered unthinkable becomes far less daunting. *Earn her trust. For Henry's sake.* KC's advice recycles. If you want justice, do whatever it takes. I reach for Henry's tiny, rigid peace offering in my pocket, and for extra encouragement, I envision Dr. Harb's wretched mug behind iron bars. I inhale and shift into character. *Lights, camera…*

"Soraya." I stare straight into her faceted pupils, resist the urge to blink, and prepare to say whatever it takes.

I picture my dad, and my eyes gloss with tears. I suck in, bite the inside of my cheek, and do what has to be done. "I'm really sorry I tried to choke you…"

Dr. Harb will rot in prison forever.

"Without giving you a chance to tell your side of the story."

He'll never have an opportunity to build another death bomb.

"Pish," she says. Her hands flutter, appearing to clear some imaginary dust in the air. "I'm the one who needs to apologize," she says, sounding particularly sincere. "What my dad did to your family…" Her fingers flit like butterflies. Tiny lines wrinkle across her otherwise perfect forehead.

Soraya stands still, arms uncrossed, without making any nervous gestures, every bit of her body language confirming her words. Her chin falls to her chest; curly hair cascades forward and covers her face. She squeaks. "I can't imagine what I would have done in your shoes."

I glance down at my hiking boots caked in red clay and then check out Soraya's designer patent flats. "You wouldn't be caught dead in my shoes."

She grabs her stomach, snorts, throws her head back, and laughs.

"You're right," she says between gut thrusts. For some reason, I crack up too, perhaps at the absurdity of lying while telling an absolute truth.

Here's my chance. I scoop the receiver booster from my pocket. "A peace offering," I explain and drop the microscopic chip into her hand. She pushes the magnet around in her palm and wrinkles her nose. But the three-hundred-million-dollar question is, after all that's happened, will she buy into the fact that I'm sharing it with her?

"Henry found another way to hack the net, didn't he?" Her pupils widen.

"Not exactly," I pinch the chip and attach it to her existing receiver. "No eyes, only ears."

Soraya wiggles her lobe as if clearing water after swimming.

"It links to the security stream," I say. "This way, we can track Chief McDunney and his cronies."

She caresses the add-on. The tip of her nose twitches. "Only the chief?"

"So far, security chatter is all I've heard."

"How…"—she gnaws her lip—"how is Henry?" Sorrow dampens her light songbird tone.

A flame of pain ignites in my gut. *As if you're not aware. All you have to do is look at him…*I breathe, picture the steady horizon line, and snuff out the kindling before it burns out of hand.

We need her help, I remind myself and suck in a second breath. "He's having a *real* bad time. The Streeters have painted a bull's-eye on his back. You only have to see his face to recognize the extent of their contempt."

"Is that why you're here?" She looks away, fidgets, and her confident stage presence wanes.

"Definitely. Henry was there for us, so we came back to help him."

"We?" What looks like hope shines in her eyes. "Trigger's with you?"

"Double or nothing," I repeat our mantra, even though in the last twenty-four hours, it feels more like every man for himself.

Soraya looks away. "Henry isn't the only one you left behind."

Are you kidding me? Her comment knocks me off balance.

"Can't say I've seen Henry around much since…" she trails off. Her eyes mist. "With both our dads gone…"

"Gone?"

"Missing. Left. I don't know." Her hands flit like butterflies again. "No one will tell us anything."

"Us?" I say.

"Henry and me."

Wait. Dr. Harb and Henry's dad aren't here? My thoughts whirl, wondering if there's any chance I might be wrong about Soraya.

"Headmaster Funkhouser has requested we spend minimal time on campus." She clears her throat. "After Pioneer shut down the student stream and beefed up security, Henry disappeared for a while." Her gaze falls to the ground, and she shuffles her pointy flats. "Listen, Tana, if anyone can relate to Henry, I can. My dad abandoned me, too."

As did mine. But he didn't run off, did he? He was taken. Murdered. In order to get you fast-tracked to Pioneer. Electricity surges through my limbs, stoking my smoldering gut fire. Fury rages. A nuclear reaction spools. *No.* I whisk away the doubt. I know who she is.

Steady, Tana. Stick to the mission. Make her believe you are friends.

After snuffing the internal reactor, I squeeze my core and ask, "Where did he go?"

"I have no idea." Tears spill from her lower lids.

"Have you spoken to him?"

Soraya sniffles. "Not since the night…that nightmare of an evening when you and Trigger left." She drags her pressed white sleeve across her nose and cheeks. "No note, no phone number, no e-mail—he just vanished."

As much as I hate to admit it, I feel connected to Soraya. I'm a regular on the wave she's riding. One minute you're going along—school, sports, friends, and family—and then all of a sudden, *bam*, everything familiar is swept away. From that moment on, you're never the same. Broken. The rage churning inside simmers as I admit, in this tiny way, that Soraya and I aren't all that different.

Hold on a second, an internal voice argues. It's not the same—not even close. Your dad was murdered, and hers, well, her father's disappearance is his own doing—running away like a gutless coward. I listen to the rationale, the black-and-white reasoning of my subconscious, and though every word rings true, I can't help but wonder if it's fair to hold a daughter accountable for the sins of her father.

Soraya's tears puddle; her face is red and blotchy. She touches her ear. A smile parts her lips. "Is there anything I can do to help?"

I swallow, understanding I'm about to become the liar, deceiver, manipulator, cheat. Through clenched teeth, I say, "Meet us at the dance." Who knew that false words could come out as easily as true? "Tonight, we'll make sure the Streeters pay for what they've done to Henry."

CHAPTER 27

If you don't pay, you can't complain, I think, jostling in the passenger seat of Pioneer's free airport shuttle, which is an open-air jeep run by McDunney's security team. Time being of the essence, I needed to get back to our bunk and report having accomplished my mission. The trap for Soraya had been set. I'd held up my end of the plan.

McDunney's crony, the hulky Number One, is driving, which in my mind is more than a good reason to feel a little anxious. I ignore his disapproving glances and think of Tuck Hunter. *Cool water on a hot summer day.* I grab the roll bar and lean outside the jeep's open frame. *Could he be a chance for a clean slate?* The afternoon sun bakes my skin. *With no you-tried-to-kill-me-in-an-airplane baggage?* I stretch as far as the seat belt will allow and extend an arm into the stiff airflow. *Is this my opportunity to get off the Trigger Flough emotional roller coaster?* The warm breeze flushes over my skin, raising every hair on my arm. *Why not? We found a way to make storms and listening boosters and convinced a master manipulator that we can be friends again. If I've learned one thing during my time at Pioneer, it's that anything's possible.*

Nominated for best actress in the pretending to be a friend category… I arch my back and plunge into the wind. I close my eyes and silently celebrate my ability to stay calm without the slightest inclination to wring Soraya's long, skinny neck. As the forceful airstream beats against my chest, grains of sandy grit prick my face. My cheeks burn.

I picture Tuck wearing his wide-brimmed Stetson and remember his neck stubble and the thick baritone cords pulsing from his muscular neck. *Why not a chance meeting with a mysterious country singer who seems to know what he wants. Me.*

Number One slams the brakes. I jerk back into the seat, and my eyes open. I grip the padded bar with both hands and swing to the ground. My feet have barely hit dirt when Number One spins both rear tires.

"Idiot," I say. The easiness I feel lingers.

As I approach the boys' tent, I notice a buzz about camp. It's different from this morning since every aisle is blurred with matching tan-and-brown uniforms. Marines are jogging—no, sprinting—with overstuffed duffel bags draped over their shoulders. The Humvees are packed with helmets and body armor. And if the unusually long line of soldiers outside Sergeant Numereau's tent is any indication, I believe something big is about to happen—something likely instigated by a tiny powder-filled capsule.

I split the Velcro and unzip the flap of our bunk, but before I have a chance to step in, I hear my name. "Welcome back, T." The voice is undoubtedly Trigger's. Keystroke sounds click.

"How did you know it was me?" I cross the makeshift threshold.

Faster than gunslinger McVie, both my partners hide hands behind their backs. Trigger beams, and Henry's cheeks puff like a scared blowfish. I tap my foot and wait until the Weatherman's skin turns bright pink. Once his flushed cheeks turn as red as a beet, he blows. Trigger's hand flies to his mouth, only allowing the slightest whimper. Henry breaks wind, and they both burst out laughing.

"Great." I plug my nose and hold the tent flap open to air out the putrid stench.

"Whoops. Piff." Henry fans his face. "Accident."

Trigger rolls on his back.

"Nice distraction," I say, nostrils pinched. "But you haven't answered my question."

Trigger rocks upright with a sat phone in hand and trades a grin with his coconspirator. "Guess we should tell her."

Henry reaches behind his back and passes over KC's cell booster.

"So?" I shrug. "Old news."

After attaching the slim magnetic booster to his phone, Trigger holds the LED screen high enough for me to see. Two digital lights pulse in the middle of three bull's-eye rings, pinging like targets on submarine sonar. One is dead center and the second on the edge of the outer ring.

I swipe the phone, angle for the door, step outside, scan the glowing screen, do an about-face, and reenter. The flashing blip in the middle matches my round robin course. "You're tracking me?" I shout.

Henry and Trigger hoot like a couple of grade school pranksters.

My internal thermostat rises to hot and irritated.

"Come on, T; don't get worked up." Henry rests a hand on my shoulder. "We're not just tracking you, but…"—he points to the second dot on the screen—"thanks to your incredible sense of self-control, we have eyes on Soraya."

"Without the intranet? How? A supersurveillance spy cloud?" I stride to the zip-out window, press my face against the bug screen, and check the weather. *Mouthwash blue from here to the moon. Great.* Now I'm being spied on too. "Are you keeping secrets from me?" Still ignoring Trigger, I stare at our in-house techie.

"No, of course not." Saliva bubbles on Henry's lower lip. "No secrets here. We only just figured out how to piggyback GPS on security's modulating signal."

"We?" I say. Although Trigger is above average at anything he tries, firewalls and backdoor hacking are not the aviator's areas of expertise.

"KC, Triggs, and me," Henry says. "We've been brainstorming all afternoon." Gone from his face is any boy-speaking-to-girl nervousness. "If you don't believe me, she's on the line right now." He makes a goofy face and hands me the cell.

"Kase, are you there?" I cradle the phone against a shoulder, hear a burst of static, and wait for an answer.

"I'm at McVie's lab if that's what you mean. Hiding from my parents. Avoiding an all-day clean-up-our-energy company picnic slated for two thousand of our family 'friends.'"

"Drag," I say, remembering how exhausting it was being the daughter of social parents.

"I told McVie I'd help him mix more storm solution if he'd cover for me with the power parental unit. Midterm makeup is what he told Mom when she checked my alibi."

Our midterm. I shrink, being reminded of the lack of progress on our storm research. "Have you made any headway?"

"Let's just say if we turned in what we have now, we'd all have failing grades."

Ugh. "That bad, huh?"

"No worries." Her voice is lower and louder, as if she has moved her mouth closer to the phone receiver. "I've got the professor exactly where I want him." Raspy, stalker breaths crackle over the line, and I consider that if a career in computers doesn't work out, KC is well-suited to be an annoying telemarketer.

"Miss McKenna," Professor McVie joins the background noise. "Protons and electrons don't combust around your social schedule."

"On my way," KC replies, in normal volume. "Anyway, the GPS add-on is pretty cool, right? You weren't lying about Henry's gray matter. Ripe." I hear her smack her lips. "USTA Prime."

"Do I want to know?"

"Universal Student Techie Association," she explains.

"I was referring to how you penetrated Pioneer's supersecure network."

"Ready to be dazzled?" She doesn't wait for a reply. "Get this. I scanned my blood cells onto my laptop and created a thousand different versions of my digital DNA. Kind of like avatars. Each chain is basically the same, but with one tweaked difference."

"New outfit, change of hair color, maybe even a few piercings?" I tease.

"Something like that." She doesn't laugh. "After a little finger magic, I sent my DNA clones marching over the bandwidth and then called in an epic favor. An insider on site who awakened an idling Trojan horse I planted weeks ago."

"Weeks? We just decided to come two days ago."

On a techie binge, KC glosses over the unnecessary details—mainly my questions. She says, "Bombarded by the army of packet sniffers—"

"Layman language, Kase."

"A program that grabs clusters of information on the Internet. The company's firewall became overwhelmed, allowing one of my avatars to capture high-level user names and passwords."

I picture lines of code twinkling like Orion the Hunter in purple-rimmed glasses.

"With an unlimited pass to access all security screens, I breezed in right through the front door of BioDynamics's storage cloud."

"BioDynamics? The drug company?"

"They designed Pioneer's upgraded receivers."

Scumbags. "So the sniffer-filter-data-stealing soldiers and the Trojan program fall within the white-hat hacker code of ethics?" I say, guessing her methods are anything but legal.

"Wearing a white hat means it's my obligation to identify threats and vulnerabilities in computer systems in order to protect unsuspecting companies from black hacks. Actually, I'm doing them a favor."

"By breaking into their system?"

"I like to think of it as testing. Look, T, when we get the information we need and are done borrowing BioD's pass codes, I'll call my insider friend and show him the cracks in Bio's firewall."

"For the record, I don't think you'd like prison. Your parents would die of humiliation, and orange isn't your color."

KC giggles. "If we use the information to bring a killer to justice and therefore quash his ability to hurt any other innocents, then how can hacking BioDynamics be against the white code?"

I take it back. KC is way overqualified to be a telemarketer. A trial lawyer would be a much better career track.

On the other side of the line, a boom thunders like a shotgun. "Miss McKenna!" Professor McVie hollers.

"Nearly standing next to you, sir," KC's voice ratchets up, and then she says she has to run. Literally. "Oh, one more thing." Her breathing quickens. "Your mom and Gunner were guest speakers at my dad's picnic," she wheezes.

Mom and Gunner? Together? Again? For two people who haven't seen each other in years, they sure seem to have a lot to talk about. "Kase, did you dig up any info on Mr. Clark?"

"Zippo," she says. "All sources report he's as normal as a next-door neighbor. Go trail Soraya. Key Kitty signing off. Over and out."

After a loud click, the line goes dead.

I touch my stomach. *So much for the gut-o-meter.*

Arms out and palms up, Henry's shoulders shift side to side, resembling a hip-hop rapper's. "So, was I trippin'?"

I wedge myself between him and Trigger and light the map on the handheld. Three concentric rings with a target in the middle appear. "Show me how this will help find Dr. Harb."

"These rings are the range." Trigger points. "Increase the speaker volume, and the map scrolls out up to twenty-five miles. Lower it, and the view magnifies down to a quarter."

Henry sets the range ring on twenty miles and says, "You're the blip in the middle, T." He snickers, and I elbow him in the side.

"And your apprentice?" I fold my arms. "Where's his signal?"

Raising a hand to his ear, Trigger twists Henry's receiver add-on a quarter turn. A third dot appears on screen and pulses next to mine. "You guys have been busy." I reach to adjust my chip when Henry bats my forearm.

"Trigger's is the only one that can be shut off. Both yours and Soraya's transmit continuously."

"Because?"

"Because you're very important to us, T, and we don't want to lose track of you."

I'm about to stick my finger in my throat to gag when Henry bounds to his feet. He angles the screen, holding the up volume button to increase the range. "Soraya's moving."

"Where?" I say.

"Don't know, but it appears she's on the edge of campus."

"Walking?"

"Must be driving," Henry says. "Her signal is moving too fast."

"Last-minute dance prep?"

"Don't think so. The auditorium is the opposite direction."

Trigger cuts in. "Any chatter on the security frequency? No one leaves Pioneer's gate without an escort."

I adjust my receiver volume to full, only to hear the dull sizzle of static. "No, nothing from security."

Trigger bunches his face. "How strange, not to have heard a single peep all day and then…"

I shoot to my feet. "What are you trying to say?"

Henry steps between Trigger and me. "I think what he's asking is, did something happen between you and Soraya?" The Weatherman spreads his arms like a crossing guard. "Is it possible you said something that upset her?"

"Really?" I blast my bangs with a huge breath. "I did exactly as you asked. Even apologized for choking her." *Which I'm not that sorry for.*

"That would have been something to see," Trigger says.

I move around Henry. If expressions could kill, the sky surfer would be well on his way to an ocean burial.

"Way to go, T." The Weatherman slaps my arm and motions to Trigger to zip his lips.

"I gave her the booster and said we'd meet up at the dance and help you solve a problem."

And meet an overflowing tank of avgas named Tuck.

"With no threats of bodily injury?" Trigger says.

I smile, pleased with my self-control.

"Impressive."

"What problem?" Henry says.

"Soraya knows." I try to pull the Weatherman to the cot, but he yanks his arm away.

"Knows what?" He adjusts his goggles over his eyes and knocks the miniwiper's cycle switch.

"About the Streeters…" I press the off switch. The wipers stop dead center. "I told her we plan to confront them tonight and put an end to this madness."

"Plan? I don't know about any plan to face Wall Street. Oh no, no, no, no. At the Aurora Celebration? Tonight? No, it's not the right time." Henry shudders.

"Whenever our paths cross, that will be the time to set those hacks straight." Trigger's shoulders rise like an angry tomcat's.

"Tana, please." Henry faces me.

I look him straight in the eye. "There is no plan to meet, intimidate, or fight the Streeters." I shoot a warning look at Trigger.

"Why do we need one?" the sky surfer says, clearly missing the cue. For two people who used to be on the same wavelength, lately we couldn't be any further apart. "When I see them, I know what to do," he says, making the situation worse.

I shake my head.

"But not tonight, right, T?" Henry's chin twitches. I'm about to reassure him when I notice Trigger's face turn red.

"Do you want them to keep pounding on you?" the sky surfer asks.

"Not helping," I say and touch Henry's arm. "That's just the story I fed Soraya." *I'm such a liar.* "To keep her close so we can watch her. Isn't that what you asked me to do?"

"Yes." Henry swipes his brow and then searches for his inhaler. As he pats his pockets, the sat phone falls between his legs. He retrieves the unit. Panic covers his face.

"Her dot is gone." He slaps the phone against his hand and brightens the screen. "Soraya's disappeared."

CHAPTER 28

"Stay calm." Even as I hear myself speak, I can't believe the words came from my mouth. Despite every internal organ wrenching, somehow my exterior holds steady, shedding a little insight to our meteorology professor McVie's say-one-thing-and-do-another behavior. "Stay calm and run for your life," he often says, all in the same sentence. His placid words are contradicted by frenzied actions, which is exactly how I feel right now.

Spinning like an F1 twister, my thoughts waft to Tuck, western music, and vintage rock, and his take on how opposite ends of the spectrum can still be similar, the uncanny way he turned two negatives into a positive.

"Our plan is working," I say to my team, sampling Tuck's approach. "Is it possible our chat prompted her to contact her dad?"

"Could be." Henry's words quicken.

"Or she's on a train getting as far away as she can from the 'friend' who nearly strangled her," Trigger says and then swipes the sat phone. He flicks the screen.

Wet blanket.

Unaffected by Trigger's half-fuel-tank-empty attitude, I search the tent for a blunt object to whack his negative state to positive. When I am about midway through mentally rolling a thick magazine, Sergeant Numereau's square jaw appears at the door.

"Attention!" he bellows like a bullhorn. Since all three of us are already standing, he follows with a quick, "At ease. Top brass is about to touch down. Surprise inspection of our progress." His uniform shirt is untucked, and his belt buckle is off center.

"If it's a surprise, then how do you know they're coming?" Henry says.

"This is the marines, not book club. Our jobs are to know things before they happen. Always be two steps ahead of your opponents. Lucky for me, I have a contact in Washington who is alert to the corps advancements."

Trigger leans in and whispers, "Military jargon for an office gossip."

"Aren't the generals on your team, sir?" Henry's forehead flexes.

"Not when it comes to performance reviews. Occasionally, the brass gets an overzealous attitude."

"Meaning they're highly motivated," Trigger interprets.

"To make sure everyone's character is beyond reproach," Mac says.

"Above the law."

"Mr. Flough."

Trigger raises his hands in the air. "They're civilians. Just translating, Mac."

The sergeant's lips press together. "Everyone I trust, my entire unit, is on high alert." Mac rests his fists on his hips. "Regardless, we have to go through the motions, show the generals how much progress we've made." He zooms in on Trigger. "Care to join us? Get a firsthand look at the pill in action?"

I'm certain Trigger will accept. How can he pass an opportunity to hobnob with senior officers?

But he doesn't.

"Man, Mac, that would be solid." I notice his ocean blues flick to Henry, appearing to trace the green-yellow lumps on his face. "But…"

The sergeant's sight line follows his little brother's, and then his head bobs like he understands.

Freaky. It's as if he and Trigger have a covert language—one with no words, only facial expressions.

"Next time then." Mac's bark lessens. For such a strict commander, Sergeant Numereau sure seems to have a soft spot when talking to Trigger.

"Fall out!" Mac belts, although there aren't any enlisted men in the tent—at least not yet.

Mac stomps across to Trigger, clasping a meaty hand around his neck. "I'll look for you when we finish." Matching his mouth to our friend's ear, he says, "You promised me an answer. End of day."

Trigger's Adam's apple drops. "Yes, sir," he answers.

As Sergeant Numereau aims at the door, I notice the time, scoop the duffel Gran packed, and hurl it over a shoulder. "Any chance the test area is near the ladies'?" If I want to get to the dance early enough to meet Tuck, I have less than an hour.

"You're in luck." Mac waves me ahead. "Ladies' head is on the way to the practice field."

I turn to Trigger. "Come get me in thirty minutes?" I say, aware of the unfavorable logistics involved with riding a dirt bike in a dress. *Emphasis on dirt.*

"On it." The ever-reliable Flough agrees and sets the timer on his chunky dive watch. He squints one eye shut, shifting perspective, perhaps trying to see past my dusty khakis and dirt-stained blouse to recall how I look in a dress. *Mind bender.*

"Here," I pull the Ziplock bag from a duffel pocket and toss it at Trigger. "Have a scone."

Outside, the sergeant's urban tank idles. Two uniformed marines occupy the rear seats, so I drop my bag on the floor and climb up front beside Mac. As before, Commander Lead Foot floors the gas, bouncing my head against the seat. Zero to sixty in a few seconds. My head jostles against the headrest. At ease or full-speed ahead, I'm learning, are a marine's only gears.

After counting twelve tents, I anticipate a left turn at the first crossroad. When the land yacht jackknifes around the corner, I feel a thud hit my seat. Twisting, I notice a soldier in back, head bent between his legs.

If I didn't know better, I'd think he was suffering fallout from an all-night drinking bender. But having met his commanding officer, I know hangovers would never be tolerated in Camp Numereau.

Mac bulldozes ahead.

The sick marine's counterpart levers him upright, revealing the soldier's pale, clammy face and glazed eyes.

"What's wrong with him?" I say, and Mac glances in the rearview mirror. He blinks and then redirects his attention to the dirt road.

"Stomach bug." Mac's nostrils flare, and he scratches the bridge of his nose.

Angling around the bucket seat, I see a sick guy, who looks like he's in a trance.

"Have to get ready for the field test," the ill soldier mumbles. He squirms in his seat. "My service weapon, armor, goggles, and helmet." His arms pantomime what looks like his gear-up ritual.

Strange, since I notice a holster hanging from his belt, and by the puffiness of his jacket, I'd say he's wearing a flak vest. *Does he think he's back in his bunk, packing for the mission?*

"Get him some water." Mac's forehead creases. "He's dehydrated." His eyebrows cave, almost touching one another.

Dehydrated. Really? I think through my experience with Nurse H_2O during our last visit. I was a little out of it but remained lucid. I knew where I was and recalled what I had done the hours before. This guy appears to be hallucinating, repeating already completed tasks.

The marine's counterpart fills the groggy soldier's mouth with water. He loosens the corpsman's neck bandana and blots the slimy sweat film from the marine's sunken features.

Streams of gritty red dust flow through the opened windows— a telltale sign we're nearing the edge of camp. *Next stop, ladies' room.* Although every part of me wants to ask the obvious—the did-he-take-the-pill question—I've witnessed Mac's intolerance for insubordination firsthand and know better than to go head-to-head with the base commander. Unless, of course, I want to be back in McDunney's grubby hands.

Go for neutral ground. My daughter-of-diplomats training kicks in. Get the information by probing with unrelated questions, ones that won't raise suspicion. "Exactly where do you practice maneuvers?"

Mac's gaze flicks from the road at regular intervals and checks the soldiers in back.

"See the second ledge resembling a ship's bow?" He aims the Humvee at the stone wedge that hovers over the ladies' head. "A clearing about ten miles square lies beyond that shelf, surrounded on four sides with sculpted sand bunkers. That's where we practice."

"Remote," I say, while envisioning the manpower it must have taken to excavate such rocky terrain. "Did your team level the area just for this project?"

"No." Mac circles the female facilities, a lap likely for surveillance. He weaves around and parks in front of the tent. "The site was cleared during the Cold War, for the Trident Missile Program, a place the Russians wouldn't look for nuclear warheads."

Countless times, I've heard my grandfather talk about the 1950s, bomb shelters, gas masks, food stockpiles, paranoia, and Americans living in perpetual fear of a nuclear attack.

"Terrifying times," Pop always says, "an uneasiness that could only be understood by living it." It was an era long before I was born.

But today, where I currently sit, inside an armored horror, near a small army of marines about to finalize a pill to end all wars, I catch a glimpse of the world from the military's perspective and wonder if I'd lived during a time like the fifties, what lengths I would go to to be safe— regardless of the risks.

For some reason, I think about Henry, battered, beaten down, his daily existence a reoccurring nightmare. I consider for a minute to what extremes I've gone to secure his safety. I've risked McVie's job and allowed KC to wear a black hat, created and flew through a volatile storm, and then chanced bodily harm with that creep Chief McDunney.

And Henry's just one person.

A heaviness descends—a dread like I felt after the explosion that killed my dad. I turn to Sergeant Numereau and wonder about the burden he must feel. Like the mighty Atlas's, I guess, since Mac seems to carry the weight of the world on his back.

"Got to go," the war chief says. "Sick marine in need of medical attention."

"Thanks for the lift." I leap out the door and drag my duffel across the sand. I take one last look at the delirious soldier and tell myself the pill to end all wars had nothing to do with his condition.

At least, I hope so. For the world's sake and Mac's sake, but most of all for Trigger's.

CHAPTER 29

Gran came through: a dress, makeup, accessories, and even the right shoes. Boots to be exact. We are in the desert after all, going to an outdoor concert, likely to meet a hostile clique of Streeters and traipse around after Soraya, all while avoiding the watchful eye of Pioneer's Chief Handsy, and there's no way I *can* run in heels—never mind *want* to. Perhaps Gran understands me better than I think.

As I wiggle my toes, I examine the worn but freshly polished slouchy lace-up boots. The textured black leather with brown undertones, takes the edge off my bold pink sheath. *A definite notch up from my chunky hiking treads, which are caked with sand and dirt.*

Spinning around, I take a look in the mirror nailed over the sink. My fingers smooth the silky fabric as I recall where I got the dress—the campus shopping district, with Soraya, before the whole choke-and-hold episode, the day she faked a migraine, and we ditched day 2 of candidate orientation.

"You have to get it," Soraya had squealed, sitting opposite me in the dressing room. "The color brings out the warm undertones in your skin."

At that moment, she'd seemed like friend material. She gifted me the dress and offered to lend me a pair of earrings.

How could I be so stupid? I swallow as thumbnails from Pioneer's old intranet slide in front of my eyes—Soraya's bedroom, the snapshot of her and her father at the airport, the glimmer of light that drew my attention to the hammered metal in the jewelry box, my birthday earrings, the moment I realized who murdered my dad.

Fury flashes through my body, reddening my skin to the shade of my dress.

I bought into it all, the entire best-friend act.

Divert and distract. I squint at my ruddy reflection in the dust-caked mirror and run possible payback scenarios. *Like what?* I track back and forth over the gritty floor. *How about when our paths cross again, I completely ignore her?*

I turn on a heel and retrace my steps. *Yeah, that would really show how over her I am.*

Better yet—I stomp over the worn path—*tell everyone on campus how the perfect Soraya Harb is an accomplice to murder.*

That's right. I hop and skip. Miss I-Have-It-All-Together would be humiliated. I stop flat-footed and gnaw a fingernail.

Problem is Soraya, Henry, and Trigger are the only ones I know at Pioneer. *And Tuck.* I swallow. *What would he think?* I'm guessing the upperclassman would see me as mean and immature. But he has no idea about the crimes Soraya and her dad committed.

As if summoned, my eyes shift to the hanging mirror. I stare into the dusty haze, and Dad's image appears.

You're not real. I look away. And then I hear his voice.

"Careful, Tana. You get back what you put out," the phantasm says.

"The way of the world according to Benjamin Lyre."

"Do you really want to bring spite, contempt, and vengeance into your life?"

"This is just part of the grieving process. My subconscious making sense of a horrible experience." I grab my temples. My rib cage contracts. I reach over the sink and, with my sleeve, wipe away every speck of dirt until Dad's face disappears. The graveyard guilt trip, however, lingers.

"If that's the case, Dad, what epic wrong did you commit to get yourself murdered?"

Coyotes howl in the distance.

All right, all right, all right. Even from the grave, Dad can still make me feel like a little girl.

I stay very still, half expecting some sort of paranormal sign that I'm on track. I listen for the wind to whip, scan around for a butterfly. I search out the window to see if lightning has appeared.

Crickets.

Did you hear me? I said I wouldn't be spiteful. I bend down, pinch some grit from the floor, and throw it against the mirror.

Nothing.

I see my reflection, now covered with hundreds of tiny dirt specks.

Be rational, Tana. I start to pace again. *Instead of throwing your energies into revenge tactics, why not use the past to gain the advantage? As leverage to turn the tables.*

I stop, spin, and lean into my reflection. *Why not make Soraya believe I wore this dress as a memento? A gesture to show how desperately I'm trying to smooth over our differences?*

Just the idea of gaining the upper hand cools the heat pulsing through my veins. My skin fades into its typical creamy color. I avert my attention to my duffel and dig for my lip gloss, when the mirror twists and swings on the nail. *It's a great plan isn't it, Dad? Besides, it's true to who I am.*

After a swipe of lip gloss, I scoop the remnants into my bag.

I've barely stepped from the latrine tent when Trigger pulls up in a loaner jeep, exactly on time. Another idiosyncrasy, I've learned, having been born with military blood. The jeep creeps forward, and Trigger cocks his head in my direction. His features are frozen and his neck stiff. With one hand on the steering wheel and the other on the stick shift, he rolls to a stop and sets the parking brake. His gaze remains unbroken.

What's up with him?

As I approach, I notice him swallow hard. *Is it the scone?* I listen for signs that the cleanse curse has begun.

"You OK?" I say. Guilt pings as I hurl my duffel into the backseat.

Trigger doesn't move. His mouth is steady; his sky blues are hidden beneath aviator shades. He groans.

Gran strikes again.

***

The diesel engine knocks, and I look closer at his *oogly* expression, realizing that the sigh has nothing to do with his stomach. His mirrored glasses fall to his lap.

It's the dress, I conclude—Trigger's favorite.

I climb into the seat beside him, and his head swivels forward. He releases the brake and shifts into gear.

"How's Brooklyn?" I ask.

The clutch snaps. The jeep bucks like a bronco and then stalls.

Red-faced, Trigger smashes the clutch and twists the ignition key.

"My foot slipped from the pedal," he explains, focusing on the dirt road ahead. "Fine," he mumbles. "Brooklyn's good. I'm assuming. I haven't had a chance to talk to her since we left." He shrugs the way guys do when they want you to think they're indifferent.

"BB must be missing you." I turn away.

"Anyway," Trigger diverts, "I've got news."

I face him. "You've joined the marines?"

Trigger grabs his side as if jabbed with a knife. "No!" His voice spikes, and he retrieves his glasses. "Soraya's back on the grid."

"So she didn't run." *Good.*

"Henry's holed up in the bunk, all four eyes glued on the sat-phone map, keeping track so we don't lose her again."

"Where's she now?"

"When I left, she was at home."

"Probably getting ready for the dance."

"Makes sense." He eyes his watch. "The concert starts in an hour. Girls take forever to do who knows what."

"The 'what' you guys pay no attention to, right?" I straighten the hem on my dress.

"Anyway"—Trigger opts to avoid—"if we want to find out if Harb is still around, Soraya's our best chance."

"If we watch her every move."

"And stay hyperaware of who she speaks to, and if she hands off anything—objects, trinkets, or paper—maybe we'll get lucky and find that scumbag."

"Right," I say, but my stomach cinches. I rest my hand on my clenched abs. *Do I want to catch Dr. Harb?* Without a doubt. Short of donating an organ, I'd do just about anything to get justice for my dad. *But is Soraya tangled up in all of this?* My instincts fire. The burning I feel inside is somehow not so sure.

As we coast along the road to Pioneer, the sun slides below the layered rocks. The vast sky is airbrushed with peach-and-pink wisps. Dust devils twist between the sagebrush as we chase daylight. The colossal orange sunset reflects off Trigger's mirrored aviators.

Paralleling our track, a freight train trumpets and speeds past. I change subjects. "Do you think it's ever right to sacrifice a few for the good of the masses?"

"A few what?" Trigger says.

"Lives."

He squirms in the driver's seat. "What are you talking about, T?"

So used to him finishing my thoughts, I forget we're out of sync. "On the way to the girls' latrine, one of the marines in the Humvee was sick."

"Flu?"

"Don't think so; he was sweating, but even though his eyes were wide open, he looked like he was in some sort of trance. Get this"—I watch Trigger for any sort of reaction—"instead of realizing he was riding in the back of the Humvee, he thought he was packing his body armor in his bunk, completely unaware he was already wearing his helmet and flak vest."

"Sweat, disorientation—he was probably dehydrated."

"That's what Mac said. Still, he was in an awful hurry to get the soldier to the medics. Kind of like yesterday when..."

"When what?" Trigger's jaw clenches.

When you were cowering against the flight lockers and had forgotten the meeting with Professor McVie altogether.

I hesitate, noticing both of his hands clenched on the steering wheel. *What's wrong with you?*

"You didn't answer my question." I do a little diverting of my own. "Is the loss of one life worth the gain of a few?"

The sky surfer says, "It depends."

"On?" my voice notches up a level.

"The situation."

I'm about to launch into the emotional atmosphere when Trigger removes his aviators and throws up a hand.

"Before you go ballistic, let me explain. Every single human life matters, Tana. It's a priceless gift whose value can't be measured or replaced. Saying that, I grew up in the reality that some of us are called to fight for the masses. Soldiers oftentimes sacrifice their lives to protect others."

My heart thumps, beating as quickly as a snare drum. "In wars and in combat," I clarify, buying time to calm down.

"In all kinds of situations. Thousands of circumstances. Some that save a few lives, others that may save hundreds."

I feel myself trembling. "Who decides?"

"Whoever is in charge."

"But how can they know how many will be hurt by their decision? And how many benefit?"

As the last ray of apricot sunlight hits his face, Trigger's sky-writing eyes soften. "Your dad didn't die for nothing, Tana." His hand leaves the shifter and rests on my knee.

I feel numb.

"No lives were saved by his death." My mouth quivers.

"He wasn't a soldier, but he chose to work for the UN." Trigger's thumb glides over my skin.

No tingle. No sparks.

"He knew the risks," Trigger says. "Knowingly put himself in harm's way to help people who otherwise had no voice."

"So?"

"Your dad sacrificed himself, his family's security—your safety—to protect the unprotected."

"Just like a—"

"Marine."

I fight the tears filling my eyes—tired of the gray area, tapped out of compassion for the greater good, and longing for the days when things were either black or white. "It's not the same," I snap and shove Trigger's hand back to the shifter.

Not another word is said until we pass through the Pioneer security gate. Nearing the base of the mesa, he reviews logistics. "Once you hook up with Soraya, don't let her out of your sight." He rolls to the curb in front of the auditorium stairs. "Tell her you two are on Streeter lookout. Make her believe we plan to confront them during intermission."

I nod and reach for my cross-body bag.

"Henry and I will be nearby, out of sight, watching on the tracker."

I start to climb from the jeep, but Trigger clasps my arm. "In case you hear anything on the security stream"—his free arm angles under the front seat, and he hands me a second sat phone—"call."

I drop the phone into my satchel.

"If you see anything suspicious, call," Trigger says. He squeezes my arm again. "If you need me for anything…"

I hold his glance for second and notice his ocean blues swirling like treacherous undercurrents.

"Tana," a deep voice twangs, and we both spin around.

Tuck Hunter strides over. Despite the darkness consuming the sky, his smile gleams. His boots, hat, and longhorn belt buckle come into view. He pauses, as if memorizing every curve of my face, looks past me, and offers a hearty hand to my seatmate.

"Tuck," his vocal cords strum.

Trigger looks as if he's somehow placed second in a flight-team tournament. He matches Tuck's grip. The veins in both hands bulge.

I'd hate to be the skin between those two palms.

"Trigger," the sky surfer says, giving me a look like "Who the heck is this guy?"

Before I have a chance to explain, Tuck Hunter takes my hand. "Ready?" His brows crunch. "Concert's starting before long, and I'm running short on time."

"Tuck is the lead singer of the T. H. Wranglers," I say over a shoulder.

"The band playing tonight?"

I nod and focus on Tuck. "I heard them practicing this morning. The beat is somewhat vintage," I say and use a hand to conceal a grin.

"You hate country music," Trigger says.

Tuck and I exchange a glance.

The sky surfer frowns.

Tuck offers a stiff forearm. I latch on and climb from the jeep.

"See you in an hour." Trigger slides on his aviators. He grinds the gearbox and shoots from the curb. I watch the jeep's abrupt departure.

Call any time, and I'll be there. I watch until the four-wheeled dot disappears. *Yeah, sure.*

"Brother?" Tuck spins me and loops my arm around his.

I shake my head.

"Cousin?"

I twist my neck "no" as he guides me toward an entrance marked "Private." He cracks the door and reaches over my head, and an unsnapped pearl button dusts my forehead. He steps in. His hips brush mine. Goose bumps rise on my arms. His eyes angle from beneath the Stetson's wide brim. He winces. "Boyfriend?"

"Friend," I say, fighting the urge to touch his chest.

"Ah," Tuck grumbles and adjusts his hat. "The competition."

CHAPTER 30

"No worries, I'm up for it." Tuck scans my dress, shudders, and then adjusts his hat. "This way." He leads me through the door to a flight of concrete steps, and we descend along bedrock walls lined with concert posters—pictures, I'm guessing, from past Aurora Celebrations. At a closer glance, however, I notice framed shots of famous musicians, sports athletes, movie stars, and politicians. I also see hand-scribbled signatures etched into the stair risers. *All Pioneer grads?* I wonder.

Tuck plods on, obviously too familiar with the wall of fame to catch a celebrity buzz. I, however, am vibrating.

The ceiling lowers as we round the last steps and arrive in a cavernous tunnel. Ahead, the open area is crowded with dozens of men dressed in jeans and black T-shirts, most with bandanas tied around their foreheads.

"This is my crew," the country singer introduces them and weaves in and out of the roadies. "Guys, meet Tana." The roadies nod and go back to devouring pizza and watching NASCAR.

We take a few more steps before we're approached by a security guard. "Hey, Tuck." A guy about Eddie's size blocks a narrow corridor.

"Here's my badge." Tuck removes the lanyard around his neck and swipes it over the scanner. "This is my friend Tana. You'll find her name on the list."

The muscle skims his tablet and then hands me a badge marked "Guest of T. Hunter."

As Tuck slides the pin through my shirt, my heart flutters.

"You're clear." The man in the security windbreaker steps aside and points to a second guard. "Please raise your card as you pass each checkpoint."

Security that would impress my mother.

The stone tunnel forks to the right. Tuck grabs my hand and ushers me into a well-lit passage. Instinctively, I count strides from the exit. From what I can tell via my internal compass, we're in a cavern beneath the stage.

"Catering room." Tuck points to the right. "Business lounge." He gestures left and then hightails it past another set of doors. We flash our badges as we pass a fourth security guard.

"Dressing rooms." Another couple of strides and his boots skid. "Finally, my room." I stuff a hand in my pocket and feel for my pepper spray. Tuck scans his badge, and the door unlatches. "After you."

Inside, a short hall opens into a rustic sitting room. Two stuffed leather couches and a driftwood coffee table are arranged on an Asian rug.

Tuck crosses the carpet and collapses onto the black sofa. I take a seat on an identical couch across from him, and my eyes bounce between the pictures of desert landscapes around the room. Two floor lamps cast an amber hue. In the background, sounds of ocean waves echo.

"This is where I'm supposed to unwind when I'm not performing." Tuck props his boot heels on the coffee table's edge. "Like I could possibly relax with the circus I travel with." He tilts his wide brim, and I see a pair of tired eyes and realize that, this time, it's Tuck who feels a little dizzy and disorientated.

"I know," I say.

I scan the trays of sushi and fruit and plates of bite-sized cookies and brownies. I notice neatly piled shirts and jeans, hanging garment bags, and rows of spare cowboy boots beside the bed—not to mention a collection of acoustic guitars poking from a rack.

"Troubling existence," I say, grinning.

"Ah," Tuck grumbles and centers his hat. "Don't get me wrong; when our second album went platinum, *whew*, wow, I was grateful. Downright stoked. I don't want to come across as entitled. It's just…"

Suddenly, it all came crashing back to me, my life before—the armed guards, June, Eddie, the behind-the-scenes tours, the black-tie parties, the privilege of experiencing the extraordinary every day, the numbness that comes with having anything you could possibly dream of at your fingertips.

"Exhausting," I finish his sentence.

Tuck jumps like he's been stung with a cattle prod. His worn Wranglers scrape across the table, and once opposite me, he removes his hat and runs a palm over a head of spiked tobacco-colored hair. "Ahhh…" The cowboy rests his elbows on his knees and squints straight into my eyes. "What does it all mean anyway?"

"Not sure," I say, quicker, I suspect, than Tuck expected.

As the rock star's chin dips toward his chest, I remember the time when I searched for the answer to the same elusive question. Although urgent in that moment, seated at some stuffy dinner with A-listers, now, I struggle to recall the last time I thought about the meaning of my life.

How ordinary I've become—eating Gran's cooking, studying with KC, and climbing out of my window late at night to hang with Trigger. No red carpets or private jets. I've traded my floor-length gowns for rain gear without an ounce of regret.

I shrug. "Maybe it's about the simple things."

Tuck's gaze rejoins mine.

"The stuff without the pyrotechnics, strobes, and spotlights. Chilling with friends, kicking around—you know, spontaneous, incidental stuff."

Tuck's hand covers mine, warming me from the inside out. As our knuckles intertwine, he reaches for my cheek, and his fingertips glide over my chin and cascade down my throat. He curls his hands around the nape of my neck and draws my mouth near his. I feel his short breaths. His full lower lip touches mine…

Boom, boom, boom. A heavy thud rasps against the ready-room door.

CHAPTER 31

Tuck's forehead knocks against mine. We split.

"Hey, man." The lock flies open. "Oh sorry." His drummer's eyes widen. "You're generally…ah…"

Tuck glares. "Alone."

"No, it's just, well, I'm not used to you having, you know," the drummer stammers. "Chicks, girls, ladies—oh heck, dude, just wanted to let you know it's time."

Tuck straightens to his feet and offers me a hand. "Duty calls."

I sense he says it for himself as much as for me. He bends my clenched palm behind his back and moves toward the door.

"I know you." The drummer scratches a lumberjack beard. "You're the girl from rehearsal."

"Tana, meet Grady, better known as Ricochet," Tuck says, and we file into the tunnel.

"Ricochet." I smile.

"Long story. If it pleases you, miss, call me Ric."

The three of us walk single file, opposite the lounge, to the farthest end of the rock cave, until we reach a second concrete staircase. I count off the paces backward.

Unlike the first stairway, in this one, the walls are smooth curves of natural stone. The risers, however, are another story altogether. The face of each ledge is painted with bright colors; the names of entertainers—Rolling Stones, U2, Bob Dylan—pass beneath my feet as we ascend toward the surface. At ground level, Tuck opens the metal door, and in less time than you can say the-ultimate-behind-the-scenes pass, we are on the edge of the stage.

"Nice to meet you, Tana." Ric nods and then joins the other members of the band.

"There's one more thing I want to show you." Tuck guides me to the sound engineer standing behind a desk covered with jet-black panels, rows of knobs, and slide switches.

"The sound system can shatter glass," Tuck says, "extinguish a candle flame, and has even been rumored to have fired a rifle by the low frequencies of its subwoofer."

"Really?" I say, watching the cowboy, who is quickly becoming the most interesting guy I know. He skims the panel until he locates a switch marked "House Mic." "I didn't know you needed this much oomph to play vintage redneck."

Tuck storms to the amplifiers and unhooks the hand mic from its stand. He jogs back to the soundboard and balances his finger on the on/off switch. "Care to repeat that last line for my fans?" A devilish look masks his Southern charms, and a second later, a mesh microphone is against my lips. "Go on; I dare you." He opens the mic.

A hot rush flashes over me; I'm certain my cheeks blush. I exhale, and a piercing screech wails over the speakers. I nudge the mouthpiece to Tuck's chest. The engineer's hand hits the kill switch lickety-split.

Tuck stands proud, aware of the fact he called my bluff and I flinched.

"What was that?" A lyrical voice screeches, pitched nearly as high as the mic. Soraya approaches. Henry and Trigger trail behind her. *So much for out of sight.*

"Technical malfunction," the engineer murmurs and pretends to fiddle with the sound switch.

"Is that all?" Apparently my faux BFF doesn't know much about electronics. "Well then, the show will go on."

In less time than it takes for the sound tech to reboot the board, Trigger and Henry are standing at my side. So close, in fact, they're stepping on my boots. "I thought you were going to stay hidden," I say to Trigger through clenched teeth.

"Thought you were watching Soraya," he says and throws a nod at Tuck. "Obviously something more important has caught your attention."

I'm about to stomp on his foot when Henry faces the up-and-coming country star. "Who's this?"

"A friend of Tana's." Trigger emphasizes *friend.*

"Since when? We're T's only friends at Pioneer."

"New friend, Aska Gu. If I'm right, there's nothing vintage about it." Trigger layers his arms over his chest. "He goes by Finn or Huck."

Henry raps, "I think I'm going to upchuck."

"Enough." I elbow both of my so-called friends. "Henry Aska Gu, meet Tuck Hunter."

"Top of not only the country charts, but the pop-music charts as well," Soraya says. "First record went double platinum."

Henry gapes.

"Pleased to make your acquaintance, Henry." Tuck offers a hand. "I squeaked by two semesters of your dad's weather-drone class."

"Sorry." The Weatherman frowns.

"No worries. I'm not all that good with names either."

"No, that's not what I meant. I'm sorry you had to have my dad for an instructor."

"OK." Ever the time tyrant, Soraya claps her hands, and before another word crosses her lips, the rest of the band prepares to go onstage. "Hand me the mic; it's time to kick off the night of redemption."

As Soraya arrives front and center, a shower of blue and purple lights cascades over her curls like a mountain waterfall. Fog streams around her feet, and a single spot lights her face. "Pioneer students…" She pauses as the crowd belts out a loud cheer. "Are you ready to make amends with the past?"

A thunderous chant echoes off the rocky walls as Soraya exits the stage. Arms wave in the air, and the rumble of thousands of stomping feet shakes the stage. Energy from the pavilion blasts like heat from an opened oven. My body temperature climbs, and my heart races, not from the sound, but from the intensity of Tuck's stare. As he is walking backward, his eyes hold mine; he ignores the laboring crowd as if we were the only two people in the stadium. His hand covers his heart, and then he tips his hat. Now in full view of his fans, he jerks around, breaks into a jog, and like a superhero, tears open his shirt, transforming into a rip-roaring country star. He slings his guitar from over a shoulder, strums a few cords, and slides across the stage on his knees.

I hold my breath.

Something offstage catches my attention—the sight of Soraya and Chief McDunney engaged in heated conversation. My supposed BFF is yelling, and the chief looks to be doing his best to settle her down.

Why is she talking to the chief? And what's she so angry about?

I whirl around to shout to Trigger only to discover him leaping from the stage. After landing flat-footed, he takes a few steps, and begins to climb the stone stairs. *Baby.*

Henry nudges me. "Go find out what's going on." I watch Trigger fade into the student mass. "We'll be up top. With the tracker." He aims toward the flat shelf on the mesa. "Where there's better reception."

I assume his next move will be to stomp off as Trigger did, but I'm wrong.

"T"—Henry steps in, blocking my view—"I don't have to remind you, we're running out of time. If you have any secret tactics in your daughter-of-famous-diplomats backpack, now would be the time to use them."

My stomach knots. "No pressure, right?"

"More angst, better result." He raises his shoulders. "Time-tested fact, backed by good science. Besides, Trigger says you're a junkie." His eyes jut away and then drift back. "As in adrenaline."

He lowers the night vision goggles from the top of his head, cycles the wipers, and hustles after his partner. Funny, at this moment, I feel closer to Henry than Trigger.

Doubling back, I retrace the steps I took with Tuck. I weave through the sound crew, pass the roadies, and arrive at the service stairs. Skipping every other step, I sprint down the corridor beneath the stage and emerge at floor level on the opposite end of the pavilion.

Percussion rattles as the band rocks on. I arrive late, just as McDunney steps away from Soraya.

Too slow, Lyre. I pant, drag my heels, take a few breaths, and then hear Tuck's voice. "I've never met a problem that can't be solved with a kiss."

CHAPTER 32

When I reach Soraya, her eyes are damp, and her cheeks are glowing with sweat. The edges of her mouth are turned down. "Smoke," she explains, even though I haven't asked. "Wreaks havoc with my contacts."

Contacts my backside. Something McDunney said upset her. And I'd bet my life it had to do with her dad.

"Stupid thing, really," she says. "The chief just informed me a few candidates got into a fight. For freshman, the momentum of the dance can be overwhelming."

That's why you're upset, a preparty brawl? I recheck her unconvincing expression. *Doubt it.* Alphas would never do anything to compromise their futures. Unless…

Streeters. I quickly scan the crowd, not seeing any familiar Wall Street faces. From the corner of my eye, I catch Soraya dab her eyes with her sleeve. Sensing she's on the edge, my instincts scream it's now or never. My thoughts scramble. If I were in her shoes, what would get me to panic?

Call it what you will, fate, coincidence, alignment of the universe, but the exact words I need to hear rumble over the state-of-the-art subwoofers. "Unspoken truths always come up at the most in-con-veeeenient moments. Even when tucked away in your favorite pair of boots." Tuck's attention turns to side stage. To me. His energy tugs in the same way I feel when I'm around Trigger. I grab my ear piercing. Cold.

I take Soraya's arm and give it a gentle squeeze. "Henry just told me we have a lead on his dad." The first unspoken truth glides off my tongue.

"Really?" Her upper lip twitches, slightly. "How?"

"Mac, I think," I say, straight-faced. "Rumor is he might still be here, hiding on campus."

Her emerald pupils expand. She doesn't blink. Doesn't breathe. She stays as steady as a porcelain statue. The actress extraordinaire surfaces. She giggles. "Right here under our noses?"

Even though Soraya is laughing, I notice a lump build in her throat. "Wouldn't that be something?" she says, the corners of her mouth waver. She checks her watch and then touches my arm. "Do me a favor?"

"Sure," I say, hoping I struck a nerve. A coin flips in my head—50 percent chance she runs to the bathroom, 50 percent chance she…

"I'm going to check the chief's progress; fighting at school functions won't do. At least, not while I'm dance chair." Her olive skin dims to the color of the rising moon. "After all, my résumé is on the line."

In a blink, she's at the exit and circles around, her fingers picking at her lower lip. "You'll stay here and keep the program on track?" Soraya's expression looks torn—half serious and responsible, the other part resembling the guilty eyes of a dutiful daughter. I should know. It's the same face I'd seen many times reflecting at me in the mirror.

"Got your back." I play along. *But only if you're telling the truth.*

"You're a real friend, Tana." Soraya's mouth sags. She pushes a hip against the door, and as she disappears into the hall, I feel conflicted. Part of me is hopeful she's checking crowd control. The other side, the dark inner skeptic, suspects the worst, hoping she leads us right to her father. I'm not really sure which side I'm rooting for.

According to plan, I ease the sat phone from my bag, clench the receiver in both hands, and shut my eyes. I listen to Tuck's deep, stretched lyrics, willing Soraya's GPS blip toward the parking area.

Ricochet's frayed drumsticks sweep over the snare drum, and a low bass picks up the riff. Tuck sings the chorus, "If you can't tell the truth, at least be a good citizen; vote to add trust to the endangered species list."

I take stock in his message, open my eyes, and speed-dial the only programmed number in memory. I suck in a deep breath and wait. In short order, Henry answers. "Weatherman here, what's your report?"

"The dust devil is spinning in your direction."

"Contact. See her, twisting like a tornado." A slight pause, a muffled exchange, and then Henry speaks. "Unless we're not where we think." He must have moved the receiver from his mouth because I struggle to hear. "What do you think, Triggs?"

"I see Soraya's signal."

"Roger, clear and a million," Henry says.

"She's heading right below you, toward student parking?" An unexpected spark of excitement tingles in my throat. Maybe this time…is it possible? Can we be friends again?

A hush settles on the line, and I hear Trigger in the background. "She's done an about-face. Definitely tracking opposite our location," Henry says. "Sorry, T, I'm afraid that cold front's coming."

She lied. Again, and although there's no wind, I shudder. "Give me her bearing," I shout and break into a sprint. At this moment, I'm certain Soraya and I will never be friends.

"Bearing zero-two-zero from…hey, man—" The Weatherman's voice cuts out.

"Tana," Trigger takes over. "I'm sure you're lit up, but hold tight and wait for us."

"Wait?" My temper flares. "Enough of the waiting, being patient, and extending the benefit of the doubt."

Check your emotions. Get control. I force a breath, attempting to recenter.

"I'm closer," I say. My heart burns. "I'll get a head start." *Logic Trigger can't argue.* Running, I hear my treaded soles clap against concrete. "Can't risk her giving us the slip."

"Right, good idea, we're only a few minutes behind," the sky surfer says. His breathing is labored. "If you catch her, promise you'll hang back until we get there?"

"Promise," I lie.

Trigger says, "Double or nothing, right, T?"

My ankle twists, and I stumble a few steps before regaining safe footing. *Double or nothing.*

Although endearing at one time, the circumstances have changed. Trigger is on the verge of joining Mac and the marines, an act guaranteed to end our friendship. *No way, my friend.* No more tugging at my heartstrings to get me to do what you think is best. I don't answer him. I allow the cell receiver to cycle with my arms. I slide my thumb and press the hang-up button.

Stretching into a full-blown sprint, I suck air through my nose and decide to do whatever it takes to keep eyes on Soraya.

Behind the stadium, I join the access road opposite student parking. I zig between the semitrailers and white catering vans and zag past Tuck's tour bus and a short line of limousines until I reach the rear stage gate. Bending over the boom, I scan as I do in the cockpit—short intervals, bracketing from left to right. My short breaths are visible in the cool night air.

Two headlights click on in staff parking.

A diesel engine cranks.

Light from the head beams angle, and a jeep comes about.

Behind the steering wheel, a head of curly hair appears.

CHAPTER 33

Lucky for me, the metal gate is chained shut during concerts.

Cornered, Soraya revs the jeep's engine. The thick-treaded tires spin, and a cloud of dust fogs the air. From the debris, the four-wheel drive jumps as if shot from a cannon. It rams the gate and splits the chained links, sending shards of metal swirling to the ground.

She's getting away.

Caked with dust and sand, I stumble to the empty parking area. *There must be something I can drive.*

I spin around once.

Twice.

"Empty!" I scream. I drop to my knees and bring my fists to my forehead. "No, no, no, he can't get away again." I thrust forward until my head rests on the dirt. "I'd give anything…"

Burrrum, bum, bum, bum. I feel a tremor. A vibration rumbles across the cracked earth. *Burrrum, bum, bum, bum.* I lift my head. I recognize the hum of twelve hundred cc's. *Ah,* I sigh. *Music to my ears.* I brush the fringe from my eyes to see a pizza-delivery boy dismount from his dirt bike.

I push to a squat, crouch, and shimmy behind a clump of snarly sagebrush. The delivery guy unhooks the steaming cardboard boxes strapped to the rear seat and heads to the pavilion door.

I tiptoe to the side of the motorbike, swing my leg over the seat, and kick the clutch. With one heel dug in the ground, I spin a half circle, and the hem of my dress lifts from the exhaust blast. I thread through the busted gate.

A hot-pink escape.

Virtually unnoticed.

Unless, of course, you count the chasing pizza-delivery boy I see in the rearview mirrors.

Ahead, Soraya's headlights slither along the steep grade, two golden lanterns, illuminating the hairpin turns winding down the mesa. I take advantage of the declining slope.

Angling forward, head and shoulders over the handlebars, I twist the throttle to max and gain speed. The gap between our vehicles closes, and I switch off the bike's headlamp to avoid being seen.

Navigating the last sharp corner blindly, I lean over farther and balance on the edges of each tire. As I am rounding the final stretch, a notch in the otherwise solid rock provides a blip of light from the crescent moon.

Grateful for nature's streetlamp, I bend the sports frame upright and bask in the good fortune. At the base, the ground flattens. The jeep ahead swerves until the all-terrain tires get traction and join the single route to and from the airport.

Going somewhere, Soraya?

I flash back to the framed photo of her and her father arm in arm, tucked behind the jewelry box, taken at London's city airfield. *What's your plan?* I consider her family history. *Blow up another plane?*

Any ounce of self-control I had explodes into a rush of rage. I hunker down on the handgrips and twist the throttle to full bore. The bike tears forward.

Maintain a safe distance, or she'll see you, I remind myself and then ease my grip and fall back until I trail behind the jeep by three car lengths. *Thanks, Eddie.* Yet another useful surveillance skill I learned from my former protector. Blowing up an airplane might provide a diversion, but it won't help Soraya or Dr. Harb escape. *Stealing an airplane, however—I* hold my speed steady—*is a more viable option.* That is, if they're trying to escape. But only if Soraya has taken up flying. *Doesn't make sense.* I weave to avoid roadkill.

Beneath me, the dirt bike sputters and coughs as if it caught a nasty cold. Glancing at the gas gauge, I notice the needle pegged on empty.

Conserve fuel! My pulse races. I estimate how much gas is left. *A gallon? Two?* Downshifting, I hope to stretch what remains in the tank. The bike may be decelerating, but my brain continues to crank—a thinking tank full of catch-a-killer fuel.

Holding at half throttle, the gap between us widens. The jeep's head cones angle ninety degrees, joining the airport ring road. Soraya darts by the first row of hangars, the altitude chamber, and transient airplane, parking without so much as a tap on the brakes. She passes the beacon tower, appearing to head to the last row of metal buildings on the field.

Trigger's plane? My heart beats like a bongo, wondering if she knows about Henry's miraculous cloaking chamois. Squinting, I focus on the rear bumper to catch the first glint of brightening taillights and tighten my fingers on the handlebars.

Soraya's jeep edges faster and drives off of the pavement, heading for the military's makeshift road. I follow, tires skidding, kicking tiny rocks and sand that swirl into a funnel of dust.

Choking in the foggy air, I squeeze my thighs against the gas tank, steadying it upright. Soraya pulls away, and I have no choice but to juice the throttle.

A dozen camouflaged bunks fly by before she knifes at the first intersection. Soraya tracks through the tent grid easily, as if she's familiar with it.

When my knee grazes the ground, I tip the bike the opposite way to maintain balance. *A right at the crossroads. A left at the flagpole.* The composite frame weaves back and forth between my thighs, maneuvers that bring me less than a tour-bus length behind her.

I check the rearview mirrors and see the comfort and security of Sergeant Numereau's camp fading into the lurid landscape. The lightless path ahead may have frightened me if I hadn't been down this dirt road less than twenty-four hours ago. Our course matches the route McDunney took the night before to the ladies' lav.

I know Soraya is an inside kind of girl and hasn't come all the way out to the desert to tinkle. So I'm not surprised when she roars past the ladies' facilities, her wiry curls waving like a Pioneer victory banner.

I'm now riding on fumes, and a rock shaped like a ship's bow whizzes past my left shoulder. The gap in between the tall stones narrows enough to create a wind tunnel.

Whish. An eddy swirls. Its powerful updraft lifts me from the bike seat. By the time I regain balance, a second tall rock arrows into my path.

Lean. I throw every pound of my body mass to one side and thread past the spear-like edge. I open my mouth to blow out, and I'm smacked with a mouthful of dirt. The grit pelts my cheeks and coats my tongue— thrown, I'm guessing, from Soraya's spinning tires.

I knuckle an eye, and when my vision clears, the jeep is gone. I search around. *How did she just disappear?*

Using the hem of my dress as a rag, I whisk the grime away to improve my vision. I downshift to first gear and stretch my feet from the bike pegs to allow them to skim the prickly brush. I glide forward and circle around the towering ship-shaped rock. After a second pass, I drag my heels into the parched earth. The bike sputters and quits.

Where could you hide in a matter of seconds?

I lean the bike on a peg. My eyes dance across the darkness. Miles of flat, desolate fields are speckled with sagebrush and porcupine cacti. I scan again. Nothing.

Get real, Tana. Soraya didn't vaporize into the arid air. I think about Henry's cloaking chamois. I take off on foot, weaving through the brush the way I'd seen McDunney's men search for Henry and Trigger. I walk a grid until I stumble on the jeep's tire tracks. Crouching, I make myself small and follow along the deep tire ruts.

Hovering near the ground, I shuffle my feet like a basketball player. After a series of sidesteps, I notice a glint in the distance.

An array of needled antennas.

My feet chop, and I get close enough to count six spindly sticks that are more than twice the height of Pioneer's airport control tower. As I approach the first pole, the shortest of the group, I notice that the cluster of antennas ascend like a flight of stairs.

Navigation antennas are horizontal. Communication antennas point straight up. Since they work on line of sight. At least that's the way it is on airplanes, and I'm thinking these aren't any different. With my neck tilted at the sky, I see a narrow platform on top. A lookout station? *But what's worth protecting out here?*

Forest for the trees. I catch myself hyperfocusing on a single element. *Toss the net wider, Lyre.*

I picture the marine camp, the future pill, and the flurry of exercises being conducted in remote parts of the desert.

There must be something here of grave importance.

I glance around again, this time from a more general perspective. I notice details—ones that don't quite fit.

Behind me, a two-story hill crests from the otherwise flat land. As far as I can see, cacti and sagebrush match the rest of the natural habitat.

It's too perfect.

Instead of growing randomly, the foliage appears to have been planted in straight rows, mimicking farmers' crops.

Was this berm built to conceal the area behind the antennas?

Every hair on my arms stands on end.

Picking up where I left off, I continue to walk the grid. I get into a groove and cover about two square blocks when a bee-like vibration pricks my hip bone. I hop on one leg, certain I've been stung.

Buzz, buzz. The sound hums again. *Calm down.* It's not a bee but the vibration of my phone.

My hand flies to my hip and removes the sat phone that Trigger loaned me. "What?" I duck behind a giant cactus, expecting to hear Henry or Trigger's nagging words. To my surprise, KC's congested voice croaks over the line.

"Found something," Go-To McKenna says. "Why are you whispering?"

"Wouldn't believe it if I told you," I say, staring at the prickly pear cactus's porcupine skin.

"Last I heard, you were following Soraya." KC sneezes once. Twice. Three times.

"I am," I say. "Until she ditched me in the middle of the desert."

"In the desert? Where?" I hear a series of sequential ticks.

I tilt on my heels, and what feels like a hundred hypodermic needles stab into my back. "Ouch," I jerk and arch my spine. "I backed into a cactus."

"Think of it as a rosebush without all the fixin's." A few more ticks, and then she sighs. "Something's jamming your tracker."

"Antennas," I figure, careful not to tilt back on my heels.

"Wi-Fi?" KC clarifies. "Thought you said you're in the middle of the desert."

"Strangest thing. While I was searching for Soraya's jeep tracks, I stumbled across six monster transmission poles, equally spaced and painted black."

"Ha." KC fake laughs. "Are you sure you haven't seen any green-skinned fellows with laser guns?"

"Not yet, but..." I take a second look at the cabled antennas. "They're as tall as skyscrapers, without any warning lights."

"Curious." KC's tongue clacks the way it does when she's solving complicated equations. "Why would anyone need to jam GPS signals way out there?"

"For protection," I say, with Mac's Project Déjà Vu in mind.

"Protection from what? Everything online says the area's abandoned."

"Or appears to be." From my periphery, I see a blast of gray-white smoke trickle from behind a neighboring cactus. Either the plant is on fire or I'm missing a post–Spirit Dance bonfire.

"Fire!" I yelp and bend close enough to see between the fork in the plant's curved arms. A steady smoke stream flows. I drop and crab shuffle across the gravelly ground.

"Must be from a lightning strike? How else would you start a fire in the desert?" KC's fingers tap on her keyboard. "Funny, I don't see any storms in your last-known position."

I check the sky and see nothing but twinkling stars. I investigate further.

Approaching a second cactus, I widen my perimeter, respecting each razor-sharp limb. I circle around and, this time, approach from the back.

Behind the prickly pear, my soles scrape against metal.

Squatting, I pat the sandy surface and touch what feels like a louvered grate. "Unbelievable." I fill KC in while verifying that I'm in fact standing on a doormat-sized piece of heavy-duty steel. "It's not a fire; it's exhaust air."

"And where there's carbon dioxide—"

"There's oxygen underground." I knock a fist to my forehead. *Of course.*

I hear KC's fingers tap. "A missile silo." She hammers. "Decommissioned, Titan II, built during the Cold War. Five miles from Pioneer."

I examine the scraggy surface underfoot with fresh eyes, scoop a handful of sand, and sift the seemingly random pebbles. *They are exact replicas of one another.* I stand, move, and retrace the jeep tracks, which seemed to disappear into a cluster of boulders. This time, however, I shimmy around the arrowhead-shaped stone, and once I reach the opposite side of the pointy face, I see Soraya's abandoned vehicle.

"She didn't vanish, Kase. She burrowed underground like a mole."

From my periphery, I catch a match-like light strike. A bright flash sparks. The ground below is lit for an instant and then softens to a dull-yellow glow.

This is my chance. I run. "Got to go," I say.

I haul toward the flat, rectangular panel of light at breakneck speed.

"Hang on," KC yells over the speaker. "I've got one more thing to tell you. It's urgent."

Arms swinging, I peg the phone receiver to my ear, wondering what could be more important than finding Soraya.

"I found proof," my friend says, "ironclad evidence that Dr. Harb killed your father."

CHAPTER 34

Like a derailed train, I stumble from the jeep's tire rut, regain balance, and charge toward another cluster of flowering cacti. "Proof? How?" I repeat the words that, if true, might give me closure.

"A text message," KC says. "Heavily encrypted, buried in an off-site cloud."

"Whose—" I start to say when *whap!*

A blunt object swings out of nowhere and whacks me across the chest. My feet lift from the ground. The sat phone flies from my hand. And once my back flattens against sand, two sturdy hands grip my ankles and drag me behind a giant cactus.

"T?" My vision steadies, and I see Henry at my side. Trigger is in front, holding my feet in the air.

"Tana?" Henry splashes water on my face and then slides his arms under my shoulders and lifts me upright.

"I'm fine." I bat at my helper and shoot eye daggers at Trigger. "Was that really necessary?"

"You we're about to blow our cover." He turns his palms up, offers a hand, and pulls me to my feet.

"What are you talking about? I found Soraya." I touch my certain-to-be-bruised midsection. "I was about to catch up with her, until you two…" My legs buckle, and I lean on Trigger's shoulder. "How did you guys find me so fast? When I left the concert, you were miles behind."

Henry points to my earring and then holds the tracker in the air.

"But KC said the signal was jammed. Interference, probably, from the antennas." Spinning, I search for the sat phone. A wave of dizziness chases me. "Speaking of signals."

"We lost you, too," Trigger says. "So I called in a favor."

"Let me guess. Mac and half the marine corps."

"Nobody knows the desert the way Mac does, Tana."

I squat down and scour the brush. "Did your military brother happen to mention that we're standing on top of a nuclear missile silo?"

Trigger's face bunches.

My foot knocks against something solid, and I reach down and feel the phone. I dust off the screen and punch the power button. The handset remains dark, so I assume it's dead. "Guess you're still on the need-to-know list," I say to Trigger.

Straightening, I toss the phone to Henry.

The Weatherman's forehead wrinkles as he catches the pass. "There used to be a silo here. But as part of the US-Russian disarmament SALT treaty, the facility was decommissioned."

"How long ago?" Trigger and I ask together, perhaps thinking the same thing.

"When I was a kid. Ten years ago." Henry's brows arch. "Why?"

I say, "Right around the time—"

"Pioneer started offering the future pill." Trigger finishes my thought.

Henry's eyes open wide and bright, like the aurora borealis. "You mean, all this time they were doing the research right under our noses?"

I have to admit, a secret like this wouldn't be easy to keep, especially at a school where students are given the ability to see years into the future.

"Not sure, but we're about to find out." Trigger bends, gathering two small backpacks.

"How?" I say, since my straight-on approach to walk toward the light was deemed a "cover breaker."

"Mac lent us...me...his security clearance." Trigger's last word dangles.

"Awfully nice of him," I say, knowing there's no way something as important as a top-secret day pass came free. "How much?"

"Huh?"

"What does Mac want in exchange for borrowing his classified pass code?"

If crickets live in the desert, the silence right now would allow opportunity to count every last chirp.

Henry averts his eyes from Trigger.

"My commitment to join him and Project Déjà Vu."

I push from the sky surfer's shoulder.

Trigger grabs my hand. "Come on, Tana. This is an opportunity I can't pass up." He brings my palm to his smooth cheek. "You know how much I want to fly fighters."

I meet his stare and allow myself to dive deep into his stargazing eyes and see the youngest pilot to ever break from earth's atmosphere.

"Please," he says. "I need you to understand."

I know what I should say, some sort of go-for-it pep cheer, but I'm not Brooklyn. Besides, I don't want to lie anymore. "Can't," I say.

Trigger's hand drops from mine. His chin falls to his chest. His shoulders roll forward.

Henry's eyes darken. His lips pinch, as if he swallowed a sour pill.

The sky surfer reaches into his pocket and passes the Weatherman a piece of Beemans gum. *Mac's brand. Of course.*

As Henry unfolds the wrapper, a long string of numbers appears.

"Call KC; give her this code." Trigger stares into the darkness. "It's our last shot to find Soraya and Dr. Harb."

Every part of me feels heavy. I'd swear my arms have filled with lead. For a second, I wonder if Trigger made a deal, a promise to Mac in exchange for Dr. Harb's location. I listen for the sound of steel drums and wait to feel the pull of Trigger's tractor beam as confirmation.

Double, with an emphasis on nothing.

Never mind. Nothing is more important to the sky surfer than flying fighter jets.

I will my arms to reach for the key, the sole link to my dad's killer.

"On it." Henry swipes the backup phone from his belt, slings his bag over a shoulder, and forges ahead. Trigger follows without as much as a look in my direction. I force my feet to move, despite the fact that I'd rather be anywhere but here.

As if on autopilot, Henry tracks past where I saw the light flicker. He beelines to an open area between the third and fourth antennas, stops, looks around, and then hustles to the nearest cluster of sagebrush. I watch as he uses a pocketknife to unearth sand and dirt. He digs until he resurrects a bundle of colored wires. He separates the yellow and green cords from the cluster and clips them in half. Using the tip of the blade, he peels back the plastic coating and twists the raw copper cords until they fit into the ports on his sat phone. The green-hued screen lights, and when the cursor prompts a password, Henry drops to a knee and piston pumps an elbow. "Yes."

"We're not in yet," I say and then hear two heavy thuds. A slow motor grinds, chased by a dropping *thump*. Before our eyes, the brown-red earth splits.

CHAPTER 35

Why not? My thoughts rewind to the in-ground turbine engines we discovered beneath the dry lake at Pioneer's airport the last time we were here.

The panels covered in sand glide open.

"Back door." Henry stands, cycles his goggle wipers, and leaps onto the first concrete stair. Trigger and I join him and descend below ground level.

Ten steps down, Henry stops flat-footed. He spins, and all four of his eyes bulge. "Burn can." He points to an unlabeled soup can nailed to the concrete wall.

In my head, a timer ticks down. *Sha-boom* echoes, and fiery flames mushroom before my eyes. My hands fly to my ears.

Trigger lunges forward. "Burn can, as in something that might blow up?" He angles between me and the perceived threat.

A charred soot scent fills my nostrils.

The Weatherman drops his backpack, lowers his center of gravity, and creeps closer. "Someone must have lit a match."

That's what I saw flicker. "Not safe," I say and turn on a heel. "We have to get out of here."

"Henry," Trigger snaps, catches my wrist, and pulls me to his side.

The Weatherman's neck twists over a shoulder. "T." He frowns. "Wait, oh, no, no, no." He pushes his goggles back on his head. He grips the ribbed aluminum can, turns the tin over, and shakes it. Shreds of charred paper drift to the floor. "See, harmless." His eyes bounce between Trigger and me. "I had no idea the cans were real. I'd heard rumors that during wartime, if the silo blast doors were secured, the only way to get word to the surface was to leave a handwritten note in the can." Henry bends and scoops the largest scraps. He stands, and wobbles on one foot, using a bent leg as a table. "Periodically, a guard would come and check, and if a note was found, he'd read it twice, and then burn it so it wouldn't fall into enemy hands." The Weatherman sifts through the clutter, arranging the edges like pieces of a jigsaw puzzle. With the last charred piece in place, Henry squints and reads the message—"They know you're here."

"Soraya," Trigger and I talk over each other. "Warning her father."

Remnants of the smoke, fire, and soot in my head disappear.

Liar, deceiver, manipulator, cheat…too good to be true. The message sinks in, allowing me to read between the lines. "Dr. Harb never left Pioneer."

At once, everything around me spins like a funnel cloud.

The sky surfer releases my hand and air boxes. "We're going to get him this time. Get justice for your dad." He thrusts a fist in the air.

Henry hops, bouncing like he's walking on the moon.

I stand still.

"Don't be afraid, T." Henry bounds to my side. "We're with you all the way."

"Scared?" I swallow and touch my neck scars. *What could be more thrilling than confronting the man who killed my father?* The wishy-washy haze of disbelief drains away and is replaced by a surge of adrenaline. What feels like sparks ignites my thighs. "Let's go get a killer."

We fly down the next forty-five steps, three stories if Henry's memory serves, and at the bottom, are faced with a set of eight-foot-thick reinforced concrete doors.

"Options?" Trigger says while rummaging through his pack.

"Only one." Henry trades his eye wipers for night-vision goggles. He attaches an alligator clip to his Pioneer ear piercing and signals to me, and I rush right over. My pulse rivets.

He clamps the opposite end of the curly copper-wire clip to the security upgrade he gave me earlier. A warm tingle burns around my helix, and I see Henry's receiver glow. Instead of student blue, though, the halo is security red. A sea of conversation floods my ears.

A few voices I recognize; others are unfamiliar. I close my eyes as they go on about formulas and number calculations. After a minute or so, the scientific chatter fades, almost as if I'd entered into a private chat room.

The subject matter shifts, sounding more like pilots ticking items off a checklist. The stern voices call out a series of numbers—four sets of eight, repeated in sequence.

What I wouldn't give to have my visual back.

Through a slit eye, I spy a red, lighted box projecting from Henry's goggles. Inside the colored rectangle, the entire series of numbers I just heard on security's stream appears.

"The combination." Henry sidesteps right and wraps his hand around a steel beam, careful to keep steady, so the access code shines on the blast doors. Between a gap in the rail, I notice a keypad. Henry wastes no time typing in all thirty-two numbers. "Boom," he says and plugs fingers into his ears.

But instead of an explosion, the door rotors grind. A thrust of air hisses. Latches unwind. With a light tap of Trigger's finger, the doors—built strong enough to withstand a three-ton nuclear blast—creak open like a screen door.

We rush through, only to find a fork in the corridor.

"Which way?" I say.

Does the access tunnel to the right lead to Soraya and Dr. Harb? Or are they hiding at the end of the cableway on the left?

My mental coin spins end over end. Heads—go right. Tails—go left.

"Right," Henry says.

Even though my imaginary coin still tumbles, I opt to follow, since, so far, the Weatherman's instincts have been on target.

Trigger tightens his pack straps and kicks behind Henry. "Let's go."

As I spin to join my tribe, the virtual coin flattens.

Tails. Left.

My coin must be on the fritz. Since we're more than thirty feet underground. Well past the limits of any compass calibration, internal or otherwise. Right?

A sharp pain pings my side.

Reluctantly, I rejoin the leaders.

Barreling forward like a trio of guided missiles locked on target, we pass through a series of oval portals and whiz by pipe-sized ducts and bundles of thick hanging wires that make my computer power cord look like a skinny string of thread.

The ceiling is getting lower. Residual static electricity from the wires lifts my bangs on end. Long spaghetti cable loops to my shoulders, making me wish I'd brought a hard hat. Angling my chin up, I see a strange blue-green glow through the portal ahead.

Trigger's thighs pump faster. He passes Henry and takes the lead. He leaps through a hatch, legs split and arms stretched overhead. His boots have barely hit ground when his body stiffens like a board. Henry plows into his back. I slide and join the pileup.

Trigger digs his heels into the slick metal surface, but the momentum of our combined weight is more than he can handle. We cannon toward the edge of a narrow catwalk, scratching, clawing, and reaching for anything to stop us from tumbling over the rapidly approaching ledge.

Trigger hits the guardrail first. The force of the impact goes straight through Henry. The jolt knocks me on my back. My friends flip over the barrier and dangle by fingertips.

The slick fabric of my dress glides like rails on a snow sled. I crash against the steel wall, pop back onto my feet, and scramble toward my friends. Bending over the safety rail, I hook my thumbs through their belt loops, pretending not to notice the fact that I'm hanging headfirst in a missile launch tube. The silo goes topsy-turvy.

Find an anchor, Lyre. I blink away the blur. My eyes dart around for something stable and connect with Trigger's steady ocean blues.

"You've got this," Trigger says.

The bobbing compass in my head rights itself. My vision clears.

I ball my biceps.

I grunt and teeter back on my heels, squat, and sit on the ground in order to lever them back to safety. Henry flips over to my side of the rail. Trigger follows. We all collapse against the perforated floor.

"Nice save," the sky surfer says. His chest heaves like he's just finished drill.

Henry sits up for a second and then flattens. "Remind me never to complain about T being explosive."

I roll over, climb to my feet, and glance over the ledge. I see the seven-story drop surrounding the 9-megaton warhead. I stumble backward, dizzy, spots speckling my view. *Will I ever get past all my fears?*

"Easy." Trigger rushes over and steadies my shoulders.

I nod, seeing three of him.

"No worries, T, every superhero has a weakness."

The sky surfer swipes bangs from my eyes and tucks the loose strands behind my ear. The distant clang of steel drums echoes. Any anger Trigger held seems to have melted away.

"Only one?" I say and grin.

Although I'm still crushed by his decision to leave with Mac, no one makes me smile as easily as Trigger. *Not even Tuck.*

Trigger says, "It was an impossible choice, Tana."

"You mean fighters or Brooklyn?"

"No, T." His ocean blues widen. His fingers drape around my neck, and his thumb glides over my collarbone scar. He lifts my chin. "Fighters or—"

"McDunney, twelve o'clock!" Henry scurries to his feet and collects our bags. "Three levels down, adjacent to the diesel generator."

"Get them!" The chief's voice rumbles off the walls of the launch duct. Trigger heaves me upright.

Henry flies by, running back the way we came. "Should have gone left."

Single file, we hop through the portals, weave under the cables, and bounce off the reinforced walls, never pausing to check who might be on our heels. We retrace our steps until we are back at the base of the service stairs.

"Straight ahead," Trigger yells, and I remember the results of my coin toss.

Tails. Left. Why didn't I trust my gut?

Edging past the service elevator, I hear a motor grind, and then a chime and guess McDunney and his crew's elevator is about to arrive.

"They're right behind us," I pant and pump my arms faster, falling in rhythm with Trigger's quick steps. Henry unloads his pack, allowing him to move faster.

Nearly at the end of the cableway, the overhead signs indicate we're almost at the control center.

A few more steps.

My heart pounds, beating from not only being chased, but also from being inches from Dad's killer.

At the entrance, we slow and line up shoulder to shoulder, blocking the doorway the same way the marines stood when we arrived last night. On the verge of crossing the threshold, I break formation, desperate to be the first to confront Dr. Harb.

I could never have expected what I saw next.

CHAPTER 36

As if I crossed the time-space continuum, the contents of the room transport me back—seafoam-green paint, suitcase-sized computer monitors, and floor-to-ceiling processors that remind me of war-game computers I've seen in the movies.

I scan the room and see disconnected servers sandwiched in the corner and workbenches in the middle and beakers, test tubes, and high-powered microscopes matching the ones in Henry's old lab.

At the far end, a man of Dr. Harb's stature hovers over a crate of test tubes, his back to me and his face covered in green plastic goggles.

There you are.

I sprint with what feels like a stiff wind at my back. I breeze by the two marines standing at the launch desks.

"Tana, no!" Trigger says.

Too late. I've already snapped away the elastic goggle band. The protective eyewear flips from the top of the man's head, and when he whirls around, I see a gaunt face, sullen eyes, and stringy black hair. Professor Gu's scolding expression sends me stumbling backward.

"Dad," Henry says, his words like a mouse squeak.

The bowtie around Dr. Gu's neck twists. His jowls flutter, and his lips purse. "What are you doing here?" He looks through me as if I'm invisible. "You weren't the swiftest genius in our group, but goodness, Hen Li, can't you take a hint?"

"Hint? What do you mean, Dad?" Henry drags his feet toward his father.

"What's wrong with you?" Professor Gu asks in the same way he might quiz in a group lecture. "I abandoned you."

"I know. You left me. Your only son. To be humiliated. Beaten. Tortured." He trembles. "Why did you leave me, Dad?"

"You're an embarrassment, a disgrace, a mutation in an otherwise pristine gene pool. All the gifts you were given and the only thing you ever wanted to do was toy with codes and stupid thunderheads." Gu waves a scolding finger. If that wasn't enough, he says, "I no longer have a son. Get out of here. I never want to see your sorry face again."

Henry shrinks. His legs collapse, and he drops on the diamond plate floor. Dry heaving, he somehow climbs to his feet and trips through the portal door.

Trigger wars forward, head down and fists clenched, charging like a battle tank. He swings at Henry's dad, landing one punch after another on Professor Gu's soft midsection.

The two marines leave their station and yank Trigger from the scientist, who's now balled on the floor. They pin the fighting Flough's hands behind his back and restrain him for a second before Trigger spears both men with sharp elbows. The guards recoil, and the sky surfer wiggles free and sprints back to Professor Gu, I'd guess, to finish what he started.

"That's enough!" a commanding voice thunders.

The mere sound of the sergeant's tone stops Trigger midstride.

Mac steps from the doorway, crosses the room, and places himself in front of Professor Gu. "No denying, he's a douche." He rests sledgehammer-sized hands on Trigger's shoulders. "But we need him. Focus on the bigger picture. You're part of this mission now, little bro."

With a flushed face, Trigger's chin quivers.

Mac says, "I'm your commanding officer."

"You are no such thing," I screech, wedge in between them, and knock Trigger free from Mac's grip. Sergeant Numereau backs away way too easily, and I know something's wrong.

Spinning, I grab two handfuls of Trigger's shirt.

"It's OK, Tana." His hands cover mine. I squeeze tighter, knowing I don't want to hear what he's going to say next. "Mac is right. I gave my word." Our eyes meet. "Fighters or you, Tana, that's what I was trying to say before."

His Adam's apple drops, and he pulls me to his chest. He holds me so tight that for a second, I can't tell where I end and he begins. I feel like I'm floating—wings spread, soaring, slicing, looping like a happy-go-lucky flitter bug. I hear his heart thump—confident and strong, making me believe every word he has said is genuine.

I push my cheek from his T-shirt to see a familiar look—flashes of joy, fear, and uncertainty rolled into one expression, explaining the sky surfer's up-and-down behavior. KC was right. Trigger is afraid.

And leaving.

Breaking our grip, I start for the door and dab my damp eyes with my sleeve, sure of one thing. Although Trigger and I were destined to meet, we aren't meant to be together. I didn't know how much I wished we might be until now.

A heartbreak I've felt only one other time tugs at every inch of my chest. I touch my forehead, cheek, collarbone, and neck. I finger the shrapnel scars. *Maybe someday I'll get over both of them.*

Divert and avoid. My defenses rise. "We have to find Henry," I say to Trigger over my shoulder. "I can't lose anyone else I care about."

I march around the corner of the last seafoam-colored desk and consider where I would go if I were Henry. As I weigh possible options, my boot smacks something stiff. My ankle rolls, and I fall to all fours. With my cheek inches from the ground, I notice something I might have otherwise missed. A single black-patent flat abandoned beneath the guard desk. Tilting on my heels, I stand, spin in a circle, and shout, "Where are you, Soraya?"

CHAPTER 37

I check behind the whopper computer servers and under the control center desks. I inspect every crease and crevice large enough to conceal my ex-friend. Tromping to the far corner of the room, I brush past Trigger and Mac and shove Professor Gu aside.

"Here I am," I hear a songbird whimper, and Soraya appears from behind a glass freezer.

"No, Sora." I see a drumstick forearm reach from the cooler filled with green-glowing syringes.

"It's OK, Dad." His daughter lures him from his protective shelter. "You're innocent," she says. "As you explained, it's all just a horrible misunderstanding."

When Dr. Harb emerges, I notice specks of gray in his hair. "Oh, Sora." He wraps his arms around her sagging shoulders. "Dear, sweet Sora."

"What is this?" Mac barks at Trigger.

"Tana thinks Dr. Harb murdered her father."

"I don't think, I know," I say and rise on the tips of my toes.

"How?" Numereau asks. "If you're so certain he's guilty, show me the proof."

"It's complicated," Trigger says. "Tana's dad was beating BioDynamics in mediation. A lawsuit, if lost, would have bankrupted the pharma company. So they asked their chief of security—Dr. Harb—to fix the problem."

"Fix it how?"

"By blowing up Mr. Lyre's airplane." Trigger grimaces. "Allegedly."

Mac chuckles and then snaps his gum. He layers his arms and assumes the Numereau-commando stance. "Quite a story, but Dr. Harb is a scientist. How in the world would he know how to build a bomb, never mind get his hands on explosives?"

"He was a bomb builder." I squeeze every muscle in my body. "In Lebanon. A soldier in a special government unit."

Mac's eyes slant to Dr. Harb and size him up. Based on what I know about Sergeant Numereau, I'd guess he's considering if it's typical for a scientist to be six foot five and as thick and muscular as the marines in Numereau's unit. His jaw tightens, and he cracks his gum. "Innocent until proven guilty, right? Do you have any proof?" He looks at me, but Trigger answers.

"Tana found her earring in Soraya's jewelry box. A match to one she lost the morning her dad died on the flight ramp."

"That's all?" Mac shifts his weight and moves his hands behind his back.

"You know how these things are. All the physical evidence gets blown to bits in the blast. It's nearly impossible to prove—"

"I have proof," I interrupt, remembering the last thing KC said on the phone.

Every head in the room jerks around.

"You do?" Trigger says.

"Lend me your phone." I unhook the sat phone strapped to his belt and scroll through the e-mail list until I come to KC's note marked "URGENT." I highlight the contents and hand the cell to Trigger. He reads the message aloud, "'Confidential—Intended only for CAH.'" He translates. "Chief Abraham Harb." He glances at Soraya and her father and then reads on, "'Your future is in jeopardy. The legal tide has turned. Initiate Plan B. If we lose, no funds will be left for your research. We're confident you'll do the right thing. Time is of the essence. Wait until after his daughter's birthday.' Signed: CAK."

Bug-eyed, jaw hanging, Trigger passes the handset to Sergeant Numereau. Mac's cheek twitches while he reviews the content on the screen. He storms over to Harb and eyeballs the former chief of security turned PHD. He makes a guttural sound from pressed lips and then speaks. "Had you figured for a coward, the way you abandoned your family and burrowed underground. But a hit man?" Mac grinds his molars. "Didn't see that one coming."

We've got him, Dad. I shut my eyes and wonder if I'm dreaming. I hope that when I open my lids, what I just heard will still be real. And when I do, I see exactly what I remembered: Sergeant Numereau opposite Dr. Harb, readying to give the order to take him into custody.

Heat burns in my chest. The pain I've buried surfaces. *Justice.* My eyes flood. *Finally, justice.*

Through blurred vision, I notice Mac's fingers flex. His neck cords throb. "Take him," he orders the two marines on guard. He buries a stiff finger in Harb's broad chest. "What a waste." He *tsks.* "A man gifted with a scientific mind, but who lacks the fundamental understanding of honor and integrity."

"Thank you," I mouth and breathe a massive sigh of relief. Tingling, I watch as the marines slap handcuffs on Harb's wrists.

Silent to the extent I'd almost forgotten she's in the room, Soraya steps away. Her skin is as white as a mourning dove. Her perfect nostrils flare. Her body weight shifts from side to side, and then she launches forward.

"You said this was all a misunderstanding," Soraya pounds her fists against her father's back. "That you had no idea who planted the bomb or ignited the trigger. Said management gave you no options. You had to cover up the evidence or they would ship us back to Lebanon."

"Sora, darling, please, everything I did was for you, your mother, our family. So you would have a different life than mine." Dr. Harb weeps as his daughter delivers body blows.

"Don't want to hear any more of your stories, Dad. I'm not your naïve little girl anymore. You killed a man." Her eyes flick to me. "Not just a man, Tana's father."

"Aaaaaaah." Dr. Harb drives his head toward Soraya like an angry bull, the best he can do with both hands secured behind his back.

She swerves from his reach, swats him away like an insignificant fly, and collapses to the floor.

"Get him out of here," Mac barks, and the marines drag their prisoner toward the portal. They're nearly through the oval doorway when Chief McDunney and the remainder of Pioneer's security force crowd the causeway.

The chief shoves the soldiers, widens his stance, and layers his arms. "The only place Harb's going is with me."

CHAPTER 38

Mac strides forward. "Harb committed murder. No one, not even someone as important as the doctor, is above our moral code. My mission, my rules. And if I were you"—he eyes the red-faced marines— "I wouldn't touch my men again."

McDunney doesn't budge. Instead he grins. His men huddle around him and solidify their position. The chief taps his ear receiver, and the red halo burns. "The marines have Harb in custody," McDunney says, staring straight ahead as if talking to himself. "Numereau is here, sir. He gave the order."

Before I have a chance to swallow the wad hardening in my throat, the sat phone attached to Mac's belt chirps. He unholsters the cell and listens.

"Yes, sir." His voice lowers. He clips the phone to his belt and works his gum. He winces.

Trigger storms to his blood brother. "Mac, hold up. You can't. What about our code? She has proof; you saw it with your own eyes."

Mac frowns, and he rests a hand on his brother's shoulder. "This is going to be hard to understand, but sometimes in pursuit of the greater good, there are casualties."

"Seriously?" Trigger knocks Mac's arm away. "You're going to give me the sacrifice-a-few-for-the-masses speech?"

"It's the vow we took when we committed to the corps."

"So you've said." Trigger nods as if he agrees, but I know different. "News flash—Tana's dad wasn't a marine and made no such promise. He was a civilian. You know, the people we vowed to protect."

"Benjamin Lyre wasn't so innocent," Dr. Harb grumbles.

I notice McDunney grin.

Oh, no, no.

"Mac, please don't—"

"Release him," Numereau says, and the soldiers unbind Harb's writs.

I squeeze my temples. I see the limp wind sock and the yellow butterfly loop. I trip. I look up to Dad standing across the ramp. He smiles, waves. Stretched seconds of a timer tick. Dad scans around. Does he hear it too? His grin fades. He glances at his chunky dive watch. He gazes into the sky, and when he reconnects with me, he touches his heart and blows a kiss. Flames explode. Smoke engulfs his image.

My scars pulse. I squeeze my skull. *He knew. He said good-bye.*

"Murderer!" I shout and charge toward Dr. Harb. "I won't let you get away. Not again." But before I reach the door, the two marine mountains block my path.

Dr. Harb says, "I'm afraid he loved something more than you."

"Shut up!" The forever-simmering volcano inside me erupts. "Liar." I thrust against the marines and reach beyond their shoulders.

They restrain my hands. "You know nothing about my father."

"Mac," Trigger says, "if you go along with this, then you're just as guilty as them."

Numereau sucks a short breath; his muscular shoulders sag. "It's out of my hands."

"Then my answer is no." The sky surfer stiffens. "I can't trust you. I'm not joining this messed-up program."

"Trigger, wait." Mac's voice softens. "Harb will never be out of my sight. I give you my word." Mac's eyes slide to Dr. Harb, and his jaw grinds. "He's integral to the mission." Numereau moves and cups a hand around Trigger's neck. "A world without war, remember? We need him. Can't afford for such an important asset to rot, useless, in prison."

Trigger swings like a home run hitter, sending the beakers and test tubes on the lab table crashing on the floor.

"Guarded, 24/7," Mac says. "Locked in a lab. He'll never be a free man again."

"Not good enough." A glassy film covers Trigger's ocean blues. He rips away from his adoptive brother, strides over, and takes my arm. "Let's go, T," he says, staring at the marines guarding the door. The soldiers hold steady, solid as steel blast doors.

"Let them by," Mac mumbles. The marines break formation, and we shove past Chief McDunney, Number One, Number Two, and then come face-to-face with Dr. Harb.

Nausea shoots up my throat. I turn away, determined to avoid Harb's smug expression.

Trigger nudges me forward, and as I pass, the man who murdered my father leans into my ear. "Ask your mother or Gunner Clark. You and Soraya have more in common than you think."

I shake my fingers free and clench my fists.

"Tana, no." Trigger's thick forearm wraps around my waist. He lifts me in the air and spins a half circle, his back to Dr. Harb.

As I flail, Trigger carries me, my feet bicycling above the ground. "Another time." He grabs my chin. "Look at me." He squeezes my cheeks, and I drag my attention from Dad's murderer. "What about Henry?"

Henry. My stomach cinches replaying the horrible words a kid should never hear from a parent, and I wonder which is worse—a father who is dead or one who's alive and renounces your existence? "I know it's hard." I focus on his sky blues and hear the reggae riff. "But I'm sure Henry's pain far exceeds your need for vengeance."

Calmness settles over me, the kind of still that comes before a thunderstorm hits.

Don't worry…about a thing…

"I'm OK," I breathe.

The sky surfer's forehead wrinkles.

"Really." I nod. "Henry needs us. Harb will be…" I cringe and choke down the venom that's scaling my throat. "He'll be locked away. Mac promised. Guarded by hundreds of marines," I say, not believing a word of it.

"Don't worry." Trigger matches his mouth to my ear. "We'll find another way."

I doubt it. I turn away and rush down the metal corridor.

Back at the crossroads, where we made a wrong turn, I jog to the stairs and stomp every ounce of anger through the soles of my feet.

I climb the final tier, cross the landing, and slap the burn can with an open hand. I smash the red door-release button, and when the steel ceiling splits, I scale the last four steps. Trigger trails.

Up top, dark skies linger—no moon or stars to light a path. The sky surfer beelines for the ship-shaped rocks, disappears, and then returns on foot. "The jeep's gone," he says, shaking his head.

Great. We're stranded. I feel my heart clench. *Cowboy up, Lyre. Enough of this gloom-and-doom attitude.*

Spinning in a semicircle, I scan around until my internal compass centers. I feel a ping in my side, stop, and point to the ship-shaped rock. "There." I take off to where I left the dirt bike.

"Awesome," Trigger hollers after me.

I arrive at the mesa to see yet another kink in our game plan. "Slashed tires," I say and notice a pair of wiper goggles lying next to the dirt bike's deflated inner tubes.

Trigger shrugs. "Guess Henry didn't want to be followed."

"Now what?"

"We could run," he says.

"Ten miles?" I touch my dress.

"Is it really that far?"

I picture the dirt bike's odometer. Five miles back to the bunks and five more to Pioneer's campus. "Half that to the marine camp, and if we're not on Mac's hit list, maybe we can borrow a set of wheels when we get there."

Trigger eyes my boots. "Ready?"

I answer with a nod.

After a couple of jogging steps, we both kick into a full-blown sprint. Ranging through the darkness, I do my best to keep up with Trigger's lightning pace.

From behind the mesa, two headlights arc like shooting stars across a black canvas. A motor rattles. A green jeep appears and lands, front wheels first, and when the rear axle touches, it squats and skids across the sand. Brakes squeal, and the four-wheeler stops inches from Trigger.

"Soraya?"

"Get in!" she shouts and gooses the accelerator. "I know where to find Henry."

CHAPTER 39

Being desperate can make crazy circumstances seem acceptable. Take the fact that Trigger and I accept a ride from the one person we know we can't trust—a girl who deceived us not once but twice, *three* times if you throw in the trap we're likely walking into right now.

"Do you really think she knows where Henry is?" I whisper to Trigger.

He turns both palms up. Knowing better than to ask the queen of manipulation, I decide to go for a topic far less controversial. Like how did she get topside so fast? Her answer—she rode the service elevator.

As we haul along the road leading back to Pioneer's campus, I study the soft lines of Soraya's serious expression and try to figure out how she has any idea where Henry went. I lean toward Trigger. "After all Henry's been through, do you really think he'd go back to campus?"

"Not sure." Trigger rubs his temples.

"You OK?" I move his hand from raw skin.

"Yeah, sure, my head's pounding." He squeezes his skull, blinks, and lets go. "Been under a little pressure lately."

Fast jets, impossibly precise maneuvers, engine off landings, Trigger is accustomed to teetering on the edge of life and death. *A headache? From stress? Unlikely.*

"Where else does he have to go?" Soraya says from the driver's seat and takes the steep road that climbs the sweet-potato-rock-pie mountain. She eyes me in the rearview mirror and then looks away.

"Perhaps the marine camp, the bunks," I say.

"New place and unfamiliar," Soraya replies. "Henry's a scientist first."

"But the music pavilion? There's nothing scientific there."

"Not at the concert venue, per se." Trigger scratches his head. "But the stage is wedged between two massive mesas. The plateau on the farthest wall stretches for miles. The western tip extending out to—"

"The airport," I finish his sentence. "The lookout spot where he took you to see the weather drones."

"His outdoor laboratory," Soraya says.

"A scientist's sanctuary. A place where no authority would look for him." As the jeep climbs the final switchback, I realize that, once again, my nemesis and I are impossibly of the same mind-set. I hear Dr. Harb's cryptic words in playback mode. "You two are more alike than you are different." I shudder and convince myself his words are just another manifestation of a babbling psychopath.

Motoring forward, Soraya pulls into backstage parking.

Trigger hops out. "He left some of his equipment up on the shelf while we were tracking during the concert. If we're lucky, Henry is still here collecting his antenna boosters."

Soraya touches a finger to her nose. "Let's go."

She kills the engine and climbs from her seat. Trigger and I leap out and jog to the restricted door. With a swipe of Soraya's unlimited-access key, the locks disengage and the gate swings open.

We burst through the stage door, scale a flight of stairs, and then barge onto the left side of the empty stage. Any remnants of the band are gone. Instruments and amplifiers are broken down and packed away by the road crew. Most noteworthy to me, however, is the absence of Tuck.

I swallow, realizing how much I would have liked to see him again. *Missed opportunity*, I think and then stare at Trigger.

Out in the stadium, clusters of students lounge, talking, laughing, while sprawled across the bench seats. I scan the cliques, hopeful one may have taken pity and included Henry. *Doubtful.*

"Ouuuuuch!" a pained shriek echoes against the stone venue, and I search the stands for the source of the shrill. At the far end of the front row, I see four students in tailored suits kicking at something curled on the ground.

"Henry!" I yell.

Trigger launches from the stage and tackles the closest chalk-striped jacket. Through the gap, I get a glimpse of the Weatherman. The Streeters found Henry. And from his lack of movement, I guess he's been beaten to a pulp.

"Help him!" I shout to the crowd. My words fall on deaf ears.

I run to help Trigger and notice the Wall Street circle has doubled in size. *Eight suits?* I count again.

Even if—and it's a big if—Soraya joins, the three of us are no match for two rings of the fit, determined future stock traders. Then, as if lightning ignites my brain, something KC said back in Tulsa sparks my cerebral cortex.

Outnumbered, but not outgunned. A tidbit of little-known information is often more useful than mounds of muscle mass.

"Microphone," I yell to Soraya, who is hovering near the soundboard. She unfastens a mic from the stand, swings her arm like a softball pitcher, tosses the mic, and then flips on the amplifier power switch.

Once metal hits my palm, I clear my throat. *Strong is better than loud.*

"Attention," I say, fighting to hold my voice steady. When the cliques continue to chat, I slap the metal mesh against my palm.

Perhaps just a little bit of loud is in order.

A blood-curdling screech cracks over the monster speakers. The students cover their ears.

"Now that I have your attention, there is something you all should know." The residual murmuring lingers for a minute and then quiets. Quizzical expressions focus in my direction.

That is, everyone except the Streeters is looking at me.

Holding their circle tight, the members alternate between foot thrusts and punching bag blows. The two suits restraining Trigger hunker down, making certain he can't break free. The lump I know is Henry lies limp, wedged between four sets of spit-shined rock crushers.

Hit them with the facts, Tana. KC's voice resonates loud and clear. *The truth always prevails.*

After sucking in a deep breath, I report the dirt our hacker dug up on the deep net. Ugly details, meant to be kept secret.

"Clayton Wilshire," I say, as if I'm reporting the weather. "Father found guilty of engaging in a Ponzi scheme, sentenced to twenty years in a white-collar correctional facility." A tall, polished, clean-shaven kid I assume is Clayton lifts his head and glares at me.

A quiet rumble comes from the student body.

"Maxwell Fitzpatrick," I continue, and the stocky redhead to Clayton's left snaps around, a desperate expression covers his freckled skin. "Father guilty of fraud and embezzlement. Fled the country. Last official sighting in the Cayman Islands." Maxwell's eyes glass; he appears to be about to bawl.

The tallest member of the financial clique shoves Maxwell aside and lifts his knee to his waist. A pile-driver stomp hovers over Henry's midsection. "Dare you." He mouths and shoots eye daggers.

I squeeze my rib cage and hold my stomach muscles tight. *It's the only way, Lyre.* I inhale and announce the final name and the facts KC discovered. My upper lip quivers.

"Michael J. Thorton III," I speak, like Kase's digital computer reader. "Father serving a life sentence in a northeastern supermax prison. Killed his wife for life insurance money. Convicted of trading fraud and murder."

What starts as a single howl from the crowd escalates into a chorus of boos. The Future of Wall Street scrambles, appearing to look for some fellow student sympathizers.

Give them a cause to rally around, Tana. KC had coached via sat phone. *Then the scales will tilt in your favor.*

What's the highest priority to a Pioneer student? I think on my feet, knowing at any second I'll lose the mob's attention. *Being better than the best.* In an instant, I know exactly what to say.

"You are the top young minds in the country." I stare at the stands without blinking. "And this is who you choose to be your leaders?" I point at the faltering Streeter circle. "Bullies. Scared little boys in tailored suits with daddy issues?"

Allowing my line of sight to survey the crowd, I notice just about every jaw drop.

Bull's-eye.

"To the future leaders of our great nation, I propose this question: Are you willing to stand idle and let this small group beat on the weak so they can feel powerful? Tarnish Pioneer's world-class reputation?" I take two short breaths. "Because if I had to judge at this moment, I'd say I've seen more integrity at my local public high school."

Almost as if a dam broke, the social floodgates let go, and waves of Pioneer students rush over the wooden benches. Cliques flow together— techies, nerds, gamers—all for one common cause: protection of Pioneer's superior legacy, their credibility not to be tainted by a rogue clique of thug-raised criminals. The raging current tears the Streeters jackets from their backs and drags them from the stadium by their Windsor-knotted neckties.

As quickly as it flowed, the student wave recedes, and with the pavilion empty, I spot my friends. Trigger helps Henry to his feet. The Weatherman is doubled over, holding his waist, a painful wince following each limping step. From where I stand, it appears Trigger fared a hair better—bloody lips, puffy cheeks, and a forehead marked by bright-red knuckle prints.

In an attempt to free my hands, I turn, expecting to throw the mic back to Soraya. Instead, I stand face-to-face with Tuck.

"You're still here," I say.

Tuck removes his hat. His boots click closer until his pointy snakeskin tips touch my steeled toes. He swallows, lowers his gray-green eyes, and says, "You are so brave."

"Me?" I laugh. "Brave?" I shake my head. "You don't know me very well."

The vintage country star blows out, fiddles with his hat brim, and rubs his fingers over chin stubble. "I know you're afraid at times. I've noticed the way you touch your neck when you're anxious or shake your bangs over your eyes when you're trying to hide. But when a friend was in trouble, you stepped up, in front of all these people, and had the guts to say what we've all been thinking."

He gets me. Finally, someone understands who I am.

Tuck grabs my trembling hand and layers it over his thumping chest. "Ever feel like you're waiting for something?" His gaze locks on mine. "But have no idea what for?"

I suspect he wants an answer, but all I can do is stare.

"I reckon I've found it." He squeezes my palm. "And now you see"—he looks off into the stadium seats, and then his gaze returns to mine—"I can't help but feel a little anxious. Troubled that I might never see you again." He lifts my hand to his lips and kisses my wrist. "When can I see you again, Tana?"

Anytime, all the time, is what I'm about to say when Trigger shouts, "Incoming!"

CHAPTER 40

I hear security chatter over my receiver. McDunney and the marines are about to storm the stadium. From the tone of the transmission, I realize they aren't coming for an after party.

"National School in Tulsa." I hold Tuck's eyes for one more second. "That's where you'll find me. I have to get out of here."

Tuck's grin stretches as if he's won a Grammy. He slides on his Stetson, winks, swipes the mic from Soraya, and skids to center stage. "Hey, anyone from Pioneer still around?" He whistles over the loudspeaker. "I have at least one more encore left in the tank."

In less time than it takes for me to turn a heel, Tuck hums and begins to sing acappella, a slow, sultry ballad—one that is meant to be danced slow and close.

Like an infantry storming the enemy, the tidal wave of students rushes back into the vacant seats. Tuck hums on, and although he's focused on his fans, deep inside, I know the song is for me.

From the top of the mesa, lines of marines file down the steps toward the stage.

"This way," Soraya signals.

With Henry and Trigger now at my side, I hesitate and turn to my friends. Averting my eyes from the cuts, bruises, and blood, I say, "Are you sure we should follow her?"

McDunney and his men approach from opposite sides of the stage.

"What choice do we have?" Trigger and Henry hobble away, and after one long look at Tuck, I run after them.

Aware that Soraya is destined to be a corporate risk officer, when she knocks twice on a hollow boulder, I'm also certain she'd make a great spy. The faux rock slides to the side, and a man in a skull-covered bandana leans out, checks either direction, and then ushers the four of us into a hidden corridor.

"Crowd control," one of Tuck's roadies explains. "If security is ever overwhelmed by fans, the band can escape through here." He leads us to a loading dock filled with black instrument cases that are about to be moved to the tour bus. "Before he headed back onstage, Tuck mentioned you might need some help, so I arranged to have four amp cases emptied."

Two bearded crew members unlatch the cases and wave us over. "In here," bandana man says. "I'm not sure what kind of trouble you're in, but I just got word the uniforms are about here."

We hop into the cases, and I hear the latches click as my box tilts on edge. After a short scrape against what sounds like metal, the case tips farther, and I guess I'm being wheeled on a dolly. Jostling against the foam interior, it's safe to assume my roadie is jogging. I hear a loud thud and a hiss, and what sounds like a door motors open.

After tumbling end over end, the case rests flat. Three haphazard thuds follow, and another motor grinds. I figure the door has shut.

"You, over there." The voice is McDunney's Number One, without a doubt. The rest of his security detail is talking nonstop over my ear receiver. "White male, road crew, appears to be loading musical equipment."

"Yes, you," McDunney shouts outside. "Have you seen four teens come through here?"

According to the security stream, Tuck's man answers, "My job is to break down and load instruments in the bottom of the bus. Not missing persons."

Number One must have believed him because the next words I hear are "Spread out."

The sounds of shuffling boots fade away. Then the security stream goes idle.

The band's tour bus motor turns over, gears shift, and the wheels begin to roll.

Where are we going?

It doesn't take long to figure our only option.

The airport. Get the plane, and fly the heck away from here.

CHAPTER 41

In any other circumstance, I might be freaked. But after surviving burial by mud, being locked in a plush instrument case feels like I'm riding in first class. That is, if the case is ventilated. I suck a deep breath and spider my fingers along the edges searching for anything that feels like fresh air. Lying flat in the dark, I sense the surrounding padding growing like a wet sponge, feeling less like plush accommodations and more like a coffin.

Stay calm. I suck in and force myself to hold the inhaled air for three seconds. *Just a little longer,* I tell myself, despite the fact I've lost track of how long we've been driving.

The bus jerks to the right, and my case tumbles. The latches must have hit the wall, because when the bus straightens, the locks jar open. I lift the lid and sit upright while sucking a big gulp of diesel exhaust. I cough, climb out, and open the remaining cases. Trigger, Henry, and Soraya rise, and when the bus jerks to a stop, we all huddle away from the door.

"Where are we?" Henry asks, his blue-purple lips swollen as thick as dirt bike tires.

"The airport," I say, as if I have some sort of pill-induced premonition. Truth is, it's the chatter over the security stream that gives up our location.

The pneumatic shocks spit pressure, and the luggage door beneath the bus levers open. We find ourselves parked right in front of the dilapidated hangar. Trigger's out first. He makes for the hangar door and hits the open button.

"They're already here." Soraya points to the rope of lights slithering around the airport's access road. She traces the caravan of approaching Humvees. "The chief will have the area surrounded before you have a chance to get off the ground."

"We need a distraction," Henry says and wipes the blood and snot from his crooked nose. He limps to the opened hangar, moving past the cloaked airplane and behind a divider. When he appears again, he's pushing a rusty dirt bike. He lumbers to the tarmac and checks the tank for gas. He faces Soraya. "There are two bikes."

Wait! No! I want to scream, but I realize Soraya is nodding as if she knows what he has in mind.

"We'll cut across the field," Henry says, "head back toward camp, and create a diversion."

I've barely processed his words when Soraya disappears behind the divider. In a blink, she returns with a second two-wheeled beater. She pauses next to Henry and lifts a leg over the torn seat.

"Hold on." Trigger grabs her handlebars.

"Henry and I will provide the distraction. Soraya, you help Tana get in the air."

"What?" I say.

"You've got this, T," Trigger assures me. "Remember, you just aced your private license test."

I swallow, glance over my shoulder, and see the field covered with motorized fireflies. "You don't have to go with Mac, Trigger. Please, come back home with me."

"OK." The sky surfer tugs on his shirt collar.

"OK?" I repeat, thinking I must have misunderstood.

"Mac lied, Tana. I can't go with someone I don't trust."

"Even if it means giving up fighters?"

"I'll become a fighter pilot, like my dad and his father before him." His chest swells. "It's just going to take a little longer."

"McDunney's nearly here," Soraya says.

"Sora"—Trigger holds the handlebars as she climbs off the bike and then wheels next to Henry—"take the jeep behind the hangar. Meet them halfway and stall."

Soraya smiles as if she knows exactly what to do. "Pretend I've gained your confidence, know the escape plan, and have come to turn you in."

Henry, Trigger, and I exchange frozen glances. If she wanted to, Soraya could do the very thing she just suggested.

"Exactly," Trigger says, his expression looking the way I feel—unsure if Soraya is friend or foe.

"It's the least I can do." Soraya shuffles her patent flats.

Trigger says, "Before you go, help us pull the plane to the ramp."

"Plane?" Sora's emerald eyes search what appears to be a vacant hangar floor.

Henry angles both bikes against the door track, hobbles around an imaginary wing, and hunkers down as if he's about to push something heavy. I stand perpendicular to him and latch onto an invisible propeller.

"On three." Trigger joins me.

Soraya widens to clear the other disguised wing.

"Three." Trigger opts for the quick count, and we heave as our friends push. After rocking back and forth a few times, the plane inches forward. I envision what KC might see if she were watching us via satellite—four heat signatures moving forward in a T formation, lugging absolutely nothing at all. My attention goes to Henry, to the top of his amazing, shaved head, and I make a decision. With the chamois-covered plane out in the middle of the taxiway, Trigger rests a hand on my shoulder and joins my view.

"I agree," he says.

I lean back against his chest. His heart pounds through my rib cage. "Reading my mind again?"

Trigger smiles and fingers my hair.

"What do you want me to do?" Henry asks.

Trigger breaks away. "You're with me, Gu. We'll take the bikes, head for the tracks, and if we're lucky, we'll catch the evening freight train and ride one stop to the next town over. And then Tana will fly the plane, land off field, and pick us up just outside the depot. Do you remember, T?" He grips my shoulders. "The checkpoint I showed you when we flew in?"

"I remember." My thoughts flip to the train tracks outside Pioneer's airfield. "Twenty or so miles east."

"That's the one." His hands squeeze tighter.

"Then what?"

For as smart as he is, Henry misses the hint.

"Then…"—Trigger snickers—"we get in the plane and fly to Tulsa."

"Got it. You and T go, but how do I get back to campus?" His skin looks green.

Trigger strides to the dirt bikes. "You're not going back, my friend. You're coming with us."

"I am?" Henry chokes a lump down his bruised throat. "I am!" He joins Trigger and mounts the second dirt bike.

"Take this." Trigger tosses his sat phone to me. "Once in the air, contact KC, tell her and McVie to activate the storm sequence. We're on our way home."

The boys kick-start the bikes, dart over the ramp, cut across the pavement, and then ride down the middle of the longest taxiway, their high beams lit in order to draw attention.

It works. Midway down the field, the caravan splits, and half the headlights break away in hot pursuit.

Soraya starts for the side door.

"Are you…"—the words tangle on my tongue—"going to be OK?"

"Don't worry, Tana," she says. "Like you, I'm a survivor."

"Who said I'm worried," I backpedal, but she doesn't appear to hear. Her designer soles have already pointed toward the exit. As she walks away, I notice that the rows of helium tanks stacked on either side of the doorway have tripled since the last time we were here. *Left over from the annual hot-air-balloon fest,* Henry had explained. But in the last twenty-four hours, I hadn't seen a single balloon in the air. *Weird.*

"See you around," Soraya says, and after a beauty queen wave, her curly head disappears through the door.

We're nothing alike. I gulp. "Deceiver, liar, manipulator…" The defensive mantra catches in my throat. The wad of undeniable facts, however, raises a very important question. *If Soraya is wicked to the core, then why did she abandon her father to help us find Henry?*

CHAPTER 42

As Soraya's jeep speeds away, I jog toward Trigger's invisible plane. I lift the camo cover from the propeller and unlatch the gull door. I crawl into the pilot's seat, don a headset, and turn the ignition key, and after a couple of prop rotations, the engine turns over.

Out of habit, I glance out the windshield, only to discover that although the chamois outwardly blends into its environment, the underside is as opaque as a concrete shower curtain.

Now what? I scan the panel. *I'll need to use the instruments to navigate to the runway*—a procedure that's rarely used on the ground.

Think of it like flying in the clouds. I take a page from the Flying-Flough's handbook and make light of an impossible situation.

I take note of the compass heading, advance the throttle, and roll forward. With no time for finesse, I jam the lever to full power.

Tires rumble over grooved metal, and I assume I've cleared the hangar door. The pavement beneath me smooths out, and I envision the invisible silhouette of a plane rumbling across the ramp. Using the tips of the rudder pedals, I make small corrections with my feet.

I tap left and then right, determined to keep the compass needle centered. After the plane gains some momentum, the edges of Henry's chamois lift and billow enough to allow brief peeks at the ground from my periphery. The surrounding pavement is as skinny as a sidewalk.

Crap, I'm on the taxiway, not the runway I intended to depart from. But if Trigger landed on the narrow strip, there's certainly enough room to make a takeoff. If I stay in the center.

Suddenly, the wing dips left.

Too close to the edge, Lyre.

I stomp on the right rudder pedal and the wings level. Once I reach fifty knots, the air swirling around the wing tips lifts the cover from the plane.

At sixty-five, the nose wheel lifts, and the plane climbs into the air. I initiate an eastbound turn and see Soraya out of the side window, leaning on her jeep's roll bar, hands flitting, all dramatic, explaining, I'm guessing, to McDunney and his team, the circumstances surrounding my unscheduled departure.

I level off at a thousand feet in order to spot the old gold-rush train tracks. I check my heading—090. *On track.* A mile or so ahead, I notice two single-light cones zigzagging to avoid the tracking floodlights atop Mac's Humvees.

They took the bait.

As hoped, the marines split from the chief.

Easing the throttle, I slow to nearly a hover and watch as Henry and Trigger trail the caboose of the evening freight train.

The marines appear to be gaining, closing the gap between the dirt bikes' rear fenders.

On the verge of being rammed by the road rhino's caged bumper, two yellow-green sparks flash and Henry and Trigger's bikes shoot forward.

The image of my friends blurs across the windscreen.

Nitrous, I assume, not the least bit surprised at Henry's latest upgrade. "Woo-hoo!" I celebrate and wonder what other cool contraptions he has stuffed in that backpack.

With the benefit of the accelerant burned out, Henry and Trigger parallel the boxcars, moving just a hair faster than the train.

They edge past the caboose and motor beside a series of coal carriers.

The Humvees stalk two lengths behind.

After clearing the coal bins, Trigger and Henry speed alongside an opened boxcar.

Fly the airplane, I remind myself. After a quick instrument scan, I refocus on the fleeing dirt bikes.

Side by side, moving as if they're one, my friends match the pace of the open-air car and drift closer to the exposed platform.

On the outside bike, Trigger takes Henry's handgrip, and steadies it, and then the Weatherman climbs to a wobbly flat-footed squat.

Barely balancing on the seat, Henry glances at Trigger. They exchange a go-for-it nod, and the Weatherman leaps. His arms and legs spread like a skydiver's. He free-falls for a second and then belly flops across the rusty metal floor.

With Henry safely aboard, Trigger releases the paralleling handlebars, and the relic frame steers away, tumbling out of control.

Trigger weaves to avoid being hit. He slows and falls back, allowing the marines an opportunity to close the nitrous-induced advantage.

When the Humvee brushes his rear fender, Trigger hunches over, matching his chin to the speedometer. He twists the accelerator and inches forward, making up lost ground.

As the sky surfer approaches the opened boxcar, Henry scrambles to secure his backpack's nylon strap around the steel frame. He loops the slack around his bicep and gives the cord a hearty tug. Anchored, Henry's torso dangles in the airflow, arm outstretched like a lifeguard's shepherd's crook.

Trigger steers the bike with one hand and uses his spare to latch onto the platform's lower rail. Connected to the train, he shimmies his fingers until he's beneath Henry's feet, bouncing and jostling as if surfing a gnarly wave.

Trigger pushes from the bike pegs, places one foot in front of the other, and balances on the seat, as I imagine he would if surfing waves on his longboard. He absorbs the bumps, knees knocking against his shoulders, lifting and then lowering to maintain balance, when a sand mound catches the tire and launches Trigger from his surfboard seat. He soars across the three-foot gap, arms cycling like propellers.

"Ah!" I gasp. The view goes under the wing, and I whip the airplane on its side.

The boxcar reappears, and I see Henry and Trigger piled on the floor.

"Woo-hoo!" I cheer again, level the wings, and move the throttle full forward.

With my friends safely on the train, I recenter the heading needle on east and search for the upcoming station—our rendezvous point, the platform Trigger spotted on our dead-stick approach last night.

After a couple of shallow turns, a cluster of city lights appears.

Found the town; now where's the depot?

Still holding 090 degrees on the compass, I double-check below to make sure I'm aligned with the tracks. With visual confirmation of dual rails, I know I'm headed in the right direction.

Call KC, I remind myself and grab Trigger's phone from the seat next to me. I speed-dial my best friend.

KC's number rings into voice mail. I leave an urgent message. "We're on our way. Get McVie, and start the storm." I smash the disconnect button and toss the cell back on the copilot's seat. *Where is that train station?*

The cluster of lights along the horizon fractures into dozens of tiny dots that speckle the ground. *Streetlights.* I follow the lighted path until the line dead-ends.

"Depot, twelve o'clock," I say out loud even though I'm alone in the plane. I veer off to the left and prepare to land in a flat, open field behind the small station.

Before starting the landing checklist, I try KC's number a second time. *Voice mail.* "Check your messages," I say. "We need to leave pronto." I cross my fingers, hoping she's camped out with McVie on Turkey Mountain with no cell signal.

I complete the final checks and then lift the nose. The airplane slows to approach speed. I lower the landing gear, extend the flaps, and pick a point where I can let down.

The wheels hit hard, and I add throttle to avoid being stuck in the gritty sand. Over my shoulder, the train's whistle blows twice, announcing its arrival to what the sign says is Silt Station.

I set the parking brake and cut fuel to the engine, and once the prop stands upright, I climb out of the cockpit to go get Henry and Trigger.

Although only twenty miles from Pioneer, I notice how quickly the weather has changed. The night air is heavy with humidity. The ground underfoot is slippery, as if it has recently rained.

I arrive at the tracks a little ahead of the steaming locomotive. The whistle shouts, the pistons slow, and the train eases as it approaches the platform, chugging so slowly that I can keep up with it at a brisk walk.

Boxcars pass like highway traffic. Counting the truck trailers, hopper cars, and flat pallets stacked with large metal pipes, I expect at any moment to see the boxcar with two familiar freeloaders. I catch a glimpse of an opening in the next car and run to meet it. But I don't see Henry or Trigger.

"Sergeant Numereau!" I shout, wishing for Henry's inhaler. "But how? Why…where are…"

He steps aside and reveals the answers to both questions.

Henry is shackled, being manhandled by two marines. At his feet, Trigger lies lifeless on the floor.

"What did you do to him?" I growl and run alongside the car.

"Just following orders, Miss Lyre." Mac's square jaw claps. "When the brass commands, even I have to listen." He moves to the boxcar's edge, bends down, and offers a hand. "You need to come with us to be debriefed. You don't want to abandon your friends, do you?" I swear I see fire in his eyes.

Beyond his dangling hand, I focus on Trigger—eyes closed, curled in a ball, and skin as white as exhaust smoke.

"What did you do to him?" I say again, my fists swatting at his extended arm.

"So you can't be counted on." Mac spits out his gum. "Guess Trigger was wrong about you." He shrugs. "Either way"—he eyes his prisoners—"they're coming with me."

A sound I've heard only once before booms from my stretched lungs. "One hair, just one out of place on his perfect head, and I will kill you."

Mac chuckles. He squares his stance, layers his arms over one another. "Dare you to try," he says through a smug smile, making me so want to punch him in the face. But before I get the chance, the train wails, gear links cycle, and the locomotive gains momentum.

"Coward," I say.

"Like I told you, having access to confidential information has consequences," Mac says. "Lucky for Trigger, you and I are nothing alike. I'll never do anything to hurt my brother. I gave my word, and whether you believe it or not, this is his destiny."

"Shut it!" I yell, but my shouting does nothing to slow the speeding train. Now in full stride, I struggle to keep the boxcar's pace.

Faster. I pump my arms. *Can't let them get away.*

The opening in the boxcar disappears.

CHAPTER 43

With my chest on the verge of exploding, I stop and crash to my knees.

This can't be happening. I can't. Won't. Refuse to lose anyone else.

Sweat drenches my face. Strands of hair stick to my cheeks. The last few cars whiz by, and I stare at the fading caboose.

"Yoo-hoo." A blood-curdling sound drifts from the platform, and I dust bangs from my eyes.

Number Two snarls and leaps from the passenger access.

Run. I shoot to my feet, my legs burning with fatigue. I swing my arms, ear to pocket, and arrow toward the parked plane. Rubbery, my thighs cycle through perpetual motion.

I slide under the fuselage.

Crawl up the wing.

I slam the hatch and latch the door.

Once buckled in the seat, I press the toe brakes.

Trembling, I grab the keys and reach for the ignition. My fingers fumble the ring, and it falls to the floor.

A loud crack slaps the side window, and I see the chief's cratered-skinned lackey pressed against the Plexiglas.

"I've got you now." He shows jagged teeth.

Hunched, I scour the floor for the tiny ignition key.

Number Two wiggles the door latch, and I use my elbow to secure the inside lever.

I stretch my fingers farther and finally feel the metal key.

Outside, the guard's kneecap piles against the window.

All in one motion, I slide in the key, turn the switch to on, and crack the throttle while releasing the parking brake. Still warm, the prop turns over on the first try. My feet slide from the brake pedals, and the airplane motors ahead.

"This is your stop," I mouth to Number Two and increase power.

His meat-cleaver hands flex on the front side of the wing, but the acceleration is far more force than the muscleman's grip can handle. He peels from the wing, and I push the control stick forward. After building speed, I loft in the air.

"Five hundred feet," I read from the altimeter. My eyes shoot outside, and I search for the train.

Not too far ahead, the locomotive continues along the same track. I peg the propeller hub to the caboose and hold a steady course.

Buzz, buzz. I hear a ringing and reach for the sat phone bouncing in the seat next to me. "KC?" I say.

"Henry," the voice replies, sounding pretty out of it. "T, it's me." His voice is weak. "Henry." He repeats. I hear Mac grumble in the background.

"I'm at five hundred feet, right behind the train. Be there in twenty seconds."

"Please, T, don't leave us," the Weatherman's words quiver. "Something about these soldiers, Mac, and Project Déjà Vu isn't right."

"Hold tight." I glance at the GPS map. "ETA, ten seconds and closing."

A piercing shrill rings in my ears. The tone is so deafening, it rattles my molars. I put Henry on speaker, drop the phone, and say, "Hang on."

A sound blasts as if a cannon has fired.

A rush ripples through the air. In its wake, a wave of turbulence flips my plane on its side.

The right wing points at the ground. I wrangle the controls and jerk to counteract.

When the wingtip's flashing strobes realign with the horizon, I blow out, my hands and legs trembling.

Steadying the yoke, I suck another breath. Over my receiver, I hear a creepy cackle. Off my wing, another airplane appears.

CHAPTER 44

"McDunney!" The chief matches my speed, piloting an exact replica of Trigger's homebuilt. He wiggles his fingers as if waving to a friend, but nothing about McDunney has ever been neighborly.

Dr. Harb sits next to him, grinning ear to ear, looking as if he's about to get away with murder—like he already has.

What are you doing? I ask with a glare.

The chief angles his propeller at mine.

Yanking and banking at the same time, I roll the wing over ninety degrees and dive toward the muddy sand.

Once the airspeed reaches redline, I pull the stick full back, and as if launched from Cape Canaveral, the plane lofts into the sky.

I soar past McDunney, his nose arrowing at the ground. I barrel roll and allow the shot of Sir Isaac Newton's natural nitrous to rocket me toward the stars.

As the airspeed bleeds off, the controls become sluggish, nearing a stall.

I lower the nose and scan the sky for the chief and Dr. Harb. I see no sign of McDunney. I locate Polaris and make a wish that he's a burning hole in the ground.

I'm about to go after Henry and Trigger when a bright light sparks from the darkness. A neon-green ribbon lights and cascades from the heavens.

"Oh, no, KC, Professor McVie, not yet," I say.

The aurora curtain drops.

The luminous sheet waves and curls into a loose funnel. The cone of light tightens. A spindly finger unfolds.

If that's not enough, my ear receiver screeches, and then I hear Chief McDunney's craggy cackling.

He lives. So much for wishes.

A second wretched finger unravels from the storm ahead. Sparks fly as it intertwines with its twin.

The sky goes black.

Lightning claps from the darkness. Thunder rumbles, and a tidal wave of rough air rocks my plane.

"I'm in charge of cleanup," McDunney says—clearly a madman who takes way too much pleasure in tying up loose ends. "Catch me if you can, scared little rich girl." The chief steers into the center of the storm.

Bolts of electricity pulse.

Sooty clouds engulf his plane.

"He's going through." My limbs shake. I steer after McDunney. Clouds build. A strong gust blows, carrying away the remnants of the freight train's whistle.

My head spins nearly as fast as the laboring propeller. From the rear windows, the glow of the locomotive's light falls from sight.

"I'm losing them!" I say. I start to twist the control stick, but my jittery hand freezes.

"And let Dr. Harb escape?" a wild, ferocious voice I don't recognize shouts from deep in my gut.

"No." Tears well in my eyes. "Of course, I want him held accountable. It's all I've thought about. All I've lived for for the last year and a half. But he's under the marines' protection. There's nothing I can do." As I gasp for air, I wonder whom I'm even talking to.

Veins of electricity ignite the sky and cast the outline of McDunney's engulfed plane against the cumulonimbus canvas. Mother Nature, I assume, is trying to get my attention.

"OK," I admit. "Technically, Dr. Harb did just fly into the storm with McDunney." *So much for Mac never letting him out of his sight.* "Yes, he'll get away again. But I can't abandon my friends."

Through blurred vision, I see a familiar face emerge from the cloud swirls.

"Dad?" I say, even though I know it's nothing more than an apparition.

"Yes, love," he answers. "Have you forgotten your promise? Remember, you gave your word." His dead voice sours.

I relive the nightmare—him waving me over, the explosion, and his charred body vaporizing in the fire. I squeeze my eyes shut, wishing I could forget. But no matter how I try, the vision is always there—me kneeling on the edge of the blast, sobbing. I swore to Dad to never stop until I found his killer. I say, "I remember."

Double or nothing. Trigger's hang-loose smile swoops in like a phantom sky surfer. Contrails stream from his mouth's edges and skywrite our mantra in cloudy cursive. "Don't forget, T." Trigger's image loops over my father's. "I saved your life. Even put myself in McDunney's slimy crosshairs."

My frozen hand loosens, and as if on autopilot, I begin a 180-degree turn.

"My friends need me," I say when Dad's ghastly image interrupts.

"Need what, Tana?" the ghost snaps. "Someone who breaks promises?"

"But…" I say and gasp, as if a knife has been thrust into my heart.

"Integrity above all or"—the sharpness of Dad's words twist the knife deeper—"or you will be destined to be alone."

Every lie I've ever told plays like an audiobook over my headset—to Mom, Gran, Soraya, Trigger, and even Eddie—and if that isn't horrible enough, the lies I told myself also.

"Things are different now," I sob. *I need things to be different now.* "I gave my word to them, too, Dad," I shout, ignoring the fact that the plane has entered a shallow turn.

"You have to choose, Tana. Family or friends."

"The way you did? Preached to put family first and then sacrificed your life for a lawsuit?"

The phantasm rolls his misty lips together. The shadow begins to fade.

"Don't you dare leave. Answer me, Dad!" I say, feeling like I'm about to split in half—part of me is loyal to Trigger and Henry, and regardless of the secrets he kept, my other side is obligated to my father.

Absent the time to flip a mental coin, I stare into the wisps of Dad's eyes, into the soul of the man who raised me, nurtured me, and taught me how to fly.

"Please, Daddy. Stay. I choose you. Family. Duty first. Above all else." *Even love.*

I yank the side stick, reverse course, and point into the eye of the storm. Dad's image vanishes.

My shoulders sag. My palms are slick with sweat. My scarred heart shatters.

A shroud of darkness consumes the fuselage, turbulence erupts, and the control stick shakes. I glance in the passenger seat and see the sat phone still transmitting.

"Henry," I say.

"Please…" The Weatherman's voice trembles. He sniffles. "I'm begging you, don't leave us."

I squint at my reflection in the windshield. *Follow his actions, not his words.* Dad did what he had to, regardless of the price. Now, so will I.

"There's still time, T," echoes over the phone's speaker. "You can save us." *My father's gone, but my friends are still here.*

I roll my wrist, dip the wing over, and try to double back. But the stick is damp and slips through my fingers. A shock of turbulence hits. The control stick vibrates.

I can't catch it.

Clouds blanket the plane.

The power fails.

The yoke slides from my hands.

All goes black.

CHAPTER 45

When my eyes open again, all I see is gray. A thick, soupy overcast sky dims Tulsa's bronze-gold landscape. The absence of sunlight makes everything appear ashen, dingy, and drab. Even the mirrored windows of the local university appear somber, sheathed in dark colors as if anticipating a funeral. I know I should be relieved. I'm alive, I'm home, but all I can think about is what I left behind.

Safely through one storm, only to face another.

Descending from the north, I parallel the winding Arkansas and follow the familiar dry patches in the riverbed until I spot Riverside Airport's green-and-white beacon tower.

Shallow ripples roll over the muddy water, suggesting the winds favor a landing to the south. I slant toward runway 19R, a track that flies over the condemned outdoor amphitheater that Trigger and I visited just two nights ago.

"Care to see a show?" I hear his voice, touch my cheek, close my eyes, and feel my head against Trigger's warm skin, chin to cheek, sprawled across the stone benches, talking about our hopes, dreams, and fears.

Overcome with guilt, I feel tears trickle down my cheeks. If I hadn't been tempted to chase Dr. Harb and McDunney, my hand wouldn't have slipped, and I'd be well on my way to rescuing my friends.

Good-enough story, I lie to myself. But the dark secret I keep buried deep in my heart is that there's nothing I want more than to kill Dr. Harb—more than helping Henry and more than having a friend like KC. It's a drive even greater than my desire to be close to Trigger or perhaps even Tuck.

Vengeance is the *only* way to end the sadness, stop the pain, and right this horrible injustice.

My thoughts shift to Soraya.

Then as if I am waking from a nightmare, reality crashes in, and I remember I'm still eight hundred feet in the air.

Fly the plane, Lyre. For a second, I fight the desire to squeeze my eyes closed, let go, and drift away in the calm, nonjudgmental air.

Not this time. I refuse to take the easy way out.

My eyelids flutter, and I squint, hoping to adjust to the low light. A loud snap overpowers the engine noise—a crackle, chased by a splintering, like ice thawing on a frozen lake. From the corner of my eye, I spy what started as a tiny dimple and is now a ragged crack spreading across the windshield. It's the mark left from the heavy turbulence when we arrived at Pioneer—the crack that I had not mentioned to Trigger and went on to forget myself.

Reaching the dash compass, the fractured vein pauses and stops, and I almost believe the thick glass will hold.

I sit still.

I breathe shallowly.

Kaboom.

The glass blows.

The window explodes and is sucked forward. Its jagged shards bombard the propeller blades. Laboring, the engine grinds as if slicing chunks of ice in a blender. When the last piece of glass lets go, the prop stops.

Warm air rushes through my hair, and I watch the pointed hub dip like the hood of Trigger's pickup topping the First Street Bridge. The plane drops like a lawn dart, and I pitch for best-glide speed, praying there is enough altitude to stretch to the airport.

No such luck.

When my view fills with more earth than sky, I realize there's no way I can make any part of the paved airfield.

Plan B. Off-site landing.

I scour a square mile for a plowed farmer's field. Everywhere I look, though, there are only dense rolling hills.

Plan C?

Checking again, I see long lengths of dry riverbeds prevalent at this time of year.

Better than nothing.

The question is, am I skilled enough to touch down on a narrow strip of sandbar mud?

Sure, I can. My mind is made up, when an annoying peep of self-doubt asks, *Without engine power?* A reasonable question that, in the end, I choose to ignore.

Focusing, I attempt to recreate Trigger's dead-stick approach into Pioneer. I parallel the snaking shoreline and then count the dry mounds between areas of pooled water. I scour for a potential landing spot and decide on the mud bar a quarter mile ahead. Committed, I shoot an imaginary string from my eye and aim for the highest point.

Skimming the Seventy-First Street Bridge, I raise the nose to the horizon, and the plane begins to drop like a meteor. Teeth clenched, palms dripping, I hold my breath until all three wheels smack the mud.

The plane jerks, how I imagine it might when landing on an aircraft carrier.

The force slings me forward, and my body sails through the open windshield, recoils, and snaps back. I slam against the headrest.

I suck air and swipe my bangs from my eyes to see two figures hopping like frogs, jumping from one mud island to another, the dry patches providing a step path across the streaming water fingers. After unlatching my seat belt, I reach for the door handle. It's jammed.

Trees for the forest. I squat on the seat. "If a gull door closes, use a window." *Or missing windshield.* Grimacing, I duck through the wide opening, crawl on the long cowling, and then swing to the ground. By the time my boots touch dirt, reinforcements have arrived.

"Tana!" KC squeals. Her skinny arms wrap around my shoulders, and I squeeze with all my might, unaware of how much I needed a hug. I linger, uncertain if after they hear about my botched rescue, I will have any friends at all.

Professor McVie approaches. "Good to see you, Miss Lyre." He tugs on his ponytail.

"You, too, Professor." I fake a smile. "By the way, nice storm."

McVie unholsters an air gun from his belt and blows on the pretend barrel. "Pretty gnarly, if I do say so myself."

Triumphant moment, scientific breakthrough, call it what you will, but I suspect the success of the geomagnetic experiment might just have earned us an A-plus midterm grade.

For the second time in the past few days, I wish a moment wouldn't end—first with Tuck and now, here with my best friend and a rockin' grade, feeling so comfortable I could almost forget—

"Tana," Mom's voice interrupts as she lands barefoot on the closest mushy mogul, platform heels in hand, Gunner by her side, tromping through the murky river as if he doesn't notice the mud.

"Thank goodness." Mom clenches my arm. "KC called and said she just happened to see your approach through the binoculars. Guessed you had engine trouble and called in the cavalry." My mother hangs her free hand on KC's shoulder and pulls us closer. "I'm so relieved KC and Professor McVie happened to be up on Turkey Mountain collecting data." She turns to Gunner. "I mean, what are the chances?"

"Dumb luck." Mr. Clark's eyes slide toward McVie.

The very last person I want to see arrives next to Gunner.

"Where's Trigger?" Professor Flough asks, squinting at his plane slowly sinking in the muck.

Mom's and KC's arms fall to their sides, as if they just realized I flew in solo.

"He's…" I say, but then I'm distracted by the fact Professor Flough isn't wearing a flight suit.

Noticing my struggle, KC finishes my sentence. "He ran into an old friend. Should be here any minute." Her purple frames search the sky.

"Not buying it, Miss McKenna." Flough pulls a toothpick from his jacket pocket and gnaws on the tip. "Trigger would never leave Tana on her own. So what's really going on here, ladies?"

KC dabs both corners of her mouth.

Without looking, I sense the heaviness of Mom's disapproving glare. I breathe deeply, aware that the homecoming celebration is about to end.

I swallow, squeeze my rib cage, and look at Trigger's dad. "He's with Sergeant Numereau," I say, committed to telling the truth—a version of it anyway.

"Mac?" Flough shakes his head and then laughs as if he's been asked a how-many-marine-corps-men-does-it-take-to-screw-in-a-light-bulb joke. "As in Sergeant Mac Numereau?" He holds his midsection. "Please, the last time I checked, reliable intel put him at the other end of the globe."

Although spoken with absolute confidence, I notice his freckled eyelid twitches.

Perhaps it was the street clothes, relaxed-fit khakis, untucked polo, or the worn pair of leather deck shoes, but the fearless flying legend who claims to be in the know appears off-kilter. Not only does he have no idea Mac is Stateside, he also seems to be in the dark about the military's joint project with Pioneer.

Maybe there are limits on your unrestricted security clearance, sir.

He glances at Gunner and then continues, "So you want me to believe that Trigger sent you back on your own in order to stay with Sergeant Numereau?"

Something like that. My gut somersaults.

I nod in agreement, and he spits a tiny wood shard. "Not buying it, Tana."

*Can't say I blame you, since the truth is Trigger really had no choice in the end. Truth is…*I try to pry my lips open and admit I left my friends in the hands of a rogue military commander. But the explanation gums in my mouth.

"Trigger took you along as a safety pilot, making the plane and its crew his responsibility. No way he willingly relinquished this obligation."

My cemented jaw finally cracks. "I didn't say he went willingly."

Flough's lips stiffen. His leathery face hardens. "You and Trigger went back to Pioneer, didn't you?"

Like two spotlights, his bright blues shine on KC and McVie.

"Oh, no, Lamar," Mom chimes in, speaking at light speed. "Trigger and Tana flew cross-country practicing for the flight team's next competition." Her brows rise. "Isn't that right, dear?"

I gulp and break a sweat. A cold front is coming. Here comes the rain. "No, not really," I answer. "Like I said before, Trigger's with Mac."

"Where? In the desert?" Colonel Flough tugs his scarred ear and makes eye contact with Gunner.

Wish I knew.

"You're asking the wrong question, Lamar," Gunner says, lines wrinkling over his forehead. "If what Tana says is fact, then what we should really be wondering is what a soldier like Mac Numereau is doing at a private prep school?"

Hold on. Did I miss something? How does a union negotiator for the Department of Transportation know about Pioneer?

"Recruiting, I'm guessing," Flough says.

"At that think tank?" Gunner grins. "Highly doubt it."

Despite the connections, security clearances, and reputations, I come to realize that a first-semester high school sophomore knows more than all of them put together.

Gunner says, "What I am certain of is if Trigger decided to stay, it must have been for something pretty important."

Like flying fighter jets? Despite multiple attempts at being honest, I don't think Flough is too interested in what really happened.

Try harder. Your friend's life may depend on it. "Sir"—I make my voice as deep and as official sounding as an enlisted soldier's—"Trigger didn't choose to go with Mac."

Gunner twists his face in an I-told-you-so manner. The man opposite him now resembles less of a living legend and more of a disoriented parent.

Flough says, "You want me to believe that my son was taken against his will? Try again, Miss Lyre. Trigger and Mac are like brothers." He shifts his jaw back and forth and then spits out remnants of a splintered toothpick. "Besides, Trigger would never take leave without telling me."

Clueless. Once again, I'm amazed at how little parents know about their children.

"They saw something…classified," I stutter. "That's why Sergeant Numereau took them."

"Classified? Here we go." Flough shakes his head. "Let me guess, some top-secret save-the-world plan?" He caresses what's left of his ear and exchanges a strained look with Gunner.

"They?" Gunner Clark says, ignoring the secret part.

"Trigger and Henry."

Professor Flough cuts in. "Gu's kid? Not possible. Henry's dad is that school's golden goose." His fast-paced speech resembles my mother's.

"They let you go?" Gunner seems not to hear anything the colonel has said.

A few more tumbles and flips, and my stomach ties into a taut, square knot. "I, well…you see, we planned to rendezvous, but Mac was on the train. The storm came, and I had no choice but to…"

Before I finish, Professor Flough stalks away. Gunner follows.

"To go through," I finish my sentence and turn to my mother, only to see a face covered in disappointment.

"We'll talk when we get home, young lady," Mom utters through gritted teeth. "Gran's on her way. If you ever want to see the inside of an airplane again, you'll make sure to be waiting for her."

"The geomagnetic curtain is only open for a short time, seconds, a minute at best," Professor McVie explains. "If Tana had waited any longer, she'd be stuck along with Henry and Trigger. Then where would we be? At least now we have some information."

"And that justifies her lying to me how?" Mom does nothing to curb her hot temper. She taps her bare foot in the mud, waiting, I assume, to hear a logical answer.

McVie rattles on about how some sacrifices have to be made in the spirit of scientific progress. "Save your technical babble, McVie." Mom sighs and stomps after Gunner.

You haven't cornered the market on questions, Mom. Here's one: Why are you spending so much time with Gunner Clark?

CHAPTER 46

"Speaking of sacrifices." Our school's headmaster approaches, and the two uniformed policemen walking alongside him circle our weather professor. "Creating volatile storms, trashing rovers, collaborating with students on an unapproved curriculum? I warned you." He points a disapproving finger at McVie. "This time, you're through."

McVie's chin falls to his chest as the officers collar our professor's arms and escort him toward a security van. Red-faced, Headmaster Buckley hikes after them.

"I object!" KC leaps to the next mushroom top. "I want an official inquiry. You haven't even heard his side of the story."

Uninterested, Mr. Buckley plods forward, doing his best not to dirty his shoes.

Tumbling from the dry lump, KC stumbles into a shin-deep mud puddle. She steadies herself and shouts, "It was a matter of national security!"

Whether it was the shrill tone of her voice or the seriousness of such an accusation, Mr. Buckley turns on a shined heel. "That's enough, Miss McKenna." His skin flushes crimson, matching the Oklahoma dirt. "You're already on shaky ground, and if you want to keep that A-plus midterm mark, I suggest you curb any reckless accusations."

KC glances at her unstable footing, likely considering how the impact of a lesser grade will affect her admission to MIT. She pushes her glasses to the bridge of her nose.

"What's it going to be, Miss McKenna?" Mr. Buckley says.

"I plead the Fifth."

"The Fifth Amendment requires you to keep your mouth shut, Miss McKenna. A skill I understand you have not quite developed." Headmaster Buckley sloshes through the water, apparently no longer concerned with the shine on his loafers.

"So…" KC shuffles a half circle, wades over, and shares my high ground. "What could possibly be so important to make you leave Trigger behind?"

Guilty, I add fuel to my own bonfire. "And Henry."

"Yeah, but you come home without we're-so-on-the-same-wavelength-he-can-read-my-mind T. Xanthus Flough?"

Two thoughts collide in my head. First, she's right, and second, until her curiosity gets satisfied, KC will question me to death. "Didn't you just vow to keep your mouth shut?" I say in a feeble attempt to distract her attention.

"That was just some legal mumbo jumbo I picked up from my dad's lawyers." Her corrected eyes sparkle. "Spill."

"Not what, but who." I've barely uttered the sentence when I notice a pair of arms waving like a hawk perched on the Seventy-First Street Bridge. Between audible caution warnings and emergency strobe flashers, I recognize the car on the shoulder—Gran's roadside-assistance-ready hybrid.

"Come on," Gran hollers, and I traipse in her direction, knowing how much my grandmother hates to wait.

"Who?" KC hoots like an owl, shadowing close enough to be perched on my shoulder. "Who could have lured you from Henry and Trigger?"

At the edge of the river, I scale the steep, weedy bank, using my hands and feet. Monkey-gripping the gnarly branches, I heave myself forward, right hand and then left, until I propel myself over the hilltop. Steady on flat ground, I spin back, latch onto KC's forearm, and pull her to solid footing.

"Dr. Harb," I say and puff out air. "He and McDunney flew a plane through McVie's storm, and I'm guessing they landed here in Tulsa."

KC's mouth gapes. It seems that think-on-her-feet McKenna is at a loss for words.

"Girls," Gran says. She trots over with an elastic bandage and wool blanket in hand. "Way to put it straight down the middle, Tana." Her orthopedic shoes inch from the ground, and she offers a celebratory high five. "Don't leave me hanging." After an explosive palm slap, Gran shakes out a gingham-checked blanket, and even though the temperature is near eighty degrees, she covers our shoulders. Gran pushes her UV wraparound glaucoma goggles up on her head and guides us toward the car. "I thought the biggest thrill of the day would be seeing which hat Carolyn Coltan wore to church."

As we approach my grandparents' mint-green hybrid, I'm blinded by the blinking hazard lights and the flashing triangular caution cones.

"Eyesore," I say.

Gran lowers her glaucoma goggles, checks both ways for traffic, and waves KC and me on like a crossing guard. "Do you have any idea how many pedestrians get hit daily while on the shoulder in Tulsa?"

No, but I'm becoming very familiar with statistics concerning the number of engine-out landings in airplanes.

"Two hundred," KC says. "Another fifty if you include areas outside Tulsa County."

I look at KC. *How does she know this stuff?*

"My point exactly." Gran opens the driver's door. "Planning thwarts accidents." She fastens her belt, motors her seat forward, adjusts the rearview, and then turns the ignition. But before shifting into gear, she reaches to the passenger side and opens a portable cooler. "Power bar anyone?" She offers two grainy bricks zipped in plastic bags.

"I'll take one," KC says, and before I have a chance to warn her, she wolfs a monster bite. "What?" She raises her brows as oats and pine nuts crumble from her lips.

"Never mind." I glance away, hoping this recipe called for less cleanse and more sugar.

"Lyre house, nonstop," Gran says. "KC, your parents called and asked if you could stay the night."

My friend devours the remaining snack bar. With chipmunk cheeks, she nods her head.

"We're off," Gran says, and after a shoulder check, she hits the accelerator.

"Just a minute," I say, buying time to come up with some excuse to swing by the airport. "I left my laptop at the hangar." The lie comes easily, signaling I'm officially off the tell-the-truth bandwagon. *That was fast.*

"Riverside Airport it is," Gran says. "But after that, I have strict orders to take you straight home."

Mom, I guess. I recall her last words, the part where she said I'm in a whole world of trouble.

CHAPTER 47

"So I was right?" Gran spins the tires, hooks a sharp U-ey, and cuts through four lanes of traffic, a move worthy of my mother's skill set.

I'm doomed. I rub my forehead, reconciling the fact that I'm destined to be a terrible driver. "Right about what, Gran?"

"The dress."

"Dress?" I point at the pink hem, and KC notices my frock.

She says, "You piloted in a dress?"

"Long story," I say.

"I've got time—besides, you know I can't stand to be out of the know."

You have to be in in order to be out, Kase, I think, as a loud moan grumbles from her midsection. Her hand slides down to her stomach. She says, "I don't feel so good."

Gran's bakery strikes again.

I straighten the wrinkled sheath that's frayed and stained with sand, dirt, and mud. "Tell you when we get home. Right now, we need to focus on finding McDunney."

"I'm guessing he came through the storm first. That's why you didn't go after Henry and Trigger, right?"

"I followed them, just as we planned. But when I saw McDunney and Harb disappear through the geomagnetic curtain, it was too much to bear."

"So you were torn." KC's speech quickens. "Your friends or your dad."

"I hesitated for a split second."

"You did go back then?"

"I tried," I say, chest heaving. "By the time I turned around, the air was too turbulent. The stick slipped from my hand, and the next thing I knew, the power was out. When my eyes opened again, I was hovering over the Arkansas River." My fingers tremble as if I were reliving the flight. "If I hadn't been so consumed with my own…" I'm struck with the moment my dad told me that *if* is not a verb. "I am just like her," I say, repeating Dr. Harb's words.

"Like who?"

I face the last friend I have on this earth and say, "Soraya."

KC touches my hand. "I wasn't there, Tana, but if I know you—and who knows you better than me?" She finds my eyes. "You did your best. You always go above and beyond." She adds a second hand to our pile. "Watching your dad's killer walk away scot-free is cause to make even the most loyal person waver." KC's tummy gurgles, and then she coughs up a sizable burp. "See"—the cockeyed expression on her face makes me laugh—"Nobody's perfect."

I curl my fingers around hers and squeeze.

"We've all done things we're not proud of, T."

Designed spy software, hacked private mainframes, peeked at a few employment records, and every now and again, planted a Trojan horse— those likely made KC's list of not-so-stellar moments. Infractions, I might add, that injured machines, not human beings.

"Now"—she adjusts her purple specs—"let's get back to figuring out how to find McDunney."

As Gran motors down the ring road, KC and I scan ramp parking for any unfamiliar airplanes. "There it is." I point to the tie-downs next to National's hangar.

Gran stands on the brakes. "You left your laptop outside?"

"Sorry. What I meant to say is Trigger's truck is parked inside the school's hangar."

"Oh," she says. "Then your computer is in the Creamsicle?"

Rescuing me from another fib, KC answers instead. "Figured it was safer that way. We all know what thunderstorms do to electronics."

Gran joins the airport access road and rolls up to the security gate. "This wouldn't have anything to do with the plane that arrived moments before you?" Her wraparounds inch over her brows.

KC and I spin and bump heads.

"Chief McDunney?" KC whispers, and I put a finger to my lips.

"What kind of plane, Gran?" I say.

"Not quite sure, my eyes aren't as good as they once were." Gran digs in her handbag and retrieves a tiny radio. "Heard the arrival on the two-way. Caught my ear because the call sign was an experimental, like Trigger's."

KC and I trade glances.

The chief and Dr. Harb are here.

"Do you know the one I'm talking about?" Gran's goggle shades reflect at me in the rearview mirror.

"Mum's the word," KC says under her breath and angles her head at my grandmother.

"Ah, who knows?" I say. "There are hundreds of takeoffs and landings at Riverside every day."

"It's 573 to be exact," KC says.

I touch my neck scar. "Could be anyone."

"Uh-huh." My grandmother appears to accept our explanation, but something in her voice hints that she's suspicious.

"We'll walk from here." I open the door. "Shouldn't take more than ten minutes."

Ducking under the wooden security arm, I turn back to see my grandmother idling outside the barrier. *I'm a liar, manipulator—*

"Any idea what we are going to do if McDunney and Harb are still in the plane?" KC asks as we jog toward the transient parking tie-downs.

"No clue," I say. That is, until I see the fuel truck chug across the ramp. A glint of sun hits the polished-aluminum tank, sparking a fantastic notion.

"Line support." I beeline for the tanker.

"T, is this really the time to chat with a ramp rat?"

Line support could be compared to rodents, I suppose. They're known to be gruff, be rugged, and scuttle around. Their domain—every paved inch of the airport. Perpetually outside, they see, hear, and know everything that happens at the field firsthand: stealth arrivals, secret meetings, planes that want to scoot below the radar, and some that don't file flight plans.

"Hey." I whistle with my fingers, and the fuel truck swerves and angles toward me. Fingering the chief's homebuilt, I nudge KC, and we join the ramp rat and track for McDunney's parked plane.

"One hundred low lead?" the fueler says.

"Actually," I hoist myself up to the window. "I'm looking for a pilot. A friend of mine who landed about an hour ago."

The rampie unhooks his clipboard that's dangling from the shifter and scrolls down the arrival list. "Yep, you're right. Arrived at nine. Took forty gallons of avgas and one quart of oil."

"Sounds about right." I swing my bangs, tuck the loose strands behind my ear, fold my arms, and rest my chin on the windowsill. "Did they go inside?" I smile wide and make eye contact.

Unlike rodents, however, line workers aren't simpleminded, and just because they have useful information doesn't mean they are willing to share.

The fueler pulls his clipboard to his chest. "These friends of yours"—an undertone of skepticism piggybacks on his words—"if they were expecting you, wouldn't they have pinged your phone?"

KC splits off and laps the airplane.

"Not if it was a surprise," I ad lib fib.

The rampie coughs, removes his ball cap, and scratches his head.

"You know, I'm not really supposed to give out information about customers' personal business."

"Oh, darn." I bunch my lips and scrunch my nose. "I understand. It's just I'd hate for my uncle to miss his surprise welcome-home party."

"Surprise party? Is that why they didn't call?"

Words catch in my throat, likely a knee-jerk kick from my conscience. *You're only as good as your word* rings in my ears, and I pretend as if I didn't hear. "Absolutely."

The rampie's beady eyes glaze. The corners of his mouth rise. *Gotcha.*

He checks his roster. "They borrowed the crew car and plan to depart this evening around eleven."

In the dark, after the tower closes—a perfect time to depart undetected.

"Did they say where they're going?"

The fueler clenches the clipboard to his chest. His tiny eyes jut over the ramp. He reaches down, and the window rises up. "Can't tell you anything else. I've already said too much." The rampie lowers his ball-cap brim, grips the steering wheel, and steps on the gas.

I jump from the doorstep, and as he pulls away, I shout, "Remember, if they come back, the party is a surprise."

"I see what you mean." KC rests her chin on my shoulder. "You're becoming a decent actress, like Soraya."

My head snaps around. "That's not a compliment." I scowl.

"What now?" KC says.

"Good news is we know McDunney and Harb are here. Bad news is we have no idea where to look." A heaviness collapses my shoulders. "Why do I get so close, only to have Dad's killer slip through my fingers?" I spin in a circle and search for something to punt.

A stiff wind blows, and the pilot in me searches for the airport's wind sock. When I twist toward the runway, a piece of paper slaps against my shins.

I bend, about to crumple the trash, when I see familiar words: "Land for auction. Ten acres. No trespassing. Violators will be prosecuted to the fullest extent of the law."

As I fold the soiled flyer into my dress pocket, saliva dribbles from KC's mouth.

"What?" she says.

"I know where to find McDunney and Harb."

CHAPTER 48

Although we are confined like two detainees inside Supermax Lyre, Warden Gran is generous and allows KC and me access to my computer. For homework, she says, and then adds, "What sort of trouble could you possibly get into with that itsy-bitsy machine?"

Kind of how this whole mess started, I think, trying to stop my eyes from bulging from their sockets. Obviously Gran is no longer following KC's how-to-work-around-firewalls blog tips.

Out of the loop? Maybe. Oblivious? No way. I know, because when the door lock clicks, the handle jiggles and reopens enough for light to shine through the gap.

"We're being hawked." I touch my eyes and then my ears.

KC nods while activating her looking-glass software, so if the warden checks another laptop, she'll see a prerecorded loop of two diligent high school students engrossed in online homework.

"Done," KC says, although I still hear the sound of keystrokes ticking.

Sprawled on my back, I stare at the ceiling, eyes tracing the branch-like cracks. "We have to get over to the old amphitheater."

"Two challenges," KC says, her eyes never leaving the computer screen. "First, we have to get around your grandmother. Second, we don't have a car."

I roll onto an elbow, hoping Go-To McKenna lives up to her nickname. "McDunney and Harb are there. I feel it in my gut."

KC's purple-rimmed eyes lift to meet mine, and she smiles while her fingers keep moving.

"Yes! I just hacked into Homeland Security's boosted satellite feed to see if I can locate Henry and Trigger's position."

"Homeland? I thought you were creating a diversion so we can make our way over to the coliseum?"

"Then what?" KC's fingers fly over the keyboard. "You said these guys are orangutans. How are we going to capture them?"

Good point. I flatten on the bed and blow the bangs from my eyes. "It won't work. Triangulating their position. Trigger gave me his phone with your chocolate-bar booster."

"Didn't you say Henry called just before you entered the storm?"

"Yes, but…" I swallow.

"Then I'll use the call's time stamp to locate your last-known position, reverse ping Henry's phone, and triangulate a virtual grid."

"Take the train's approximate speed," I say, catching on. "And figure how far and in what direction they could have gone."

"If they stayed on the train—"

"We'll be able to zone in on a few possible locations."

A faint flash lights up the room.

"Storm's coming," KC says, and as I turn to look for lightning, a white paper airplane darts through the open window.

I snap up.

Could it be?

CHAPTER 49

I bound to my feet, chase the folded paper until it lands on the floor, drop to my knees, and fumble the bent edges.

"UFO?" KC says.

I quiet her with a shaky finger, straighten to my feet, legs tingling with pins and needles, and read the single handwritten word—*downstairs*.

I read it again, my heart hesitating to beat. I cross the room at breakneck speed and push open the window that leads to the fire escape.

"Tana," KC calls.

I don't answer, assuming I know what she's going to say next. House arrest means indoors. Yes, I heard Gran's rules. But when she speaks, what comes from her mouth isn't at all what I expected. "Hold up. Where are you going? I just found—"

"Trigger's here," I say, swinging a leg over the windowsill.

"He's what?" She rechecks the computer screen and then hurries to my side.

"Downstairs." I point to the front yard. "By the big magnolia tree. His usual spot."

A rush of excitement raises goose bumps on my skin, but the information slayer's face appears anything but thrilled.

"Can you believe it? Trigger and Henry are back!" I grasp her shoulders with both hands and shake. "Kase, what's wrong?"

"It's just…" She rattles her head as if clearing water from her ear. "Doesn't make sense. There must be some mix-up with the GPS signal."

With my entire body now outside the window, I wrap my feet around the thick metal joint on the copper gutter drain and lean against the sill. "I'm not sure what you're talking about, but our friends"—I glance down into the banana leaves of the plush magnolia tree—"are waiting, and I can't afford to miss another opportunity."

"Right behind you, T." KC half grins, and once I shimmy far enough down the drainpipe, she follows through the window.

The rough, flat roof of the sunroom scrapes my bare feet. I ignore the pain and think about a heartfelt apology. Spinning around backward, I descend the fire escape rails. At the bottom, I leap from the last metal tread and land flat-footed on the freshly sprinkled grass. Curbing my desire to run to the sky surfer, I twist and assist KC to maneuver the final stair.

"Over here." I wave like a third-base coach egging a runner to home plate.

The damp blades of fescue tickle my toes, and as I approach the thick trunk of the budding tree, my entire body prickles.

Out from the foliage cover steps a hulky shadow. It's obscured mass strides in my direction. "Trigger?" I say.

When the glow of the porch light meets the veiled face, I realize it's not Trigger at all.

"McDunney!" I squeal and dig my heels into the ground. My damp feet, however, continue to slide. I crash into the chief's pecs. His meaty arms coil around my body and lift me in the air. "Did you really think we'd let you go after seeing our master plan?"

KC screeches and rakes her fists against his forearms. The chief swats, knocking Kase on her bottom.

A door hinge creaks.

Steel heels clop over pavement, and I hear a loud, distinctive *click-clock* sound.

McDunney whirls and recoils, acting familiar with the universal sound. He faces the front door, and we see Gran pumping a twelve-gauge shotgun. She raises the butt to her shoulder, the barrel to her cheek, and closes an eye. "Release her. Now." Gran's index finger hovers over the trigger.

McDunney squares his feet and positions my torso as his shield.

"Tana!" KC hollers, and I see Gran's opened eye drift to her.

"Don't move, Kase," Gran says. She secures the gun against her shoulder, walks forward, and squints down the long barrel.

"One more step, old lady, and I'll snap your sweet thing's neck."

Gran's boots flatten against the stone steps. She holds the gun barrel steady, her finger inching closer to the kill switch.

I hear tires squeal.

McDunney swivels, me still pinned to his chest, and I see three black Suburbans jump the front curb.

Doors burst open, and my mother appears. She whisks up the pavers, Gunner Clark a step behind, clawing after her. "Linnea, wait. McDunney is dangerous."

Mom slips through his grip.

Gunner knows the chief?

McDunney's steel fingers clamp around my neck.

Mom's palms fly up. "Slow down." She maintains a safe distance. "Everyone take a breath. So far, nothing has happened that can't be undone."

CHAPTER 50

McDunney's finger clamp holds steady, not tightening and not loosening, making me believe he is at least considering what Mom has said.

Mom lowers her hands, walks toe to heel, minimizing the clopping of her high heels. Alongside my captor, she says, "Tell us what you need, sir, and we'll see what we can figure out."

Despite her even demeanor, I notice Gunner's free hand drop to a holster on his right hip.

The chief's heart beats—*thumpety-thump*—so quick and strong, I can't differentiate it from my own pulse. He shifts toward Gran to see her still clenching the junior Remington 870. He wastes no time turning back to face Gunner and my mother.

At once, everything shifts.

Mom shoots forward, and Gunner draws his weapon. Gran springs from the steps, the long barrel a foot a head of her.

The chief's grip ratchets tighter, crushing the veins on my neck. I swear I hear steel drums playing, a calypso rhythm. A powerful tug yanks my heart against my spine.

"Release her. That's an order," a commanding voice booms from behind.

Sergeant Numereau?

Startled, McDunney's fingers slack long enough for me to thrust an uppercut and knuckle his exposed wrist. I twist like a tornado and spin from his grip. By the time he realizes what's happening, I've taken two quick steps and come face-to-face with...

"Henry? Trigger?"

CHAPTER 51

My visual field narrows. The sounds, landscape, and people fall away. I feel the way I do when being deprived of oxygen in the pressure chamber. I'm solely focused on one thing. In this case, it's Tana.

Even as I stand opposite her, hands clenched, my head about to explode from my shoulders, I can't stop my eyes from outlining every inch of her face. *What's wrong with me?* I touch my throbbing forehead. *Why, when I see her, does the landscape tilt?* At times, I have to cock my neck just to see level. *Am I an idiot? Or a masochist?* Because despite the lies, disappointment, and rejection, I'm still drawn to her. I love the fact she's a pilot and that she never tires of airplane talk. She understands my drive to practice flight maneuvers to perfection. Not to mention, she couldn't care less about getting her hands covered in oil and avgas. Truth is, she challenges my pilot sense, my common sense, and my intuition. And when I'm at what I think is my limit, she pushes me further. Forces me to step up. Challenges my thinking. Holds me to my word. And even though she's the last voice I want to hear at night and the first thing I think about in the morning, this time she's gone too far.

"Trigger!" Tana yells as McDunney's orangutan arms stretch and snag the hem of her dress. I'm guessing the fabric is silk since it slides from his clumsy grip.

She runs full speed, her legs hammering, until she collides into my torso. She throws her arms around my neck and squeezes me against her.

I close my eyes and breathe.

For the first time since we met, I feel nothing—not even the desire to protect her.

"I'm so sorry," Tana says. "Soooo glad you're back." Her embrace tightens, and she buries her face in my shirt. She relaxes her grip and raises her eyes to mine. "You don't have to choose." She smiles, a look that used to make me feel all mushy inside. "Go fly fighters. I'll be here when you get back."

My arms hang at my sides. My hairline burns as if on fire. I tighten my jaw. "I've seen this movie before, Tana. It's a horror story." I glance at my father. "A nightmare. Not a happy ending."

Tears fill her eyes.

I take one last look at what might have been. I memorize her pained expression. Suddenly, I notice every one of her shrapnel scars. "I'm done," I say. I bury my hands deep in my cargo pockets and walk away.

"Trigger," I hear her say. "Henry, please, what's wrong with him?"

"You went too far this time, T," the Weatherman says. "Way too far."

CHAPTER 52

"I can explain." I move around Henry to track after the sky surfer when the doors to the second black SUV click open.

My mouth slackens.

Shoulder to shoulder, Professor Flough and Mac Numereau climb the walkway steps.

"Professor, no, he's not who you think…"

I jog forward to warn him when, from behind, McDunney releases a thunderous wail. "Colonel Lamar Flough."

The chief knows Trigger's dad? I stare at the back of Trigger's head. *Is this what's between you and McDunney?*

Professor Flough spits a toothpick. "Colin McDunney." He trades a look with Mac. "If my math is right, you should still be locked in a cell."

McDunney snorts like a bull readying to charge.

Mac says, "How *did* you get out?"

"Good behavior," the chief answers.

Mac looks at Flough, and the living legend shakes his head. "Doubt it."

The chief stomps a foot and flips his ratty eye patch from his head. "You did this to me, Lamar." He points at a thick scar that splits his cloudy pupil. "You know what they do to a man like me in prison?"

"My fault?" Flough retrieves a fresh toothpick from his pocket. "That's right; you never could take responsibility for your actions."

"Come on. She slept with every guy in the unit." McDunney's words mix with spit. "We were drinking. It was her word against mine."

"Words!" Professor Flough says in a tone that makes everyone shudder. "The cuts and bruises on that young girl's body…" The living legend's sky blues darken.

The chief tugs on his shirt collar. "I could have been—"

"An engineer? A patriot? A decent human being?" Mac fills in the blank.

"You were the most promising airman basic I had at the time, Colin. A standout in the force's alternative energy program." Flough blinks at Mac. "He had ideas. Ones no one else had."

The chief's barrel chest expands. "You were my superior. You should have backed me up."

Flough's eyes remain trained on Mac. "We had proof." He spits a gnawed shard. "Your DNA."

Chief McDunney's balled fists rise, looking as if he's preparing to fight, when Gran pumps a twelve-gauge memory jogger into the air. The chief lowers his dukes, licks his lips, and eyes Henry and Trigger. "Ask Mr. Gu and your son about my DNA, Colonel."

Mac and Flough snap around. "Trigger?"

The sky surfer lowers his head.

Henry raises his sweat shirt hood.

"Leave it alone, Dad." Trigger's shoulders sag. "It's nothing." His voice wanes. "He's trying to rile you up."

Flough and Mac crowd around the sky surfer.

"If you so much as touched these boys…" Professor Flough clenches his jaw.

McDunney laughs.

Flough and Mac surge forward. "You're coming with us."

Gran fires a second shell.

All three men freeze.

I scan the yard. Mom is beside the mysterious Gunner Clark. Trigger and Henry are huddled with Mac, seeming unfazed that a few hours ago, he'd threatened me and held them captive. *Total mindbender.* If that isn't enough, the last Suburban's rear door opens, and Dr. Harb's silhouette appears.

My entire body vibrates. I knew McDunney and Harb came through the storm. I saw them. But standing opposite him again, in person, ignites a fire inside me that would rival the eruption of Mount St. Helens. On autopilot, I dart at Dr. Harb.

Mom and Gunner scramble and block my path. Mac backtracks, latches onto Harb's arm, and drags him under the trellis.

"Let me go." I swing my arms and glare at my mother. "He killed Dad."

"Trust me, Tana. Gunner and I have a plan." Mom's eyes lock on Dr. Harb's smug grin. "He has friends. Very influential friends."

I squint at Gunner Clark and see nothing notable—average height, stocky frame, and a face that would blend into any crowd of adults. Friends? I doubt it. Nothing about Gunner Clark leads me to believe he was ever the most popular guy at school; so what's so special about this union negotiator?

Gunner stands tall. "Are you ready to make the exchange Numereau? You get McDunney in exchange for Trigger and Henry?"

Guess I was wrong.

Gran trades a look with my mother and holds her steel barrel steady.

Professor Flough gnaws his toothpick, his sky-writing blues scribbling across the overcast cloud layer. "I've changed my mind." His eyes trace another sky writing loop de loop. "They both are coming with me."

CHAPTER 53

Mac's cheeks flush red. "We had a deal, Lamar. I bring you Henry and Trigger in exchange for the chief."

Professor Flough hangs his thumbs from his belt loops, rolls his lips together, flips up the collar on his bomber jacket, and raises his shoulders like he couldn't care less. "You kidnapped my son and held his friend against his will. Even after Trigger told you he wasn't going to be bribed with a fast-track promise to fighters. From where I'm standing, Mac, you're in no position to negotiate."

"I explained the circumstances, Lamar." Sergeant Numereau speaks through a locked jaw. "Trigger and Henry required an official debriefing after being privy to classified information. I had no choice. Top brass's order. General Yvelington's."

"I'll handle Yvelington," Flough says.

"No denying—McDunney is creek scum, but the future of a highly classified project lies in his hands."

"A criminal's hands. I know about Project Déjà Vu, Mac, and I don't really give a zero-g wing-over about a project that pumps soldiers full of pills. McDunney is a killer, and the code I serve under holds no exceptions."

"Brass will never stand for this." Mac's forearms flex.

"I'm not afraid of Conrad Yvelington."

"You will be." Mac smirks. "Like you, he's good at making empty promises."

"As if you have any business passing judgment," Flough says.

"Always black or white with you, isn't it, Lamar?"

"What's right is right." Colonel Flough's gaze returns to the murky sky. "Gray was never one of my favorite colors."

"Things have changed. They aren't as simple and clear-cut as they were back when you were out saving the world."

The living legend kicks, lobbing a hunk of grass onto the sidewalk. He eyes Dr. Harb and the chief. "The world hasn't changed as much as you think, Mac. Murderers still go to prison."

Tears dampen Mom's eyes, and Gunner rests a comforting hand on her shoulder. Strangely, Mom places her hand on top of his.

"Now," Colonel Flough booms.

The chief stomps forward, with the help of Gran's shotgun in his back. Mac shoves Dr. Harb, who stumbles a few steps and then stops opposite McDunney.

Flough latches onto their arms. Gunner strides forward and lends a hand.

"It's over." I exhale. Mom and Gran rush to my side, squeeze against my hips, and smash me as if I'm the strawberry jelly in their love-nut sandwich. When Mom pulls away, I see her grinning ear to ear.

"What?" I ask and track her sight line.

KC and Henry stand inches from one another. Kase's small hand reaches for the Weatherman's Pioneer piercing. She rubs her fingers over his receiver and then slides her hand, like a comb, over his stubbly head.

"Beefy," she says, the edges of her mouth twitching.

The Weatherman looks as if he might pass out.

Like any good wingman, Trigger digs in Henry's pack and offers an inhaler.

After he sucks a steroid shot, the color returns to the Weatherman's skin. He offers KC his hand. "Henry," he says, his palm steady as Kase offers hers in return.

"My friends call me Code Killer."

Henry mouths her hacker sign.

Although there isn't the slightest breeze, the bushes rustle, leaves shake, and sticks crack. The bustling foliage splits, and soldiers emerge.

A stern voice shouts, "Nobody move."

CHAPTER 54

The uniform that appears to be the leader shuffles forward, his cheek stuck to an AK rifle. He stops, lifts his hand from the gun butt, and signals, and a dozen men fan out in the yard. "Secure the assets," the leader commands, and each soldier's laser scope finds a target.

Dr. Harb, McDunney, Mac, Trigger, and Henry all have red dots painted on their chests. After a quick glance at my midsection, I find myself in the same position—with a tiny laser bull's-eye over my heart. One move and I could be dead.

"Who…" I say, and Mom's hand covers my mouth. Gunner Clark steps in front of my mother.

The leader's visored eyes sweep the perimeter, and then he sidesteps over to Sergeant Numereau.

"What's with the theatrics?" Mac says and lifts an arm to swat the gun barrel from his torso. Before he connects, two soldiers twice his weight scramble over and secure his arms behind his back.

"No need to get gruff." Professor Flough jogs from the walkway and hurls his body weight forward, hooking an arm around one captor's throat. He stomps a foot and grapples the kid, who is half his age, to the ground. Mac breaks free, elbows the remaining marine, stutter-steps, bends, and joins his mentor. Fists fly, and blows strike flesh until the unit leader rushes over and pushes his gun tip into Professor Flough's forehead.

"Enough," a voice says over a loudspeaker.

Headlights burn, and a convoy of Humvees and jeeps circle our property. Spotlights lap over the front lawn. A figure leaps from a utility vehicle, and when his torso slices the light's crosshairs, three shiny gold stars glisten on his breast pocket.

"General Yvelington, sir." Mac climbs to his feet and raises his surrendering hands near his ears. He eyeballs the man holding a gun to his temple, and after a stretched second, the soldier lowers the weapon.

Mac salutes as the three-star general approaches. Yvelington acknowledges with a tense nod, bends, and offers Lamar Flough a hand. "Forever the living legend."

Flough ignores his extended palm. "Hate to disappoint you after all these years."

"Sir, why are you here, sir?" Sergeant Numereau says.

"Your mission has become a security risk."

"Project Déjà Vu is under control," Mac says. "You have my word."

The general's line of sight shoots from Dr. Harb to McDunney to Professor Flough, and if the disapproving expression is any indication, I'd guess this group of men wasn't meant to be together. Yvelington studies Henry and then shifts to Trigger. "Brass doesn't agree."

Trigger grabs his skull, falls to his knees, and cringes.

There is something wrong with him. Seriously. I break from Mom's grip and haul down the walk. My arms swing, and my bare feet clap against the cool concrete. When I'm by his side, Trigger's head lifts, and he shoots me a don't-you-dare look.

"Stay away from me," Trigger says. "I choose *nothing.*" He winces and presses his temples.

It is as if every bone in my body splinters. My lungs collapse, and my heart erupts in my chest.

Trigger rests his head on the ground. His dad rushes to assist him.

I'm about to take another step when I feel a tug on my dress. Gunner Clark yanks me back toward Gran and my mother.

"Round them up!" Yvelington hollers. The marines nudge their captives as ordered. Mac, McDunney, and Dr. Harb march toward the Humvees. "I'll handle Trigger."

Professor Flough cuts between Yvelington and Trigger. He drops to his knees and crouches over Trigger. "Not my boy."

"Out of the way, Lamar," the general says. "You're still a national hero; be careful not to make us change the public's mind."

"Don't threaten me, Conrad. You know I couldn't care less about all that bull. You've taken a lot from me." Flough rubs a thumb over his ring finger and then tugs on the helix of his ear. "I won't let you take Trigger."

The general widens his stance, double shoulder width. He puffs out his chest and hangs his thumbs on his utility belt. "You're right, Colonel." He looks down at the living legend. "I owe you." A snarky smile crosses his lips. "In the spirit of the old days, let's play a game of give-and-take."

Deep lines wrinkle across Flough's forehead. His Adam's apple drops. "Active duty. Volunteer. Go on the road and recruit for the reserve program you're spearheading. I'll do anything for my son."

"I'm not talking to you, Lamar. I'm talking to her." Yvelington points a crooked finger.

"Me?" I say, trembling. I avert my eyes from Professor Flough and Trigger. "What could I possibly have that you would want?" My voice quivers.

Yvelington rolls his lips together and rocks on his heels. "Nothing." He grins, appearing to be enjoying himself. "I hold the two things you want most. The man who murdered your father and the boy"—he blinks at Gunner—"I understand, who is close to your heart."

My stomach knots. I feel lightheaded.

"Justice for your dad? Or freedom for a friend?" General Yvelington teeter-totters his hands. "Which one will you pick?"

"I can't." The landscape tilts the way it does when I look over a tall edge. "Won't." I stomp a foot against the topsy-turvy pavement. "It's an impossible choice."

"Therein lies the give part. Trigger or justice for your dad?" Yvelington clicks the timer on his chunky dive watch. "You have thirty seconds."

Still frames pulse like light from a camera flash.

Dad and our homebuilt. *"Tana and Benjamin Lyre—off to save the world."* Flash.

"Ready to fly solo?" The London City Airport. Flames. Smoke. I flinch as shrapnel reslices my skin.

Flash.

The inside of the ambulance. *"Wasn't an accident; it's murder."*

Flash.

National school orientation. Trigger. *"Nice to meet a fellow aviator, reluctant or otherwise."*

Hundreds of coins of chance flip in my mind. Heads—I choose Dad. Tails—I choose Trigger. Frames continue to pulse.

"You promised, Tana"—Dad's ghost mouths against the inky sky—*"to find my killer."*

"Double or nothing." Trigger eases my hand from the homebuilt's throttle. *"We're in this together, T."*

Soraya's bedroom. With Dr. Harb. *"What wouldn't your dad sacrifice for justice?"*

Pioneer's honor bond. The beacon tower. Swallowing the pill. A glimpse into my future.

Trigger. McDunney. The sky surfer trades his life for mine.

The mind coins sail through the air, end over end. I squeeze my eyes shut and cover my ears. The memories pulse like paparazzi bulbs on the red carpet.

Mac. A chance to fly fighter jets. The thrill of afterburners in the sky surfer's eyes.

Cowboy boots and a rolled Stetson. A country singer named Tuck. *A fresh start?*

The train. The storm. A choice. McDunney and Dr. Harb or Henry and Trigger.

"*Family above all else.*"

"*You, Tana. You or fighter jets.*"

"*A deathbed promise, my love. You gave your word.*"

Flash, flash, flash…

"*Stay away from me. I choose nothing.*"

The yes-no coins fall and settle flat. I don't want to look.

The scent of smoke fills my nose. Heat burns beneath my eyelids.

I no longer feel my pulse.

I exhale, crying.

Professor Flough's commanding voice cuts in and says, "There's no honor in vengeance, Tana."

His words drift, fading like the wail of a departing train whistle.

I suck in air and tighten my rib cage. I open my eyes wide and say, "I'm sorry, Professor. I choose Dr. Harb."

The ferocious, fighting Flough shoots to his feet.

The general ticks his neck, and two marines intercept Trigger's father.

"Game over, Lamar. She's made her choice. Brass gets what they want. Your boy will be safe with Mac, flying fighters, as he has been groomed for his entire life."

Professor Flough lashes like a caged animal. The stout soldiers restrain him without breaking a sweat.

Yvelington says, "Calm down, Lamar, or I'll tell Trigger the truth." He smiles. "By the way, Callie sends her best."

Flough's neck cords throb. He swings bunker-busting fists. His efforts are thwarted in a matter of seconds. Marines drag the living legend toward the Humvees, hands cuffed and a gun pointed at the back of his neck.

General Yvelington spins and eyeballs my mother and me. "Agent Clark," he says.

Agent Clark? I don't trust my ears. *Is this why KC couldn't find any background on Gunner?*

Agent Gunner Clark's expression is blank. "Sir, Linnea possesses diplomatic immunity and that protection extends to her daughter. Tana stays here."

The general pauses, and his lips press together. He latches onto Trigger's arm and speaks through a clenched jaw. "If anything happens, it's on your head, Gunner. Finish the job, and meet us at the rendezvous," Yvelington orders and then nudges Trigger to his jeep.

Gunner's view falls to the pavement, his gaze avoiding my mother's. He moves to KC.

"Kellan Catherine McKenna, you are under arrest for corporate espionage, hacking private networks, violating privacy rights, accessing government satellites, and posing a threat to national security." Gunner pulls KC's wrists behind her back, securing them with a plastic zip tie.

"Mom." I glare at my mother.

My mother runs to Gunner's side. "This is crazy. KC's not a threat. She's a sixteen-year-old kid."

"This has nothing to do with you, Linnea. You got what you wanted. Closure. The man who killed Benjamin will go to prison forever." Agent Clark carries KC toward the SUVs. "Besides, you don't want to play this game anymore, remember?"

Mom chases alongside. "As you may recall, Mr. Clark, no one is as good at the game as I am."

With KC and Agent Clark inches from the first Suburban's passenger door, I know this is my only chance. I have to do something big, because I will *not* abandon another friend.

"Tana!" I hear Mom shout as I run past. Arriving at the black Suburban, I'm greeted by Gunner Clark's solid chest.

Smack. I bounce, tumble backward, and fall on my butt.

Bigger, I coach myself and scramble to my knees. I dive at his calves in an attempt to bring him to the ground. As I charge, he shifts, and my head slips in the gap between his calves. Before I know what has happened, his knees close around my neck.

"Let me go," I say, my head trapped. I stretch my arms around Gunner's shins.

"Help me, Tana." Kase swats at my hands.

I twist my neck and grunt. Then I feel the tension on my neck release. "On my way," I say, but before I can get traction, I'm lifted by my dress collar.

"I don't want to hurt her, Linnea, but there's no getting around the fact that serious crimes have been committed. Miss McKenna is coming with me."

"No," I twist, my arms flailing through the air. Mr. Clark tightens his grip. When Mom is within arm's reach, Gunner releases my dress. I fly forward, regain footing, and curve to circle back.

Mom has other plans.

She pinches the joint between my forearm and elbow, and my legs buckle as if broken in half.

She kneels by my side. "Believe me, we'll find a way to help KC and Trigger. Not here. Not now."

Engines crank, and just as fast as it came, the armored convoy clears. The leaves are still. The red-orange glow from the harvest moon matches the burning in my chest. I kept my promise. Justice has been served. The pain remains, though, and aches twofold. I cover my heart with my hand and face the empty pavement. *What have I done?*

E.L. CHAPPEL

www.elchappel.com